PERSIAN ROSE

Part 2 of the White Lotus Trilogy

LIBBIE HAWKER

Running Rabbit Editions

INTRODUCTION

In the fifth century BCE, Egypt is the greatest civilization known to mankind. But with a foolish king on its throne, the Nile Valley is ripe for conquering.

Amid this climate of danger and strife, in the alleys and brothels of Memphis, an extraordinary young woman comes of age. To spare her siblings from starvation, Doricha is sold into prostitution. But she has gifts beyond mere beauty. Through wit and determination, she works her way into the realm of the hetaerae—courtesans of exceptional refinement.

As a hetaera, Doricha has access to the schemes and negotiations that shape the world. But the rich and powerful also have access to *her*, and Doricha soon finds herself in the Pharaoh's harem, caught up in his reckless schemes. When the Pharaoh sends her off to his fiercest enemy, thinly cloaked by a dangerous ruse, Doricha must become a double agent if she hopes to survive. Caught between the Pharaoh and the Persian king Cambyses, it is Doricha—once a slave, now a woman of great but secret power—who will determine Egypt's fate.

Persian Rose is Part 2 of the *White Lotus* trilogy.

I

PHARAOH'S DAUGHTER

RAISED UP

"RHODOPIS, COME FORWARD."

Pentu's voice was pitched low—calculated to carry just above the rumble of conversation in the feast hall, and to travel no farther. The Pharaoh's chief steward was ever deliberate, always precise, and his sharp black eyes missed nothing. By the dim, guttering light of a single clay lamp—the only light to illuminate the chamber behind the feast hall, where the Pharaoh's women waited—Rhodopis could see the sharp pinch of impatience on Pentu's face. She stepped out from behind the last concubine in the queue and hurried toward him, the linen of her pleated gown rustling softly, a trail of whispers following her down the length of the chamber.

The private chamber was separated from the festival hall by a dark, heavy drape, thickly woven of char-black wool, embroidered all its great length with blue-winged scarabs and the spikes of red lotus flowers. The drape reached up to the soaring, wood-beamed ceiling of the palace and touched the painted pillars that stood either side; the curtain's folds shut out the light of the feast hall completely, but not the scents and sounds of the Pharaoh's grand party. Laughter and conversation filled the room beyond, underscored by the gentle plucking of a three-stringed lute. Sweet cinnamon mingled with the smell of rich roasted onions, overpowering even the perfumes of the Pharaoh's women. The smell made Rhodopis' mouth water.

She lowered her face humbly when she reached Pentu, waiting for his instructions.

"Fourth place in line," the steward said, making no effort to soften his snappish tone.

Rhodopis was grateful for the dim amber light; none of the Pharaoh's women could see how her cheeks reddened. It was not a blush of pleasure, but rather the hectic heat of embarrassment —or perhaps fear. Murmurs of protest rose from the line behind her, but Rhodopis did as Pentu directed, and took the fourth position in the queue of immaculately dressed women and girls. She stood just behind the king's chief wife, Khedeb-Netjer-Bona, and her two young daughters. By custom, the women of the king's household entered the feast hall in order of their favor, so those dearest to the king's heart were also closest to his hand. Rhodopis did not need to look at the chief wife to know that her back was straight, her shoulders stiff with offense. She could all but feel the sickening quiver of Khedeb-Netjer-Bona's outrage. She was grateful she could not see the faces of the women behind her— Amasis' minor wives and concubines, all of them no doubt glaring their hatred at Rhodopis that very minute.

She understood the women's indignation. She had lived among them, an ornament in the king's harem, for merely three months. Why should a newcomer to the harem be placed so well? And why should a *Greek* stand so high in the king's regard? The harem was populated by true Egyptian women, the daughters of ancient families, whose blood could be traced back more than three thousand years to the court of the first Pharaoh. For countless generations, those noble houses had supported the throne by giving a daughter to the king. Yet now this interloper—this jumped-up foreign courtesan, who had draped herself across the couches and beds of countless rich men—thought to supplant them.

It isn't my doing. Rhodopis desperately wished she could tell the women as much, but Pentu's eyes were upon her, and if she spoke out of turn, no doubt Khedeb-Netjer-Bona would slap her for the impropriety. *I've no control over the king's whims. He only likes me because I'm Greek… can't you see it? He would dote just the same on any girl, so long as she came from Thrace or Athens or Lesvos.*

The women waited. Pentu listened for his signal. Rhodopis did her best to remain still, though the urge to fret and fidget was almost irresistible. Would this sudden rise in status prove dangerous? The king's women carried themselves with great dignity; they were the most elevated women in Egypt. She doubted the Pharaoh's concubines would lower themselves to the hardscrabble tactics of the girls in Xanthes' Stable. Violence seemed unlikely—nor were the women likely to mock her openly or treat her with overt cruelty. Such pettiness was beneath them. But that was not to say the women were *friendly*. Rhodopis was no fool: she knew there were dangers besides flailing fists or knives in the dark. It had been three months since she had presented the rose-gold slipper to Amasis in the market square—three months since he had whisked her away from Xanthes, away from an increasingly grim life among the hetaerae. But she felt little safer here, in the Pharaoh's palace, than she had felt in the Stable.

No sense in trying to fool myself. The gods intend me to be here. Why else did they send the king's falcon to take my slipper? But just what they mean by putting me here—among all these women who'd rather see me vanished like a puff of dust on a breeze than let the hem of their dresses brush my own—I'm sure I can't begin to guess.

The sharp, observant Pentu nodded briefly to himself; he had detected the signal he'd been waiting for. With a quick motion, he flicked the heavy drapery aside with no more effort than if it had been made of the finest, sheerest linen. Light from the feast hall—from its dozens of large lamps—flooded into the chamber. Rhodopis blinked in the sudden glare.

"You may enter now, my lady," Pentu said to Khedeb-Netjer-Bona. But the chief wife was already moving, sweeping into the hall with her head high, allowing the bright light to glitter across the golden, downward pointed wings of her traditional vulture crown.

The file of women followed the chief wife to their gallery, a painted platform near the king's dais. There they would sit slightly higher than the Pharaoh's guests, but not as high as the king. It was not the first time Rhodopis had climbed the steps to the women's gallery, but never before had she felt so thoroughly displayed. The sudden increase in status removed her from the rear of the gallery, in its most shadowed and inconspicuous corner, placing her squarely before the eyes of every noble and servant in the hall. There was no escaping their scrutiny.

Isn't that the point, and all? Rhodopis thought as she sank quietly into the scooped seat of her wooden chair, smoothing her linen dress across her thighs. Most women in the harem held the official title "Ornament of the King." They were little more than pretty baubles to King Amasis, symbols of his wealth and power. Their chief purpose was to be seen—to be displayed, quiet and complacent, beautiful and envied.

Rhodopis gazed rather dully down the length of the feasting-hall. How its grandeur had awed her, on that first fateful day when Amasis had claimed her in the name of the god Horus, and she had stepped inside the palace for the first time! Then, the ranks of pillars—fat near the ground, but slender as the boles of young trees where they touched the ceiling—had sent a thrill up her spine, for they had reminded her of giant soldiers standing at attention, awaiting the command of the king. The hall's smooth polished floor was as dark as Nile water, and a thick spice of incense smoke had flavored the air, though Rhodopis had seen no censers burning. It was the perfume of ages she had smelled

—the echoes of innumerable feasts and festivals, stretching back through Egypt's long history to its distant, shadowed past.

Now, though, the feast hall no longer excited her. In three short months, she had come to realize that the room, like most of the Pharaoh's palace, was a tedious and disappointing place. As an Ornament of the King, her status was even higher than that of any hetaera. Far from enjoying the autonomy of a freed courtesan, Rhodopis soon learned that her life was more restricted than ever before. She was no longer a slave, yet she longed for freedom. She sighed softly, watching the guests laugh and raise their cups; she laced her fingers together in her lap so she would not give in to the temptation to lean her elbows on her small table like a wistful, brooding shepherdess. Khedeb-Netjer-Bona would not be impressed with such carelessness, and Rhodopis was already treading on dangerous ground where the chief wife was concerned.

But how she hungered for freedom—for any small measure of it! Even the opportunity to drift from table to table, as a hetaera might do, would be a welcome novelty now. How she yearned to talk to the men at Amasis' feasts—to engage with them on unexpected topics, to make them laugh with delight as she slipped another of Aesop's clever talking-animal tales into the conversation. She would have gladly brushed elbows with the women, too. Amasis still made some effort—nominal though it may be—to keep up old Egyptian ways, and so the feast hall held almost as many women as men. Wives and daughters of the Pharaoh's esteemed guests, they moved at will through the crowd, conversing with the men, laughing and singing, entirely at ease. There was no andron here, no gynaeceum—no separation of the sexes. Separation was a Greek custom, through and through.

Wonder what the women talk about, when they're right there alongside the men. Do they know as much about the world as their husbands and fathers do?

And might those Egyptian women hold the key to some

crucial knowledge, some unique perspective on Memphis—on the world—which Rhodopis had never thought to consider? The *newness* of it all called to her with a powerful voice, tantalizing with visions of all the intrigues she might learn... if only she could be down there, out of this gods-cursed gallery, among the guests in all their fascinating variety.

Since coming to the king's harem, there had been little opportunity for Rhodopis to learn, to expand her skills—to challenge herself as a conversationalist. For a young woman as bright and social as she, the seclusion and careful dignity of harem life were intolerable drudgeries. Worse still, she'd had little opportunity to dance. Oh, Amasis often asked her to dance privately for him, and his musicians were excellent. *Practically the best in all the world*, Rhodopis thought. But it wasn't the same. Nothing Rhodopis had yet experienced could compare to the exhilaration of performing before an adoring audience. *One man simply doesn't count as an audience, no matter how much he might desire me. No, not even if he happens to be the king.*

Amasis sat alone on his high dais, lounging easily on his gilded throne, smiling down at the feast. He always seemed to smile, whenever ceremony didn't demand a stern, noble countenance. From her days as a hetaera, Rhodopis knew well that many men took Amasis' easy temper to be a sign of softness. To those who did not respect the Pharaoh, his smile was the brand of his weakness—an outer mark of all his inner failings. Rhodopis hadn't yet decided whether the king's detractors were correct. Perhaps, after all, he did lack fortitude—what else could lead him to disregard the greatness of his Egyptian people, and favor Greek culture instead? Perhaps, as his admirers said, he was forward-thinking, cleverer and more adaptive than any Pharaoh had been before. Only one thing was clear to Rhodopis: Amasis was an aging man, and therefore set in his ways, as all older people were. He was unlikely to change his heart or his habits now, no matter how his priests and nobles implored him. As he leaned from his throne to murmur some order in Pentu's ear, the blue-and-saffron cloth folds of the Nemes crown slid over Amasis' shoulders—shoulders that were still broad and strong, but spotted by the sun, and beginning to show the roundness, the subtle stoop of great age approaching.

Pentu nodded at the king's command, then stepped forward, raising his hands before him. The raucous din of the hall quieted a little; guests elbowed one another for silence or turned in their seats to watch the shaven-headed steward.

"The Pharaoh calls for his dancers!" Pentu cried.

Cheers flooded the hall; cups raised high above guests' heads. Rhodopis sighed again. She bit her lip as a troop of dancers appeared through the hall's massive doorway. They made their way along the aisles, weaving between the tables. The dancers ignored the shouts of acclaim that greeted them; they looked only at the king. This troop was composed of both men and women, each of them naked but for the traditional dancing belt, a slim bit of linen girding their groins and trailing the long, colorful tassels of their trade.

What Rhodopis would have given to be among them! Gladly would she part with all the silk gowns in her dressing-chest, all the necklaces and bracelets of gold and silver, emerald and turquoise and bright, translucent carnelian. She would have surrendered every gem-studded belt, every rare purple sash— even her rose-gold slippers, if any of the trappings of a harem girl could buy the pure pleasure of dancing for an audience.

Why did the gods send me here, if not to dance? For it's sure I don't do anything better than dance. I'm just about useless now, far as I can see. If the gods hadn't intended her to dance in the king's palace after all, then why had they subjected her to such danger? The threat she felt from the king's other women may be vague, impossible to define... but it was no less real for that.

Rhodopis glowered down at her fingers, still knotted tightly in her lap, as the dancing troop made their obeisance to the king.

She could look at them no longer; the bitterness in her stomach was enough to choke her, and she had no desire to gag and retch there in the women's gallery, before the eyes of every guest at the feast. Now that she had no duties, save for an occasional visit to Amasis' bed—and nothing to occupy her mind, except learning to spin flax for weaving—Rhodopis found herself with ample time to languish in the garden, or in her private chamber, mulling endlessly and bitterly over her fate. Anger haunted her, day and night, but she could never quite decide why she felt so frustrated, nor could she say who was the focus of her anger. Was it the Pharaoh? He had swept her away, transporting her into a life that was supposed to be better than the one she'd lived before. Instead, he had all but abandoned her to the isolation of the harem, leaving her to stew in boredom and idleness. Was it the other women, the King's Ornaments, who tormented her with their subtle stares, their whispers... who chilled her with their rejection? Perhaps it was Xanthes. Or Iadmon, who, after all, had plucked her from her family and transplanted her to this strange world, the very heights of Memphian society. The only thing Rhodopis could feel certain of was this: now, as an Ornament of the Harem, she was barred from every good thing she had ever known: dance; the freedom to move about, to speak with whom she pleased; the hope for a future she alone would control. And —the loss that still stung most painfully—Aesop, the only person who had ever been Rhodopis' true friend.

The music began with an upward rush from the reedy, nasal-toned pipes the Egyptians loved so well. Rhodopis kept her eyes fixed on Amasis, for she couldn't bring herself to watch the dancers. The Pharaoh leaned against the backrest of his throne, smiling broadly. A familiar, distant softness clouded his eyes as he gave himself up entirely to the pleasure of the entertainment. His foot tapped inside its curved, golden shoe, keeping time with the music.

Maybe it's Egypt itself I'm so angry with, Rhodopis thought as the king beamed mildly down at his celebration. *And why shouldn't I be? Wasn't it Egypt—all the great, disordered mess that it is these days—put me where I am now? Wasn't it Egypt drove my family into poverty, and made a man desperate enough to kill my father, and made us all suffer from empty bellies and no hope to be had, no matter where we looked?*

Rhodopis felt a thump on underside of her chair's seat. She glanced back over her shoulder, meeting the narrowed eyes of Nebetiah, a fellow Ornament.

"Best wipe that scowl off your face before the Lady of Teeth and Claws sees it," Nebetiah said, cutting a quick glance in Khedeb-Netjer-Bona's direction. Nebetiah spoke in her native Egyptian, of course. No one in the harem dared to speak Greek— nor any other language—lest they incite the wrath of the chief wife.

"I'm sorry," Rhodopis said hastily. She had gained some skill with the Egyptian tongue since coming to Memphis, but she still spoke it with a noticeable accent. "I didn't mean to offend."

Now that the music had swelled to fill the great hall, the women in the gallery were free to speak to one another. Minneferet, seated to Nebetiah's right, blinked in a mocking way and imitated Rhodopis' accent. "I'm sor-*ree*. I *did*-ent mean to off-*fent*." She nudged Nebetiah with her elbow. "Don't fret over this one, Nebet. She isn't worth your worry. If Khedeb-Netjer-Bona tries to punish her, the Pharaoh will fight off his own chief wife with his crook and flail."

Rhodopis blushed.

"There go her cheeks again," Minneferet said. "Red as carnelians."

"How very charming," said Iset drily. She was seated to Nebetiah's other side, and had already reached the bottom of her cup, as was her habit. She raised it, drawing the eye of the servant with the wine pitcher. The servant filled it dutifully and backed away.

"Turn back around," Iset said to Rhodopis. "My wine isn't as entertaining as the dancers."

Minneferet said slyly, "It is very fascinating, though, how quickly you can drain a cup."

Henuttawy, a regally self-possessed woman in her late thirties —of an age with the chief wife—sat to Rhodopis' left, at the front of the gallery. It was she whom Rhodopis had displaced in the king's favor. Henuttawy seemed remarkably unaffected by the change, giving no outward indication that her place in the world had shifted like dunes before a strong wind. She ignored Rhodopis as completely as she ever had, but she could not ignore the bantering of the young women behind her. She turned her head only a fraction and said, just loudly enough to be heard, "Be quiet, all of you. I'm in no mood to listen to the hissing of a flock of ill-behaved she-geese."

Minneferet sighed and leaned back in her chair, arms folded below her bare breasts. "It's all one to me. I'm in no mood to hiss, anyway, except at Rhodopis."

"That's a fact." Iset stared gloomily into her cup. From the corner of her eye, she noticed Rhodopis watching her, and kicked her chair as Nebetiah had done.

Rhodopis turned to face the feast hall, and picked up her own wine cup, taking the tiniest of sips. She allowed her eyes to unfocus—giving all appearance of watching the dancers, but seeing nothing of their performance. All her attention remained fixed on the women behind her, who had gone on speaking quietly as the servants presented the first course.

"Things have gone from bad to worse," Nebetiah said. "It almost seems an affront to the gods to sit here, feasting as if everything is well, when there are riots out there in the city."

"The riots are none of our doing," Minneferet said. "Why should we feel guilty, and deprive ourselves of a rare joy?" But despite her words, she sounded as grim as the others. Rhodopis resisted the urge to turn in her seat again, to read the expression on Minneferet's face.

"None of our doing," Iset agreed. "But do you suppose that matters to the gods?"

"It's not the gods I'm worried about," Nebetiah said.

"More fool you."

Nebetiah went on as if she hadn't heard Iset. "It's the ordinary people that concern me—our fellow Kmetu." Rhodopis blinked; it was the native word for Egyptians. "It seems an effrontery, doesn't it, to be here in the palace, feasting as if nothing in the world is wrong, when we all know too well that everything is wrong."

"I wouldn't say *everything*," Minneferet muttered. "Always so dramatic, this one."

"I'm not dramatizing," Nebetiah said patiently. "You'd agree with me, if you paid more attention to what happens beyond the palace walls."

"Go ahead, then; enlighten me." The words should have been light and playful, but Minneferet's voice was dull, as if she dreaded what Nebetiah might say.

"My mother wrote me again this morning," Nebetiah began. "There has been another riot. One of the largest yet, I am sorry to say."

"How many is that, now?"

"Seven since the start of the year. But the number hardly matters; even one is too many. There hasn't been unrest of this sort for more than a hundred and forty years."

"Thoth Incarnate," Iset said, poking fun at Nebetiah. "Behold her majesty; she knows all."

"You'd know a thing or two, if you ever took your nose out of the wine jug and put it in a scroll instead. I tell you, these riots should trouble all of us. Riots aren't *maat*."

Even before she had come to live in the Pharaoh's palace, Rhodopis had understood maat. It was the Egyptian word for sacred order, the perfect balance of all things the gods had made. Egyptians held maat in the highest regard. If ever the righteous balance was disturbed—if any aspect of life were *not maat*—then chaos would be sure to follow. She swallowed the stewed apricot she'd been chewing with a painful gulp.

"Where was this riot, and when?" Minneferet said.

"Last night. It was just below the north side of the city, near that big market square. You know the one, don't you?"

"I think I know. Near that Greek fellow's place, is that it?"

"Which Greek fellow?" Iset interjected wryly. "Memphis is crawling with them, worse than lice on a Canaanite."

"The one who owns all those prostitutes," Nebetiah said.

Their conversation died in a sudden hush. An itch tingled between Rhodopis' shoulder blades. She could feel the women's eyes on her back, could feel their silent judgment, the laughter they barely kept in check. She spooned up another apricot, slowly and gracefully, waiting for its juice to cease dripping from the bottom of the spoon—as if she hadn't heard a word the women had said.

After a moment, Nebetiah resumed her story. "That's why Mother wrote to me; she didn't want me to fear. This riot came closer to their estate than any has before. My family has always lived on the north side, you know."

"Yes, we know," Minneferet said. "You've said as much before, any number of times."

"More people were killed in this riot than any before," Nebetiah went on. "These eruptions are growing more violent all the time. I tell you, Kmet is heading toward darkness. I've no idea how we might find the light again."

Rhodopis set her spoon aside. What little appetite she'd had fled from her now. So a riot had finally reached Xanthes' very doorstep. Vividly, she recalled the panicked moment when she and Xanthes' other girls had thought a riot was about to encircle their master's estate. Her heart pounded; her skin flushed at the memory. She wondered distantly how the girls of the Stable had fared. Surely they had survived—or so Rhodopis hoped. Xanthes' wall was impressive, his guardsmen plentiful and strong—the best money could buy. Bastet, Persephone, Callisto... they had never been her friends, but she had lived side by side with them, had shared with them a life most other women could never understand. Fate had forged a bond among the girls of the Stable. Rhodopis could not bring herself to wish them ill.

She blinked, trying to dispel a sudden mist from her eyes. Through the blur of unshed tears, she watched the dancers whirl and sway, the bright tassels of their belts spinning gaily to music that now seemed obscene in its joyfulness.

Egypt is heading into darkness. And I've no way out, no way to save myself.

Rhodopis looked to the Pharaoh again. He came sharply into focus, leaning casually in his throne, surrounded by the naïveté of his feast, his pointlessly glad celebration. In the aging stoop of his shoulders, Rhodopis seemed to see the whole of his nation, the whole of his world. Egypt was little more than a crumbling façade now—a shadow of the astonishing empire it once had been. In the streets of Memphis, when Rhodopis had been free enough that she could speak to the city's influential men, virtually all of them had agreed: Amasis was at best a disappointing king—at worst, a catastrophe poised to befall the nation. Egypt wavered on the knife's edge. Who could restore the balance of maat? Who *would* restore it, with Amasis on the throne, with all the vast power of Egypt's gods and armies in his uncaring hands?

Rhodopis forced herself away from such dark thoughts. They would not help her now. Returning as she often did to the careful training Aesop had given her, she calmed herself and sharpened her ears, listening once again to the women's conversation.

"Well, you can only expect riots," Minneferet was saying, "when there's so much disparity. Outrageous wealth for some—"

"And nearly all of them Greeks," Iset interjected.

"While others have fallen into poverty."

"Or into low-class whoring," Iset said. "If you want to know why I drink so much, here's the reason for it: two of my cousins have turned to *that sort of work*, if you take my meaning. It's bad enough that anyone from our family should resort to such a thing, but *two*...! We may not be from the north side of Memphis, but mine is the wealthiest family in Annu, with a long and respectable history. And yet here we are, with minor daughters of a noble house forced into men's beds for silver. I swear to Hathor, it's fortunate each of us was born when she was—first daughters of our families, or near enough to first. Otherwise, we wouldn't have been sent off to Amasis, would we? We might very well have found ourselves facing the same choice, but instead we're protected, and want for nothing, even if our days do get rather dull."

"Don't be so certain a whore could never find her way to the Pharaoh's harem," Minneferet muttered.

Rhodopis didn't like the edge of humor in her voice. The spot between her shoulders itched and prickled again.

"You're right about the disparity," Nebetiah said. "There has never been a time before, you know, when we've stood so far apart."

"When who has stood apart?"

"The rich and the poor."

"Surely that can't be true."

"But it is. I've read all about it," Nebetiah insisted.

"Didn't I tell you?" Iset said with a delicate snort. "Thoth Incarnate."

"Not even when the Assyrians invaded. Nor even long, long before, when the heretic king Akhenaten ruled. We've never seen a Kmet like this one. Only the gods know what we should expect. Anything may happen—anything at all."

"I fear violence," Iset said darkly. "Worse than we've already seen. What's coming is sure to make the riots feel like a day on a pleasure barge by comparison."

Minneferet said, "I doubt that. This king can't last much longer—the gods won't allow it."

"Keep your voice down," Iset warned. "The chief wife will punish all three of us if she hears you say such things!"

Minneferet did lower her voice, but she went on doggedly. "Once the gods set things right, and settle old Amasis in his tomb, then we'll have Psamtik on the throne. He'll put Kmet to rights, and no mistake."

At mention of the Pharaoh's eldest son, Rhodopis glanced across the feast hall to where Psamtik stood, leaning one shoulder casually against a pillar. Her eyes fastened on the heir instantaneously, as if, like some shy, tiny creature cowering in the undergrowth, every unconscious instinct made her aware of the hunter's presence. Psamtik had made Rhodopis feel wary and insecure since she had first arrived in the palace, though he had never deigned to speak to her. He didn't need to speak; he had *looked* at her often enough, more often than Rhodopis could stand. His gaze was always intrusive. No, it was more than intrusive, *worse*. It was possessive. Psamtik made little effort to conceal his contempt for Rhodopis—for all Greeks, perhaps—and there was something starkly predacious in his eyes whenever he sized her up with one of his lazy, condescending stares.

Psamtik bent over a nearby table of guests, making to join their conversation. But he broke off suddenly and looked up, as if he could feel Rhodopis' eyes upon him. She looked away quickly, lifting her wine cup to her lips, feigning unconcern. But she found herself taking a long, deep draft from the cup, drinking more than was prudent. She hoped it would calm her unsettled nerves, or at least deaden the crawling sensation that chilled her skin.

Unrest on the northern side of the city—all I can do is pray it won't touch Iadmon's house, and Aesop and the rest of his household.

Did Aesop know about last night's riot? Surely he must. Rhodopis gritted her teeth, fighting down another swell of bitterness. If only she could be of some *use* here in the harem—if she could extend the Pharaoh's protection over Iadmon's household.... But it was useless to even to think of it. She was powerless here, a bird in a cage. She was weaker and more helpless than she'd ever been before.

The music reached its end; the king's dancers spun to their final positions and held graceful poses, regally still while shouts and applause thundered all around them. Rhodopis set down her wine cup and applauded dutifully, but her gaze strayed back to Psamtik. He was watching her from across the hall, arms folded, baring his teeth in a stiff, malicious grin.

Rhodopis shut her eyes and prayed until the servants carried out the second course.

2

DANCING IN THE DARK

THE FEAST STRETCHED LATE INTO THE NIGHT. LONG BEFORE THE king rose from his throne, dismissing his guests and his women, Rhodopis' back had begun to ache from the strain of sitting still and upright on her hard, wooden chair. If only she could have danced...! It would have been a welcome relief to remove herself from the women's gallery, for when the Pharaoh's concubines were not murmuring about the riots in the city, they lapsed into an icy silence. The back of Rhodopis' neck never ceased to tingle with the sickening certainty that they were casting evil thoughts in her direction. She could feel their hostility like the prick of a poisoned needle, small and cold and subtle, but no less dangerous for that.

As the Pharaoh departed from the feast hall, his cadre of stewards and guards fluttering around him, the women of the harem seemed as eager to leave as Rhodopis. Khedeb-Netjer-Bona stood abruptly, allowing her linen napkin to slide from her lap to the floor. The rest of the women rose with equal readiness. None of them could enjoy a celebration when Memphis wavered on the verge of chaos, and maat was nowhere to be found. In a quick rustle of gowns and a cloud of myrrh-sweet perfume, the women

shuffled impatiently behind the railing of the gallery, waiting for
their chance to step down and follow Khedeb-Netjer-Bona from
the great hall.

Never had the walk through the night-time corridors felt so
long, so oppressively dim. Rhodopis had seen these walls, these
pillars, countless times before; she knew each turn of the route
she traveled. Yet the bright murals and long, brick-floored corridors seemed to meld into one—an endless monotony of stone
and lamplight, of the same stiff, painted figures staring down
from every wall. For all Rhodopis could tell, she walked forever
through the unchanging endlessness of Hades' realm—as if the
gods had condemned her to trudge eternally in that file of
Egyptian women, never escaping the anger and hatred of those
behind her, seeing nothing but the stoically turned backs of
Khedeb-Netjer-Bona and her two daughters at the fore.

When the high, familiar, green-and-blue arch of women's
corridor stretched overhead, Rhodopis sighed with relief, not
caring a speck who heard. The line disintegrated; the women's
ceremonial silence was replaced by growing murmurs as they
sorted themselves into groups of friends. The corridor filled with
motion and color as the Pharaoh's wives and concubines hurried
toward the leisure rooms or the welcoming sanctuary of the
communal bath.

Rhodopis knew better than to try to join any of the women for
a game of senet or invite herself into the bath. At the best of
times, none of the girls were enthusiastic about her presence. But
now, newly raised to fourth among all women, she knew it would
be especially foolish to try. Instead, she slipped quietly through
the crowd with her eyes fixed on the floor, heading for the seclusion of her private room. Its stillness and simple comforts would
make a welcome change from the noise and tension of the feast.
She hurried along the corridor, past a series of painted arches,
each leading to the various common spaces—the game room, the
music room, a quiet library whose shelves were stacked with

scrolls—until at last, she reached the door to her small chamber. She pushed it open, edged around the gap, and shut it as forcefully as she dared, leaning her back against the door as if her slight weight could bar all the women's seething disapproval from flooding in after her.

When she had first arrived in the palace, Pentu had admitted to Rhodopis that this chamber was one of the smallest and meanest in the women's wing. "There is nothing to be done about it," he'd said briskly, as if expecting that Rhodopis would complain. "No other room is available at present. You're lucky *any* room was free; otherwise, you would have been sent off to one of the Pharaoh's harem-houses in another city. Best to be satisfied with what you've got here, if you want my advice."

Rhodopis had not asked for Pentu's advice in the matter, but the smallness of the apartment made no difference to her. In fact, she had quite liked it from the start. After the tiny sleeping alcove she'd had at the Stable, this chamber seemed a palace all its own. It was several times larger than her room at Iadmon's had been; the furnishings were a good deal less impressive than those the other women enjoyed—Rhodopis had caught glimpses of their lavish accommodations through open doors—but the simple, sensible things the king had provided were comfortable enough to please a Thracian farm girl.

She sighed again, deeply, alone in the dusky dimness of her private sanctuary. She leaned her head back against the door, squeezing her eyes shut. *Amasis, what were you thinking?*

The air still seemed to crackle around her with the affronted silence of the concubines. No doubt the bath would soon be boiling with the heat of the women's anger. Rhodopis pictured them floating about the sunken stone tub like a lot of par-cooked fish in a simmering stew. She could have laughed at the image, but the memory of their silent anger was still too near.

And now what am I to do about living among them? Reckon it was bad enough before, when they just didn't like me because I'm Greek.

Now they purely hate me. It's just about enough to make me wish for Vélona and the Stable again.

Rhodopis pushed herself away from the door. Her small bronze ember box was glowing faintly on the table, the carefully packed wood-coal within twinkling through delicate piercework holes. She flipped back the box's hot lid with deft fingers and touched a dry reed to the coal, then carried the tiny flame to the wick of her oil lamp. The sweet oil caught at once; a rose of light blossomed and unfolded, filling the chamber with cheer.

By the dancing lamp-flame, Rhodopis worked her fingers into the tight knots that held her Egyptian gown in place. She wrenched at them until they gave way. The linen dropped to the floor, and Rhodopis left it lying where it fell. The chamber servants would tend to it in the morning when they brought her breakfast. She removed her jewels with greater care, laying the necklace and bracelets aside on her dressing table. The carnelian set had been a gift from Amasis—and although she felt no particular affection for the Pharaoh, she was always cognizant of the great honor he'd done her, in raising her up from bondage in Xanthes' household. Amasis was a complicated, sometimes infuriating man, but he had always been kind and generous to Rhodopis. She thought she could have mustered genuine respect for him, if his frequent lapses in judgment had not confounded and frightened her so.

Blessedly naked in the warm air, Rhodopis stood for a moment beside the garden window, allowing the gentle, scented breezes to cool the light sheen of sweat from her skin. She drank in the heady scents of night-blooming jasmine and the yellow, star-like flowers the harem women called "moth blossoms," for they attracted flitting, white-winged insects that danced dizzily in the moonlight. The soft whisper of a breeze among the garden leaves soothed her. The tension she felt around the king's other women always affected Rhodopis, souring her stomach and setting a hard lump in her throat. She did her best to disguise her discomfiture, though, denying the other girls petty victory. But no matter how she tried to prevent the women's hostility from clouding her mind, she could never quite escape it.

Reckon there's no hope of avoiding it now, she thought morosely. *Now that he's gone and made me favorite. Gods help me; he's raised me up almost as high as his chief wife!*

Suddenly she was overcome by restlessness, a need to move— to shake off and outpace the pained, tense silence of the feast, of the women's hall behind her, where she could still feel the disapproval of the wives and concubines weighing her down like a cloak of wet and stinking wool. A walk in the garden—alone, of course—would be just the thing to settle her mind and loosen the knots from her limbs. She found a simple linen tunic in one of her trunks, pulled it on and belted it, then shook down her hair until it tumbled around her shoulders in rose-gold waves. Briefly, Rhodopis considered going back through the quarters to the proper garden door, but almost at once she rejected the idea. She had no desire to show herself in the corridor now—to hear the whispers and hisses as she passed by the other women. The window was plenty wide enough to admit her, and its stone lip was smooth and cool. She vaulted up to it, turned about carefully on her bottom, and paused for a moment, swinging her legs in the pale-blue starlight. Then she dropped down to the flower bed below.

Rhodopis crouched among the tangled jasmine vines, listening and waiting. The garden was perfectly still, save for the insects and frogs that trilled, endless, high, and monotonous, within its shadowed depths. The bleak mood that had dominated the women's quarters—a mood that had no doubt been helped along by Rhodopis' unexpected promotion—seemed to discourage the wives and concubines from venturing out tonight. Perfect peace beckoned, a solitude unspoiled. She struck out into the garden, grateful for the chance to be both alone and uninhibited in her movements. It was a pleasure she hadn't enjoyed for far too long. The paths lay silvered by starlight, and every sweet flower stood out in sharp relief against the darkness, nodding and luminous on their slender stems. Here and there the pale moths fluttered in clouds, brushing Rhodopis lightly with their powdery wings as she moved among them. The churring of frogs took the shape of music in her head, revealing to her rhythms and melodies she alone could hear. She danced along the garden path, stretching and reaching, turning and bending in time, allowing her fears and anxieties to slide away while she gave into that fleeting moment of joy.

Rhodopis went wherever the music of her heart directed. She followed the curves of lily beds, cartwheeled beneath trained arches dense with roses, and danced lightly at the edge of the lake, moving forward, then back along the brick retaining wall with deft, sure-footed steps, playing games with her pale reflection in the wind-stirred water. She sprang hand over foot across a lawn of plush grass, delighting in the tickle of the freshly cut, sap-scented blades against her palms and the soles of her bare feet. Rhodopis moved without regard for where she was—for the women's garden was vast, and anyhow, a high, white-plastered wall circled the palace, its top patrolled by guards both day and night. She had nothing to fear.

As she was kicking and twirling her way across a small, moonlit courtyard, a rough burst of laughter startled her to stillness. Breath heaving, Rhodopis stared wide-eyed around the dark garden, trying to find the interloper. The voice had been distinctly male, rough-edged and low. But it was not Amasis; Rhodopis knew that at once. There was always a certain gentleness, a deferent hesitation in the Pharaoh's voice and manner. There had been nothing gentle or soft about the laugh she had heard.

"Who's there?" Rhodopis said, turning slowly in a circle. She gazed up at the wall—perhaps it had been a guard, looking down on her—but the wall was too far from where she now stood.

There was no chance a guard's voice would have sounded so disconcertingly near. "Show yourself at once!" Then, blushing, she realized she had been speaking Greek. She repeated the command in Egyptian.

The tall, blocky shadow of a man stirred, shifting along one of the paths that radiated out from the courtyard. A chill settled in Rhodopis' stomach. Even before he left the deeper shadows and stepped into honest moonlight, she recognized Psamtik, the king's son—knew him by his slow, confident gait, by the starlight flashing off his teeth, bared like an animal's in an arrogant and possessive grin.

"Quite a dance, little Greek girl," Psamtik said, amused.

Rhodopis drew herself up, facing him squarely. He may be the king's son, but she was the king's favorite. She had no reason to fear him. "What are you doing in the women's garden? You aren't allowed here without guards to accompany you. No one but the Pharaoh is allowed."

Psamtik laughed again. "I'm not in the women's garden. And neither are you." He gave a short, directional nod.

Though she didn't like to turn her back on Psamtik, Rhodopis chanced a quick peek over her shoulder. There, flanking the widest path, stood the two great stone urns that marked the boundary between the women's private gardens and the Pharaoh's. She had wandered beyond her place. Wrapped in the ecstasy of dance, she hadn't noticed the urns as she passed them.

Rhodopis turned back to the king's son, lowering her face contritely. Her cheeks flamed. "I'm sorry; I didn't know. I... I shouldn't have scolded you."

"Don't be afraid, little Greek girl." Psamtik chuckled deep in his throat. He slid closer. "I won't hurt you. But you are charming, aren't you, when you blush that way? I can see why my father likes you so well."

Not knowing how to answer—whether any response at all could be considered either safe or sensible—Rhodopis maintained her silence. But she would not allow Psamtik's words to beguile her. He may be all smiles and quiet laughter now, but Rhodopis was no fool. Every bitter glare he'd ever cast in her direction repeated in her mind; the predatory glint in his dark eyes flashed at her, bright and cold as light on a sword's edge.

"What are you doing out at night, by yourself?" Psamtik asked casually.

Rhodopis glanced behind once more, trying to work out exactly where she was in the garden, and how long it would take her to return to her chamber.

Psamtik tried another approach. "You aren't thinking of flitting away, are you, when we've only just begun to talk? Why don't you stay and keep me company? I hear you are well versed in the arts of entertaining men."

At once, Rhodopis turned her back on the heir and strode toward the twin shadows of the urns—and the women's realm beyond. But a heartbeat later, Psamtik seized her hard by the upper arm; he spun her about roughly.

"Don't touch me," Rhodopis spat.

Before she could say more, Psamtik's huge, hard hand closed painfully around her jaw. He lifted her face, forcing Rhodopis to look up into his eyes—and she stifled a gasp, for she saw the slow fire of an unpleasant promise there, the smoldering embers of cruelty. For the first time since that terrible night when she was caught out in the marketplace, alone and unprotected while the Egyptians and Greeks clashed around her, Rhodopis' stomach churned with a cold, queasy wave of panic.

"Smile," Psamtik said smoothly. "You of all people should know that men like to talk to pretty girls who smile."

Rhodopis clenched her jaw. She stared at Psamtik levelly, giving him nothing, praying he would release his grip. Her legs screamed at her to run; her heart pounded with a fear that throbbed in her ears, but she forced herself to watch Psamtik's face coolly, dispassionately.

"You are pretty, even if you don't smile." He paused, but when Rhodopis remained unmoved, his voice slouched lower, an oily whisper. "What, don't you like compliments? Kmetu women do. But maybe it's different for you Greeks." Suddenly, he shook Rhodopis hard; her neck tensed in resistance, and pain shot down her back and shoulders. She bit back a harsh cry. "But a Greek whore like you... maybe you only like one thing—maybe you only understand one thing."

He stepped back, toward the shadows of the garden, dragging Rhodopis along. "Just as well," Psamtik said. "Perhaps my father's not the fool I think him, after all. Perhaps he has the right idea. Kmetu women for good and honorable work, but for convenient usage... well, your kind will do."

Rhodopis seized his wrist, digging in with her nails, trying to break his grip on her face—but his arm was like the corded heft of a ship's rope, too taut and cumbersome for her to move.

He laughed at her struggle. "Of course, you've only been with old Amasis since coming here to the palace, haven't you? Then you don't know what a real Egyptian man feels like—a true Kmetu, blessed by the gods, not a limp old rag like my father. But you'll know after tonight... what a real Kmetu man is, how powerful we are."

Beyond Psamtik's thick shoulder, Rhodopis saw something pale and low resolve out of the darkness. The chill in her blood redoubled when she realized he was hauling her toward a stone garden bench. She mustn't let him force her down on that bench —it would all be over, then. She rolled her eyes desperately toward the wall, pale and impossibly far off in the moonlight. Ought she to scream, and alert the guards? Would they even hear her, at this distance? And if they did... her heart leaped higher in her throat... even if they did hear, would they bother to come to her aid? The Pharaoh's guards were all Egyptian, too—for prominent families were as eager to send their sons to the king's service as they were to send their daughters to his harem. How could she expect an Egyptian man, a son of an old, noble, and thoroughly embittered family, to stop Psamtik from doing whatever he pleased? No—Rhodopis understood at once that an Egyptian guard would never lose a moment's sleep over a Greek girl raped and defiled... even if she was the king's favorite.

I'm on my own, and no mistake, she thought frantically. She braced her bare feet against the courtyard stones, trying to resist, and bit back a whimper as Psamtik dragged her ever closer to the bench; the skin of her soles scraped away, stinging and bleeding. *Gods preserve me... gods, give me some idea...!*

A memory flashed in her mind, bursting upon her so bright and clear that her head ached with its sudden vividness. She recalled dancing at Xanthes' party—that first time, when she had still been with Iadmon. The Maiden of the Reeds. She remembered the slap of Iadmon's hand against her cheek—could feel the sting even now, beneath Psamtik's brutal grip. She saw the wash of moonlight in Xanthes' courtyard, Iadmon's litter vanishing through the vine-wrapped gate. And Archidike, her strange blue eyes intense in the darkness, her low voice murmuring. About knives.

With a force of will she didn't know she possessed, Rhodopis released her desperate grip on Psamtik's arm. She fumbled her hands in her belt of her tunic, just long enough to be convincing. And then...

Her hand shot toward Psamtik's body with startling force. Her long, lacquered nail pressed hard into his rib; she bore her weight upon it, twisting. He paused, tensing, and stared at her wide-eyed.

"I've got a knife," Rhodopis gasped. "Release me, or I'll spill your blood!"

Psamtik let go of her jaw; he flinched back, recoiling instinctively. That brief moment was all Rhodopis needed. With a speed and deftness only a dancer could possess, she twisted and spun away from him, throwing herself beyond his reach. Then she pelted back along the path toward the two stone urns.

"You gods-cursed slit!" Psamtik roared behind her. She could hear his pounding footsteps as he gave chase, could feel each leaping stride reverberating through the earth as he sprinted ever nearer.

Would he follow her into the women's garden? Rhodopis had no reason to believe Psamtik would respect the boundary of the urns. She would have to out-maneuver him if she hoped to remain free.

Two years of dancing had made her body athletic and resilient; she was nimble, too, and as soon as she passed the stone urns, Rhodopis left the garden path and crashed through the flower beds, weaving and dodging around bushes and trees, slipping through narrow gaps between vine-covered trellises, seeking to put every obstacle she could find between herself and the beast who hunted her. Pain shrieked up from her injured soles with every desperate stride, but Rhodopis ignored it. She thought of nothing but Psamtik, lumbering and crashing as he tried to give chase through the thick, tangled beds of the garden.

The windows of the women's quarters came into view, glowing ember-red against the darkness. Psamtik's sounds or pursuit faded, then stopped, and only his coarse, cruel laughter followed Rhodopis through the darkness.

She didn't stop running until she broke free of the last flower bed, the one that stood nearest the great door to the women's wing. There she pulled up short, bracing her hands against her quivering knees, sobbing for breath. Nebetiah, Iset, and Minneferet were lounging on the short grass, enjoying the sweet breezes and the plate of honey cakes that lay between them. They broke off their conversation, staring up at Rhodopis in confusion and surprise.

Rhodopis looked down at herself, the torn, stained tunic, her legs scratched by the thorns of the garden. Droplets of blood stood out clearly against her pale skin. She limped a few steps, strangling a cry of pain, then halted again and stood mutely before the women.

"Mother Hathor save us," Iset said. "What happened to you? You look like you've crawled up out of the Duat!"

Nebetiah clambered to her feet. "We heard the running, but we thought some of the king's hounds had got out and were chasing each other through the garden. Rhodopis, what's the matter?"

Rhodopis opened her mouth, prepared to tell them every-thing. The next moment, she shut it again decisively. The three women might believe her if she told them what had happened, but she was not confident they would feel any sympathy. She was the favorite, now, after all... surely they would find some opportu-nity in her misfortune and act upon it. What would Rhodopis do if they spread tales that she had enticed Psamtik in the garden? *Easy enough to make me fall from my place, if anyone was to believe such a story. And who wouldn't believe? I'm nothing but a Greek whore to these women. I don't belong. They'd be glad to see me done in.*

She shook her head at the three women and limped past them. Nebetiah reached out for her, but Rhodopis flinched away from her hand. She slipped into the women's hall and made her way painfully down the corridor, heedless of the bloody foot-prints she left behind. The passage was empty, thank the gods; the rest of the women were still lounging in their baths, or, more likely, had gone off to their beds.

Rhodopis found the door to her chamber and hid away in that private sanctuary for the second time that night. And for the second time, she leaned against the door from the inside, shud-dering and weeping where no one else could see.

3

GOSSIP

RHODOPIS WAS SURPRISED TO FIND HERSELF WAKING IN A BEAM OF morning light, for she had been certain she would never fall asleep—*could* never sleep again, for the darkness of her chamber seemed to hide the shape of the leering, laughing Psamtik in every corner and shadow. She had lain awake for hours, clutching the cover-sheet to her chin, straining to hear the crackle of twigs or a heavy footfall over the sound of night insects—any sign that might mean Psamtik was coming through the garden, pursuing her, *hunting* her. She groaned at the noise of two maids carrying her breakfast tray. Even their subdued chatter and soft laughter hurt her head, which felt as if it were stuffed full of wadded linen. The early light was intense on the window sill; its glare made Rhodopis squint and cringe. She raised a hand up to shield her eyes from the slashing light.

"My lady," one of the maids said, dropping the tray onto Rhodopis' table with an unfortunate crash, "what in Sekhmet's name has happened? Your feet—!"

In her sleep, Rhodopis had kicked the sheets askew; now her battered feet lay exposed on the mattress. She tried to hide them again, but the sudden movement made her wince and hiss with pain.

The maids edged closer to the bed. Both women eyed her bruised, bloody feet as if they were a pair of cobras coiled on the mattress.

"Mistress Iset, have mercy," the first said. "You're hurt, my lady!"

"Of course I am." Rhodopis didn't intend to be snappish with the maids, but a dreadful humiliation was sinking deeper into her bones with each passing moment. The servants' attention made her feel weak and helpless, as if she were an animal in a menagerie, caged for display. She shook her head impatiently. "Don't worry about me; I'll be all right."

She made as if to stand. One of the servants restrained her with a gentle hand on her shoulder. Rhodopis sank back against her cushions, secretly grateful; the mere thought of putting weight on her feet made her ache and shudder. To stand would have been agony.

"You must have a physician, my lady," the maid said. "If those cuts aren't cleaned properly, they may never heal."

Rhodopis sighed. "You're right. Suppose you ought to send for the physician, then."

The two servants exchanged wary glances, brows raised under the dark, straight-cut fringes of their hair. Their silence was heavy as an overfilled wine skin. Then the one who had kept Rhodopis in bed shook her head slowly. "Oh, no, my lady—not us. Only the chief wife can send for the court physician. But don't fret; Khedeb-Netjer-Bona will be here in a twinkling, and once she's seen your injuries for herself, she won't hesitate to have you treated."

"Khedeb-Netjer-Bona." A new wellspring of anxiety filled Rhodopis' stomach. "But I—"

It was too late. The women had already gone, bustling away with their new errand. Rhodopis could do nothing but wait for the chief wife to arrive. Khedeb-Netjer-Bona was the last person she wished to see at that moment, but she could hardly leap up from the bed and flee the room. She lay with her trembling hands folded across her stomach, pressing her belly to ward off the queasiness of worry. At last, she heard the chief wife's light but confident tread at the threshold of her door.

"Chief Wife," Rhodopis said, a polite greeting. She pushed herself up until she was sitting, propped against her cushions. "Forgive me for not standing."

Rhodopis knew that Khedeb-Netjer-Bona was in her late thirties, but if no one had told her so, she would have been hard-pressed to guess the chief wife's age. Khedeb-Netjer-Bona was one of those smooth-skinned, serious-eyed women whose faces refuse to mark any passage of time—at least until they've achieved a truly venerable state, and then they seem to age all at once. The chief wife was not beautiful, exactly—her nose was far too bold, with a sharp hook like a falcon's beak; her cheeks and chin were quite narrow, her eyes set rather close together. But in her unshakeable poise and proud bearing, she carried all the exquisite loveliness of a dozen goddesses. Regal and imposing despite her short and slender frame, Khedeb-Netjer-Bona stood in silence for a long moment, allowing the force of her presence to fill the room. Her dark brows were arched curiously; long, lacquered nails tapped in a thoughtful rhythm against Rhodopis' little table with its untouched tray. The chief wife's lips pursed as she considered the Greek girl, but her expression was unreadable. Rhodopis willed herself not to fidget under that silent scrutiny; she bit her lip, waiting for the chief wife to speak.

"The servants tell me you have injured yourself," Khedeb-Netjer-Bona said. Her voice was smooth as well-polished wood, low-pitched for a woman—a surprising sound, coming from such a small body. She drifted closer, peering down at Rhodopis' feet, though without any of the recoiling horror the maids had shown. Only a flicker of startled disgust passed across her features, instantly quelled. "What in the all the gods' names did you do to yourself, girl?"

"I..." Rhodopis swallowed hard. "I was running, Chief Wife."

"Running."

"Without my sandals."

"I can see that. What possessed you to do such a thing?"

Rhodopis lowered her eyes, fixing a dull stare on her clenched fists. Did she dare confess that she had left the women's garden? She had done it quite by accident, of course, but that would make little difference. Even if Khedeb-Netjer-Bona forgave her for venturing beyond the stone urns, would she believe that Psamtik had menaced her—had tried to rape her?

Still the chief wife waited, silent with expectation. Rhodopis could feel Khedeb-Netjer-Bona's sharp eyes resting on her, weighing her, judging her. The insistence of that stare pricked like a hundred needles.

"I was running from... someone who wanted to hurt me."

"Ah." Khedeb-Netjer-Bona folded her arms beneath her small breasts and walked to the garden window. Her back remained turned to Rhodopis, yet still her voice managed to fill the room with ease. Its tone was flat, devoid of sympathy, but at least the words were understanding. "You needn't say any more, girl. I take your meaning. There are certain dangers lurking in this palace; no one knows that better than I." She spun abruptly on her heel, so suddenly that Rhodopis flinched. Khedeb-Netjer-Bona stared at her with that same sober, indecipherable composure. "I am not inclined to like you, Rhodopis—but I believe you know that already. However, I can find no fault in your actions. What happened to you last night could have happened just as easily to any woman under my care."

Khedeb-Netjer-Bona sighed. Her shoulders sagged a little—as much a display of desperation as the chief wife ever permitted. "I've often prayed for war, you know. Wicked of me, yet I won't deny it. And do you know why I pray for war, girl? So *that* one will be sent off to the battlefield. If the gods were merciful, they would remove him from my path entirely."

Rhodopis blinked at the chief wife in surprise. "But isn't he your son?"

Khedeb-Netjer-Bona laughed—a hoarse, rattling cough that seemed too deep and cynical to have come from her small, delicate body. "Gods, no. Amasis had another chief wife before me. She succumbed to a fever and left her vicious whelp behind to plague not only my days but my every waking thought, too. Psamtik is *her* son, not mine. But he is *my* problem, never the less, and not only because he chases the Pharaoh's women about like a leopard after gazelles. Someday he will take the throne, you see. On that day, I must give him one of my daughters to wed."

Rhodopis sat up straighter. "But *must* you, Chief Wife? I wouldn't like to be married to that man, and... oh, I hate to think of your daughters, young as they are—"

Khedeb-Netjer-Bona cut her off with a wave of her hand. "You come too close to impertinence, Rhodopis."

"I'm sorry." Her cheeks heated; she sank back against the cushions again. "I didn't mean it."

"No, I don't believe you did. But it's true: I must marry one of my girls to the king's son. It is the way of things—the tradition we've kept here in Kmet since time past remembering. If I were to rebel against a tradition so old, so revered, it would be..." The chief wife made a lost, grasping gesture, her empty hands sifting uselessly through the air as she searched for the right word.

"Not maat?" Rhodopis suggested.

Khedeb-Netjer-Bona offered a tiny smile, the merest curve of one side of her mouth. "Exactly. It would not be maat. I don't like it any better than you do. And yet, I can't help but feel that whichever of my daughters goes to Psamtik's marriage bed is the lucky one. For I know—I see already—that the other girl, and I, will be in far greater danger on the day Amasis dies."

"How can that be, Chief Wife?"

Khedeb-Netjer-Bona returned to the garden window. She gazed out at the greenery for a moment, the placid leaves and cheerful blooms bathed in warm morning light. She said dully, "Do you know what young lions do, Rhodopis? Out there in the desert? When they depose an older male from his pride—or when they kill him—they maul all his little cubs to death. It makes the lionesses receptive, so the new males may sire their own get upon the females. Psamtik will take no chances; no one with any claim to the throne, no matter how slim, will be left alive to oppose him."

Rhodopis shuddered. In Khedeb-Netjer-Bona's slender body, in the stillness of her posture, she read a new vulnerability, where before she had seen only icy and carefully maintained dignity.

The chief wife glanced at Rhodopis again. Her mouth turned down in a thoughtful frown; she seemed to understand that she had said too much, gone too far in confiding to the Greek newcomer. She brushed her hands together, a gesture that said, "Let us turn to our task," and headed toward Rhodopis' door with a brisk step, gliding beyond the reach of their dark conversation. "I'll send for the physician," she said. "It will be painful, I think, to clean and treat those injuries. But you'll bear it, I expect. You seem a tougher and more sensible girl than I've given you credit for."

❧

IT TOOK NEARLY two full weeks for Rhodopis' feet to heal—two weeks of unpleasant ministration from the king's physician, a pinch-faced old man whom the gods had not seen fit to bless with gentle hands. Two weeks of swabbing with concentrated wine—it burned like a malicious fire—and salving with thick, noxious-smelling oils. In all that time, Rhodopis was half convinced she would never dance again—indeed, that she would never walk again without limping and crying out piteously—

though every day the physician reassured her that her feet were healing exactly as he expected.

Finally, though, the worst of her lacerations closed and the raw, red scrapes hardened with scab. If she moved with care, Rhodopis found she could walk well enough, and soon she was even permitted to trade the linen wraps that bound her wounds for ordinary sandals, though the doctor admonished her to keep them impeccably clean, and to bless them with the smoke of myrrh incense morning and night, which would prevent foul spirits from clinging to the soles and reintroducing infection. The fear that she would never dance again fled from Rhodopis' mind. The departure of that constant dread left her feeling lighter and more joyous than she had since her first day in the Pharaoh's palace.

Buoyed and glad, Rhodopis found herself craving for interaction with the other women. The yearning for company—for conversation and laughter, if not true friendship—seized her with a grip as powerful as the worst hunger she had endured as a child. Most of the women still seemed to dislike Rhodopis. She was Greek, after all, and were not the Greeks the source of all Egypt's troubles? But she was determined to find her feet among them, to make the most of her situation.

Spinning linen threads was the traditional pastime of the Pharaoh's women. For thousands of years, the king's household had occupied itself with spindles and distaffs, transforming the long, pale-gold fibers of the flax plant into soft, pliant threads. Women of senior standing wove the threads on their large, intricate looms, producing vast lengths of fine linen, pale and flowing as moonlight on water. Amasis' women took their work very seriously indeed—for now more than ever before, it seemed critical that they preserve the old ways, the customs and honored traditions that had defined them as Egyptians for uncountable generations.

Rhodopis threw herself into spinning with earnest enthusiasm. She was quite hopeless at the work. She wielded the distaff no more gracefully than a child playing with a wooden sword. Her fingertips cracked and blistered from the friction of the dry flax stems, but despite her sacrifices and dogged determination, her threads remained abysmally kinked and marred by ugly slubs. The other women gossiped and joked and sang their songs, and all the while perfectly smooth and uniform threads seemed to sprout from their fingertips like seedlings from the dark Egyptian soil. They achieved what Rhodopis could only dream of, and apparently without the least bit of exertion or concentration. She would have been envious, if not for the pleasure she took in their company. For though they still disapproved of the Greek girl whom the king had dropped among them like a pebble carelessly tossed into a jewel box, the women seemed to approve of Rhodopis' dedication to her spindle and distaff. She may not be Egyptian, but she seemed bent on learning the ways of a true Egyptian woman—on taking a proper role within the harem. For now, it was reason enough for them to tolerate Rhodopis' presence.

One bright, humid morning, in a circle of white stone benches beneath the shade of a rustling sycamore, Rhodopis sat with the harem girls, spinning in the sweet garden breeze. The women chattered and jested as always while spindles dropped from their hands and rose again, dropped and rose in a steady, soothing rhythm. The twirling spindle weights flashed their blurred colors against the pure white of the women's skirts. Rhodopis listened to their conversation, trying to concentrate more on their talk than on the feel of her threads, which were embarrassingly rough, as ever.

"Did I tell you," Nebetiah said, "I've had another letter from my mother?" Her thread seemed to form itself between her deft fingers. She spun easily as she talked, a spider casting out its gossamer web.

"Not yet," Iset said, "but I have a feeling we'll hear about it now."

"The riots in the northern end of the city have been quelled— at least for now. That's what Mother said."

"Good news," said Sobek-Neferu.

Iset emitted a tiny, delicate snort. "*Is* it good news?"

"Why wouldn't it be? You don't want violence and destruction, do you?"

"Mm," Iset said noncommittally. She shrugged as she caught her spindle and dropped it again. Her eyes never left the weight as it whirled at the end of her thread, but she spoke rather forcefully, and loud enough for every woman to hear. "No one wants violence and destruction, but neither do I want to see good and true Kmetu people roll over like dogs in the street, with their bellies exposed."

"It's not the same thing," Sobek-Neferu protested.

"Like *dogs*," Iset said. "Whining in their throats, tails between their legs, pissing on the spot, out of pure terror of their masters!"

Nebetiah laughed. "You do paint a vivid scene. I'd hardly call the Greeks masters of any Kmetu."

"Oh, wouldn't you?"

At Iset's wry murmur, other women in the spinning circle nodded. "She's right," someone said from the other side of the small courtyard.

Iset went on. "If there are riots, at least it means our people fight back."

"Fight *back*?" said Sobek-Neferu. "No—they are only *fighting*. Fighting solves nothing."

"Surely you're right," Iset said airily. "That must be why the Pharaoh keeps such a large army: to accomplish nothing whatsoever."

"Stop it, both of you," Nebetiah said. "You hiss at each other like a couple of vipers. What good does it do?"

Sitmut, a plump young woman who was always quick with a

jest, tossed out a careless laugh. "Better a hissing viper than a whining dog with its belly exposed. Am I right, Iset?"

"You'd rather see riots than peace." Sobek-Neferu sounded weary and sad.

"It's not that we want riots," Sitmut said. "But how else are Kmetu to find any justice? We're all here in the harem at the pleasure of the Pharaoh. But you know he cares nothing for justice or peace."

"That's not true." Sobek-Neferu didn't sound convinced by her own words.

"The time for peaceful negotiations is long past," Iset said. "Negotiations with Greece... negotiations with our king..."

Sitmut kicked a pebble in Iset's direction. "You had better take care. If the chief wife hears you say such things—"

"What can she do to me?" Iset said defiantly. "Throw me out into the street? Very well; I'll join the riots!"

Nebetiah chuckled as she pulled more flax from her distaff.

Iset rounded on her. "Do you find something amusing?"

"Nothing at all." Nebetiah shrugged, but she couldn't keep the smile from her face. She broke out in full-throated laughter, nearly dropping her spindle and distaff as she rocked and shook. "It's only... the thought of *you*, pounding up and down the streets, shouting and throwing stones! You'd break off a fingernail, and then, gods help us all!"

"Gods help the Greek pestilence," Iset growled.

All laughter died on the instant. Rhodopis felt a dozen pairs of eyes turn in her direction, but she couldn't have said whether those looks were apologetic or challenging. *Reckon a bit of both is about right*, she thought. Her cheeks heated, and she kept her own gaze downcast so she wouldn't be forced to meet either an accusing stare or a sympathetic one.

"Don't stop talking on account of me, girls; you mustn't," Rhodopis said. "Anyway, I don't disagree—not with any of you. Of course I don't like the riots—who does?—but it just about looks as if the... the Kmetu have been pushed past what anyone can bear." She smothered a sigh. She had very nearly called the native people *Egyptians*, and none of the Pharaoh's girls—proud Kmetu, one and all—would have looked kindly on such an error.

"See?" Iset said, triumphant. "Even the Greek pestilence agrees with me."

A week ago, Iset's words would have been nakedly barbed. Now she sounded friendly, almost jovial. Rhodopis peered up through her lashes and offered Iset a shy smile. The dark-eyed young woman grinned back and bumped Rhodopis' shoulder with her own.

"Somebody teach this poor flea how to spin, though, for the sake of sweet Goddess Nit! Look at her threads; they're like a ship's lines."

"It's true!" Rhodopis laughed helplessly. "If we send my thread to the weaving house, the older women will think we're trying to play a terrible joke on them. You couldn't weave a grain sack from my spinning!"

Nebetiah eyed Rhodopis' thread, trying once more to hide a smile... and failing. "Your thread might make a serviceable fishing net."

"Not even that! I'm about as much use as a two-legged horse."

"The important thing is that you're trying," Nebetiah said. "With enough practice, you'll learn."

The women's conversation drifted on, all question of riots and pestilence forgotten for the time being. But the placid smile faded slowly from Rhodopis' lips as she played her companions' talk over again in her mind. What she'd told them was true: it was clear as daylight to any blind fool that the Egyptians of Memphis —and elsewhere in the Pharaoh's lands—had endured more than any people ought. How much longer would they tolerate their king's outrages? And when they'd finally had enough, what could Amasis expect? What could any Greek in the city expect? The mere thought was enough to make Rhodopis shudder with dread. She held no affection for Egypt. Indeed, Memphis society had taken much from her: she could only pray that her family had made it back to Thrace safely, for she had no way to contact them now; nor had she a friend in the world, thanks to the hard culture of the ever-warring hetaerae. Egypt could fall as fast and hard as hail from the Thracian sky, and Rhodopis would never shed a tear. The country was nothing to her; it was merely the place where she had washed ashore, the culture in which she found herself embedded and unwanted, like a sliver of wood in tender flesh.

But when it all boils over, they'll come for the Greeks, the moment Amasis is pulled from his throne...

Iset roared with laughter at one of Sitmut's jokes; Rhodopis looked around, smiling as if she'd heard the jest and understood it. She had not, of course. Nothing her companions said had penetrated the cloud of her bleak thoughts.

"Don't you wish it!" Iset howled, while the other girls giggled and shrieked. "Can't you just picture Sitmut here, with her hair unbound and her breasts out in the wind, standing up there on the wall and shouting—"

"Hush!" Nebetiah waved a hand frantically; the spinning circle fell silent. Nebetiah's eyes widened; she nodded significantly toward the ornate doorway that led from the garden into the women's quarters. "King's guards," she whispered.

Rhodopis turned, as all the women did, to peer curiously at the pair of guards as they stepped out of the shaded portico. Bright sunlight bounced off the blue-and-white stripes of their kilts and glinted, cold and sharp, on the hilts of their sheathed blades. Both men were broad and vigorous as bulls. Armored pectorals, made from overlapping bronze scales, covered their chests, but the solid, blocky form of their muscles was evident through their stiff uniforms.

"My, my," Iset said appreciatively.

"They're looking for someone," said Sitmut.

"I hope it's me."

"It's not, Iset, so wring out your skirt and hang it up to dry."

"The chief wife?" Minneferet suggested.

"Where is the chief wife?" Nebetiah peered around the circle, her eyes narrowing suspiciously. "I haven't seen her all day."

"I saw her," Minneferet said. "She was strolling in the garden, not an hour ago."

Iset grunted softly. "How pleasant for her."

"Iset's jealous," Sitmut said, laughing. "*She* wants to be the chief wife."

"May all the gods preserve me from such a fate. I'm too young yet to go sour."

"You've already gone sour, like goat's milk in the sun." Sitmut punctuated her comment with a loud, goatish bleat.

At that moment, Khedeb-Netjer-Bona appeared, material-izing among the lush flower beds like a mist, placid and drifting. The spinning circle silenced itself again; backs straightened and faces stilled, and the women's spindles dropped and spun with renewed vigor. Rhodopis watched as Khedeb-Netjer-Bona approached the two guardsmen with her usual unflappable poise. The chief wife spoke to the guards—no more than a few words—then turned to look at the spinning circle. A definite frown creased her brow, shadowing her narrow features. Her sharp black eyes fastened on Rhodopis, and the frown deepened. An uneasy chill prickled down Rhodopis' arms.

"Rhodopis," Khedeb-Netjer-Bona called. "Come here, girl."

The thread slipped from Rhodopis' fingers; her spindle dropped to the ground, clattering across the courtyard's paving stones and rolling in the dust. She scrambled to pick it up with clumsy, tingling hands. The king's guard—sent for her? It wasn't unusual for Amasis to send for Rhodopis, of course, for she was his favorite, although the king had deprived himself of her enter-tainments while her injured feet were healing. *He's heard I can walk again, and wants to lie with me—that's all.* Again and again,

Rhodopis tried to convince herself it was true. But something about the circumstances gnawed at her mind. It was mid-day, and Amasis preferred his affections at night. Something had changed. Something had disrupted the routine of the palace. Has it come so soon? *Are the Egyptians clamoring round the outer gate? Are they calling for my death—for all the Greek pestilence to be stamped out?*

Rhodopis bit her lip as Minneferet helped her gather up the ruined thread and spindle. Don't be a fool, she told herself sensibly. *When the revolt against Amasis comes, you'll hear the shouting outside the palace walls long before any guards come to take you.* It was a comforting thought, though the gods knew such a possibility should have comforted no one. *I've landed in a strange time, a strange place. Wonder if I'll ever find my way out again, into a world that's safe and makes sense, the way any world ought to do.*

Rhodopis hurried to Khedeb-Netjer-Bona and bowed low. "How can I be of service, Chief Wife?"

"It seems you're wanted in the Pharaoh's audience hall."

"His hall? Not his bed chamber?" Khedeb-Netjer-Bona cleared her throat, and Rhodopis blushed. "I... I'm sorry, Chief Wife. That was not discreet."

"No, but I suppose it can be forgiven. It is no secret, what purpose you serve in the king's household."

Rhodopis bowed again. She didn't know what else to do, how she might respond. "I will go to the king at once, of course."

"I'll come along," the chief wife said. "Only to accompany you to the king's door. My legs could use a stretch." That, of course, was untrue. Khedeb-Netjer-Bona had been walking in the garden for the gods alone knew how long. She called out to the spinning circle, though her words were affectionate, not harsh. "The rest of you: back to work. Yes, I know you're all trying to listen to our conversation. I'm well aware that you're a pack of shameless gossips. The flax won't spin itself."

The chief wife turned abruptly and headed for the portico. In the blink of an eye, she was lost amid the deep-blue shadows.

Rhodopis and the two guards hurried to catch up with her. She may have been a small woman, but Khedeb-Netjer-Bona had as stride like a conquering general. Rhodopis positioned herself a modest half-pace behind the chief wife's shoulder, but she nearly had to skip to maintain the woman's stubborn pace. Quiet and obedient, Rhodopis rushed through the brightly painted passages of the harem. The only sound in the corridors was the rapid clip of Khedeb-Netjer-Bona's hard-soled sandals against stone.

When they had passed beyond the great green arch that marked the interior entry to the women's quarters, Khedeb-Netjer-Bona spoke so suddenly that Rhodopis stifled a squeak of alarm.

"Your feet seem to have healed well." The chief wife did not look around as she spoke. Her dark, narrow eyes remained fixed on the gilded halls and pillars ahead.

"Yes, my lady," Rhodopis managed, "thanks to you."

"Thanks to the physician. I had nothing to do with it. Perhaps Amasis wants to see you dance now that you've mended."

"But he never sends for me when the sun is up. I don't understand it. I wonder, Chief Wife, could something be amiss?"

Khedeb-Netjer-Bona turned her head, just enough that Rhodopis could see the woman's sparing, almost grudging half-smile. "You are a bright girl. I've noted that about you."

Rhodopis smiled tentatively.

"This is a strange turn," Khedeb-Netjer-Bona said, "a disruption, an alteration of the king's routine. Any disruption concerns me. I am sure I don't need to tell you why."

Psamtik, waiting like a lion in the desert for his chance to leap and tear. No, the chief wife had no need to remind Rhodopis why she was unsettled. Rhodopis merely nodded.

"That is why I've come with you to the king's hall."

"You are the chief wife, and may go wherever you please, of course."

"Of course I may. I was not asking your leave, girl."

"No; I didn't think..." Rhodopis fell silent again. She didn't know how to speak to this woman—this greatest, most influential of women in the whole vast and ancient land of Egypt. Since the day when Khedeb-Netjer-Bona had come to her chamber and seen her wounded feet—since they had shared their mutual dislike of Psamtik—Rhodopis had sensed a subtle softening in the chief wife's demeanor. She was under no illusion that Khedeb-Netjer-Bona liked her. But the almost imperceptible thawing of the chief wife's habitual iciness might indicate something akin to respect. Was that enough? Could Rhodopis speak to the chief wife freely without fear of undue rebuke? The urge to explain herself swelled in Rhodopis' chest, rising uncomfortably to her throat. She wanted only to unburden herself of the guilt that had hung so heavy on her heart since the most recent feast. She took several deep breaths, intending to confess to Khedeb-Netjer-Bona everything that roiled in her mind, but the right words evaded her. Each time she opened her mouth, she could feel the chief wife's sideways glance, could sense the woman's growing expectation.

"Let it out, girl," Khedeb-Netjer-Bona said shortly. "Whatever is plaguing your heart: speak."

"I didn't mean to harm anyone, Chief Wife," Rhodopis said in a rush, her words suddenly freed.

"Harm?"

"That is to say, I didn't intend to set any woman back."

"Ah. You refer to your rapid rise as the king's favorite."

"Yes, my lady," Rhodopis murmured.

Khedeb-Netjer-Bona strode on, quiet but thoughtful. Finally she said, "No; I don't suppose you meant any harm. Some women would have intended great harm, you know. Some would have whispered in Amasis' ear, convinced him to increase their fortunes at the expense of some harem rival. But you seem entirely too innocent for such scheming." She fell silent again and directed the full force of her piercing stare at Rhodopis as they walked. Rhodopis' face burned under the chief wife's scrutiny.

"Innocent," Khedeb-Netjer-Bona said, musing, "and yet there is something shrewd about you. One doesn't find such qualities often in girls of your age."

"I've never thought myself shrewd, Chief Wife."

"Perhaps it is not exactly the right word. Let me see... No, I'm not prepared to call you 'calculating.' That's not the correct word, either. Watchful, perhaps. Yes. Observant."

Not knowing whether the chief wife was criticizing or complimenting her, Rhodopis said nothing.

"I wonder," Khedeb-Netjer-Bona said, "what will you do with that talent?"

"Talent? It's not a talent, is it, to be observant?"

"Indeed it is, girl. A rare and useful one, too."

"But what can I do, with this talent or any other, shut up in the harem as I am?"

Khedeb-Netjer-Bona smiled tightly. "Doesn't harem life suit you?"

Rhodopis swallowed hard. She could think of no response that was both safe and honest.

The chief wife shrugged lightly at Rhodopis' silence. "You could gossip. A sharp-eyed thing like you, seeing and understanding even the smallest details of the most seemingly mundane exchanges... your tongue could be legendary. You could even put Sitmut to shame; the spinning circle would fall at your feet, Greek or no. Good gossip could make you popular with the other young women. Perhaps then you would no longer be so lonely."

They rounded a massive pillar and turned down an adjoining hall. There before them stood the door to the Pharaoh's audience room. The likeness of a great winged scarab was carved into its surface. The beetle's domed carapace was a brilliant lapis-blue;

the angular forelegs were outstretched, rolling a gilded, glittering sun-disc across the flat cedar plane of the sky. There was no more time for conversation; they had reached their destination. The two soldiers guarding the scarab door straightened abruptly at sight of the chief wife; one turned and rapped on the door, and a moment later it swung open.

On the threshold of the Pharaoh's hall, Rhodopis paused, taking in the scene before her, wondering at Khedeb-Netjer-Bona's sudden stillness. The chief wife had gone tense as a harp string the moment her sharp stare landed on the two young women who stood trembling before the Pharaoh's throne.

❧ 4 ❧

A GIFT OF BRIDES

OVER THE COURSE OF HER THREE MONTHS IN THE PHARAOH'S
harem, Rhodopis had fit together the history of Amasis, piece by
piece. He had been born a common man in the southern territory
of the Nile, but had risen to prominence in the army—first as a
bowman, then as an officer, and finally, a trusted general of Ha'a-
Ibre, the previous king and father of Khedeb-Netjer-Bona.

From the beginning of his reign, Ha'a-Ibre had thrown his
efforts into defending the farthest extremities of his empire—or
what remained of it. The vast expanse of Egyptian power,
conquered some fifty generations before by the sword of Thutmose the Third, had long since passed into history or legend. But
Ha'a-Ibre was determined to retain the final outposts in Tehenu
and Swenett, at all costs. He dreamed of restoring the empire, of
taking back every land Thutmose the Third had once claimed,
from those two precious strongholds to the reaches of the four
horizons. But one Greek onslaught after another had proven
more than Egypt could bear. Egypt's army and wealth were, after
all, still sadly depleted after rule by foreign Kushite kings,
seventy-five years before Ha'a-Ibre's time.

Soon the depleted army realized that Ha'a-Ibre could not

even retain his hold on nearby Tehenu and Swenett. Fueled by shame and anger, they turned on their king. When Ha'a-Ibre had fallen, the High Priest of Horus, the falcon-headed god of war, chose the general Amasis for Egypt's throne.

Amasis had been quite content with the role of general, or so the women of the harem had told Rhodopis. Never had he coveted the king's power, nor dreamed of holding the throne. Despite his ferocity in battle, he was a humble man with simple, pure ambitions. He wanted only to live well and honestly, to protect what was his, and, upon his inevitable death, to pass with ease through the dark labyrinth of the Duat and stand untroubled before the gods of judgment.

That humble demeanor was precisely the trait that had caught the eye of the High Priest of Horus. Perhaps the priest believed Amasis' earthy ways would make him the very best of kings, clear-headed and thorough in thought, with his ears always open to the hear voice of the people. Or it may have been like most of the harem women believed: that the god Horus truly had appeared to the High Priest, and called Amasis king. Perhaps (so Rhodopis had mused, the first time she'd heard the tale) the priest had assumed Amasis' lack of personal ambition would make him easy to control, so that he and his fellow priests could manage Egypt's affairs—and its great wealth—from the shadows. Whatever the High Priest had planned, he had announced the god's will before the whole gathered army, and with so many witnesses to the word of Horus, the fates of both Amasis and Ha'a-Ibre were well and truly sealed.

With a commoner's unquestioning faith (and no small amount of superstitious awe), Amasis accepted the priest's claim that Lord Horus himself had chosen him for the throne. Amasis led the army's revolt against Ha'a-Ibre and, when Memphis fell easily before him, he gave the king a swift and dignified death. That same day, he'd married Tentu-Kheta, who had been the chief wife of Ha'a-Ibre, and later that year, he also wedded the young King's Daughter, Khedeb-Netjer-Bona. If Khedeb-Netjer-Bona had objected to Amasis' coup, or to marrying her father's killer, she gave no indication of distaste. Rhodopis had often wondered why. Perhaps the involvement of the High Priest—or of the god Horus himself—had put her mind at ease.

But Amasis soon proved himself a poor choice as king, shattering whatever secret ambitions the Cult of Horus may have nurtured. During his many campaigns against Greek forces, Amasis had found ample opportunity to observe Egypt's most problematic enemy. Years of fighting Greek soldiers, of devising tactics to counter their best generals, would have embittered most men, and made of them inveterate Greek-haters. Not so Amasis. Open and honest to a fault, he could only admire the organization and will, the remarkable precision of his opponents. Thus began the tide of Greeks, flowing like a second great river into Egypt—and the erosion of the Kmetu way of life.

But the Nile rose admirably under Amasis' reign, year upon year. The grain stores were always full to bursting, the valley rich and green. The gods were clearly pleased, and what Egyptian would risk opposing the will of a content and pacified god? A coup against one Pharaoh was terrible enough; to oust another, especially when the river rose and fell untroubled and the fields prospered, would surely defile maat.

Rhodopis watched Amasis across the length of his audience hall; she could not help but see him through the prism of all she knew about him, his humble origins and his manufactured rise to power. He seemed to her a lap-cat resting in the rightful place of a lion—well-intentioned and even sweet, but by his very nature hopelessly unfit for his position. Amasis looked up at the squeal of the scarab door's hinges. The ornaments of royalty—the tall, red-and-white double crown with its single curled plume; the falcon pectoral spread across his chest, glinting with the fire of gold and polished carnelians—lent him the imposing and dignified air one expected of a king. But he did not sit easily on the carved and gilded throne. He never did. It seemed even Lord Horus couldn't make a king as readily as that. The kingly poise, the natural authority that should be a Pharaoh's by right, were lacking entirely in Amasis. All one had to do was look past the gilded trappings, and his hesitant nature—his palpable unsuitability—were clear for all to see.

A misty, half-sheepish, half-baffled expression hung across his face like a woman's veil, but Amasis brightened when he saw Rhodopis standing in the doorway. "Ah! There she is. Come, Rhodopis." He beckoned her forward.

Rhodopis left Khedeb-Netjer-Bona standing near the scarab door. She moved carefully through the crowd that filled the audience hall, glancing about surreptitiously as she went. There were, of course, the usual contingent of stewards and ambassadors, nobles and petitioners to the throne, all thronged at the foot of the dais, shifting and jostling subtly in their attempts to maneuver themselves to the fore, where they could gain the king's attention and his judgment. But as Rhodopis moved through the crowd, she noted that it was denser than usual. There were many more people gathered today than usually stood before the king's seat. They parted to make way for her, stepping backward or sideways, and she glanced at each person's garb as she passed. There were a great many people dressed in dark robes, long yet bulky, the cloth lacking the smooth, flowing quality and crisp pleats of Egyptian linen. Most of them had skin a paler shade of brown than she typically saw, too. Most of these people were foreigners, then—and by the simplicity and sameness of their robes, she determined that they must be servants or slaves.

The last row of supplicants parted; Rhodopis stepped out into empty space, to stand in the Pharaoh's gaze. She bowed low to the king first, holding up her palms after the Egyptian fashion. Then she turned at once to the two women beside her and bowed to them in turn.

They must be the mistresses of all these servants, unless I miss my guess entirely. And only very important women could command so many servants.

Rhodopis straightened with a shy smile, and at once cast her eyes down to the polished malachite floor. But she took in every inch of the women as her gaze lowered. Both were young—no older than their early twenties. Their black hair was straight as an arrow's shaft, quite unlike the tight curls of most Egyptians. Olive-brown complexions made the women too pale to pass for native-born Kmetu; even if their clothing had not marked them out as foreigners, the difference would have been obvious to any observant person. Robes of lightweight wool, heavily embroidered in a riot of colorful flowers and birds, fell straight down to their sandals; the robes closed in the front with a series of small metal clasps, quite unlike Egyptian gowns, which were draped and knotted into place, and ornamented with a hundred fanciful pleats. The robes had heavy sleeves that hung down past the women's elbows, baring little of their flesh and giving scant relief from the thick, humid heat of the Nile Valley. Each wore a long shawl draped over one shoulder, doubled back and knotted low around her hips. The shawls swung with layers of many-colored fringes and tassels—which, swaying and dancing, had the unfortunate effect of amplifying each woman's trembling. They held themselves with an unmistakably regal bearing—indeed, they seemed more naturally powerful than Amasis on his throne—yet there was no mistaking their strained expressions. The younger of the two was red-faced, her lips pressed tightly together. She seemed on the verge of bursting into tears.

Rhodopis turned back to the throne, her eyes still on the floor. "How may I be of service, my king?"

Amasis spoke in Greek. "I present to you, my ladies, Rhodopis of Thrace. She is one of the Ornaments of my harem, and a treasure to my heart. She alone of all my women speaks your tongue."

That was not strictly true. Several of the harem women could speak Greek ably; they had confessed as much to Rhodopis, and sometimes teased her in her own language. They merely chose not to speak the language, as a point of pride—and they especially avoided using Greek outside the harem, where any Kmetu might hear. The last thing the other Ornaments of the Harem wanted was to be thought un-Egyptian. But Rhodopis, of course, did not correct the Pharaoh.

"Rhodopis," Amasis said, "these beauties are Ninsina and Shamiram. They are daughters of Cambyses. You know who Cambyses is, do you not?"

"Yes, my king," Rhodopis said. "He is the ruler of Persia."

"Indeed, he is. Their father has sent them here to Egypt—to me—that they might become my wives." He paused; Rhodopis glanced up. A slightly foolish half-smile played about the Pharaoh's face. Clearly, it delighted and flattered him, to have more beautiful women in his household. "With our marriage," the king resumed, "we shall have a bond of kinship between Egypt and Persia. That's very good, don't you think?"

Rhodopis' cheeks heated. What did it matter, whether an Ornament of the Harem—the youngest and newest, at that—approved of Amasis' diplomatic marriages? Greek may be an unpopular tongue among members of the Pharaoh's court, but most of them had no trouble understanding the language. What would they think of their king, for having sought the blessing of a harem girl? Embarrassment on behalf of the kind but bumbling Pharaoh flooded her; she felt dizzy and weak with the force of it. But he had asked her a direct question. She could not avoid answering.

"I place my trust, as always, in the good judgment of the Pharaoh," Rhodopis said. "If it pleases you, my king, then how can I be anything but glad? I am your servant, and servant to the gods who love you."

"Yes," Amasis said briskly, oblivious to his lapse. "It seems these fine ladies do speak a bit of Greek—enough to get by—but they do not appear to know much Egyptian, if any. You will help them settle into the harem, won't you, my jewel? I know they will be grateful for your kindness."

Rhodopis turned to the Persian women, only to be met with a glower from the elder. The dark brows drew down like the fork of a bird's foot; her painted lips pursed, and for a moment Rhodopis wondered if the woman would shout, demanding someone else for the task. Rhodopis was suddenly aware of the sheer linen draping her body, the openness of its weave, her flesh on display. It had never troubled her before; it was simply the Egyptian style, and she, a former hetaera, found no shame in nudity. But she was an Ornament—a concubine—whereas these Persians came to Memphis as wives.

It occurred to Rhodopis, too, that if she were to go about attached to new women of such admirable status, it would only serve to set her higher still among the harem. *The women will all begin to hate me again, when I've only just found my feet among them.* She could not accept the assignment. She must make the king change his mind.

"I... I have never worked as a translator before, my king," Rhodopis said carefully. "I fear I am not worthy of the task."

Amasis waved his hand dismissively, brushing away the rote demurral he expected at every new appointment. But Rhodopis had been quite sincere in her objection.

"Nonsense," Amasis replied. "You'll do the task admirably; none is better suited."

Rhodopis bowed her head. Had they been alone in his bed chamber, she might have convinced Amasis to choose another woman for this delicate work. But here in the audience hall, where so many had heard the Pharaoh's words... Rhodopis had no choice but to obey. "I shall be glad to serve you, my king."

"Very good," Amasis said, beaming. He raised his hand, beckoning across the length of the chamber, and spoke loudly—in

Egyptian, this time. "I see my chief wife is here. My heart warms. Khedeb-Netjer-Bona, come forward."

The crowd cleared a path for Khedeb-Netjer-Bona far faster than they'd done for Rhodopis. The chief wife glided easily toward the throne. She did not bow when she reached the foot of Amasis' stepped dais; she merely stood looking up at him, serene and patient.

"You, my wife, must find whatever servants we have who are proficient in the Greek tongue. And any who may chance to know the Persian language, too. They will be useful in settling all these new servants here in the palace. As you can see, each of my new wives has brought her own household! We must make a place for them, yes?"

"Of course," Khedeb-Netjer-Bona said smoothly. "It is fitting, that the daughters of a king as great as Cambyses should travel so well equipped. I shall set to work at once." She turned without waiting for Amasis' dismissal and left the hall, shadowed as always by her pair of guards.

"I have already instructed Pentu to prepare two good apartments for our new beauties," Amasis said to Rhodopis. "Take them to the women's wing now, won't you? I am sure they're very tired from their long journey."

Rhodopis bowed to the king again. Then, turning to the daughters of Cambyses, she gestured to the path through the crowd, the swath of respectful space that remained in the wake of Khedeb-Netjer-Bona's passing. "If it pleases you," Rhodopis said carefully, quelling her Thracian twang with an effort, "follow me, my ladies."

The elder woman—the frowning one—barked a few words in her native tongue. A small group of Persian servant-women detached themselves from the crowd, falling in behind their mistresses. Rhodopis led the way out of the audience hall.

"You must have traveled for many days," Rhodopis said when the scarab doors had closed behind them. The murmur of the audience hall was muffled now; the corridors of the Pharaoh's palace were serene, pleasantly dim and perfumed by myrrh smoke. "I don't know exactly where Persia is, but—"

"Not 'Persia,'" the elder snapped. "That is what you call it, you Egyptians."

Rhodopis smiled timidly. "I meant no offense, my lady. What is the proper name for your land?"

"Haxamanishiya. You *can* say it, can't you?"

Rhodopis opened her mouth, prepared to try, but the woman never gave her a chance.

"No, of course you can't."

"Was the journey long from... your land?"

"Longer than I care to say. Longer than I care to remember. It has been a trying time. And now here we find ourselves, in a place where no one even speaks the proper tongue. I would call this place the home of uncivilized wild things, but for the city itself. And this palace is good. The art is garish—everything looks as if it were painted by a child!—but at least your architects know how to build. The city is almost as fine as Babylon—what little I saw of it. Your king's palace cannot compare to my father's, but I suppose it is the best one can hope for in a place such as this."

"The palace displeases you?" That seemed impossible; the Pharaoh's palace was the finest estate Rhodopis had ever seen, and she had been to more than enough rich men's homes to be a judge of quality.

"Simple bread can only displease, after one has feasted on honey and spices for all of one's life."

"Haxamanishiya must be a very splendid place, if it can outshine Egypt."

The woman turned to Rhodopis, one black brow arched in amusement. "So you can say it. Though your pronunciation leaves something to be desired."

"I will do my best to make you happy, my lady. You must be worn out."

"The journey was trying. The less said about it, the better."

Rhodopis kept quiet and led them on. Had she been less observant, she might have taken the new brides' stiff dignity for arrogance. But she noted their cheeks, pale as if long travel had wrung the blood from their bodies like water from a rag. She saw the thinness of their tight-pressed lips, the frightened shifting of their eyes, the shivering of their tasseled shawls. Their distress was plain to read. It brought back uncomfortable memories of Rhodopis' own homesickness, when she had been a young girl newly arrived from Thrace.

At least I had my family with me then—Mother and Aella and the little boys. Father, too, when he still lived. These two have only each other, unless you count their servants.

If their dignity was feigned, the Persian brides seemed genuinely unmoved by the grandeur of the Pharaoh's splendid halls. They followed Rhodopis in stiff silence, casting only the most cursory of glances to the left or the right as they passed towering murals three times the height of a man, depicting kings of the past in their war chariots, or striding across the land with the flail sigil in their fists, trampling tiny enemies beneath their feet. A forest of lotus pillars, tall and graceful like the trunks of Thracian pines, filtered glittering strips of mid-day light from the garden beyond the portico, but the new women hardly blinked at the beauty. The great blue-and-green archway that led into the women's quarters left them similarly unimpressed. The elder of the two did not even look up to take in the brilliant color. She simply glided beneath the arch's curve, fanning smoke of myrrh incense away from her face and coughing with a small, dainty sound that yet managed to fill the hall with an ostentatious ring.

Pentu had left the doors to the new wives' apartments standing open. Sweet incense, burning on polished braziers within, drifted out into the hall. Rhodopis gestured to the first open door, and the women filed in.

The chamber was considerably larger, and far more beautifully appointed, than Rhodopis' own. Plush rugs woven in bright patterns of red and blue nearly covered the floor, yet wherever the rugs did not reach, cheerful blue and green tiles peeped through, revealing a pattern of lotus leaves floating on a smooth pond. The furnishings were made of ebony wood, gracefully carved and well worked so that each slender curve shone with reflected light. Two broad dressing closets stood against the far wall, each so wide that half a dozen children could have hidden comfortably within. Their double doors were decorated with rows of turquoise cabochons and painted with the image of Hathor, goddess of love and beauty. The women stared in astonishment at the bed, for its mattress sloped head-to-foot, as all good Egyptian beds did. They did not seem best pleased, despite its stuffing of soft camel hair and goose feathers, and the fine, soft weave of the bright blankets and shawls spread across its surface.

Rhodopis pressed her own lips together rather firmly as she watched the women's chamber servants inspect the room. With brisk efficiency, they took the measure of its closets, exclaimed over the small private bath that adjoined the chamber. A dreadful little thrill of envy rolled in Rhodopis' stomach; she quelled it with an effort. These women were the daughters of kings. She may be the Pharaoh's favorite, but she was only a hetaera, and a Greek one at that. By Pentu's reckoning—and that of most of the harem—Rhodopis had barely risen from the puddle of back-alley piss where Amasis had found her.

Pentu told me my room was the only one left. She recalled the conversation with no small amount of bitterness. Yet no woman had departed the harem since Rhodopis' arrival. Pentu had lied to her; there was no way around it.

But I won't weigh on these poor ladies' hearts by complaining. Not now.

She watched the younger bride as the woman stared about the room. Those great, dark, red-rimmed eyes were both distant and painfully confused. She seemed hopelessly lost, and past the point of surrendering dully to a miserable fate.

"This is a very fine apartment you have here," Rhodopis said cheerfully. "It's ever so much grander than my own. Why, the chief wife herself can hardly have better, though I admit I've never seen her chambers before. Look, you've got two windows, and doesn't the breeze from the garden smell lovely?"

The elder sister shut the door abruptly. Its thud reverberated hollowly in the large room. With the corridor cut off from view, an unexpected sense of isolation came over Rhodopis. Her skin prickled with an anxiety she couldn't name. She did not fear the new brides, but their stoic dignity and the quiet shuffling of their servants left her with a sinking feeling of futility.

"I'll show you how to get out into the garden, shall I?" Rhodopis' voice was too loud in the silence of the chamber. "It's very pleasant at this time of day. There's plenty of shade under the trees, and—"

The elder woman cut her off with a great, huffing sigh. "Can't you be quiet, you tiresome thing?"

"Don't be harsh with her, Shamiram," said the younger—the one with the tragic eyes. "At least she is kind. It is good to see a friendly face in... in this strange place."

A thick quiver distorted the younger woman's voice—She's Ninsina, then, Rhodopis thought. Both of Ninsina's smooth, bejeweled hands flew suddenly to her mouth as she struggled to hold back a sob.

"Don't start," Shamiram said, not unkindly. "Not again. You know you must retain your dignity, little sister."

With a wail of despair, Ninsina threw herself into her sister's arms, weeping against the bright pink silk of Shamiram's embroidered shawl. Shamiram barked a few quick words to the servants. They filed swiftly from the room; a moment later, Rhodopis heard the muffled thump of the other chamber door closing behind them.

Still crying like a baby torn from its mother's arms, Ninsina slid weakly to the floor. She huddled beside the bed's ebony footboard, her knees gathered to her chest, rocking and keening in her grief. Shamiram bent over her sister, speaking tightly in Persian. Rhodopis could not understand the words, but all the kindness had fled from Shamiram's voice. She was rapidly losing patience.

Rhodopis hurried across the chamber to the bed. She dropped to her knees beside Ninsina, wrapping an arm around the woman's shuddering body, pulling her close. Ninsina babbled in her own tongue, her mouth distorted by weeping, her face so red it was almost purple. Shamiram, crouching in front of her sister, answered her harshly. Rhodopis caught the older woman's meaning easily enough, even if the words were foreign to her. *Brace up*, Shamiram seemed to say. *Remember that you are a daughter of Cambyses.*

But Ninsina went on wailing, shaking her head and pressing her face against her knees. The bright threads of her embroidered robe were soon spotted with tears.

Shamiram raised her hand; Rhodopis saw at once that she meant to strike her sister, to slap the sense back into her. Rhodopis reached up quickly, took Shamiram gently by the wrist. "Please don't, I beg you."

"You dare to touch me—you, a concubine? Perhaps I ought to strike you instead!"

Ninsina looked up. "Don't do it," she said. "You leave her be. She is kind. That is more than we can say for Fate."

Shamiram jerked her wrist from Rhodopis' grasp, but she lowered her hand, giving Ninsina no harsher treatment than a disappointed glower. Ninsina leaned into Rhodopis' embrace. Rhodopis held her, murmuring into her ear until at last the flood of tears subsided.

When Ninsina was calmer, Rhodopis pushed her gently back until she could look into her eyes. "Are you well now?"

Ninsina sniffled, wiping her nose with the back of her hand. "I will never be well again. How can I? We shall never see our home, our families—nevermore!"

Rhodopis leaned back against the smooth, cool wood at the bed's foot. After a moment, Ninsina did the same, swallowing her hiccups and dabbing the tears from her cheeks with the edge of her shawl. Shamiram sighed, and scooted around on her backside until she, too, was leaning against the bed.

"Tell me about your home," Rhodopis said. "I've never been to Haxamanishiya before, nor even heard tell of it. What is it like there?"

For a long moment, Ninsina did not speak. A wagtail piped in the garden, its piercing, insistent call chiming over the distant splash of water and faint peals of laughter as the harem women took their leisure in the pond. Ninsina's silence stretched on, but at last, she drew a shaky breath and spoke.

"Haxamanishiya is a vast empire, but Babylon is the place we call home. It is a very fine and grand city. Shamiram did not lie, when she implied that your Memphis is not as beautiful. Nothing can compare to the splendor of Babylon—no city man or gods have made can touch it! Its walls are surrounded on all four sides by the river Purattu, and the river flows through the center of the city, too. It shines like electrum in the sun. And every building is as tall as a tree, with great windows that take in the whole of the world. In the evening, the desert out beyond the walls and the river turns violet as the petals of a flower. There is a gate—the great northern entry, which we call the Ishtar Gate—all tiled in blue, with bulls and lions of gold. It is the grandest, finest thing you will ever hope to see. And everywhere you look, there are the winged lions that are our sigil—Babylonians' sigil, that is— crouching all throughout the city."

"Except where there are lions with the heads of eagles," Shamiram added. It was the first time Rhodopis had seen her smile. She had a remarkably pretty smile; it set her dark eyes to sparkling with a light that would have been called mischievous, in a less dignified woman.

"And the gardens," Ninsina said. "Every building reaches up to the sky, and each one is terraced, just like the ziggurat temples. Every terrace spills over with greenery—long vines that spill down the sides of buildings like water flowing from a fountain. And flowers—everywhere, flowers! The air is perfumed with their scent, through every season of the year."

"You have a style with words," Rhodopis said with real appreciation. "I just about feel as if I was there." She blushed at her slip—the unrefined, country speech of a Thracian peasant, which neither Iadmon nor Vélona had managed to drive entirely from her tongue. But the Persians did not notice, or did not care.

"The palace gardens are the best of all," Ninsina resumed. "Terrace after terrace—lush greenery that smells delicious in the sun, and flowers to rival the colors of a sunset. And water that pours from one terrace to the next. You can climb and explore all the day long, and never see the whole of that garden. The birds and butterflies that are drawn to the flowers—oh! The gods themselves must envy it."

"Your father must be a very clever man, and a great king, to have made it."

Shamiram gave a small, self-deprecating laugh. "Our father Cambyses did not make the Great Gardens, nor anything else in Babylon. Our grandfather Cyrus conquered the city when Ninsina and I were just little girls, hardly past the age of weaning. After he died, our father inherited all he had won." She drew herself up against the bed's footboard, suddenly defensive, though Rhodopis had offered no criticism. "Our father is a very great king, though—make no mistake about that. As a young man, he learned all from Cyrus, and now he is as powerful as our grandfather ever was. Before Cyrus took Babylon, our father and his household were all but nomadic, moving from one conquered city to the next. But Babylon is his by right—*ours* by right. It suits him; it is his just reward from the gods. It is the place where we belong... not here in Egypt."

"I didn't start out in Egypt, either," Rhodopis said. "I'm from Thrace, far to the north."

"Is your father a king, too?" Ninsina asked.

Rhodopis giggled, surprised by the question, glad for the relief of levity. "Gods have mercy, no! My father was only a simple man. We came to Egypt looking for work. He thought to earn a good, fat lot of silver, and take it back to Thrace after a year or two, and buy a farm. He wanted to have something to pass along to my brothers, you see, when they grew up—something to keep them secure all the rest of their days."

Rhodopis fell silent. A part of her heart was always full and warm with the memory of her family, but she hadn't truly *thought* about them for a long time—longer than she cared to admit to herself. She had sealed the most tender memories off, hiding them away from herself, where they could cause her no pain.

"But how did the daughter of such a simple man end here, in the Pharaoh's harem?" Shamiram said.

Rhodopis swallowed the lump that swelled larger in her throat with each beat of her heart. "My father was killed. Thieves... they attacked him, though it was plain to see, just looking at him, that he hadn't any money. We had been in Egypt a long time by then—two years—and the silver my father had hoped for... well, it wasn't working out as he'd planned."

Rhodopis could feel Shamiram and Ninsina staring at her. She didn't dare raise her eyes to theirs. She couldn't have borne their sympathy at that moment. She swallowed again, and went on, surprised that her voice did not waver. "We were starving by then. It was hard—there was no work in Tanis anyway, but without my father to provide, there was little my mother could do to care for us. So she... So I..."

"I see." Shamiram's voice was thick with understanding. "You became a whore."

Rhodopis blushed. "Not in the way you think. I was taken in by a kind and generous man. He educated me—taught me how to be a hetaera."

"A what?"

"Don't you have hetaerae in Babylon?"

"We have plenty of whores there, if that is what you mean."

Ninsina laid a hand on her sister's arm. "Don't berate her. Rhodopis—that is what the Pharaoh called you, isn't it?— Rhodopis is a kind, good girl, and the only friend we have here." She turned back to Rhodopis. "Please, speak on. I want to know more about you."

"Hetaerae are more than mere whores," Rhodopis said, with no small amount of defense. "We entertain the richest and most powerful of men. We sing, we dance, we converse. We have more freedom than any other Greek women, too."

"So," Shamiram said, softening only a little, "the Pharaoh took you into his harem after you... *entertained* him?"

"No," Rhodopis admitted. "How I came to be here in the Pharaoh's household is a story almost too strange to be believed. Amasis received a sign from Horus, his patron god, indicating that I—of all women—should be his."

She fell silent, wondering how to explain the falcon and the rose-gold slipper. Surely the women would think her mad. Or worse, they might think her a malicious story-teller, trying to trick them into looking like credulous fools. She thought it better to let her explanation stand on its own.

The memory of the falcon returned to her powerfully— the blue streak falling like a thunderbolt toward the water, snatching up her slipper in a wink of golden light. She shivered in uneasy awe at the recollection. Would she ever understand what the falcon god had meant by his myste- rious sign, by his choice of *her* for the king's harem—a commoner, a Greek, an unfortunate, barely raised above the status of a bed slave? Surely the god intended her for more than this monotonous confinement in the Pharaoh's gilded cage.

"We are three of a kind," Ninsina said. "All of us uprooted from our lives, our homes, and brought here at the whim of the Pharaoh."

Shamiram rolled her eyes. Rhodopis could see plainly that she resented Ninsina's words, resented any hint of fellowship with a common whore. But Shamiram held her tongue, and for that Rhodopis was grateful.

Ninsina took Rhodopis' hand. "I am glad you are here with us. It's good to know we are not alone, that someone understands."

Sudden tears burned Rhodopis' eyes. This was the first real kindness she had felt since coming to the Pharaoh's harem. She squeezed the new bride's fingers. "It is good to know we aren't alone."

Shamiram rose abruptly from the floor. She stretched her arms above her head, the bracelets on her wrists rattling. "Now that you have composed yourself, Ninsina, perhaps we will see this garden. It *does* smell nice, though I am certain already that it cannot compare to our terraces of Babylon."

Rhodopis led the sisters through the women's corridor. When they reached the garden, it greeted them with a burst of color—the rich, shady greens of vine and leaf, the scarlet and gold of flowers in glorious profusion. Birdsong chimed among the branches of the sycamores; a wind stirred, laden with the cool, silty odors of the river, whispering among the feathery fronds of palms and the glossy foliage of covered arbors. The garden always brought joy to Rhodopis, provided she stayed well within the boundary of the women's side. But Shamiram was obviously unimpressed. Even Ninsina looked rather disappointed that this was the best Egypt had to offer.

"Your terraced gardens in Babylon must be marvelous," Rhodopis said. "But wait until you see the pond. It's more like a lake, in truth—big enough for swimming or boating, and the water is a luxury during the hottest months of the year."

They strolled along pathways paved in white bricks, toward the great expanse of the lake. Contained within limestone walls, the surface of the water winked and shimmered in the afternoon sun. Flat, round lotus leaves carpeted the lake around its edges; here and there the first of the lotus flowers held their bright heads up above the water. The spikes of their petals seemed to glow like lamps, flame-gold or sunset-pink, and the air was sweet with their honey-rich scent. A pair of red boats drifted near the lake's center, far beyond the field of lotuses. Rhodopis could not see which of the harem women reclined in the boats, for the curtains were drawn on their square-topped shade canopies, hiding the occupants from sight. But she could hear the music of harps and intermittent laughter.

"It is lovely," Ninsina admitted. "Perhaps not as pretty as our terraces, but pleasant still."

"I have had enough of boats," Shamiram said drily. "If a lion were to appear in the garden just now, it wouldn't be enough to force me onto another boat. I would rather the lion ate me."

"You'll come to enjoy boating, with time," Rhodopis promised. "It is a good distraction on a hot day."

Shamiram turned away from the lake, gazing out toward the garden's farthest boundary. "What is there? Those two great, black, rounded things?"

Rhodopis followed the direction of her stare. "The stone urns," she said uneasily. "They're only decorative."

"But quite large. I will go and see them."

Rhodopis heard the note of command in Shamiram's simple words. She was expected to accompany the Pharaoh's new wife; to refuse would be an offense, and a mere concubine could not risk angering a wife of Amasis. But the very sight of the urns, and the boundary they demarcated, left a queasy sensation deep in her stomach. She scars on the soles of her feet itched, and she could all but see Psamtik's face looming close to her own, could hear his arrogant, threatening laughter in her ears.

"There is nothing special about the urns," she said. "Just two great stone vases. The lake is ever so much nicer—"

"There is nothing special about the lake, either." Shamiram rolled her eyes. "Water, water—you Egyptians and your water! We have a great river in Babylon, too, you know. If you have seen one garden pond, you have seen a thousand."

Shamiram turned on her heel and strode toward the urns. Rhodopis cast a desperate look at Ninsina; the younger sister shrugged. "Shamiram feels out of her depth, and it brings out the worst in her. But she is a good, kind woman. You'll come to see it, once she has settled here in the Pharaoh's household."

Ninsina set off across the garden, hurrying to catch up with her sister. Rhodopis had no choice but to follow.

The three women covered the distance in silence. Before they reached the boundary, Rhodopis could already detect the tell-tale sounds of Psamtik practicing with his spear: the whisper of its flight, and a moment later, the vibrating thud as it sank into the bale of flax stems he used for a target. Each impact sent a shiver up her spine. Her heart pounded faster with every step, until, by the time Shamiram stopped between the stone urns and stood gazing into the king's garden, Rhodopis felt as if her chest might burst from the frantic pressure of her own pulse.

Timidly, she peered beyond Shamiram into the king's garden. There was Psamtik, exactly as she had dreaded. He was perhaps a hundred paces away. His back was turned to the women, but power and pride were evident in his every movement. He braced his foot against the bale to wrench the spear free, and his arms and back tensed, the muscles of his body swelling with the force of a brutish, animalistic strength. Rhodopis swallowed the bitter taste rising in the back of her throat.

Psamtik's spear came free from the target with a sighing sound

—like the sigh of a creature surrendering its life, Rhodopis thought grimly. The king's son turned, propping the bronze-tipped spear against one shoulder, and began prowling back across the garden to take aim and hurl his weapon again. He caught sight of the trio of women between the urns. Psamtik paused, grinned— and even at a distance, Rhodopis felt the chill of his smile.

"Who is he?" Shamiram asked.

Rhodopis couldn't tell whether Shamiram was merely curious, or whether something about the king's son drew the woman. *Better not to be pulled in by that one*, she longed to say. *You'll end like a moth in a lamp's flame*. But if she mistook Shamiram, if she offended her...

Rhodopis' mind raced, testing and discarding every possible response she might make. "He is Psamtik," she said slowly, carefully. "The king's son and heir. It is best to avoid him, my lady. He is dangerous."

"Dangerous? How do you mean?"

Rhodopis shrugged uncomfortably. The memory of the conversation she'd had with Khedeb-Netjer-Bona came back to her. *He is dangerous like a young lion, savaging the offspring of the one who came before. He is dangerous like a leopard, hunting in the night, chasing you through the darkness, through the brush and thorns of the garden...*

A faint call, far back in the depths of the women's garden, rescued her from the need to answer. "Rhodopis! Rhodopis, where are you?"

It was Minneferet. Grateful for the excuse to turn away from Psamtik, Rhodopis hurried back along the path. She cupped her hands around her mouth, calling, "We're here!"

Minneferet appeared on a distant path, around the shoulder of a thick-blooming hedge. She waved urgently.

"Come along, if you please," Rhodopis said to her companions. "We must be wanted—or at least, I am wanted."

When she reached Minneferet, she was nearly out of breath. The Persians trailed more languidly on the path behind her.

"What is it?" Rhodopis said. "Is something wrong?"

"Only that Pentu wants you at once," Minneferet said. "He was peeved, not to find you in the new brides' rooms."

"They wanted to see the garden."

"Best tell *him*—not that he'll care. He said the Pharaoh wants to see you right away, this very minute. Otherwise, I wouldn't have troubled myself to come and look for you."

"The Pharaoh... again? Has something angered him?"

Minneferet grunted in annoyance. "How am I to know? No doubt Pentu will tell you all about it. He's waiting inside the corridor. Hurry up now, or you'll lose your status as the king's favorite." Minneferet did not seem troubled by that prospect. "I'll see the new wives back to their quarters."

Rhodopis cast one quick glance at the Persian sisters, offering them a smile, which she hoped they would take for an apology. Then she lifted the hem of her skirt and ran toward the palace.

5

THE FALCON'S PURPOSE

FOR THE SECOND TIME THAT DAY, RHODOPIS LEFT THE WOMEN'S quarters flanked by a pair of the Pharaoh's guards. Still flushed and half breathless from her sprint through the garden—and from her conversation with the terse and scowling Pentu—she walked as fast as propriety allowed, yet still she felt her speed was not sufficient in the guards' estimation. They remained precisely abreast of Rhodopis, careful not to step ahead of the king's favorite, but their hard-set jaws and tense bodies spoke of their haste and impatience. There was no chance of her going to Amasis to entertain in his bed. She knew as much, even when the guards turned down the corridor that led away from the audience hall and toward the king's private chambers. If this had been a routine summoning to the king's bed, the guards would never have been in such a state.

The reason for their agitation revealed itself a good fifty paces away from the king's door. A man was shouting inside Amasis' chamber, roaring like a bull beset by a cloud of stinging flies. Rhodopis' eyes widened. *It must be Psamtik, attacking the old lion at last, just as the chief wife feared.* Her courage and poise both failed; she faltered, paused.

"Don't be frightened," one of the guards said. His words were clipped with impatience. "The Pharaoh is angry, all right, but he's not cross with you."

"The Pharaoh?"

"Of course, my lady." The guard chuckled. "Who else would dare to shout inside the king's rooms?"

Rhodopis had no time for relief. A new anxiety filled her as she started forward again. Amasis never lost his temper; for all his shortcomings, he was reliably gentle and composed. To hear him now, bellowing and cursing, made her nearly sick with worry. If ever anything flew in the face of Egyptian maat, it was Amasis pushed beyond composure or control.

"I won't have it," the king cried, his voice muffled behind his door. "I tell you, I won't!"

The guard knocked; Amasis fell silent on the instant. After a moment he said, "Come." The word was thick with effort; even without seeing his face, Rhodopis knew he struggled to marshal his dignity, his self-control.

The door swung open. Rhodopis stepped inside, ready to go to the king at once, to do whatever she could to soothe the storm of his anger. But again she paused, frozen tensely on the threshold. There in the center of the room stood Khedeb-Netjer-Bona. Her arms were folded below her breasts. Those shrewd, all-seeing eyes tracked Amasis as he paced from one end of the spacious apartment to the other. The chief wife, dressed in an intricately pleated, blood-red gown and crowned by the simple yet elegant golden circlet of the rearing cobra, stood as a pillar of serenity amid the Pharaoh's unexpected rage. When she heard the door squeal on its bronze hinges, she glanced over her shoulder with a casual toss of her head. Khedeb-Netjer-Bona nodded, pleased to see Rhodopis trembling on the threshold.

Amasis, too, took note of the newcomer. The surprise on his face was quickly replaced by pleasure, followed by a welcome cooling of his temper. *But he was startled to see me*, Rhodopis thought as she made her way to his side. *It wasn't the king who sent for me, after all.* As she passed Khedeb-Netjer-Bona, she cast a questioning look at the chief wife. Khedeb-Netjer-Bona only shrugged, her expression unreadable, and looked away.

Rhodopis bowed low before the Pharaoh.

"My little treasure," Amasis said. "How glad I am to see you! If any creature the gods ever made can soothe my ka, it is you."

As she rose from her bow, Rhodopis took his hand and kissed it. Then she peered up earnestly into his age-lined, anger-reddened face. "Whatever is the matter, my king? What has upset you so?"

Amasis sighed. He tugged his hand from Rhodopis' own and thrust an accusatory finger at a nearby table, where several scrolls and scraps of papyrus lay. It seemed to be Amasis' typical clutter of office—notes on the proclamations he would send to his scribes, missives from ambassadors and nobles to which he would eventually attend. A few tablets—hard, dark wax pressed atop neat squares of stone—held more official and urgent communications.

Rhodopis blinked; she looked more closely at the mess. A single tablet lay apart from the others, one corner hanging over the edge of the table as if the king had dropped it in a fury. She stepped closer. *This must be what's put him in such a state.* She glanced over the tablet, taking in the sharp, angular markings of cuneiform writing. Cuneiform was the script of the northern empire—the Persians. Rhodopis had once learned to read a bit of it, under Aesop's teaching, but she could make no sense of it now. Below the blocks of cuneiform, the elegant, curving lines and occasional picture-symbol of Egyptian hieratic filled the remainder of the tablet. Rhodopis assumed that whoever had written the letter in cuneiform had reproduced its contents in Egyptian script. The author had taken special pains to ensure the king of Egypt would not mistake the letter's contents.

Rhodopis was not a strong reader—not of any form of

Egyptian writing, nor even of her native Greek—but she could make out enough of the final hieratic scrawl to discern exactly who had sent the letter. The tablet was signed, *Cambyses, Lord of the Empire of the Sun, King of*—. She couldn't read the final word, but she could guess it readily enough. *King of Haxamanishyia.*

"A letter from the Persian king," Rhodopis said. "The father of Shamiram and Ninsina, your new wives."

"Yes, indeed." Amasis stormed to his table and picked up the tablet. "Shall I read it to you? I hardly have to look at it now; I've read it so many times, *disbelieving*, that I can almost recite it from memory."

"What is the point of riling yourself further?" Khedeb-Netjer-Bona said. But she sounded entirely unconcerned, perhaps even eager for the Pharaoh to enflame his anger again.

"'To Amasis, King of Egypt,'" he read, "'I send my greetings and respect. I have sent you also two of my beloved daughters, to beautify your home and make glad your heart. Now a bond of family ties us tightly together, and we must never meet as enemies on the battlefield. But I know that one bond is easily broken. Even two bonds may break in an extremity of circumstance. But three bonds are strong enough to withstand any threat. Therefore I insist, for the sake of our respective empires, that you send me a daughter in return. I will take her to wife, and vow to treat her as an equal among the women of my household. My marriage to your daughter will ensure that Egypt and Persia remain allied for all time.'" Amasis drew a ragged breath, as if bracing himself to perform a particularly unsavory task. After a moment, when he seemed more or less composed, he continued. "'My friend, do not deny my request. For if you do, the alliance between us will shatter, and Persia, with all its considerable might, will fall upon Egypt.'"

The tablet dropped onto the table with a clatter. Rhodopis jumped at the sound.

War. It was a naked threat. The very ground beneath

Rhodopis' feet seemed to tremble; she swayed, for she felt as if she was on the crumbling lip of a pit, so cold and deep that if she fell into its depths, she might never emerge. The present unrest in the streets of Memphis was frightening enough. But war with Persia...! Rhodopis could scarcely imagine what war might mean for her —how it would alter her life as a woman of the king's harem. *But one thing's sure, and no mistaking it: war never brings good to anyone—not even to the people who win.* She had learned that much from Aesop's teachings.

"The audacity of him," Amasis shouted. "Cambyses!" He spat the name.

The Pharaoh spun on his heel and began pacing again, tracing a path across his chamber, dodging the grand silk couches and chests of ebony and cedar, his fists clenched uselessly at his sides.

"The letter is terribly audacious, my king," Rhodopis said carefully. Now more than ever before, she struggled to speak like a woman of refinement, for she sensed that her simple, country manner would seem ridiculous now, an insult to the gravity of Amasis' situation. "But can you not send him a daughter all the same? Surely he is right about one thing: marriage to one of your daughters would preserve peace. It's not my place to say it, I know —I hope you will forgive me, my king—but things aren't as they should be in Memphis. Not just now. What greater strain can your kingdom bear? Can you risk war with Persia, when Egypt is already so damaged? It would be worth it—wouldn't it?—to give Cambyses one of your daughters, and prevent a war."

Rhodopis risked a swift glance in Khedeb-Netjer-Bona's direction. She expected the chief wife to be pleased by Cambyses' offer —no, his *demand*. The letter may be an insult to the Pharaoh's dignity, but at least Cambyses' proposal would put the chief wife's second daughter well beyond Psamtik's reach. Instead, Khedeb-Netjer-Bona had shed her air of serene unconcern. She scowled back at Rhodopis. "Never before has Egypt given a daughter to a foreign ruler," she said. "Never—not once—in all the long history of Kmet. We will not break *that* tradition... not now."

Amasis turned to his chief wife. His fists were still balled so tightly that his knuckles paled with the pressure, but Rhodopis could read the desperation in his soft, haunted eyes. "Yet this alliance with Persia is crucial. And fragile; you know that, my wife. The Two Lands have been weakened terribly by so much internal strife. It shames me to admit it, but it is true: we will never withstand Cambyses if he chooses to attack."

"The gods will not abandon Kmet so readily," Khedeb-Netjer-Bona said.

Amasis barked a dry and bitter laugh. "I fear the gods have little to do with it now. For more than a hundred years, Greece and Persia have been like starving beasts. They have swallowed up one kingdom after another, made each in turn a part of their respective empires. Like Ammit, eating the hearts of the dead. Whatever land the Greeks do not own, the Persians do. And as their empires have expanded, ours has receded."

"I know all this," Khedeb-Netjer-Bona said. She waved one hand airily, dismissing the Pharaoh's fears.

"Do you, though? Do you truly *understand* it?"

Rhodopis absorbed herself in a study of her sandals. She wished fervently to be anywhere but in the king's chamber, playing the unwilling witness to their argument. Khedeb-Netjer-Bona was a prideful woman; she would resent Rhodopis for having seen her this way, chastised by the king.

Amasis said, "Kmet has always been a sovereign land. Even when foreign elements have held the Horus Throne, still the kingdom itself has remained intact. I cannot allow it to fall to Cambyses."

"Then do not allow it to fall," Khedeb-Netjer-Bona said.

"Ah," Amasis laughed. "As simple as that! It's a good job the gods sent you here to advise me, Khedeb; otherwise, I might not have thought of such an elegant solution."

"Your irony is noted," the chief wife said coolly, "and unnecessary."

"Persia's strength is too great." Amasis sounded weary with despair. "If Cambyses descends on our northern border, I will not be able to stop him. If the gods wish to prevent Persia from invading, then they must send several thousand more men for my army."

Egypt was a shadow of its former greatness—that much was true. Yet it was still, Rhodopis knew, among the most populous and wealthy kingdoms in the world. Surely if it were united, Egypt could withstand an attack by any foreign king. But the country was half torn apart already by the conflict that still raged between native Egyptians and Greek interlopers. Rhodopis bit her lip, maintaining careful silence. Neither the Pharaoh nor his chief wife would welcome her opinion now. *If Amasis never encouraged the division of his own nation—by favoring Greeks like me—then he wouldn't find himself trapped in this mire.*

A brief but unbearably tense silence fell over the room. Rhodopis glanced up from her sandals. The Pharaoh stood with his eyes squeezed tightly shut, pinching the bridge of his nose as if to dispel a particularly vicious headache. She laid a hand gently on his arm. "Please don't be upset, my king. Surely there's some way to make this King Cambyses happy—keep him satisfied enough that he'll leave your kingdom alone."

"But how?" Amasis muttered. "What am I to tell him? What answer can I possibly give? Khedeb-Netjer-Bona is right; this tradition is far too old. We must not break it now... not now, with the city—indeed, the whole nation—warring over every move I make."

Khedeb-Netjer-Bona stepped confidently to the Pharaoh's side. The chief wife's unshakable poise seemed to precede her, sweeping across the room like a flood, a palpable force of confidence, of feminine power. Rhodopis shuffled backward, shrinking in awe as the chief wife's potency reached her—as it pushed her aside.

"I'll tell you how to answer Cambyses," Khedeb-Netjer-Bona said. "Send him a daughter."

Amasis dropped his trembling fingers from the bridge of his nose. A rebuke seemed to hover on the tip of his tongue—*Are you deaf to your own words, woman?*—but when he noted the sly light in Khedeb-Netjer-Bona's eyes, he fell silent.

"You needn't send any of our daughters," she said. "As long as Cambyses gets a woman from your harem, one who claims to be of your own blood, he will never question it. We will preserve the alliance, and better still, none of your Kmetu subjects will be offended by the action."

The sudden shock of realization jolted through Rhodopis' body, sending cold fire racing down every nerve and vein. She swallowed hard as a wave of nausea struck her. *There it is, then: the chief wife's purpose. This is why she called me here.*

Amasis, too, seemed to grasp Khedeb-Netjer-Bona's meaning —though the crucial detail of her plan dawned on him more slowly. He drew a shaky breath, then turned to gaze at Rhodopis. His soft eyes were deep, troubled by regret. "It will pain me to lose this one. Lord Horus himself brought her to me."

"Lord Horus brought her for a reason," the chief wife said quietly. "Think of it, Amasis: if you were to choose any other woman for the task, you would alienate her family—and that is a risk you cannot afford now, with Memphis seething and the rest of the country not much better off. But no Kmetu will be offended if you send this Greek girl away from your harem. The falcon dropped this gem into your lap exactly for this purpose, my king. What else could Lord Horus intend by his strange gift?"

Rhodopis' thoughts raced. No, she wanted to shout. *Choose anyone else, not me! I'm too young, too insignificant, too...* But what protest could she safely raise? She stood before the Pharaoh of Egypt. She was entirely at his mercy.

Amasis turned his back on both women. He stood very still as he considered the chief wife's proposal. The silence stretched, then drew itself out, ever tighter, until Rhodopis was certain it must snap, certain that something must break and relieve this terrible tension or she would scream and scream...

Amasis sighed heavily. He turned again, his face stony with acceptance. Slowly, he nodded. "What you propose, Khedeb... it *is* a solution to my predicament. I must admit, it cleans the whole mess up rather neatly. But Rhodopis... you have been my delight, my comfort. I will take no pleasure in sending you away."

"She has been your delight," Khedeb-Netjer-Bona said, "and your loyal servant. Rhodopis has pleased all of us, I am sure, although she is an outsider. You mustn't think of her as being gone from your presence, my king. She will take a journey in your service—to glorify and strengthen your works. Take comfort in her loyalty to you, and know that she is still with you, even if she works from afar."

Amasis drifted toward his garden door, despondent and subdued.

"My king," Rhodopis said timidly.

But she didn't know what else to say. She could feel Khedeb-Netjer-Bona beside her still, looming in her power, as present and keen as the gods themselves.

Amasis did not turn back, did not take one final look at the joy of his harem, his comfort and delight. He only waved one hand in curt dismissal. "See to it," he said to Khedeb-Netjer-Bona. "it is the only way to keep Cambyses from breaking down my door."

The blood roared in Rhodopis' ears. Her knees quivered, threatening to drop her to the hard stone floor, where she would surely break into a thousand pieces, a fragile faience pot fallen from careless hands. But Khedeb-Netjer-Bona swept an arm around Rhodopis' shoulders. Before she was even aware that she'd been walking, the chief wife had guided Rhodopis out of the king's chamber, into the corridor beyond. Khedeb-Netjer-Bona's grip was firm... unbreakable.

ف

THEY DID NOT RETURN to the women's wing. Instead, Khedeb-Netjer-Bona diverted from the route and pulled Rhodopis into the audience chamber.

"Remain outside," she said curtly to her two guardsmen. "Allow no one inside until we are done."

The hall was eerily empty. The two women's footsteps sounded small and hollow within that vast, echoing space. An oppressive silence lingered in the shadowy recesses between pillars. A few lamps, left over from the day's audiences, still burned fitfully; the guttering light illuminated the vast chamber just enough to throw a ghostly reflection up from the well-polished floor. Rhodopis watched her own distorted image—pale and rippling, sadly hunched—slink along the malachite tiles with Khedeb-Netjer-Bona striding beside her, upright and strong as a warrior-goddess.

Rhodopis hesitated when they reached the stairs of the dais. For a moment, she thought the chief wife would climb those steps and seat herself upon the Pharaoh's throne. But Khedeb-Netjer-Bona released her grip on Rhodopis' shoulders and sank comfortably to the edge of the dais. She motioned for Rhodopis to join her; Rhodopis melted at once onto the steps.

"You aren't weeping," Khedeb-Netjer-Bona observed.

"Weeping seldom does any good."

Khedeb-Netjer-Bona digested this in silence. After a pause, she said, "But aren't you afraid?"

Rhodopis suppressed a shiver. "Very much, Chief Wife. I've no say in this, no way to protect myself..."

Another pause. Khedeb-Netjer-Bona said quietly, "And yet, the idea isn't wholly disagreeable to you."

Rhodopis held her tongue, considering the chief wife's words —here, and back in Amasis' chamber. What indeed had been the falcon's purpose? Why had the bird—and the god it served— brought her to the Pharaoh's household, only to leave her languishing in captivity? She looked up at Khedeb-Netjer-Bona, and to her surprise, a little of her anxiety drained away. "It is not entirely disagreeable to me—no, Chief Wife."

Khedeb-Netjer-Bona did not smile; her hard, narrow face gave no sign of satisfaction. "Why?"

"Going away to Persia—well, it will get me out of the harem, for one thing."

"So, life in the harem truly does not suit you."

Rhodopis shrugged uncomfortably. "The king has been terribly kind to me. And the other girls—well, they've come to accept me, I suppose, even if they aren't always kind. It's an easy life, but it isn't a free one."

One side of Khedeb-Netjer-Bona's mouth curled in a wry smile. "You weren't free before, Rhodopis. A hetaera is practically a slave. And a hetaera is a whore, for all the gods' intents. Life in the harem surely brought you far more honor than you had in Xanthes' household, working on your back for a few stray bits of silver."

"That's true," Rhodopis admitted. "But I was nearly free. I would have earned my freedom before much longer, if Amasis hadn't taken me, and then I would have been on my own, able to go where I pleased, do what I pleased... and make whatever sort of life I fancied."

"It was the god Horus who took you, Rhodopis, not Amasis."

Rhodopis watched the chief wife's face for a moment, but her expression of stoic assurance never flickered, never altered. "You truly believe that, don't you, my lady?"

"You do not?"

Rhodopis sighed. She hugged her knees to her chest. "I'm not sure what I believe. Seems to me, nothing about my life can be credited at all. If I was to tell a stranger about my life—" Blushing with shame at her slip, she corrected her speech— "If I *were* to tell a stranger, my lady, they'd laugh and call me a liar. I don't know what to make of my life, or the falcon, or anything else. All I know is I want to be free, and do what makes me happy, and live as the gods intend. If I must go all the way to Persia to do it, well then..."

Khedeb-Netjer-Bona tilted her head to one side. Her braids slid across her shoulder with a whisper and a faint clatter of beads. "You won't be free in Cambyses' court, either, you know."

"I suppose he keeps his women in much the same way as the Pharaoh does. Secluded, like. On display."

"I can't speak to how he keeps his women," the chief wife said, brisk and business-like. "I have never been to Persia, let alone been inside a Persian king's harem. I mean only this: even in Cambyses' court, you will owe loyalty and allegiance to Kmet—to Amasis, your true king. You must live as the Pharaoh's daughter; you will be the Pharaoh's daughter in all things. Cambyses' letter was a clear threat, Rhodopis. You're an intelligent girl; you know what that Persian dog meant. You could read what was written between the lines of his letter—not that he was subtle about it. We must know where Cambyses stands, what he plans to do. And most of all, we must learn how Amasis can keep him at bay."

Khedeb-Netjer-Bona fell silent, but her sharp black eyes locked with Rhodopis' own. She stared, and the quiet of the audience hall seemed to draw around them like a thick cloak, stifling and dense, isolating the two of them from the rest of the world. Rhodopis saw an image of her present reality emerge from the depths of the chief wife's gaze. She could read that vision, that inescapable truth, like one of the picture-stories painted on the palace walls. Every conversation she'd had with Khedeb-Netjer-Bona, ever since the day the chief wife had sent the physician to tend her feet, resolved before her mind's eye with sickening clarity. It all made sudden, heart-shivering sense: the chief wife's praise for Rhodopis' skills of observation; her idle wondering what Rhodopis would do with those skills.

The royal family of Egypt had a task for Rhodopis—and she had no power to refuse. She would be expected to work on behalf of the Egyptian throne, and if she did not do her work well— flawlessly—she would find herself on the sharp end of a Persian spear.

Rhodopis could no longer suppress her trembling. "My lady, I—"

"You'll never hear me say it about another Greek," Khedeb-Netjer-Bona broke in coolly, "but you can be useful, Rhodopis. I, too, have pondered over the omen of the falcon. Many times, I've wondered why the gods would send you into my husband's heart, into his life. But now we know, don't we? Now we see Lord Horus' purpose."

Rhodopis shook her head, a desperate denial. "I'm not fit for the task. I—"

"Nonsense. Who better? This unassuming slip of a girl— Pharaoh's daughter, small and delicate and charming. No one will suspect you; you're clever enough to make sure of that. And it *will* remove you from the harem. I cannot say what Persia is like; you may find more freedom out there, in Cambyses' lands, than you could ever hope for here in the harem. You may even find more latitude than you would have attained here in Memphis, as a freed entertainer."

Tears stung Rhodopis' eyes. She blinked them away before the chief wife could notice. "P'raps I'll find less freedom," she muttered.

"And," Khedeb-Netjer-Bona added with dark emphasis, "there is no Psamtik in Persia."

"There might be someone worse than Psamtik. Who can say what dangers wait in Persia, my lady? It's so far away, so different..."

"The gods will protect you," Khedeb-Netjer-Bona insisted.

Rhodopis wished she could feel a fraction of the chief wife's confidence. "They have chosen you for this task. It is what you must do. What's more, you *will* do it; I command it of you. Your king commands it."

Rhodopis could no longer keep the tears at bay. She sniffed, surreptitiously at first, but louder as the burning intensified behind her eyelids. One hot tear spilled down her cheek, then another. She knew Khedeb-Netjer-Bona was right; she could not refuse the Pharaoh's direct command. *I'm still as much a slave as ever I was. Gods of the earth and sky, will I ever be free?*

"Don't cry," Khedeb-Netjer-Bona said. But she sounded satisfied, as if she'd been waiting for Rhodopis to break, to reveal her weakness and vulnerability. The chief wife rose from the dais and extended her hand. After a moment, Rhodopis took it, and Khedeb-Netjer-Bona pulled her to her feet. "You said yourself: weeping seldom helps."

Rhodopis nodded. She wiped the tears from her cheeks with the back of her hand. She had shown the chief wife enough weakness, enough insecurity. She followed Khedeb-Netjer-Bona back across the audience hall, and did not allow another tear to fall.

6

THE LION IN THE NIGHT

In the dimness of her chamber, Rhodopis sat alone on her bed, listening to the falling, mournful call of a night bird through the garden window. A small lamp burned on her table, casting a fitful light over stacks of chests and cedar crates, over a small mountain of rush baskets with their lids tied shut. In a matter of hours, the harem apartment had been transformed from home to a foreign place, filled with unfamiliar shapes and faint, shadowy echoes. Khedeb-Netjer-Bona had ordered a cadre of servants to pack up all of the Greek girl's belongings the moment she'd secured Rhodopis' assent to embark on the dangerous mission to Persia—not that assent had been necessary. It was, Rhodopis knew, merely a formality, a way for the Pharaoh to soothe his conscience and comfort his turmoil at sending his favorite away.

After picking at a supper she was too anxious to eat, Rhodopis had studied the baskets and boxes for well over an hour, pondering over what goods they might hold. There were far too many of them stacked and stuffed in the small apartment. Rhodopis had received plenty of gifts from Amasis, and had kept most of the goods she had earned as a hetaera—the necklaces and bracelets, the jeweled baubles that would have bought her freedom, had she remained in Xanthes' Stable. But she knew her small fortune would never have filled so many crates. Khedeb-Netjer-Bona must have increased Rhodopis' modest wealth tenfold at least, adding fine gowns, jewelry, unguents and perfumes to the holding. There were likely several small pieces of furniture packed in the crates, too—footstools and tables, tripods for lamps and incense braziers. Any why not? Rhodopis would not go to Cambyses as a Greek girl, a jumped-up whore who had landed, by chance or by whim of the gods, in the Pharaoh's harem. She would go to Cambyses cloaked in Khedeb-Netjer-Bona's lie: as a King's Daughter of Egypt. And surely a King's Daughter of Egypt was entitled to a magnificent dowry.

A short refrain of song drifted near Rhodopis' apartment door. The voice was high and sweet—Minneferet, she thought, or perhaps even Iset, who could sing beautifully when she was not drowning in a jug of wine. The song passed quickly, losing itself in the deep, sonorous murmur of the women's quarters, the low voices engaged in gossip, the melodious laughter of women accustomed to a soft and easy life. Rhodopis sighed. Never had she felt so distant from the women of the harem, not even when she had first come to live among them. And never, not even during her first weeks in Egypt, had she longed so desperately to feel at home.

Couldn't I have stayed yet a while longer? she silently pleaded of the gods—whichever gods deigned to listen. *Only it's all so sudden, and just when I was finding my place, too.* She wondered despondently what would become of the Persian sisters, the Pharaoh's new brides. Would the harem girls treat them kindly, or would they offer the same brusque dismissal they'd initially given Rhodopis? She hoped the harem girls would be kinder to the Persians. Rhodopis liked Ninsina, and thought she could come to like Shamiram, given enough time. *Who will be their friend now that I'm going away? Who will make them feel safe and welcome in a foreign land?*

Come to think of it, who will make me *feel safe and welcome in a foreign land?*

No—she pushed her thoughts firmly back from that terrifying precipice. She would go to Cambyses' court. Whether it was the will of the gods or the chief wife made little difference to Rhodopis; she had no power to alter her fate, either way. Khedeb-Netjer-Bona had already found a companion of sorts to accompany Rhodopis on the journey—a girl fluent in the Persian tongue, and sufficiently educated to write out the messages Rhodopis must send back to Egypt. That girl would pose as handmaid to the King's Daughter; hers would no doubt be the only companionship Rhodopis would enjoy. *I must hope for the best, that's all—and pray my handmaid is the friendly kind, not a boor like Iset or a treacherous thing of Archidike's sort.*

Rhodopis hadn't the first or faintest idea what she might expect from Persia itself. Her conversation with Shamiram and Ninsina had revealed only the smallest and most rudimentary details. This apartment—the Pharaoh's palace—indeed, the whole of Egypt was not her true home, yet a terrible pang of homesickness wracked her all the same. If she succeeded in her mission, she would spend the rest of her life in Persia, tied forever to the Egyptian throne as its secret eyes and ears. If she failed, she would die—Rhodopis was clever enough to understand that there could be no other consequence for failure.

It's Amasis and Cambyses who will say whether I live or die—and if I live, Amasis has already decreed that I must be forever alone and unhappy. A swell of resentment soured her stomach; the smell of burning lamp oil was suddenly too close, too thick and choking. *And before Amasis and Cambyses, it was Xanthes who determined my fate, and before him, Iadmon.*

When, she wondered hopelessly, would the gods relent? When would they allow Rhodopis to become the mistress of her own life, her own destiny? She saw no end to the pattern that seemed to spread itself out before her: one wealthy, powerful

man after another forever controlling her freedom, her body—
her very life. That bleak future stretched before her mind's eye
like a featureless path paved with identical stones.

In the morning, the guards would come for her baskets, the
chests full of dresses, her jewelry and fine unguents, for all the
dowry goods of the King's Daughter. The guards would take her,
too, bundled up like a woven rug or a basket of trinkets, down to
the royal quay. There she would board one of the Pharaoh's fine
ships and sail north. North, and farther northward still, past the
slow-moving waters of the lush green Delta, past the cities on the
edge of the sea. She would take to the ocean waves again, just as
she had done with her family, years ago on the trek from Thrace,
but now she would track north and east along the coast, to the
city of Gebal.

Khedeb-Netjer-Bona had explained it all to Rhodopis, while
the latter had sat stunned, still half disbelieving, on the edge of
her bed, watching the chief wife's servants sort and pack her
things. From Gebal, Rhodopis and her false dowry would be
borne by a caravan of camels along the ancient trade routes,
through the great oasis of Tadmor, over the desert to Cambyses'
stronghold of Babylon. It was a very long journey, Khedeb-
Netjer-Bona had assured her. It would surely be most trying.

At that grim assertion, Rhodopis had only nodded silently.
She had seen how the same trek had worn on the nerves of
Shamiram and Ninsina. She had said nothing, only listened
obediently as Khedeb-Netjer-Bona issued her instructions. But
all the while, Rhodopis had fretted and quailed inside. She hadn't
been out of Egypt since she was ten years old. The prospect of
venturing to a new land, leaving behind Memphis and the king's
palace—all that was familiar to her!—would have sickened her
with dread, even if she hadn't found herself pitched all at once
straight into the mouth of danger.

"Egypt." Rhodopis said the word aloud, wondering at the
aching, hollow feeling it made inside her chest. It was not her

home... and yet, after so many years away from Thrace, Egypt was the only home she knew. For her, it had always been a place of great loneliness and uncertainty. But it was the place where she had found herself, the place where, like refuse on the river's shore, she had washed up and stranded.

This was the last night she would ever spend in Egypt. This was the last time she would hear the harem women murmuring beyond her door, the last time she would hear Iset or Minneferet sing. The next time she heard a night bird's call, the sad, repetitive sound would not come from the shady sycamore. She would never again hear the frogs call from the leisure pond, nor see exactly the same slant of starlight fall upon her window sill.

All at once, the seclusion of her dim apartment was too much for Rhodopis to bear. She leaped up from her bed and hurried to the chamber door. The hall outside was bright with dozens of lamps; the sting of freshly burned myrrh was in the air, and a great gust of laughter spilled out from the game room, where the harem girls were arranged around their senet boards. The corridor, thank the gods, was empty.

Rhodopis lifted her skirt above her ankles and ran through the hall, out beneath the garden portico, where the crisp bite of fresh night air greeted her. The open space of the garden soothed away some of her pain and emptiness—enough that she lingered there, leaning against one pillar, shutting her eyes tightly, breathing deep the rich, green smell of the garden and the wide river beyond. When she opened her eyes, she saw that the moon had just begun to rise. The barest glow of silvery light spread along the top of the palace wall; in a few moments more, the moon itself would edge into view.

I'll watch the moon rise one last time over Memphis, Rhodopis decided, *or the king's palace, at least, since it's all of Memphis I can see.* It would be one peaceful memory to carry with her into Persia—a land that could offer her nothing but a constant threat of death.

Rhodopis drifted alone through the garden. Purple shadows enfolded her, but thought the night was cold, and the sky seemed somehow vaster and more distant than it ever had before, she did not feel afraid. What fear could rival the danger she would soon face? What could be more terrible than Cambyses, the great conqueror who thought nothing of sending open threats of war to the king of Egypt? Nothing could touch her here, on this final night in her home-that-was-not-a-home—so long as she avoided the great stone urns and stayed within the safety of the women's garden.

It is often the case that, when we know ourselves to be in grave and unavoidable danger, the fog of panic dissipates, and we find ourselves looking on our own circumstances more clearly than we ever have before. Such was the thoughtful stillness that descended upon Rhodopis. With her fate fixed before her like some blood-red star, she settled into the calm of acceptance. She began to think and plan as she wandered the garden paths in the spreading, pale light of the moon.

I must send a letter to Aesop, she decided, *this very night, or early in the morning, before the Pharaoh's men come to take me to the ship.* If she was to leave Egypt with no hope of returning, she could only do so comfortably if she felt assured that Aesop, her one true friend, knew everything that had happened to her since the day they parted. She wrote with a poor hand, but she could scratch out enough to be understood in a pinch.

Of course, she mustn't tell Aesop anything about the Persian scheme. One of the king's stewards, or perhaps Amasis himself, would read the letter; if it contained any hint of Khedeb-Netjer-Bona's plot, it would never reach Aesop's hands. She must tell him only that the Pharaoh had sent her away on an important mission, and that she must now serve Egypt from afar, never to return. Yes, she decided—that would suit. Aesop would know she was well, but it would leave him out of danger. He would know, too, that Rhodopis was no longer in Egypt, so he would waste no time in looking for her. Perhaps if she dug one of her less ornate bracelets out of the dowry baskets tonight, she could use it to pay a messenger, and he could carry the letter the next morning—

A rough hand closed around Rhodopis' upper arm, biting into her flesh. In the moment of contact, she felt no urge to scream. Her body did not even jerk with involuntary fright. A cold, slick sensation of inevitability fell across her, sinking into her skin, turning her bones to ice. Somehow she knew—somehow, it made a mad, terrible, sickening kind of sense that the gods would not let her leave Egypt as easily as that. She turned in his grip, searching the darkness for the two stone urns, certain she must have wandered beyond them again in her state of distraction. But no—there the urns stood, still some distance ahead. The moon lined their dark curves with a glow whose very serenity mocked her. It was he who had violated the boundary this time— he who had come hunting, like a great fanged cat in the darkness.

Psamtik wrenched at her arm, spinning Rhodopis around to face him. An improbable pulse of calmness beat smoothly against her rising fear. She sucked in a deep breath, filling her lungs to the bursting point, ready to unleash a loud and deliberate scream. But the moonlight flashed—a bolt of lightning flickering before her eyes, reflecting off the thing Psamtik clutched in his other fist—something smooth, hard. Metallic. A heartbeat later, the hot prick of the knife's point settled against her throat. This was no trick, like the one she had employed against him. The blade was sharp and all too real.

"Not a sound, little lotus—not a sound."

Rhodopis closed her mouth.

"Going away so soon?" Psamtik leaned close, whispering in her ear. "You're off to Persia, I hear. But you won't leave before I have a taste of you. No, not before."

She swallowed hard. Buoyed on the strange, cold calm that infused her, she spoke quietly, levelly, looking straight into her captor's eyes. "I'm part of the Pharaoh's plans now. If you try it—if you hurt me—you'll ruin everything. Amasis will never forgive you; it all must come off perfectly, or there'll be war with Cambyses. You know Egypt can't win if Persia attacks. Let me go now, and I won't scream; Amasis need never know what you've done."

Psamtik's laugh was hoarse, carefully stifled, so it carried no farther than Rhodopis' own ears. "Do you think I care about the Pharaoh's plans? My father is an old fool. Whatever scheme he's concocted to handle Cambyses, it won't come off, anyhow, whether your skin is intact or not." The point of the knife pressed her throat again. "I'll spill your blood without a second thought, you Greek bitch. And if my father objects, then I'll kill him, too."

Rhodopis tried to speak again, but Psamtik twisted the knife. A streak of pain shot upward, burning the side of her face with its cruel fire. A hot trickle of blood ran down her neck, snaking over her collarbone and down the front of her dress. She shuddered; the strange illusion of her calm shattered in slow motion, the pieces dropping like winter leaves before her mind's eye. She tried to cringe away.

"Do you think any Kmetu will bat an eye if Amasis dies?" Psamtik hissed. "By the gods, every one of my father's subjects would thank me! The priests would set the calendar with a new feast in commemoration. I'd be lauded as a hero throughout the Two Lands."

"It would anger the gods," Rhodopis said breathlessly, "to kill their chosen king. The Nile would never rise again. The gods would—"

Psamtik jerked her arm hard; the knife bit into her neck again, and a fresh stream of blood slid down her neck. She choked back a scream.

"Nile?" he spat. "A Greek word, a Greek name! The river is called *Iteru*. That is its proper name, its Kmetu name. Say it." He wrenched at her again; she stumbled, terrified the blade would slice deeper, and nearly lost her footing. "Say it!"

"Iteru," Rhodopis sobbed.

"The Greek stain will soon be blotted from this land, make no mistake. When my father is dead, I will restore what is ours by right—what is Kmetu. What is true and maat."

Rhodopis trembled in his grip. She could feel the blood soaking into the neckline of her dress. The linen clung, heavy and wet, sticking to her skin. The salted-metal smell of her own blood filled her nostrils and singed the back of her throat.

She never knew where she found the courage to speak again. She didn't even know she had spoken until her own words were ringing in her ears, too late to call them back. "When your father is dead? Do you plan to kill Amasis, then?"

Psamtik's laugh was slow, oily. "What if I did? No fear of the Iteru failing; I have every confidence that the gods would laud me for *that* deed, too, just much as my subjects would."

Rhodopis' heart was racing now pounding loud in her ears. But even as panic flooded her mind, shrieking at her to break free at all costs and run, to scream no matter what Psamtik did with his knife, still one small corner of her mind remained sheltered, level and observant. *He's told me of his desire to kill his father,* she thought. *He won't let me live. He'd be a fool, to let me go now.*

If that was true—if after all the gods intended her to die— then Rhodopis had nothing to lose. Psamtik was an impulsive and prideful man; if she antagonized him deftly enough, he might make some brief misstep, might give her just enough time to break free before he could sink his knife in further. It was the only hope she could cling to now, thread-slender though it was.

"Then why don't you do it?" Rhodopis said. "Why don't you kill Amasis, and let Kmet and the gods alike shower you with their praises? You'll be a hero, won't you? Do it; go on and do it this very night. Or can't you muster the courage? I don't believe you can do it. I think you're afraid of him, afraid of all his guards. You'll *never* do it, Psamtik—never!"

In the pale, cold moonlight, Psamtik smiled at her—a slow,

satisfied curling of his lip. "Everything in its due time, little lotus. All in its time."

The knife lowered. Rhodopis' heart leaped—with hope this time, not with fear. But the thread of hope snapped when Psamtik pulled her off the garden path. A circular grove of trees waited for him—for *her*—the trunks like stoic sentinels, or like the bars of a cage, eerily luminous in the moonlight.

Rhodopis, choking back her sobs, went along with Psamtik, never daring to shout for help. She could sense his ruthlessness, his predatory resolve. If she emerged from that grove with her life, it would be a blessing from every god of the earth and sky.

7

LADY NITETIS

RHODOPIS LEANED HEAVILY AGAINST THE RAIL OF THE PHARAOH'S great ship, staring down at the quay below. Amasis' servants carried the last of the cedar crates up the ramp; they stored her false dowry on the ship's broad deck, lashing the goods in place with great lengths of damp, twisted, fish-smelling rope. The whole quay smelled like fish—old fish, dead and rotting, with a pervasive undertone of decaying plants in watery mud, a stench like too many cattle held in a tiny pen. Why had she never noticed before how the river reeked, how its odor coated her nostrils, her throat? The river—the Nile. She would not think of its Egyptian name, would not remember the sound of the word on Psamtik's tongue, the way he'd forced her to say it, too. She would not remember. She would *not.*

The sun was far too warm already, though the morning was still young. It raised beads of sweat on her skin. The ship's painted rail was so hot, it seemed enough to burn her skin. She let her body sag against it, let the heat soak into her flesh. She ached and stung in half a hundred places; Psamtik had left her hurting all over, though he had been careful to leave neither bruises or wounds—an experienced hunter of women. But bruises or no, Rhodopis felt every blow, every violation, every repulsive touch. Everything Psamtik had done repeated endlessly in the memory of her body, if not in her stubbornly closed mind. If she hadn't been so tired, so pained, she would have screamed and screamed from the torment of it.

When Psamtik had finally released Rhodopis—when she understood that he would not kill her, after all—she had stumbled out of the grove of trees and back to her apartment, guided by a swath of moonlight. The women's quarters had been perfectly dark; not even the smallest servant's lamp still glowed. Psamtik must have held her captive for hours. She had staggered through the unlit hall, tracing her way through the corridor with one trembling hand against the cold brick wall, until at last, she returned to her chamber. There she had huddled on her bed through the remains of the night, staring into the darkness, too shocked and horrified to cry, too stricken to sleep. When the sun rose, the Pharaoh's guards had come to take her away.

The handful of servants who would accompany Rhodopis to Babylon milled about the deck, muttering among themselves. It was obvious to them all that their mistress was distraught, yet what could any of them do? Khedeb-Netjer-Bona had carefully selected the servants from outside the palace; each believed that, despite her pale complexion and red-gold hair, Rhodopis was truly a daughter of the king. None would presume to comfort a member of the royal family in a setting such as this, with the eyes of so many Kmetu upon them. And a true King's Daughter of Egypt would take offense if she were maneuvered into a public display of weakness. The servants could do nothing but watch and whisper as their new mistress slumped against the ship's rail, mired in misery.

Dull and detached, as if she observed from some unimaginable distance, Rhodopis watched the final preparations on the quay. The rowers boarded the ship, filing up the wooden ramp in an eager line. Their laughter and shouts would have offended her ears and cut her to the heart, had her spirit not been drifting in its comfortable absence. The captain shouted his orders; the great, heavy lines were drawn in, the ramp lowered to the shore, and the oars reached out from the ship's sides like the probing legs of some great, garishly colored beetle. Memphis and the Pharaoh's palace pulled away as Rhodopis was carried steadily to the center of the vast, green river.

"Good-bye," Rhodopis said curtly to the city—to Egypt itself.

She was glad to be leaving. To think she had ever thought she would miss this place, this land that had given her nothing but grief and loss and imprisonment! Unknowable dangers waited in the court of Cambyses, but at least there she would be well beyond Psamtik's reach. He was every bit the monster Khedeb-Netjer-Bona had feared. Rhodopis realized, with a chill of sickening certainty, that this mission to Persia was the only thing that had saved her from death at Psamtik's hands. She had witnessed his treasonous words against the Pharaoh—his own father!—but why should he bother to kill Rhodopis, when Cambyses was sure to do it? And surely Psamtik, with his black heart and dispassionate scheming, saw clearly that Rhodopis could be of use to Egypt in Cambyses' court. No, why should he do away with her, when she might serve the very throne he would secure with his father's death?

If I am to die, she thought bleakly, *I'd rather die at Cambyses' hands.* There had been something so cold, so strikingly inhuman about Psamtik in the grove of trees. He had gone about hurting her methodically, almost without thought. Once he'd set to his terrible work, all his gloating anticipation had fled. Rhodopis felt sure that he took no pleasure in the act; he had done it merely because some dark impulse compelled him. Had a demon possessed him? Worse—had he worked the will of a god? With a grim knot tightening by the moment in her stomach, she wondered whether any act, no matter how horrible, brought Psamtik any measure of joy.

Rhodopis squeezed her eyes shut, lowering her brow to the sun-struck rail of the ship. The oars splashed and pulled through the water in a steady rhythm; the scent of the river was sweeter here, far from the shore—cool and clean and shadowy. She breathed it in greedily, then breathed deeper still, though her injured ribs protested with a stab of pain. She wanted to crowd Psamtik out, drive all memory of him from mind and flesh. *If only I could chase him away, get him out of my thoughts.* Somehow the residence Psamtik had taken up inside her mind seemed a worse violation than the rape. His presence, his violence, had infected her very thoughts and feelings. Perhaps Psamtik would never leave her; perhaps she would never be free of him, no matter how far the ship carried her from the Memphian shore.

The memory of one of Aesop's little stories sprang up unbidden in her heart. It was a sweet, short tale about an old woman with a wine jug. The woman could not stop herself from smelling the jug, though it had long been empty. But the scent left inside was redolent with the memory of the wine's surpassing quality. "How nice must the wine itself have been," the old woman said, "when it leaves behind in the vessel which contained it so sweet a perfume!"

Rhodopis hung her head. Would the memory of the outrages Psamtik had inflicted upon her linger all the rest of her life? Would her mind and body reek with the stench of his remembered violations?

A jolt of painful realization made Rhodopis lurch up from the rail. *Aesop!* In her fear and despair, she had forgotten the letter. "No, no!" she cried, reaching out across the rail, her hands straining toward Memphis as if she could catch the city and pull it back, hold it close to her heart.

The servants appeared at her side almost at once; they had been waiting, she realized, for the right moment to crowd around her, to offer whatever comfort they could give. A few of the women clucked in sympathy, patting her shoulders and back.

"My lady Nitetis," the oldest servant said, using the false name Khedeb-Netjer-Bona had assigned, "please don't shout and cry. You'll only weaken yourself, and you must keep up your strength for the journey."

"Poor thing," another woman said. "She misses her father already, and her sisters, too."

Rhodopis shook her head wildly, batting away their hands. She wanted no one to touch her, could tolerate no one's body so near her own. How could she explain? What could she say to these bumbling fools to make them understand—and why would they not get *away* from her?

"Dearest Lady Nitetis, the sun shines so brightly this morning. Come into the shade. Look here; we've a nice cabin prepared for you, and it's cool and dark inside."

Rhodopis shrank from the women's hands, pressing her back against the railing. "Aesop—Aesop! I must tell him —I must!"

"Who is Aesop?" the oldest servant asked patiently. "We don't know that name, my lady."

The old woman reached for Rhodopis again; she pushed away the age-spotted hand. "Leave me be!"

"You heard her," a voice barked from among the servants. It was low, dark as a smoke-filled temple, but distinctly female. "Back off, all of you; give my lady room to breathe."

The others edged away. Rhodopis heaved a deep, cool breath in the circle of empty space; her trembling calmed. A tall woman stepped forward, some twenty years old, slender and poised. Her deep-brown skin was well oiled, so it glowed like a perfectly polished stone; a rich, herbal scent emanated from her body, at once soothing and compelling. She smiled lightly. Beneath the heavy fringe of her braided forelock, her eyes were steady, unblinking—and faintly conspiratorial. "Now scatter," she said to the other servants. "I'll take Lady Nitetis to her cabin and remain with her there. I'm sure the rest of you can find useful ways to occupy your time. If you can't, I'll be sure to tell the chief wife as much when next I write to her."

The servants dispersed. The tall one watched them go with a satisfied air, one fist propped on her hip. Then she turned to Rhodopis, flashing a grin. "Come on, my lady. Old Tia'a was right about one thing: the sun is entirely too hot. You'll like the cabin. If you don't, I'll make them tear it apart and rebuild it to suit you."

She started off across the deck; Rhodopis followed her in a daze.

"Amtes," the woman said over her shoulder.

Rhodopis blinked at her back. "What?"

"My name. And you—" Amtes pulled the red linen curtain of the cabin aside, gesturing for Rhodopis to enter— "are Lady Nitetis, King's Daughter of Kmet."

Rhodopis sank onto one of the cushions that had been strewn rather casually around the cabin floor. She stared up at Amtes, torn between horror and relief. There was no mistaking the way the woman had spoken. She *knew*.

Before Rhodopis could reply, Amtes let the curtain fall shut behind her. A dim, ruddy light filtered through its cracks and the slubs of the linen's weave. By that strangely intimate light, Amtes rummaged through a small case made of hardened and intricately carved leather. She pulled out two items: a faience jar with a tight-stoppered lid, and a heavy pouch with its mouth tied securely shut. Amtes tossed the jar to Rhodopis; she caught it, just barely, with numb, fumbling hands.

"My oil," Amtes said, holding up her arms to show her meaning. "It smells good, doesn't it? Not to mosquitoes, though; they hate it. It will keep them off you. They're a plague out here on the river."

"You've..." Rhodopis sniffed, choking back a hiccuping sob. "You've sailed the river before?"

Amtes offered no answer, save for a sly little smile. She held up the pouch by its tie-strings. "And this is for your hair. It will turn it black as the sacred bull—your eyebrows, too. Keep your-self plucked there, under your skirt, for it's much harder to dye that hair, and if your new husband sees golden hair in the Valley of Iset, the whole game will be over and done."

"So... you *do* know."

Amtes shrugged. A large jar of water that squatted in the cabin's corner; she lifted its stopper and splashed a handful into a shallow bowl. Then she trickled a bit of dark powder from her bag. "I know how to dye hair, if that's what you're asking." It was certainly not what Rhodopis had been asking—they both knew it. "Some King's Daughters have had pale skin like yours, but no Kmetu has hair like that. We'd best turn you properly dark, don't you think?"

Rhodopis nodded. She poured some of the fragrant oil into her palms and rubbed it over her skin, watching as Amtes stirred the dye with a small wooden spoon.

"You're the one who will write for me, aren't you?" Rhodopis asked.

Amtes nodded. "I've a good hand. Anything you tell me will go safely to the Pharaoh and the chief wife—nowhere else. That, I am willing to swear by any god you please. I've been well paid, and I know my work. I do it better than anyone else."

She took a square of soft linen from her leather case and wiped Rhodopis' cheeks. Her touch was gentle, almost maternal —a startling contrast to her rough, low voice and brusque manner. "It's a good thing you haven't any kohl on today," Amtes said, "or half your face would be blackened by your tears. But you must paint yourself tomorrow—or I'll do it for you, if you prefer. Otherwise, the rest of the servants will begin to wonder and whisper among themselves. A King's Daughter seldom goes about with her face unpainted."

"I don't care," Rhodopis said dully. "There is nothing I care for less right now than painting myself up like some pampered bit of royalty."

Wordless, Amtes took Rhodopis by the chin and lifted her
face gently. She stared at the raw, red marks on Rhodopis' neck—
the cuts from Psamtik's blade. They were the only visible marks
he had left on her body, though he had left all too many unseen
scars behind. Amtes' mouth turned down in an angry frown. She
released her hold on Rhodopis' chin and turned away,
rummaging through her case with a vigor that spoke of helpless
fury—a state it seemed all women knew too well. "Paint yourself
when you're ready, then," Amtes said shortly, but not unkindly.

She produced a fine-toothed comb from her case. "Turn
about; put your back to me. The dye is ready now."

Rhodopis turned. Amtes scooped a bit of the dye onto the
crown of Rhodopis' head. With the comb, she worked it gently
through the red-gold strands of hair. The woman's hands were
both deft and careful; the comb never snagged or pulled,
although that morning, Rhodopis had given her long, unbraided
locks only the most cursory and distracted attention. The dye was
cool where it touched her scalp—cool and soothing, with a faint
tingle that was not unpleasant. Amtes had mixed in some
fragrant oil of lavender and sacred basil; the pungent herbs
nearly covered the smell of the dye, which had a distinct ammo-
niac bite—most likely derived from urine, Rhodopis thought
with a shudder.

She held quite still as Amtes did her work. The gentleness of
the woman's attentions, and the low murmur of the lullaby she
hummed, filled the dim cabin with a peace Rhodopis had never
expected to find again. Her task was as dangerous as ever, but
with the competent and composed as Amtes by her side,
Rhodopis felt slightly less convinced that the work would lead
inevitably to a violent death. Yet she could not think of Amtes as
a friend. She had made that mistake with Archidike, but she
would never stumble so badly again. She had only one friend in
all the world...

Aesop. She recalled him with a stab of pain so deep and cold that it stole her breath away. She tensed; Amtes took note, the comb pausing in her hair. The woman's humming died away. Amtes did not move. She seemed to be waiting for Rhodopis to speak, but Rhodopis could never have done it. She pulled her knees up to her chest, huddling into her own body despite the pains what wracked her. Rhodopis listened to the sound of the oars as they splashed and pulled, splashed and pulled, carrying her far away.

Amtes began to hum again, soft and low. The comb slid gently through her hair.

8

BABYLON

RHODOPIS LAY FLAT ON HER BACK IN THE STIFLING HEAT, DOING HER best to ignore the rhythmic tread of the camels—the slight sifting sound as the creatures' thick, hoofless feet slid through the sand, and the swaying of the litter she rode in. Gods, that endless rocking—side to side, tilting and tipping this way and that, until her neck and back were sore from the tension of resisting the slow, monotonous sway. Sitting upright only made the strain in her neck worse. She found it less painful to lie on her back amid the silk cushions, but the litter, perched high upon her camel's back, was barely large enough for Rhodopis to lie flat. She was obliged to orient her body corner-to-corner across the platform, or risk her feet poking out of the litter's shade curtains. Such a display would have been most undignified, though after twelve days of enduring the litter's sway amid the fire of the desert sun, Rhodopis was well beyond caring for her dignity. She was, however, loath to burn her feet; the sun was so hot here, so eye-watering bright that the whole of Egypt seemed, by comparison, plunged in the dampest and most frigid shade. Surely only a few moments beneath the brutal onslaught of the desert sun would be enough to scorch her red and raw, and she was likely to remain that way for the rest of her days.

She concentrated on the hum of flies to distract herself from the rocking motion. Those damned clouds of black flies had followed the great caravan of the King's Daughter over the sands from the city of Gebal. But she listened gratefully to their buzzing, just for the diversion—and to the huffing groans of the camels, which managed to sound both patient and grievously put-upon at the same time. Rhodopis had to focus on the sounds —camels' feet through sand, the incessant droning of the flies— or all her thoughts would be consumed by the sway of the litter. The sway, the sway... the gods-be-damned, never-ending *sway*!

Once her ship had left the lazy waters of the Nile's northernmost delta, it had taken to the open sea. Never in her life had Rhodopis felt so ill; the ship had floundered and rolled, struggling to breast every wave, even the smallest. And the waves had been numberless, each one conjured up by a malicious Poseidon who seemed bent on tormenting Rhodopis to the fullest extent of his powers. The trip from Thrace to Egypt had never been so trying. But then, she and her family had traveled on a Greek boat. The Egyptian ships, Amtes had explained as she'd held a bowl for Rhodopis to vomit into, were designed to sail upon the river. They were not best suited for sea travel.

When, after three days of suffering, the ship had landed at Gebal, Rhodopis had fallen to her knees and kissed the warm, unmoving stones of the quay. She'd had no care for the judgment of others, no concern for the decorum of the Pharaoh's daughter. She had survived the sea—barely, she was certain—and she would give thanks to whatever merciful god had seen fit to preserve her.

But the camels—the camels had proven themselves a fresh and novel sort of misery. They were frightening beasts, each twice the size of a horse, and some even larger than that, with long yellow shards of teeth exposed in their constantly moving jaws.

Their eyes were peevish, their thin, upcurved necks all too quick
to swing and strike. She had wanted nothing to do with them, but
Amtes had assured her that there was no other way to cross the
desert—not with the burden of Lady Nitetis' rich dowry. And so
she had climbed into her litter, drawing the sun-dimming
curtains tightly shut so no one could see her frightened tears, not
even Amtes.

As the days rolled slowly by—slow as a camel's steps—
Rhodopis' fear of the beasts was replaced by annoyance. Despite
their grumbling complaints and intimidating size, she learned
that the camels were docile creatures. Yet Rhodopis felt certain
the numbing monotony of their swaying gait would drive her to
the brink of madness—if the unchanging flatness of the desert
didn't manage to rob her of her wits first.

The caravan was led by a pair of Arabes, brothers from one of
the many warring tribes that fought for supremacy over the vast,
brown barrenness that was the desert. The brothers had been
hired by Khedeb-Netjer-Bona to guide Lady Nitetis to her bridegroom in Babylon—they, and a full complement of Arabes
guardsmen, who carried wickedly curved swords at their belts
and daggers strapped to their wrists, well hidden beneath the
sleeves of their light, flowing robes. At every sunset, the brothers
called a halt in their rolling, strangely musical tongue, and the
camels knelt in the sand.

While guides and guards and servants erected the tents, made
from light but sturdy silk, Rhodopis and Amtes hid behind the
tawny bodies of the camels. Amtes would play upon her little
bone flute—she was not an especially skilled musician, but it
made no difference—while Rhodopis danced. What a relief it
was, to move and stretch and spin in the rapidly cooling air, to
shake away all the pains and frustrations that had settled upon
her throughout the day, heavy as an unwanted duty. The
elemental joy of music and movement drove away the specters of
her pain and fear—for a short time, at least. The desert, colorless

and sere by day, blushed a thousand shades of violet and pink as the sun sank below the earth; under the stars, the desert was like smooth, dark silk, or a platter of silver, luminous at every bend and fold of its terrain. It seemed to reveal its hidden beauty to Rhodopis alone, confiding in her the divine secret that things were not always as they seemed—that hope emerged, even from the bleakest of circumstances.

But in the morning, she always faced the caravan again, and the wearying sway of the litter.

Seven days into the trek, the caravan passed through the city of Palmyra, rising improbably from the barren sand like beautiful Aphrodite emerging from the featureless sea. Palmyra was a great, bustling spread of temples and glorious palaces carved from pale-golden stone—a wonder of high, intricate, square-topped arches, of horse-racing circuits and outdoor theaters, where women danced in long, billowing veils of every imaginable shade. The caravan paid tax on its goods at the city's main gate—even the Pharaoh's daughter was not exempt from the fee. Palmyra's great wealth and magnificence came from the collection of trading and transport fees—indeed, what else could make such a haven of art and beauty in the middle of the desert? There was no river there to silt the earth so that crops could grow; there were no mines for silver ore or precious stones. The passage through the thrilling noise and bright exuberance of Palmyra marked the only time when Rhodopis tied back the curtains of her litter, heedless of the sun, for she wanted to see it all as she passed—take in every fleeting detail of that fantastical place.

All too soon, Palmyra was behind her. The caravan spent a pleasant day in the vast green oasis of Tadmor, luxuriating in the damp shade and allowing each camel to drink its fill from the turquoise-blue spring. But Tadmor vanished in the caravan's wake as quickly as Palmyra had done, and the monotony of desert travel set in again.

Had it been six days since Tadmor? No, seven. Rhodopis tried to count the days, but they had all blurred, one into the next, for each was as featureless and dull as the others. Eight... nine, she counted morosely. *Could even be ten, for all I can tell. Oh, will this journey never end?*

Rhodopis heard the muffled drumming of a rider's heels against a camel's flanks, followed by the creature's indignant grunt. A moment later, the shape of a camel's head loomed above her, a violet shadow through the cloth of her curtains. The tassels of its bridle swayed; the whole image rippled, distorted by curtains and hot, merciless light.

"My lady!" Amtes said. There was a distinct note of joy in her voice—and relief. "My lady, look! It's Babylon. We've arrived!"

Gasping, Rhodopis rolled onto her stomach, then clambered about on hands and knees, fighting the side-to-side roll of her camel's gait. She seized the curtains of her litter and threw them aside. There, far beyond the camel's twitching ears, tiny in the distance, she could make out the regular, blocky shapes of a city rising above a reddish haze. Below the haze, a white shimmer like some great lake stretched along the land, seeming to separate the city from the earth below it. By now Rhodopis knew that the water-like image was only a trick of the eyes, a common deception of the desert. But even accounting for the mirage, there could be no mistaking the city on the horizon. It truly was there. She had come to Babylon at last.

Rhodopis dropped the curtain; Babylon vanished behind its weave. She crouched in the litter, every muscle and nerve of her body suddenly taut with a terrible, compelling energy. She pressed one of the silk cushions to her face and screamed into it, long and hard until her throat was burning. Her howl was one of pure emotion, composed of a hundred clamoring feelings in one great rising, bursting bubble of expression. She screamed her rage at Psamtik, her anxiety over the task that lay ahead of her— more inescapable now than ever before, with her destination looming to the fore. She screamed out her regret, her fear, her confusion—and her relief that she would soon leave this litter behind for good. All of it came pouring out at once, unstopped like a jug of sour wine.

"Are you ready, my lady?" Amtes said.

Rhodopis let the cushion fall. She steadied her breath, then, when the flush had faded from her cheeks, pulled the curtain aside once more and smiled at her maid, hoping to reassure her. Had Amtes heard her muffled shriek? "I'm ready as I may be. Now let whatever will come to me, come."

For the remainder of the journey, Rhodopis sat upright in her litter with the curtains drawn aside, watching Babylon creep ever closer. Amtes—who, like the rest of the Egyptian servants, had adopted the flowing robes of an Arabes trader for the duration of their travels—drilled Rhodopis in the Persian language. They had practiced Persian often over the course of the trek, but now even the simplest words felt foreign on Rhodopis' tongue. With every rocking stride, the camels bore her closer to her fate. It was all she could do to keep breathing, let alone master a new language.

Rhodopis and Amtes both fell silent when the caravan made its final approach to Babylon. A broad avenue stretched from the fringe of outer villages toward the city's massive walls. The road ran straight as a new-made arrow between high brick fortifications. Great blocky ramparts stood at regular intervals, each crowned by a row of bright-blue points, like the fangs of some huge earth-demon tearing and rending the sky. As the camels strode between the walls and those strangely made ramparts, a shadow fell across Rhodopis' litter, cooling her body—but the shade did not feel like a kindness. She was going straight into the mouth of the beast, deep into its devouring maw.

At the end of the avenue, two high, flat-topped buttresses flanked the road; to either side, Rhodopis could just make out the gray-blue flash and gleam of water. She recalled Ninsina's description of the city—it was encircled by the river Purattu, and bisected by the river, too, thanks to a system of man-made canals. So the great buttresses must be the two sides of a bridge, Rhodopis realized—a thing seldom seen in Egypt, except for simple planks of wood that crossed irrigation ditches in farmers' fields. No construction of brick or stone could ever span the Nile. Yet she had seen bridges of stone in Thrace; the memory of their moss-covered arches returned to her with such sudden and vivid force that for a moment she thought she could smell the moss, the rich clinging carpet of green holding tight to dampened stone. How strange, to find any kinship between her cool, shaded homeland and this blistering waste.

Beyond the bridge rose the northern gate—the Ishtar Gate, Ninsina had named it. Its two broad, straight towers rose impossibly high, stretching great clawed arms into the sky, as if offering a scouring flood of worship up to Ishtar herself. Layers of ramparts stacked one upon the other, towering eight or nine times the height of a man, so soaring that the archway at the gate's heart—at least double the height of the tallest camel— seemed no larger a mouse-hole by comparison.

And the gate was *blue*. Ardently, wildly blue, its every surface covered with glossy tiles, each one fired in a different shade. A dozen expressions of absolute blueness clamored along those lofty towers and spike-topped walls—lapis and sapphire, indigo and deepest turquoise, the blood-dark blue of falling night and the blue of the Nile on a summer afternoon.

The only features that relieved the great wash of blue were the animals—rows of roaring lions, bulls with proud heads raised high… and some other creature Rhodopis could not identify, long of neck and tail, with a curling snout and a wild eye. The animals repeated in golden yellow and fiery orange, each looking as fierce as the last. It seemed as if those tile creatures strode out to do battle with one another, fighting all across the great surface of a blue, blue sea.

"By all the gods," Amtes muttered in appreciation.

Rhodopis could only shake her head, muted by awe.

She cringed in her litter as the caravan passed beneath the Ishtar Gate, ducking her head and peering shyly up at the black underbelly of the arch. So vast was the gate, she half expected to see stars twinkling in that darkness, but a moment later the dark arch gave way to clear sky—it seemed a wan, unsatisfactory blue after the miracle of the gate's many tiles—and Rhodopis found herself within Babylon proper.

The avenue opened out, with no walls to either side—only one startlingly tall brick building after another, lining the wide road up a slight incline toward a massive palace in the distance. Tumbles of green fell from every rooftop, every terrace, every long, black slit of window. The air was rich with the scent of greenery, of water and growing things. How improbable it all was: such beauty and lush life in the middle of the desert! The glories of Babylon made Palmyra seem dull and rustic by comparison; great stone statues adorned every crossroads, lions or eagles or tall, proud gods, and all around was the splash and bright, sweet perfume of fountains.

Word had spread of the Pharaoh's daughter; crowds lined the street, shouting in excitement, gazing toward the caravan with anticipation. Some of the people tossed flower petals into the avenue; others called and sang from rooftops, throwing yet more petals, which drifted on the desert breeze in great clouds of motion and color.

A contingent of Babylonian guards stepped out from a road-side toll-house; one of the Arabes brothers drew a token from beneath his robes and passed it down to the guards. Rhodopis watched the men keenly as they examined the token, talking together in hushed tones. They wore a version of the straight robes and one-shoulder shawls she had seen on Ninsina and Shamiram, though the soldiers' versions were plainer and shorter, so as not to interfere with their weapons. Every man— the soldiers and the men looking on from the alleys and rooftops

—sported a long, thick beard. At length, the leader of the guards nodded and returned the token to the caravan guide. He called out his command, and the camels proceeded along the route toward the palace.

The cheering of the crowds intensified, rising to a roar as the caravan delved into the heart of Babylon. The camels jigged nervously at the sound of the crowd; Rhodopis clung to the poles of her litter, doing her best to look serene, no matter how her heart raced. But Amtes remained steady and unconcerned on her own mount, even when it threw its head, sending the tassels of its bridle flying. If her handmaid was unconcerned, then Rhodopis was determined to remain just as fearless. She watched the people of the city as her litter swayed through their midst. The men and women dressed so much alike that she stared at them in open wonder: both sexes wore the long robes and shawls—although of course, the common people's garb was of drabber colors than Shamiram and Ninsina had worn. The women wore their hair long and unbraided, whether they were still children, too young for marriage, or grandmothers with wrinkled faces and bent backs. It was a simple, entirely natural style, the only adorn-ment a colorful band tied across the forehead. The men's beards fascinated Rhodopis, for every male who was old enough to sprout one wore it as proudly as a forest-fowl sported his tail. The eldest Babylonian men seemed to place great emphasis on their beards; cascades of neat ringlets spilled down their chests. Some had even woven flowers into their beards and mustaches. Rhodopis couldn't stop herself from staring. In Egypt, native men and Greeks alike preferred a shaven face. She had rarely seen a bearded man since her childhood in Thrace, and even then, she'd never witnessed such intricate grooming of a man's face.

Elevated as she was above the crowd, Rhodopis could see a lone rider approaching from the direction of the palace. The man was mounted on a lively gray horse, trotting confidently down the center of the avenue. The rider's garb rippled about him, and a fresh cloud of golden dust rose with each fall of the gray horse's hooves. The man's robe and shawl were brightly dyed—red and blue—and the shawl swung with the weight of a thick golden fringe. If his clothing stood as any indication, he was a man of means and importance. Rhodopis never took her eyes from the man as he rode boldly toward the lead camels of her caravan. The gray horse did not waver; it seemed determined to collide with the camels until, at the last possible moment, the rider reined the horse aside and continued down the column. When he reached Rhodopis' litter, he wheeled the horse about and fell in beside her. She stared down at him; the man pressed one hand to his chest, bowing in the saddle. He smiled up at her through his black beard, a stiff array of perfectly like-sized, well-oiled curls.

"Lady Nitetis of Egypt," he said, "I welcome you on behalf of King Cambyses, Lord of the Empire of the Sun, Ruler of Haxam-anishiya. Er—do you speak our language, my lady?"

To her great relief, the Persian she had studied with Amtes on the long journey returned easily to her tongue. "Yes, my lord—a little. I thank you."

"No doubt Egyptian suits you better." He shifted languages as easily as a man changes his sandals. His Egyptian was flawless, as far as Rhodopis could discern. That surprised her, for he was the perfect image of a Babylonian noble, from his striped, conical hat to the long red shawl slung over one shoulder. "The king is eager to see you, my lady. He has anticipated receiving an Egyptian bride for some time; his heart rejoices that you have come at last."

"My lord and king Cambyses honors me with this marriage— and honors my father, the king of Egypt."

The man's smile froze on his face—only for a heartbeat, but Rhodopis did not fail to note it. Nor did she miss the quick dulling of the man's eyes, as if his mind had turned suddenly inward, regrouping—startled by something. But what could have robbed such a man of his composure? In the next moment, his smile seemed genuine once more; those dark eyes brightened and sharpened again. But Rhodopis' pulse quickened. She had been in Babylon less than half an hour, and already she had raised suspicion. She must do better, and she would, if only she knew what had exposed her. She resisted the urge to touch her hair, wondering if the natural red-gold color was already showing through the dye.

Then she understood. *My accent. I don't sound like a native Egyptian, do I?* Inwardly, Rhodopis cursed Khedeb-Netjer-Bona— how could the chief wife have overlooked such a crucial detail? Then she cursed herself just as roundly; she ought to have known her accent would give her away. She should have prepared for this possibility.

"You must forgive my speech," she said, thinking quickly. "My father loves me so well that he sent me to be reared in a country estate, where I could remain far from the city and its evil air. He did not want me to catch a sickness, you see, for when I was a small child I was frail. I believe he also worried that I might fall under the influence of unsavory people within Memphis, for it is a wicked city in many respects. But my mother died when I was very small, and the nurse who reared me was a Greek. She taught me to speak—indeed, she was often my only company—and I fear I sound more like my nurse than a proper King's Daughter. I loved my nurse dearly, but still, it is a source of great embarrassment to me. Many times I have prayed that my father would relent and allow me to live with him in Memphis, even if it is a wicked place, for there are many more entertainments in the city. Country life is very dull, especially when one has only a Greek nurse for companionship."

"It is no matter, my lady," the man said. "You will soon learn to speak Haxamani as readily as if you'd been born to it. And you will find that Babylon brings you more excitement than Memphis ever could, I am sure. My name is Phanes. I am chief physician, and a steward of sorts to the king—honored to be one of his most trusted advisors. He has asked that I take special pains with you, and see to it that you have everything you need to feel welcome and comfortable here in Babylon. If there is ever anything I can do for you, no matter how insignificant you may think the task to be, you have only to ask, and I shall see it done."

"I thank you for your hospitality, Lord Phanes."

Rhodopis could say nothing more. She felt a curious heat and pressure building inside her chest; she fought down a shriek of hysterical laughter. She had dodged the sword-swing of fate with that improbable tale about her childhood; it was all she could do now to maintain a straight face. She sounded so refined, so dignified—I thank you, Lord Phanes! Listen to yourself!—but now more than ever before, she knew she must quell her instinct to natter like a mud-soaked peasant. The Persian court might accept a King's Daughter with a distinctly Greek accent, but they would certainly suspect her authenticity if she let slip a single, undignified "reckon." *I never could control my tongue and speak like a proper lady in the harem. I'd best learn to do it, and right quick too, here in Babylon. Else I'll find my head rolling off across the ground without my body attached.*

Rhodopis and Phanes rode on in silence, even after they passed the last group of cheering Babylonians. They crossed a second bridge, spanning a pale turquoise-green canal that flowed straight and tame between its stone-lined banks. The king's great palace was quite near, towering above the avenue like an Egyptian pyramid, tall and symmetrical against the lapis-blue sky. Rhodopis could see the gardens well, lying along its stone terraces. They were shockingly green and lush amid the dryness of the desert, flourishing from every wall and rooftop of the sprawling palace. Ninsina had told the truth about the gardens; even from below, they seemed so varied and profuse that Rhodopis could well imagine a person might explore them for weeks without coming to the end of them—or might get lost entirely in those forests of palms and rose bowers.

A slant of violet shade fell across the avenue, the shadow cast by the soaring tiers of the palace. The moment the shadow engulfed Phanes, he urged his gray horse to a canter and returned to the head of the caravan. The palace gate was just ahead, dark with aged wood and black shadow, emblazoned with the lions of Babylon. Rhodopis could hear Phanes calling out in Persian—a greeting or a command to the guards who kept watch on the gate. A great, hollow groan thundered through the air as the gate's two massive doors swung open.

Rhodopis' camel followed the others through the gate. Phanes re-appeared at her side, grinning with a deferent air. "If you will be so good as to join me, Lady Nitetis, to the side—there, beneath those palms. Their shade is most pleasant, and I have already sent for cool drinks and food to refresh you. I know your journey has been long and difficult."

"Am I to see King Cambyses now?" Rhodopis said.

"Not yet, I am sorry to say. The king's stewards must inspect your dowry and your servants first. You understand, of course."

Rhodopis nodded. Cambyses had threatened Egypt with war. Naturally, he would be suspicious of every person, every crate and basket the King's Daughter had brought with her into Babylon. Indeed, he would cast a narrow eye at every bracelet and scrap of linen on her body until Rhodopis had earned his trust.

"I will bring my handmaid Amtes with me," she said. "I am sure you are a trustworthy man, Lord Phanes, yet still I must be certain that no one has any cause to question my loyalty to my husband." Again she fought down the threat of hysterical laughter. Here she was, riding a camel straight into Babylon's lion-jaws —yet somehow, she managed to speak exactly like a true King's Daughter of Egypt. *Except for the Greekish sound of me.* That thought only made the laughter harder to contain. She bit her lip hard when Phanes turned away. *I believe he's bought the whole bill of goods. P'raps the gods haven't abandoned me after all.*

Amtes made the camels kneel, and gratefully Rhodopis slid from the litter. Her body ached with disuse; cramps flared suddenly in her legs, and her hips were so stiff she half expected them to creak like the timbers of a ship as she moved. She could still feel the swaying of the camel's gait, even as she stood on solid ground. *Never again*, she promised herself grimly. *I'll either die here in Persia or live out my days in Babylon as the wife of this King Cambyses, but I will never ride a camel-litter through the desert ever again. No, not even to save my life!*

The cluster of palms at the courtyard's edge did provide a sweet and soothing shade. Rhodopis shared one fleeting look with Amtes as servants hurried toward her, bearing cups of wine and a bowl of sliced fruits. "You're in one piece so far," Amtes' wry glance seemed to say. And Rhodopis answered silently, "We will see what the future holds."

Both she and Amtes drained their cups of wine, rather faster than propriety allowed. It was cool, sweetened with honey and fortified with some tangy herb that at once made Rhodopis feel braced and refreshed. She hadn't known she'd been so very thirsty. The moment the wine settled in her belly, she reached for the fruits, chewing the crisp, tart slices just for the sake of distraction. Phanes was content to remain quietly to hand, near enough to be called should the lady Nitetis need anything, but engrossed in the spectacle of the dowry. He and Rhodopis both watched as the king's troop of brisk stewards unpacked, tallied, and repacked each box and basket with fascinating speed and efficiency.

When the final containers were unpacked and approved, Phanes turned to Rhodopis with another of his mild, patient smiles. "That's done, then. Now if you'll follow me, my lady, I shall take you to your royal husband. He is most eager to meet you."

Rhodopis followed her host across the courtyard, into the shade of a pillared portico not unlike those she had seen so often in Memphis. The pillars were square-sided, though, rather than round; instead of crowns of lotus flowers or papyrus fronds, these were topped by images of crouching bulls, their great, thick necks bent to bear the weight of the palace between their pale stone horns. Beyond the portico, Rhodopis found the palace hall well-lit by tall, narrow windows, with long runners of flat-woven carpets brightening the floors. The walls were lively with color, but the vast mural was not painted on the walls, as was the custom in Egypt. Instead, the hall was covered floor-to-ceiling with the same intricate, brightly glazed tiles that had adorned the magnificent Ishtar Gate. Strange trees with golden trunks seemed to climb the full height, their odd, round leaves curling like ostrich plumes. Slender gazelles played about the forest floor, oblivious to the lion that stalked them with gaping jaws and hungry eyes. A garden flourished near the peaked waves of a river—fantastical blooms nodding above the water, vivid fish darting below. The many hues of blue and green, of scarlet and crimson and deep blood-red, seemed too spectacular even for the gods to have made.

Phanes drifted past the forest mural without so much as a glance. "I do believe, Lady Nitetis, that you will find Haxamani ways rather informal. I hope our customs are not a disappointment to you."

"No," Rhodopis said. "No, I shall be most glad to take part."

They left the tiled forest behind. Phanes turned at another square-sided, bull-crowned pillar; Rhodopis stepped quickly to catch up. The floor sloped gradually upward; they began to climb a subtle ramp.

"I have no doubt you will be a commendable wife to our king," Phanes replied. "Yet Babylon—indeed, all of Haxaman-ishiya—shares little in common with Egypt."

"That is no more than I expect, of course. I am devoted to my father's cause and glad to be of service, even if I must live in a place that bears little resemblance to my home."

Phanes issued a tiny laugh—a mere gust of air through his nose, whispering against the hairs of his upper lip. "Of course," he said quietly, "Egypt itself bears little resemblance to Egypt these days."

Rhodopis stared straight ahead as they progressed up the ramp. She had no idea whether Phanes had intended her to hear what he'd said—and no idea how a King's Daughter ought to respond to such a comment. It was safer to hold her tongue, to make believe she had heard nothing. She pressed her lips together tightly, resisting the urge to cast a conspiratorial glance at Amtes.

The sloping passage found level ground at the mouth of another portico. Beyond the pillars, the bright sun beat upon the flat, utterly bare ground of another courtyard. The glaring light was so intense, the threat of a sneeze prickled Rhodopis' nose. The courtyard was devoid of the touches she had seen at the palace's entrance; no fountain splashed in a stone basin, no palms offered kindly shade against the heat of day. But there were people, arrayed in a ring about the open space. A handful of ladies, dressed in the same beautifully embroidered robes and shawls Shamiram and Ninsina had worn, clustered beneath cloth sunshades held up by servants or slaves. The women sipped from horn cups, chattering and laughing with one another, while men dressed as richly as Phanes grinned and shouted in the full force of the sun, unaffected by the heat.

Phanes raised a hand, stalling Rhodopis well within the shelter of the portico. As he did, one great roar of gleeful anticipation went up from the courtyard crowd; a moment later, two men burst into view, bare-chested, arms locked around one another's bodies, tussling and scrambling in the ferocious light. Each had the beard of a proper Babylonian, though the neat curls suffered for the fight. Neither man wore anything more than a short, brightly colored kilt of linen, not unlike those Egyptian men wore, and simple sandals tied to his feet. Rhodopis squinted against the glare, watching as they twisted and shoved, each striving to hurl the other into the dust while the crowd cheered them on. One man, the shorter of the two, hooked his ankle around the other's calf; he nearly succeeded in sending his tall, broad-shouldered opponent sprawling. But the tall man righted himself, and with a roar, he slung his challenger across his shoulders, turned him about, and tossed him to the courtyard floor as if he'd been no heavier than a sack of barley. The crowd laughed, stamping their feet in approval; the victor bent and clasped forearms with his foe, pulling him back to his feet, clapping him solidly on the shoulder.

Phanes seemed poised on the balls of his feet, waiting for just the right moment to proceed. Rhodopis craned her neck, trying to see past the pillars, to take in more of the courtyard. Was the king there—seated on a shaded throne, enjoying the spectacle of the wrestling match? If only she could see him; if only she could make out what sort of a man he was before she must speak to him... or lie with him. She was gripped by sudden nausea and cold, surging dread.

"Come," Phanes said, satisfied that the time was right to proceed. He stepped out from the shelter of the portico, into the bright sun. Rhodopis had no choice but to follow.

As soon as she revealed herself, the courtyard erupted in a startling sound—a piercing ululation from the tongue of every woman present. Wide-eyed, shuddering with the shock of it, Rhodopis stared around her at the Persian women, each of whom saluted her with a raised cup. Phanes led her toward the tall man, the victor of the wrestling match. Sweat beaded on the man's thick arms and trickled down his broad, straight back; it sparkled like gold in the sun as he turned, reacting to the women's cries. When he found Phanes, he grinned, showing straight, white teeth—and when he saw Rhodopis at the physician's side, he lifted his bearded chin in an expression of satisfaction.

Phanes bowed low before the man. The breath seized in Rhodopis' throat—this was the king of Persia? This strange, sweating bull of a man who wrestled nearly naked before his subjects? But she reacted swiftly, bending in a bow of her own, presenting trembling palms to the king in the Egyptian fashion.

The king moved toward her; she heard his sandals scuff against stone, then saw the sandals—frayed ties, well-aged leather—and the deep brownness of the king's skin between the crossed straps. There was a pinkish-white scar above one toe, and a sprinkling of fine, dark hairs along the tops of his feet. Such ordinary feet—an ordinary man. And yet he was the king.

No king is ever ordinary, is he? Not even soft old Amasis.

"Rise, beautiful one," the king said.

Rhodopis straightened slowly. She kept her eyes downcast, fixed shyly on his feet. Conscious of her accent, flushing with embarrassment, she said in the Persian tongue, "My lord and ruler, Cambyses, king of Haxamanishiya. I am Nitetis, daughter of Pharaoh Amasis, king of Egypt."

"Of course you are!" Cambyses boomed out a happy laugh. "My new bride," he called to the people gathered around him. "She has come at last. Egypt has given up a daughter—a thing never done before. Let history remember me as the only king so great and desirable that I won the heart and hand of an Egyptian princess." There was something distinctly ironic in his words. A few of his subjects chuckled, and Rhodopis flushed still deeper. Did his people know that their king had only secured this daughter of Egypt with an open threat of war?

She dared not raise her eyes to Cambyses' face, yet she could feel his appraising stare as he surveyed her, taking in every feature of her body from the crown of her head to the soles of her slippers. Rhodopis was suddenly conscious of her clothing, wrinkled and dust-marred from the long journey. It would have been a kindness, if she had been allowed to wash and dress in a fresh gown before meeting the king—perhaps to comb and arrange her hair, too, for it was surely mussed and sandy after hours lying in the camel-litter.

But Cambyses gave a grunt of approval; he seemed not to

mind her disheveled appearance. "What do you think, my ladies?" he called to the gathered women.

"She's a pretty thing," one of the ladies called back. There was no hint of envy in her words. "What a shame Egypt has been stingy with its daughters for so very long!"

"Aye," another said, laughing, "and she looks meek—not likely to cause trouble."

An older woman called out, "She's got slender hips and small breasts—hasn't had any babies yet, I'll wager."

"The king will soon fix that," a lady shouted, and the whole courtyard laughed.

When the laughter died away, one of the women said, "Be kind to her—she is shy. Anyone can see that. The poor dear is far from home."

"I don't know but the shy ones are easiest to get along with," said the one who had criticized her hips and breasts. "She will do nicely, even if she's not yet proven herself as a mother."

There was a general murmur of assent among the women; again they raised their cups toward Rhodopis.

Cambyses lifted his hand. Silence settled over the courtyard. "I believe you will do nicely," he said to Rhodopis. "Very well; you are my wife, Nitetis of Egypt. Phanes, take her to the women's quarters and give her whatever she desires. Nothing is too good for my women, eh?"

The women in the courtyard cheered again; some repeated the strange, high-pitched, warbling cry.

Phanes bowed again to the king, then gestured for Rhodopis to follow him. She hurried from the courtyard gratefully, stifling the urge to gasp in shock. *I'm married to the king, then? Easy as that? Phanes wasn't half wrong: Persia is a good deal less formal than Egypt.*

As she followed the physician through the sloping halls of the palace, an unsettling thought crept into Rhodopis' mind... then sank lower to settle, cold and bleak, in the pit of her stomach. She had learned how to navigate the currents of Memphis—well enough, at least, to become a hetaera. But in a place so different, so utterly strange—a place where a woman could be married to a king with nothing more than a word and a nod of the head—how could she ever hope to steer her way to safety?

🌸 9 🌸

A TURN OF FATE

THE HAREM HOUSE OF KING CAMBYSES STOOD WELL APART FROM the remainder of Babylon's great palace. Separated from the warren-like halls and chambers of the palace proper by a long stretch of blooming garden, the women's quarters were a haven of peace and beauty standing high above the vast, bustling spread of the city. Rhodopis gazed about in stunned fascination as she crossed the garden terrace toward the women's wing. Every bed and alcove, every stone retaining wall overflowed with color—the tumbling emeralds and citrus-greens of vine, leaf, and stem, the cascades of flowers so vibrant and many-hued she could scarcely find names for the colors. Sunset pink, carnelian red, a rich fig-brown that looked soft as a kitten's fur; an array of violet-blues like the sun refracting from the facets of a well-cut stone. There were a dozen shades of yellow, from pale cream to the deep, reddish intensity of the evening sun—and even the white flowers thrilled Rhodopis with their arrays, for their petals were crimped or smooth, star-like or all of one piece, and their throats were speckled or striped with bright pink or flecks of black, with streaks of purple as deep as good wine. Ninsina had told the truth, back in Memphis—and yet, she hadn't told the half of it.

The gardens of Babylon were like nothing Rhodopis had imagined. Certainly, the Pharaoh's gardens paled and wilted by comparison.

"Your goods are being delivered to your apartments as we speak," Phanes said. He conducted Rhodopis and Amtes toward yet another bull-pillared portico. "I believe you will find the accommodations here every bit as pleasant as in Egypt. We lack for nothing in Babylon."

"I can see that," Rhodopis said, still rather shaky from the twin shocks of the glorious garden and the rather precipitate marriage. "And I thank you. But may I bathe? I am still covered in dust from the journey."

"Indeed; you will find a bathing pool here on the women's terrace. It is well screened for privacy, but if you prefer to bathe inside, the harem servants will bring you water and a copper tub. There is no better way to—ah!" Phanes interrupted himself as they entered the portico. "Speaking of the harem servants, here is Naramsin, chief of the eunuchs and overseer of the women's quarters. All who serve the king's women answer to him. Naramsin, this is Lady Nitetis of Egypt, the king's newest bride."

Screened by the rich blue shadows of the women's palace, the chief eunuch leaned at ease, one shoulder resting against a stone pillar. He was an exceptionally tall man—perhaps even taller than the king—with curling black hair, a reed-slender body, and a beardless face. He wore a robe of pale yellow with a leaf-green shawl; the flowers and vines embroidered on his garments were so delicate they appeared out-of-place on a man's clothing. Such adornments seemed better suited to a woman.

Naramsin nodded a sober greeting to Rhodopis, but spoke to Phanes. "I was heading out to find you, Chief Physician, but I saw you coming across the terrace."

"All is well, I hope," Phanes said.

Naramsin shrugged. "Lady Freni is complaining of unbearable pain with her women's flux again."

"She is not vomiting again, I hope."

"No, but she is out of the herbal tea that eases her pain." One of Naramsin's precise black brows raised. "Again."

Phanes sighed. "I warned her that she must only drink it when her time is upon her. She had grown to enjoy the effect too much. I shall have to give her a less effective treatment this time—no more tea for her, until she learns to control her appetite for it." He turned to Rhodopis with an apologetic smile. "I will leave you in Naramsin's capable hands, my lady, while I see to Freni. In the meantime, I believe you will be pleased with the arrangements I've made for you. I shall join you again this evening after you've had time to bathe and settle in. You will tell me then if anything is amiss, will you not?"

"Yes, Master Phanes. I thank you again for your hospitality."

Phanes bowed to Rhodopis, nodded briskly to the eunuch, and departed.

"I see you speak Haxamani, my lady," Naramsin said.

"Only a very little," Rhodopis said slowly. "I don't suppose you know Egyptian."

"Some," Naramsin admitted, "though I wouldn't embarrass myself by attempting it. I would make a butchery of your tongue. Come along."

He led Rhodopis into the depths of the women's palace. It was every bit as grand and colorful as the rest of Cambyses' massive estate, but here the air was perfumed with the spicy tang of incense, with cinnamon and roses and the lingering sweetness of honey. The low, soothing notes of a harp drifted from someplace Rhodopis could not see—a hidden passage, perhaps, or behind a closed door. The music meandered without aim, coloring the air with its gentle, contented placidity. From another quarter, a baby cried faintly, and was quieted by the cooing and shushing of a kind female voice. In that soft and beautiful place, some small measure of fear ebbed away from Rhodopis' spirit, leaving renewed hope and quiet fortification in its place.

"Here is your new home," Naramsin said, gesturing toward an open door at the end of the corridor.

Rhodopis stepped inside. Many of her dowry goods had already arrived, borne up the palace's maze of ramps by Cambyses' quiet, efficient staff. The Egyptian women who had accompanied her from Memphis were busy unpacking the chests and baskets, sorting through her clothing and cosmetics, tucking them away in the great, free-standing closets and massive trunks that lined the walls. The chamber was huge—easily thirty paces across, even larger than the rooms that had been allotted to Shamiram and Ninsina in Memphis. Carpets woven in a hundred colors covered the stone floor, a patchwork of garishly clashing hues that nevertheless managed to feel cheerfully refined. In the two corners farthest from the door, Rhodopis could see arched entryways, each leading to an additional room. The size of the place made her feel markedly dizzy. *What under the moon and stars will I do with two more rooms? Especially considering the size of this first one.* How Shamiram and Ninsina must have cringed at the meanness and cramped space of their chambers in Amasis' harem!

"It's all so beautiful," she said rather breathlessly. "But please, Good Man—may I bathe?"

Naramsin looked rather amused. "You do not need to ask me, my lady. You may tell me what you wish. I will see to it that your needs are fulfilled. Do you prefer to bathe inside, or out in the garden?"

"Outside," Rhodopis said at once. The chamber was too imposing in its size and bright colors for her to feel comfortable there. At least the garden, vivid though it may be, was roofed over by the open sky. The sky made sense to her; Babylon did not. Not just yet.

"Very good," Naramsin said. "Follow me, my lady."

Amtes, thinking quickly, snatched a fresh gown from a nearby

basket of clothing. Then she and Rhodopis hurried after Naramsin, back toward the women's terrace.

The eunuch led Rhodopis toward a free-standing wall of dark
vines with fat, glossy leaves. Sky-blue flowers, flared like the end
of a musician's horn, smiled among the foliage. Naramsin and
Rhodopis stepped behind the wall of vines; a bathing pool
revealed itself suddenly, sunk into the flat stone of the terrace. The
pool was fed on one side by a fountain that splashed at regular
intervals, like the beat of some strange, silver heart. On the other
side, a shallow, brick-lined trench guided excess water off into the
garden, where the green things could drink their fill. The wall of
vines curved nearly all the way around the pool, blocking sight of
the garden, the palace, the city below. Phanes had spoken truth-
fully: the outdoor bath was remarkably well screened from view.
The bathing place a sanctuary of quiet, a welcome escape from
the awe and fear that still clamored in Rhodopis' spirit.

"The water is warm," Naramsin said, "heated by the sun, but
you will not find it unpleasantly hot."

He moved as if to undress her; Rhodopis shrank back from
his touch, and turned to Amtes instead. Amtes made quick work
of the knots and sashes that held the pleated linen dress together.
It fell away, leaving the soft breeze to brush Rhodopis' skin. She
sighed in relief; already she could feel the sweat and grime and
monotony of the long desert crossing drifting away from her.

Amtes helped Rhodopis step down into the bathing pool. The
water was indeed warm—just warm enough, a comforting
embrace that Rhodopis sank into gratefully until she was
submerged up to her chin. Amtes sat on a nearby stone bench to
wait, but the handmaid jumped to her feet again with a wordless
squawk of protest.

Rhodopis turned about in the water, searching for whatever
had startled her handmaid. Naramsin stood on the edge of the
pool, one foot lifted, frozen in the act of stepping down into the

water—and he was naked. He had shed his robe and shawl with surprising speed; they lay neatly folded on the bench behind him, in the shadow of the blue-flowering vines. He held a curved copper skin-scraper in one hand, a bottle of cleansing oil in the other. He looked at Rhodopis, half amused, half wary, waiting for her to speak.

Rhodopis' eyes darted down to his groin. She gasped—the man was fully intact.

Naramsin chuckled. "Phanes called me a eunuch—and so I am—but you were expecting something different, I suppose."

"Yes," she said faintly. Her arms had tightened reflexively, defensively, around her body, naked and vulnerable below the water.

"There are some eunuchs in Haxamanishiya who are cut," he said. "Those are made eunuchs, created by mankind. The best of us are *born* eunuchs, created thus by the gods."

Rhodopis said nothing, watching him tensely. She had not been in the presence of an undressed man since that terrible night in the garden, before she had left for Babylon, when Psamtik had... No, she would not think of it. Remembering did no good. Naramsin's unexpected manhood hung limp and soft, but still, he might try to...

"My lady," Naramsin said patiently, "you understand what I mean, do you not? I have no interest in your body, except to care for it, and that I will do in a most excellent fashion. I take great pride in my work and my position. But lovely as you are—as all the king's women are—I do not find any temptation in your nudity." He smiled wryly. "I'm afraid you lack the requisite parts to set my blood stirring."

Amtes laughed, hoarse and low. She returned to her bench with an air of satisfaction.

"Of course," Rhodopis said, blushing. "In Memphis, the Greek men... they often... that is to say..." She burst out with laugh of her own. "Of course, Naramsin. You must forgive my reaction."

The eunuch stepped down into the pool. "No forgiveness is necessary. It's not the first time I've surprised a woman in this way."

He approached her slowly through the water, as one might approach a skittish colt or a growling dog. Rhodopis turned her back to him, stood, and held her arms wide. Her skin still crept with fear—she could not trust a man who intended to touch her, even if he claimed no carnal interest—but she was determined to fit into Babylonian life, to do her secret work as well as Naramsin did his.

His hands were both gentle and efficient. He worked with a business-like detachment that soon put Rhodopis at ease, massaging the rose-scented oil into her skin, working out the knots and kinks that had formed in her muscles over the course of the long and trying journey. By the time he scraped away the oil—and the dust and discomfort of the desert trek—with his copper blade, Rhodopis had begun to feel quite comfortable in the eunuch's presence.

Women's voices came steadily toward the pool, murmuring and giggling on the other side of the vine wall. A moment later, three dark-haired beauties, barely older than Rhodopis, peeked around its edge.

"May we join you?" one of them asked, smiling. Her plump cheeks flashed beguiling double-dimples.

Naramsin waved them away curtly. "Bathe later," he said, but Rhodopis stopped him.

"Please let them come in," she said. She liked their air of friendly curiosity. "I would be glad of more company."

Naramsin shrugged and rinsed his scraper in the pool. "As you wish, my lady."

The three girls bounded toward the pool, eager as pet cats pouncing on a string. They giggled and shrieked with glee as they disrobed, then splashed down into the pool with such vigor that the irrigation trench gushed and overflowed its little brick-work banks. Naramsin clicked his tongue in annoyance, gathered up his oil, and climbed out of the bath with ponderous dignity. He dried himself with a linen town and dressed while the newcomers introduced themselves.

"I am Karânî," said the dimpled one.

"And I am Iobia." She was tall and slender, with hair that retained its curl even when wet.

"I don't have a name," the third said. Her eyes were mischievous, her grin conspiratorial. "The gods dropped me here from the middle of a great sand storm. I am probably the daughter of a goddess, but who can say? I've no memory of the time before the sandstorm. It is all a great and beautiful mystery."

Iobia rolled her eyes. "She *does* have a name: it's Faidyme, and she makes up the most ridiculous stories about *everything*. Never believe a word she says."

Faidyme laughed and splashed her friend. "Never believe a word I say, except when I tell you the truth. Then you should most definitely believe me."

Rhodopis smiled timidly. "How will I know when you're telling the truth?"

"I'll grow very serious," Faidyme said, "like this." Her trickster grin vanished in an instant, replaced by a mask of such perfect sobriety that Rhodopis couldn't help but laugh.

"You are the lady Nitetis," Karânî said. "Princess of Egypt."

"I am." Rhodopis prickled with shame at the lie, for she liked these girls already, and took no pleasure in deceiving them.

Faidyme waded to one edge of the pool, where several glazed pottery jars stood in a row. She pulled the stopper off one and sniffed it. "Jasmine," she said. "Who wants jasmine oil?"

Karânî made a face. "I'm tired of jasmine. Find me something spicy."

Faidyme went on sampling the bath oils until she found one that would suit. She passed the jar over to her friend.

"I'll take the jasmine," Iobia said. "If I can annoy Karânî with my smell, I'll consider it a battle won."

"You always annoy me with your smell," Karânî said. "Feel free to parade around the terrace with a victory banner."

There was no spite in the girls' banter. In fact, their teasing held a distinct current of warmth and affection that startled Rhodopis. She could sense already that the three Persian girls were far less competitive, less mistrustful than any group of women she had known before. She thought she could like them easily enough, but still she felt wary in their presence. The weight of her duty to the Egyptian throne never left her; danger seemed to drift all around her like an unseen mist, cold and oppressive.

Iobia rubbed the jasmine oil into her shoulders and chest. "Is it true that Egypt has never sent a royal daughter to any other king?"

"Yes," Rhodopis said. "That's so."

"Never? Not in a thousand years?"

"Well... not that I know of."

"It must feel strange," Faidyme said, "to be the first to leave Egypt in such a long, long history."

"It's... very strange indeed," Rhodopis said faintly. *You've no idea how peculiar I feel.*

"Did our brides reach Egypt before you left?" Karânî asked eagerly.

"Oh, yes," Rhodopis said. "I met them—Shamiram and Ninsina. They were very beautiful and kind. I hope they will be happy in Egypt."

Faidyme said, "I hope the same. We were good friends with both, and we miss them terribly. All the women here in Cambyses' house are good friends: we are determined to be, even though Iobia snores at night and you can hear it from the Ishtar Gate."

"Do you never quarrel with one another?" Rhodopis asked.

"Oh, now and then," Iobia said. "But we never let a quarrel last long. Living together as we do, and sharing one man among us... everything is easier if we are friends rather than enemies."

"Do the women in the Pharaoh's harem fight terribly?" This from Faidyme, who seemed eager to hear a scandalous "yes."

"They didn't—that is, *we* didn't—fight, exactly," Rhodopis said. "But the women seldom trusted one another, and they were not as kind and quick to laugh as you. They were... dignified, I suppose."

The three girls burst into laughter.

Rhodopis blushed, realizing what she had said. "I didn't mean to imply—"

"It's all right," Karânî said. "Don't apologize. We are *not* over-burdened by dignity here in Cambyses' household—not by an outsider's estimation. But we do look out for one another, and we enjoy our days."

"And our nights," Faidyme added. "Up until Iobia starts in with her snoring."

Rhodopis said shyly, "You seem to have an enviable life here, in the king's household. I pray that I will fit in."

Karânî threw her arm around Rhodopis' shoulder. "Nitetis, my sister—you fit in already. You are one of us. We accepted you down there in the practice yard, did we not? And the king took you for his wife. That means you're one of us."

"But the poor thing feels out of place," Iobia said. "We must remedy that."

Faidyme clapped her hands in anticipation. "Feast! Tonight!"

The other girls clamored in eager agreement.

"Oh—no, I couldn't," Rhodopis said. "Not tonight. I'm so tired from the journey. I can barely keep my eyes open now."

"If you fall asleep at your welcoming feast," Iobia said, "we will understand. And we'll make Naramsin carry you back to your chamber and tuck you into bed like a sweet little babe. But you must let us celebrate, Nitetis. We're all so glad you've come."

Rhodopis shook her head in wonder. Even the party the girls of the Stable had thrown, when Rhodopis became a woman, had never felt as warm or genuine as this. And certainly, the Pharaoh's women had found no cause to celebrate Rhodopis' coming. That this offer of a welcoming feast came from three girls who were all but strangers to her struck Rhodopis mute. She nodded her assent, unable to speak a word, for she feared anything she tried to say would come out as a croak of tearful gratitude.

She stood, took Naramsin's hand, and climbed rather shakily from the bath. The eunuch toweled her dry and held her gown while Rhodopis arranged its drapes and knots.

"Tonight, then," Iobia said. "Naramsin, will you see to preparations?"

❧

THE WELCOMING FEAST stretched far too late into the night. By the time she and Amtes stumbled back to the vast chamber, Rhodopis felt weak from too much dancing. Her head was light and dizzy from the wine; her cheeks ached from hours of immoderate laughter. Long after moonrise, she had finally managed to convince Cambyses' wives and concubines that she could stand no more celebration. "The journey was too long," she said apologetically, turning away another round of sweet cakes and yet another full cup of wine. "If I don't find my bed soon, I'll fall down dead from exhaustion."

Amtes yawned, rubbing her eyes as she shoved open the heavy door to Rhodopis' three fine rooms. There they found the lamps burning, the whole lavish place dancing with light. It gleamed on the brightly tiled walls, illuminated the sheen of silk on every cushioned chair and long, stuffed couch. The servants had made quick work of the dowry; everything had been unpacked and put neatly away. Someone—Naramsin, perhaps—had delivered a polished table with a row of tiny drawers along its lower edge. It stood against the wall opposite Rhodopis' bed, crowned by a great, round electrum mirror. Every pot and vial of Rhodopis' cosmetics stood in orderly rows across the table's surface.

"At least we don't have to do the work of unpacking," Amtes said, her jaws cracking with another long yawn. "Nor must we put away all those fine things sent along from Egypt."

"We don't know where anything is, either," Rhodopis pointed out. "And it's cold; never would I have thought the desert could be so cold. It wasn't like this on the journey over, I swear."

"Wintertime is coming. The desert is bitterly cold at night in the winter, or so I hear. Oh, these Persians make much of their River Purattu, but it's nothing like our river back home. The Iteru takes the edge off the cold on winter nights, so it stays warm—more or less—throughout the season. It keeps the valley cooler than it ought to be on summer days, too." Amtes added with a mocking wink, "That's how you know the gods of Kmet are the *true* gods, and love the Kmetu best of all people."

Rhodopis wrapped her arms around herself, shivering. "I wish for a hundred of our rivers now, then; I'll freeze in another minute. Help me find something warm to wear in bed."

The two young women searched fruitlessly through closets carved with eagles and she-cattle until at last they found Rhodopis' warmest robes in a trunk of simple cedar, strapped with bronze. Rhodopis pulled out a plain green smock made of thick wool. She pressed the cloth to her face. A sweet, camphoraceous scent—the wood of the chest—clung to the wool. She breathed it in deeply.

"Dress quick, Mistress," Amtes said. "It is cold, and the sooner we're both in our beds, the happier we'll be."

Once Rhodopis was dressed in the wool smock, Amtes sat her on a little stool before the new cosmetics table. She combed out

Rhodopis' hair, inspecting it carefully. "We must dye your hair again soon. Tomorrow or the day after, assuming those wild girls leave you alone long enough, and we can have a bit of privacy."

"I'll see to it that I am left alone," Rhodopis promised. "If these ladies of the harem won't leave me to my own devices, I'll make them believe I'm sick from my monthly flux. That should buy us an hour or two alone, at the very least." She paused. "But it was a good time, wasn't it? I've never had so much fun at a feast before."

Amtes laid the comb aside and squeezed Rhodopis' shoulder. The two women looked at one another in the mirror's surface. "You did well today," Amtes said. "You are young, but now I understand why the chief wife chose you. You're quick." Amtes tapped Rhodopis' chest, just over her heart—the place where all Egyptians believed thought and emotion resided.

Rhodopis smiled at her handmaid's reflection. "Thank you."

"The servants made a little bed for me in that room—there, to the left of the window. If you need me, come and wake me. Now —into bed with you, or you really will die of exhaustion."

Rhodopis climbed into her bed. It was so soft and warm, she groaned aloud with relief; every muscle and bone in her body seemed to melt into the mattress like soft cheese in the sun. Amtes blew out the nearest lamp, then made her way across the chamber, snuffing each lamp as she came to it. The great chamber sank into peaceful darkness.

Anxiety still gnawed at Rhodopis' mind—how not, now that she was in the belly of the lion? But the day had been so thoroughly exhausting that sleep claimed her almost at once. The green wool robe and the lavish silk covers draping her bed were warm enough to wrap her in a sense of luxurious comfort; her eyes closed heavily and her breathing deepened the moment her head found a cushion.

A knock on her chamber door jerked her from the peaceful realms of half-sleep. She stared into the darkness of her chamber, straining every nerve and sense, wondering whether she had truly heard it, or whether it had been the misty beginnings of a dream. But then the knock came again, cracking through the lightless chamber, short and terse—and all too real.

Rhodopis cowered, pulling her covers up to her chin. She waited for Amtes to rise from her bed in the far adjoining chamber, but there was no shuffling of blankets, no footstep on the carpeted floor. A moment later, Rhodopis heard her maid's soft but emphatic snore.

Blast it all, she thought petulantly. She wanted sleep—more desperately than she'd ever wanted anything in her life. And she had no desire to face whatever grim surprises the Persian night might offer up—whether it was an assassin's long knife or another cup of wine and a round of dancing from the harem women.

Again, the rapping sounded... and still Amtes slept on.

No choice but to face whoever's out there, Rhodopis thought, her belly going sour with fear. *Best get it over with, if I'm ever to sleep... and no matter now whether I sleep in my bed or my grave.*

She slid from beneath the silk covers, into the cold night air, and groped for a moment near her bed for her slippers. They were nowhere to be found; she abandoned them altogether, padding across the chamber on bare feet. Just enough starlight seeped in through her window to limn the brass handle of her door; it offered a pale glimmer, guiding Rhodopis through the darkness to whatever fate the gods had prepared. She drew a deep breath and twisted the handle before fear could overwhelm her and send her back to cower in her bed. The door creaked open, barely wide enough for Rhodopis to peek out into the corridor.

Phanes stood before her. In one hand, he carried a small oil lamp, hanging from a short wooden dowel. The lamp was suspended by three slim chains; it swung side to side in the space between Rhodopis and her visitor, causing a patch of orange light to slide across Phanes' face and retreat again, leaving him in darkness. His visage appeared and disappeared rhythmically, first visible, then not. The effect was otherworldly; when Rhodopis shivered, it had nothing to do with the winter's cold.

"Can... can I be of some aid?" Rhodopis asked, faltering.

"May I come in, my lady?"

She pushed the door further shut; only one eye peered out at him. "How can you ask such a thing? It is not appropriate! I'm the wife of the king!"

The swinging lamp slowed. She could read Phanes' expression for longer, now. There was a certain forbidding stillness to his features, yet his tiny smiled seemed almost wry. "My lady, every person in Babylon knows the king trusts me more than any man in his service. No one will suspect any disloyalty from either of us. And I swear by all the gods—of Egypt and Haxamanishiya —that I have no designs on you."

Rhodopis did not open the door one hair's breadth wider. She prayed frantically that Amtes would wake and come to her aid, but an abrupt snort from the maid's chamber, followed by the resumed purr of her sleeping, proved that prayer was not to be answered.

"Very well, then," Phanes said coolly. "If you will not let me in, then I shall cut right to the matter—out here in the corridor, where anyone may hear my words. Who are you truly? I will know, for if you are a danger to the king, I shall see to it personally that you never approach him again."

Rhodopis' face burned like a forge-fire. All at once she was grateful for the cold air; without the winter night to cool her, she felt she might have burst into flames. She pulled the door open wide enough to admit Phanes, grabbed him by one arm, and hauled him quickly inside. Then she closed the door quietly behind him.

"I don't know what you're talking about," Rhodopis whispered. "I'm Nitetis, of course—daughter of Amasis, king of all Egypt."

Phanes tipped his head to one side, fixing Rhodopis with a dry, judgmental stare. Clearly, he was not convinced, but she couldn't disavow her claim. Any admission that she was not the Pharaoh's daughter would mean immediate death. The cold of the room receded; a strange warmth of certainty, of ominous acceptance, enfolded her. She hadn't expected to survive this mad gamble—not truly—but she had never imagined the end would come so soon.

"You are not Egyptian," Phanes said. "I can tell by the way you speak. You're Greek, aren't you?"

"Thracian," Rhodopis said shortly. Again, she cursed Khedeb-Netjer-Bona—but what could she do, other than sling her useless imprecations up toward the gods? There was no hiding the truth from Phanes.

"Thracian—yes, I can see it now. That hair color—yours by nature, or a dye?"

Rhodopis lifted her chin defiantly. She would not answer his question.

"Tell me who you are," Phanes said.

She replied flatly, "I'm the Pharaoh's daughter." Her voice was far steadier than her legs; they trembled with fear and sudden weakness, but somehow she remained standing, uncomfortably and absurdly aware of her bare feet, their vulnerability.

Phanes stared at her a moment longer, hard-faced, searching. She thought he would shout for guards, thought she'd be hauled away to some terrible confinement and questioned—or put to the sword at once, without even a chance to defend herself. But then, in the next heartbeat, Phanes' stern countenance crumbled. He sighed, shutting his eyes briefly in a manner that almost implied relief. He turned, set the lamp carefully on one of Rhodopis' tables.

"Let me tell you," he said quietly, "how I came to be here in

Haxamanishiya. Perhaps my story will give you the courage to tell me the truth. Look at me, Nitetis—or whatever your true name may be. Look, truly look, though I know the light is dim. If I were to shave off this Haxamani beard, and let these made-up curls out of my hair... if I were to dress only in a pleated white kilt, would I not look rather..."

"Egyptian," Rhodopis said. Of course. Why hadn't she seen it before? Phanes had all the features of a native Egyptian—dark skin, broad nose, obsidian-black hair—but they were masked by his Babylonian style. She should have known—should have suspected, when he spoke the Egyptian tongue so flawlessly at their first meeting.

"I haven't always been Phanes," he said. "My mother named me Udjahorresnet. I was born in Halicarnassus, far to the west of here, and across the Great Sea from the Nile Delta, but family was Egyptian. My father was a trader; his outpost in Halicarnassus was a good one, very profitable, but he was Kmetu through and through. He kept the faith of the true Egyptian gods, and raised me to know the Two Lands before ever I set foot there. When I was old enough to be educated, he sent me back to Egypt to live with his cousin; my father wouldn't see me brought up in the Greek traditions—no, not for all the silver in the world. And so, I went to Memphis as a boy, to learn Kmetu ways. My father hoped I would rejoin him in the north, and take up his trade. Before I reached manhood, though, both my father and my mother fell victim to a terrible plague, and I was left alone in the homeland.

"But my father had been a man of means, and I received the best schooling his wealth could buy. First I learned the scribe's arts. Then, when I knew I was an orphan and had no family to return to, I chose to stay on in Memphis for more education. I turned my attention to medicine; I apprenticed myself to the best physician in the city, and from him, I learned how to combat all manner of disease—especially the illness that had claimed my parents' lives.

"I was dedicated to my art, and developed something of a reputation, even from a young age. When Amasis was new to the throne, he heard of my skill and appointed me to serve with the army. Not as a soldier, you understand—I have no skills of that sort, thank the gods—but as a healer and surgeon, caring for the sick and injured on the king's campaigns. I served for several years in Amasis' fleet, tending to the health of all the men who manned the Pharaoh's ships and fought at his command. Dangerous work it was, too.

"But after a time, the Pharaoh ceased campaigning. There were fewer battles—again, I thank the gods—and less use for a man like me. I thought perhaps I would go south to Waset, the old capital, and take up work there as a physician. But Amasis heard tell of my dedication and skill; he brought me to the palace to serve the royal family instead. I welcomed the stability, for I was eager to start a family of my own, and I wished to provide for them as well as my father had provided for me.

"I soon saw that wish granted." Phanes smiled, though a veil of sorrow darkened his face. "I fell in love with a young woman from a noble family—Muyet is her name, though I suppose she is young no longer—nor am I. She will always be a young and lovely girl in my mind, though... in my memory. She was beautiful, intelligent, sweet-tempered, with a laugh like music... everything a man could desire. Everything any man could desire, including the king.

"I'd heard rumors that Amasis had hoped Muyet's family would dedicate her to his harem. But her parents never made mention of such plans; nor did Muyet express any desire for harem life. We were in love—madly and stupidly in love, for we both should have seen the danger; we both should have been more cautious. Ah, but young love is never cautious, is it? Nor is it wise. We were married as soon as the arrangements could be made. We went together to the Temple of Hathor and swore our love before the goddess. It was the gladdest day I'd ever known.

"Amasis never mentioned Muyet to me—never rebuked me, nor treated me any differently. I had no reason to suspect the Pharaoh was displeased. Rumors continued to drift about Memphis—indeed, they circulated around the palace, too—the same old tale that Amasis had fallen in love with my wife, and wanted her for his own. I ignored the rumors; Amasis was always pleasant and fair to me. I enjoyed my life, and rejoiced in Muyet. We were happy together; indeed, I thought no man could be happier than I, until Muyet fell pregnant. Then I knew true joy.

"From early in her pregnancy, it was clear to me that Muyet carried twins. She grew as large as the full moon." He laughed fondly. "The day our sons were born, the midwives allowed me to help with the delivery. It's a privilege men don't often enjoy, but as I was a well-known physician, well..."

He fell silent, smiling in a gentle, reminiscent way. But Rhodopis could sense the sadness hanging all about him. Drawn by the mystery of his sorrow, she said, "What happened?"

"Well, my sons were born, of course. I've never felt so proud, in all my life. When I held my boys for the first time..." He shook his head, unable to speak on.

A memory surfaced in Rhodopis' mind, rising with painful force. She remembered the warm weight of Bolin and Belos, her twin brothers, as they lay in her thin, childish arms for the first time. She swallowed hard, willing away her tears.

After a moment, Phanes resumed his story. His voice was stronger now. "Our sons grew—they thrived like green shoots in the sun. But I soon noticed that Egypt was not thriving. Amasis' love for Greek culture was like the weeds of the fields, or like a vine wrapping itself round a fig tree—choking and strangling, blotting out the true identity of Kmet. Memphis grew restless— even dangerous, as the Kmetu chafed under Amasis' rule. I saw that unless the Pharaoh changed his course, soon the tree of

Egypt would fruit no longer. It would wither slowly, dying a death by degrees, so incremental it would hardly be noticed by anyone, until it was too late to revive the blighted roots.

"I was one of Amasis' most trusted advisors, and so I turned my hand to a new line of work. I tried to make Amasis see the folly of his ways—gently, you understand. One must always handle a king gently, even a king as pleasant and easy-going as Amasis. But I... I fear I over-stepped. In my desperation to save Egypt from its fate, I became too vocal an opponent of the Pharaoh's policies. As carefully and conscientiously as I worked, still I was too dogged, and the Pharaoh soon realized I was trying to influence him. Amasis exiled me. Well—that is not exactly true. He did not exile me; he merely re-assigned me, sending me off to serve indefinitely at Shali. Do you know where Shali is?"

Rhodopis shook her head.

"It is far to the west of Memphis, over the barren desert of the Red Land. It's a remote military outpost, a place barely clinging to life around the Siwa oasis. I wouldn't have minded practicing medicine there, if Amasis hadn't sent me off without my wife or children." He paused and turned away, contemplating the flickering flame of his tiny lamp. "Amasis imposed on me a sentence of isolation and loneliness... an exceptionally cruel fate, to cut me off from my wife and children. I was powerless to stop him— what can a mere physician do when the Pharaoh has spoken?— and equally powerless to convince him to allow my family to come with me.

"I knew then that the rumors had been true all along; Amasis had indeed wanted Muyet for his own, and had never forgiven me for marrying a woman he regarded as his by right. Perhaps he had only been waiting for an excuse, some reason to wreak his vengeance upon me.

"Perhaps if I'd never meddled in his Greek affairs, I would still be happy with Muyet and our sons... I don't know. It's useless to speculate; I know that now. My fate is what it is. I cannot change it."

Phanes raised his head; he looked at Rhodopis directly, his eyes burning with sudden fire. So startling was the change in his mood that she nearly stepped back, unsure whether she was frightened or awed by the physician's transformation.

"But neither could I serve a king who could do something so cruel," Phanes said. "Nor could I serve a king who would destroy Egypt for the sake of his own idle interests. I knew if I did not report to the outpost at Siwa, word would eventually reach Amasis. I would be branded a traitor; I would never return to Egypt—never see my family again.

"I lost all loyalty to the Egyptian throne at that moment, when Amasis passed his cruel sentence upon me. Oh, do not mistake me: I am loyal to Egypt itself—to Kmet, the Two Lands, my people. My father cultured that loyalty in me; it has never left my heart. But Amasis—bah! He is no king of mine. I knew it was true, knew it was my own personal maat, even as I stood before Amasis with my head bowed, listening to his decree that I should be cut off forever from my family.

"I went, of course. I left Memphis, as the king directed. What else could I do? If I had refused his orders, I would have been killed. The king's soldiers probably would have done the deed before the eyes of my wife and my infant sons. I couldn't burden them with such a memory, so I went placidly enough, though inside I was afire with anger. I sailed north, but when I reached the small town where the caravans struck out west for Siwa, I boarded another ship and kept sailing.

"By then, my resolve was set. I knew the Pharaoh had the power to separate me from my family, but he had no power to control me from afar. I could still be useful to Egypt; the gods imbued me with purpose, even if my role in this world was no longer that of a father and husband. I had learned enough of politics and war during my early years, caring for the Pharaoh's soldiers; I knew Cambyses was the only man in the world who posed any real threat to Amasis—who could wrest him and his unworthy family from the throne. For if Kmet is ever to be restored, and heal from the damage that has been done already, the line of succession must be broken. An entirely new king must ascend to the throne."

Phanes lapsed into silence, but still he held Rhodopis' gaze with his own—those fervent, fiery eyes. Both his passion and his sorrow seemed real enough. But Rhodopis did not know this man; she had no reason to place her very life in his hands. Awed as she was by Phanes' gripping tale—and his willingness to share it with her, a perfect stranger—Rhodopis heeded the thrill of caution that tingled along her spine. Persia was unknown territory; even the friendliest-seeming companion could prove a deadly enemy. Until she found her feet in the palace, the city, the king's esteem, she must presume danger at every turn. She must hear the threat hidden behind every kind and flattering word. Real as it all appeared, Phanes' story could be a whole-cloth lie, calculated to entrap her. She would place no trust in this man—nor any other—until she had ample reason to do it.

The silence stretched between them. "Tell me," Phanes said at last, a conspiratorial light shining in his eye, "how did a young woman from Thrace come to be the Pharaoh's daughter?"

Rhodopis only shrugged with the fluid grace of a dancer. She blanked her face, giving Phanes nothing—no emotion to read, no meaning to mistake in her perfectly neutral features. If the physician was so clever, then let him puzzle out for himself how Rhodopis ended up the Pharaoh's daughter. She hungered for freedom, for an easing of the terrible tension that squeezed like a fist around her, sleeping and waking, night and day. But she was not free—not yet. She was still duty-bound to the Egyptian throne, still haunted by the possibility that Khedeb-Netjer-Bona —or Amasis himself—might silence her forever if she did not deliver the information they expected.

"Very well." Phanes picked up his lamp; it swung again, sending its orange light flying about the room, a dizzying, disorienting flare. "You don't have to tell me anything if you don't wish it. But know this, Nitetis: I will learn the truth sooner or later. I always do."

"And what will you do with the truth, once you learn it?" She did her best to sound flippant, unconcerned. But her throat was dry from fear, and her voice was as a shaky croak.

Phanes stood in silence for a moment. Then he moved quietly toward the door. He paused with his hand on the latch, looking back at her, all the passion and sadness burned out of his eyes. There was nothing left but naked honesty. "That depends on what you intend to do—why you're here, in Cambyses' court. It all depends where your loyalties lie... Lady Nitetis."

He left her then. The door creaked as it opened; it swallowed the glow of his lamp. When it shut again, Rhodopis was plunged into darkness. She shivered in the winter's cold.

❧ 10 ❧

BEHIND THE LION DOOR

THE DAYS PASSED EASIER THAN RHODOPIS HAD IMAGINED THEY
would. As an agent of deception, embedded in Persia like a viper
beneath the hot desert sand, she had small reason to hope for
comfort. With Phanes suspecting her secret—or at least knowing
she had a secret, however obscure—she was doubly certain of
anxiety, of danger and strife. Yet life in the harem was unaccount-
ably pleasant. Cambyses' women welcomed her unstintingly, as
her bathing companions had insisted they would. The women
brought Rhodopis into their work, their gossip and their games
as readily as if she'd been a distant cousin or a long-lost sister,
forever remembered and cherished, yet seldom seen until now.
Everyone in the king's harem, from concubines and wives to
industrious servants, took great pains to ease her transition into
Persian culture. They were generous with their warmth, and even
with their belongings, taking it in turns to dress her for each meal
and social occasion, showing her how to affect a Haxamani style
with shawl and perfume, paint pots and hair combs. If they
laughed at her accent or her broken attempts to speak the Haxamani tongue, there was only warmth and encouragement in their
amusement—nothing unkind.

Rhodopis picked up the daily rhythm of harem life as quickly and naturally as she had learned to dance. There was a comforting kind of simplicity to harem days. Each morning, Rhodopis rose with the sun and join the other women in the garden, where the sun-god Ahura-Mazda—foremost deity of Haxamanishiya—received his due praise as he rose from the eastern horizon. Then Rhodopis dressed for the morning meal, which the women almost always took together in their private feast hall, a large room with communal tables, where all mingled freely, regardless of station or standing, gossiping and jesting over their simple yet satisfying fare of bread, fruit, and spicy, smoked meats. As the sun climbed toward its peak, the women assembled in support of Cambyses, appearing in one great flock wherever the king's duties took him on that day. It did not matter whether he sat in solemn judgment on his throne, hearing the petitions of his subjects and issuing decrees, or whether he wrestled in the courtyard with a friend, or trained with sword and spear. Every woman who was well enough to leave her bed—and not occupied with a new infant—attended Cambyses, each standing proud and confident in his presence, each a symbol of the king's wealth and power.

More than a week passed in this way. Although Rhodopis had yet to spend any time alone with her husband, through observation of the man in his element she came to know Cambyses' temper and personality. Cambyses was not only physically strong and powerful of will—somewhere in his early forties, he was easily as vital as a man half his age—but the king was also wise and good. He was quick to laugh with everyone who stood before him, from generals and guards to women and eunuchs. Indeed, he even smiled at the meekest slaves who bowed low at his feet. When he was required to pass judgment on those who had violated Babylonian law, he did so with careful thought and deliberation. Never did he revel in the suffering of others—not even the basest criminals.

As the days passed, Rhodopis began to realize (with no small measure of surprise) that she *liked* Cambyses. She tempered her instinctive pleasure in his presence with a healthy dose of caution and deliberate reserve. She may find his character appealing— what she had thus far seen of it—but still, she knew almost nothing about the man. When the eyes of his women and subjects were not upon him, Cambyses might prove a very different king. Yet what she saw of his public persona fostered a genuine respect in the king's newest bride. Comparing Cambyses to Amasis, Rhodopis often marveled at the differences in their personalities and politics—even in their bearing. The gods had never made two kings as starkly dissimilar as Cambyses and soft, old Amasis.

And of a certainty, Cambyses was nothing like Psamtik— nothing whatsoever.

Throughout the week, after his unsettling visit to her chamber, Phanes took scrupulous care to avoid Rhodopis, despite Cambyses' instructions that the physician must see to her every whim. Phanes' absence suited Rhodopis well enough, for her strongest desire now was to avoid him. When the routine of the harem brought her near Phanes—when she passed him in the halls or when they stood at opposite ends of Cambyses' throne room—she kept her eyes fixed on the floor and pretended with all her concentration that he did not exist, that she had never seen him before, that she had never admitted him into her chamber, nor listened to his disconcerting tale. She had mentioned his visit to no one, of course—not even Amtes. At the morning praises to Ahura-Mazda, Rhodopis' most oft-repeated prayer was that the god would never give her cause to speak to Phanes again... that he would forget about her entirely, allowing her to recede into the anonymity of the harem until she vanished from his memory.

As the days shortened and nights grew longer and colder, Rhodopis took to walking on the women's terrace, wrapped in her heaviest woolen shawl, alone with her thoughts and the ever-pressing weight of duty. One especially cold and windy evening, when the sun was just beginning to set, she stood at the terrace's edge, watching Babylon glow with the final fire of day. Soon the shadows of night would fall across the city, blotting out color and damping down the faint sounds of industry and song that drifted up to her on the fitful breezes. A strong gust of wind caught her shawl and whipped it out behind her; the long, bright fringes tossed and tangled as she gathered it tightly round herself once more. What a beautiful place the city was, even in wintertime. Did she dare to hope that her unwanted duty to Egypt would never require her to return to Memphis? Perhaps, if she did her work well—if she gave enough information to satisfy Amasis—she would be freed from her task and abandoned here in Camby-ses' palace. It was expensive, after all, to travel across the desert. Surely the Pharaoh would prefer to leave her where she was. If she could only appease him with the right reports of Cambyses' doings, his weaknesses—

"Lady Nitetis."

Rhodopis jumped and spun away from the view. Guilt over her treacherous thoughts heated her cheeks. Naramsin was coming toward her across the terrace, bundled as she was in a heavy shawl.

"Yes?" she said, rather weakly, when Naramsin approached.

"The king has sent for you. He wishes to see you alone."

Rhodopis' stomach lurched with fear. Had her doom come, then? Had Phanes gone to the king, told him that he suspected the new Egyptian bride of some foul deception? Heart pounding, she nodded in a silent daze and went with Naramsin toward the women's palace, her feet numb and clumsy.

"You should beautify yourself, of course," Naramsin said, "but don't take too long, and don't put in too much effort. Cambyses prefers a natural sort of beauty. If you would like my assistance, I stand ready. I do know what pleases the king best, of course."

She gave a small, shaky laugh of relief. Cambyses had not sent for Rhodopis to pass judgment—to condemn her for her crimes. He merely wished to bed his new wife. *That's work I can do well, and no mistake.* A warm swell of confidence restored feeling to her limbs. The path ahead was so blessedly familiar that she felt positively giddy, eager to return to the hetaera's trade.

"Only tell me what I ought to wear," she said to Naramsin, "and I'll be most grateful."

Half an hour later, the sun had vanished in the west, leaving the first scattering of white stars to shine down upon Babylon. Rhodopis emerged from her chamber braced and ready, dressed as Naramsin suggested in a simple robe of red silk embroidered with golden vines at the hem. Her shawl was equally modest: white as a new lamb's fleece with a pale-blue fringe. She had let down her hair, binding her forehead with a strip of beaded silk, after the Babylonian fashion, and had scented her body with Egyptian myrrh.

Naramsin, waiting in the corridor, nodded his approval the moment he saw her. "You are sure to delight the king."

Rhodopis followed Naramsin out of the women's quarters, into the palace proper, and up a ramp that led to the very apex of the structure. This was a part of the palace she had never seen before—the private quarters of the king, his haven from the trials and harsh obligations of rule. Images of Psamtik reared up in her mind, threatening to overwhelm her confidence and readiness. She banished those dark memories with a will. Cambyses was *not* like Psamtik. New to Babylon as she was, Rhodopis could feel sure of little—but she was certain that the king of Persia bore no resemblance to Psamtik, that cold-blooded creature with a hunter's stare. To distract herself from all thought of that hateful beast, Rhodopis recalled the first time she had been obliged to lie with Xanthes. At worst, this encounter with Cambyses would be much like the time she'd spent in Xanthes' bed. How Xanthes had sweated and grunted, just like the girls of the Stable had said he would! Rhodopis had found that work easy enough, once she'd set to it. Xanthes had been no chore at all, except that she had struggled to keep herself from laughing. The memory was enough to conjure up a smile as she approached Cambyses' door.

But as she and Naramsin turned the final corner, the smile slid from Rhodopis' face. There stood Phanes, stiff and sober as a proper guardsman in front of the king's chamber. His hands were locked behind his hips, his back straight as an iron rod. He watched Rhodopis with sober, wary eyes. On the instant, her stomach turned to a mass of fluttering moths.

"I will see Lady Nitetis into the king's presence," Phanes said to Naramsin. "Thank you; you may go."

The eunuch turned away.

"Wait," Rhodopis cried impulsively, reaching out quickly to catch Naramsin by the arm.

He paused. "Is there something else you need, my lady?"

"She needs nothing," Phanes said shortly. "Leave us, Naramsin."

Still, Naramsin hesitated. Phanes stood high in the king's regard, but his status gave him no authority over the chief eunuch of the harem. Naramsin's meticulous brows raised in a silent question; he waited for Rhodopis to say more.

What could she tell him? That Phanes had come to her room in the middle of the night and interrogated her—that he had guessed already that she was not who she claimed to be? There was nothing Rhodopis could say, nothing she could do to ward Phanes away. She forced herself to release Naramsin's arm.

"I am afraid," she muttered, blushing. "I have never... never been with a man before."

Naramsin smiled. "There is nothing to fear. The king will be good to you; all the women agree on that point. The king is always good, and kind, and gentle." He offered Rhodopis an encouraging pat on the shoulder, nodded to Phanes, and disappeared around the corner. Rhodopis was left alone in the corridor with the one man she had hoped never to speak to again. She swallowed hard. She could not bring herself to look Phanes in the eye. "What do you want with me?"

Phanes turned aside from the great lion-marked door—the entry to the king's chambers, Rhodopis assumed. He gestured to another, small and narrow as a closet's opening, standing open across the hall. "Step inside."

Rhodopis balked at the close darkness in the chamber. "I will not!"

Phanes sighed. "We have visited this subject before, I think. I have no designs on you, *Lady Nitetis*. My only wish is to carry out the duties my king expects."

"I'll call out to him; I'll make him come and see that you intend to drag me alone into some dark, narrow room!"

"Will you, truly?" Phanes lifted one brow. "Do you think the king will take your part—you, a newcomer to his palace —or mine?"

Rhodopis glanced at the lion door, then at the narrow closet. She swallowed again.

"Let us be done with this," Phanes said. "The sooner, the better."

"If you try to hurt me, I'll—"

"I will not hurt you. You have my word on that. If I try to do you any harm, you may scream all you like for the king; you have my blessing on that count."

Rhodopis clenched her jaw and stepped into the small room. She had no idea what purpose it served, unless it was a resting room for the king's guards. A small, hard-looking, spartan bed took up most of the space; between bed and wall, there was barely enough room for Rhodopis and Phanes to stand face-to-face without touching. Despite Phanes' assurances that he had no interest in her body, the presence of the bed made her heart leap.

With a sickening shiver, she remembered Psamtik's hand clenched tight around her arm, his hot breath in her ear.

"Raise your arms," Phanes said.

"There isn't room enough. The wall—"

"Do your best."

Rhodopis raised her arms reluctantly, holding them above her head at an awkward angle. Phanes moved her shawl aside and patted her with business-like abruptness, touching her ribs, her hips, the front and back of her. She jerked away from his hand when he felt her breasts through the red robe, but his impatient sigh reconciled her to keep still.

"What in all the gods' names are you doing?" she said.

"Checking you."

"For what?"

"Weapons. Knives, daggers... weaving needles... whatever you might think to use."

"Use a weapon—on the king? Are you mad?"

He looked up at her sharply. "Are *you* mad? You're playing some game, Nitetis. We both know it's true. I will not allow you into the king's presence if there is any chance you will be a danger to him. You of all people know how important Cambyses is to me—how I've thrown in my lot with him. I won't risk his downfall by some sly trick of the Pharaoh."

Rhodopis gave a disgusted grunt. "Amasis couldn't dream up a sly trick if his life depended on it."

The physician pulled back suddenly, locking eyes with Rhodopis. She couldn't look away from the intensity of his stare. "Then who?" Phanes said quietly. "Who, if not Amasis?"

She pressed her lips together and did not respond.

"Let me see your hands," Phanes said.

Rhodopis lowered her arms and held out her hands, palms up. "Empty, as you can see."

Phanes turned her hands over roughly. He picked and pried at her finger-rings, jerking and twisting each one in turn.

"Ow!" Rhodopis cried. "You've hurt me! What do you think you're doing now?"

"Searching for hinges and clasps," he said. "Hollow rings. Anything that might hold poison. Let me see your necklace."

She held the emerald bauble out to him; he pried at it, but the ornament revealed no hidden compartment, no deadly phial that might take Cambyses' life.

"Are you satisfied now?" Rhodopis said. "I've got no weapon, nor any poison. And if you don't let me go in to the king, who *has* summoned me, after all, he'll be looking for the reason why."

Phanes backed out of the room. "Very well. You seem safe enough this time. But I will learn the truth of you, Nitetis. Don't think you can put me off forever."

She jerked her chin high and strode past him, pulling her clothing back into place, burning with fury and fear.

Phanes rapped on the chamber door.

"Come," Cambyses called.

Rhodopis was all too glad to put the lion door between herself and Phanes. When it closed, she breathed a quiet sigh of relief and looked upon the king's private chambers for the first time. Rhodopis had thought her accommodations spectacular, but next to the king's, her rooms seemed as quaint as a peasant's mud-hut. Cambyses' rooms were so large, they seemed to occupy the entire upper story of the palace. Half a dozen doors ran down opposite walls of the chamber, each one leading (Rhodopis assumed) into another room. A huge table of ebony wood dominated the great chamber; it was covered with neat stacks of tablets and baskets of scrolls. A small wooden rack on the table held a variety of writing tools: an ink brush with fine, pointed hairs, a variety of styli and tiny stone chisels. Did the king eschew scribes, and write his own letters? If so, this was the very desk on which Cambyses had composed his threat to Egypt. Rhodopis shivered and looked away from the table. Two groups of couches ranged to either side of the room. What any man—even a king—

would need with two separate sitting areas, Rhodopis could not begin to imagine. There was a corner strewn with cushions, half-screened by small fig trees that sprouted from clay pots. Through the figs' leaves, she could see a rack that held several strange instruments, with round, bulbous bodies made of polished wood and long necks, up which ran pale strings like those of a harp.

Across a veritable sea of matching blue carpets, Cambyses stood with his back to the chamber, gazing out one of a series of tall, rectangular windows. The stars had brightened, multiplied; their pale glow graced the desert through a curtain of purple-dark night. A damp, greenish scent of garden fountains drifted in through the window. Although the great wooden shutters were folded back and tied, the king's chamber was not cold. Several large braziers burned on golden tripods; the air above them wavered with heat, and the wood coals within crackled, emitting coils of resinous smoke.

Cambyses raised his hand, beckoning without turning to look at Rhodopis. She crossed the vast room rather timidly and stood silently beside the king.

The city of Babylon spread itself across the desert below. Lamps flickered to life throughout the city, illuminating every window, blossoming like red flowers on the rooftops. Pinpricks of fire danced and moved along the streets; the commingling of many individual lights set spires of temples and ziggurats apart from the blackness of the desert. The city's subtle glow warmed the huge, pointed mounds of the ice-houses, great storage domes like the hives of enormous bees, where blocks of miraculous, milk-white ice were preserved intact against the desert clime, even in the killing heat of summer. Beyond Babylon's walls, beyond the faint silver strip of its river, the desert was an expanse of wool-soft blackness, stretching like an unending sea toward the invisible horizon. It was beautiful, that uninterrupted, untamed land. But the serenity of the view did nothing to calm Rhodopis' fears. Her heart only seemed to beat all the harder as she gazed out at the placid scene. Blackness was all around her. She was surrounded by enemies; soon Phanes would learn her secret, one way or another, and then it would all be over. Perhaps this would be the last beautiful thing she ever saw—this quiet night, this undisturbed peace. Then the blade would drop, and no one—not Aesop, not her lost family—would know where she had gone, or what had become of her. Perhaps not even the gods would know, for this was not Thrace, not Egypt. It was the land of Ishtar and Ahura-Mazda—strangers to her.

Cambyses turned to her suddenly; Rhodopis lifted a hand, trying to dash away her tears before he could see. But it was too late. He touched her shoulder with surprising gentleness. "Nitetis. Why do you weep?" A broad smile shifted the curls of his beard. "Ah—you are a virgin, and afraid. Is that it?"

Rhodopis hung her head, hoping the posture made a convincing display of bashful innocence. She could think of nothing to say to him.

"You need not fear," Cambyses said softly. "I will be good to you."

"I have heard." She could manage nothing louder than a hoarse whisper.

Cambyses chuckled. He pulled one of the folding shutters across the window. "My ladies in the harem have been educating you. I am glad to hear it. Have they made you feel welcome?"

"Yes," Rhodopis said, quite honestly. "They are most kind and generous, my king. I... I like them quite a lot."

"Good. I'm glad to hear it, though I expect nothing less of them." He pulled the other shutter closed, secured it tightly to its mate with a leather cord, then set to work shuttering the rest of the windows. "We are one family here, one body, one heart. I trust them all, you know—all my women. That first day, when you saw me wrestling in the courtyard—" He laughed again in remembrance— "You must have been shocked to find me in such a state, but even a king must have his leisure... and his due distraction from more serious matters. On that day, if the women of my house had not approved of you, I would have sent you back to Egypt."

She blinked up at him, startled. "Would you truly?"

"Yes." He brushed her cheek lightly with his thumb, wiping away a stray tear. "The happiness of all my wives and concubines is of great important to me, Nitetis—yours not the least. I shall place as much trust in you as I place in them. After all, you undertook a long journey to join me here. I know your coming was an act of loyalty to your father, and to Egypt—but I value the sacrifice as much as if you had done it all for me."

Stabbed again by shame, Rhodopis lowered her gaze. Cambyses' eyes were too earnest, too kind for her to look at him any longer.

"What unusual eyes you have," he said. "They're pale-green as the river. I've never seen an Egyptian with such eyes."

"Many people have told me that my eyes are unusual," she muttered. "But I am as the gods have made me."

"So you are. And the gods have made you beautiful."

Gently, he lifted her face. Then he bent and kissed her. His beard tickled, but his mouth was soft and slow. Even so, Rhodopis tensed, recoiling—remembering Psamtik's brutal assault with a vividness that stirred a terrible revulsion in her gut. She trembled, trying to master her body and her emotions, willing herself not to cringe away from the king's embrace.

Cambyses seemed to take her flinching and fidgeting for young woman's inexperience; his hands moved with careful purpose up and down her back, soothing her as he might have done a skittish hound. When she relaxed, his hands roamed farther, playing softly over her hips, the roundness of her backside, straying up beneath her fringed shawl to warm the bare skin of her arms.

The longer he touched her, the calmer and more reassured Rhodopis became until, all at once, the heat of desire ignited inside. She raised up on her toes and kissed him back, twining her arms around his neck, pressing her body against his in mute insistence. Rhodopis didn't know whether she was stepping into her expected role—as she had done so often as a hetaera—or whether the king had tapped some true well of fire within her. Perhaps it was only the fear and tension of her encounter with Phanes, working its jittery way out of her bones down the only path presently available. But when Cambyses picked her up and carried her to his lion-footed bed, for the first time in her life, Rhodopis found real pleasure in a man's hands, in his flesh, in his tongue.

§▲

RHODOPIS HAD no way of keeping time in the king's chamber, but when Cambyses finally sank into exhausted sleep, she thought at least two hours had passed. Never had she entertained a man for so long; she ached between her legs, and a terrible thirst left her feeling wobbly and half-sick, yet she was also suffused with a delicious warmth of satisfaction. She had enjoyed her time with Cambyses—honestly enjoyed it, without the need for any artifice or pretense. She smiled as she listened to his deep, rhythmic breath, then rolled from his bed and began hunting for her robe and slippers. Two of the braziers still burned; by their dim light, she could see that Cambyses had made a mess of her garb, strewing every stitch of her clothing across the patterned carpets and under the furnishings.

She dropped to her knees, groping beneath a couch, trying to recover her silken sash.

"Nitetis," the king called softly.

Rhodopis lurched to her feet, clutching her shawl up to her chin, trying to cover her nakedness. Cambyses laughed at the sight of her. "What are you doing, girl?"

"Dressing, my king!"

"Why?" He chuckled again. "And why in Ishtar's name do you cover yourself? Haven't I already seen every bit of you?"

She blushed, lowering the white shawl slowly.

Cambyses lifted the corner of his wool blanket. "Come. Get back into bed."

She hesitated—only a moment, for the king had given a clear command. She went to him, eager but confused. Only Charaxus had ever stopped her from leaving once her work was done. Even Amasis never kept her back for mere affection.

She slid beneath the blanket, glad in the solid comfort of his strong, warm body beside her.

"Talk to me," Cambyses said.

It was such an unexpected request that she laughed aloud. She couldn't help it. "About what, my king?"

"Anything. Tell me about Egypt. What is your father like? I have never met him face to face, you know. What kind of a man is he?"

She turned to him with a playful smile. "Are you plying me for secrets? Do you think to use this information against my father?"

"Yes, quite." Cambyses grinned, warming to her game, and kissed her on the tip of her nose. "Why do you think I sent for an Egyptian bride in the first place?" His hand stroked her hip, then roved up her side to caress her shoulder. "It was all a ploy learn Egypt's secrets. Certainly, it had nothing to do with getting a beautiful woman into my bed."

"You've got plenty of beautiful women already in your harem, so it must be true. You're only hoping I'll betray my father and tell you something *interesting*, if you can manage to take my breath away in this very bed and make me too dizzy to think before I speak." She pressed close to his beard again, and kissed him.

"How right you are," Cambyses said, his voice low and purring. "Is it working? Tell me everything—everything!"

His voice was playful enough, his smile gently teasing, but

Rhodopis was quite sure there was more than a little truth in the words themselves. She pulled back and looked at Cambyses gravely. "You know I can't betray my father's interests, my king. What kind of a daughter would I be? Disloyalty is not a trait any man values in his wife."

Cambyses took her hand, stroking it gently. "Nitetis, I swear to you—I'll swear by any god you please—that I will not harm your family. I will never ask you to betray them. But I must expand my empire however I may—that is the task the gods have given me, and I cannot deny them. But for the sake of our marriage, I will deal with Egypt peacefully, if that is what you wish."

She swallowed, blinking back the burn of sudden tears. His earnestness moved her—and surprised her. There had been truth in his letter, along with the threat of war. Cambyses honestly intended the marriage with Egypt to seal peace between them.

"Of course I wish it," she said. It was true; she wanted no harm visited on any person, Egyptian, Greek, or Persian—except for Psamtik. Every god in the heavens and earth could curse *him* to a thousand eternal deaths, and scatter his bones to the jackals, and she would never feel the least prickle of remorse.

"Then it will be so. But I must know more about Egypt, one way or another—for now we are the two greatest empires in the world. We will meet as enemies, sooner or later. If I am to navigate that clash as peacefully as possible, I must have information about your father and your homeland."

"Must you?"

He gave her a confused half-smile. "I must have information."

She shook her head. "That's not what I meant. Must you... meet as enemies? Must there truly be a war?"

Cambyses sighed, a long and weary sound. "I hope to avoid a war. Wars are always costly, both in wealth and in men's lives. But a conflict—ah, that is inevitable, I'm afraid. This is the way the gods have made nations and men. The pattern is predictable: we strive for ever greater power, some of us are conquered, some do the conquering. Sooner or later, there are only a few left standing —as there are now: Egypt, Greece, and Haxamanishiya. We will meet as enemies, but that meeting need not be violent. It won't be, if I can do anything to prevent it—if the gods will allow it. But I swore I would treat your family gently, and I shall, no matter what may come."

"You have ambassadors to teach you about Egypt," Rhodopis said. Her duty to Amasis and Khedeb-Netjer-Bona was already taxing enough; she wanted no part of whispering into Cambyses' ear. "Why make me betray my family in this way, even if you have sworn to be gentle?"

"I have ambassadors, yes—but which of them can I trust more than my wife?"

"Your Egyptian wife."

He kissed her nose again. "My wife may be Egyptian by blood, but she is Haxamani now, by marriage."

Rhodopis drew back from him, wide-eyed, smiling with mock disbelief. "Do you call that a marriage? That day in the practice field, you half-naked and sweating, and simply proclaiming I was your wife?"

"I'm *fully* naked now, and every bit as sweaty. Do you find me disagreeable in such a state?"

Rhodopis giggled. She sank back on her cushion, pressing herself closer to Cambyses. "Very well. Since you swore gentle treatment, I will tell you about Egypt and my family—whatever I can tell." Anything she *could* say of Amasis was likely to be common knowledge, anyhow, Rhodopis reasoned. What did a concubine of only a few months' standing know about the Pharaoh of all Egypt, even if she had been his favorite? She could do Amasis no harm. And she liked lying beside Cambyses, liked the feel of his strong, solid body, his beard brushing her skin. Wasn't it worth keeping the king of Persia happy, when he made her feel so very safe?

✵ 11 ✵

ISHTAR'S REPLY

THE NEW MOON HUNG LOW IN THE SKY, A SLIM CRESCENT SAILING
like a golden boat through a river of stars. Rhodopis paced slowly
along the edge of the garden terrace, contemplating the sky. Jubi-
lant songs and ululating cheers came intermittently through the
night—the women were enjoying another feast, this time to celebrate the birth of a healthy baby. Rhodopis had joined in the
singing and dancing, clapping her hands and raising her cup to
salute the newborn child, but after a time, a spell of melancholy
overtook her. She had slipped off into the darkness when no one
was watching, craving whatever silence she could hope to find
tonight.

Her thoughts were a hopeless tangle, and whenever she tried
to follow one twisted thread, it led inevitably back to Cambyses—
to the first night she had lain with him, nearly a full month ago. It
seemed impossible that she had truly lived in the king's harem for
little more than a single turn of the moon. So much of her life, of
her *self*, had changed. She had formed bonds among the women
that might be called friendships, if she could stand to draw a little
closer. It seemed to her impossible that she would ever have a
friend again, after Archidike's betrayal. Nevertheless, she enjoyed

playing her part of the harem's busy, bright, joyful routines. She had often been called to Cambyses' bed, but she received no ill treatment from the other women on that account. And as for the king himself... Rhodopis shivered with a delightful anticipation that was tempered by chagrin. There was no denying that she enjoyed playing her part in Cambyses' bed, too. The pleasure she found with him was all too real—unlike her experiences with other men, the clients she had entertained back in Memphis.

The raspy, gurgling cry of the new baby drifted across the terrace, followed by a collective "Ah!" of admiration from the women. Rhodopis smiled rather sadly at the sound. For all the forays into Cambyses' bed, she had taken precautions to ensure that she would never personally enjoy a party like this one; Amtes had come prepared with a variety of teas, tinctures, and pessaries, each more potent than the last and guarantees to ensure that Lady Nitetis remained as barren as the desert sands. It was better this way, she told herself firmly. After only a month, Babylon already felt far too much like home. She mustn't get too comfortable here, for the gods alone knew what might be in store for her. If she were to send out tentative, fragile roots here in the king's palace—if she were to become the mother of one of the king's children—it would only make the inevitable separation more painful, impossible to bear.

Rhodopis stared down at the city for a long while. It looked just as it had that first night with Cambyses, quietly glowing in hues of honey and old, aging gold. A sudden frown creased her brow. *Why shouldn't I root myself in this soil, after all?* She was happy here—far happier than she'd imagined she could be. Amasis and his damnable, pinch-faced chief wife had fretted so over why the falcon god had chosen Rhodopis. Had neither of those fools ever considered that perhaps the falcon hadn't intended to move Rhodopis about, a pawn for the Pharaoh? Perhaps Horus—perhaps all the gods—were working on

Rhodopis' part, not on behalf of the Egyptian king. *Maybe the gods maneuvered me along this strange path so I would end up here, in Babylon and in Cambyses' household... where I can finally find peace and happiness. And don't I deserve it, after all I've suffered?*

It seemed an unforgivable arrogance, to assume that a common girl's happiness mattered one whit to the gods. And yet... *If they did mean for me to come to Babylon for my own sake, wouldn't it be a terrible defiance of their will if I refused to settle in and enjoy my life?*

For one glorious moment, while the flush of certainty warmed her, Rhodopis believed it could be true, must be true. But in the next heartbeat, that wild hope ebbed away. Stout sensibility—a trait it seemed she could never shed, no matter how many beautiful dreams it spoiled—prevailed.

Even if the threat of an Egyptian assassin didn't constantly hang over her neck, Rhodopis still couldn't allow herself to feel too much at home in the harem. Cambyses did not trust her—not yet, not entirely. She knew it was so; she could sense his emotional distance in the way turned so brusquely to his business when their lovemaking had finished. He never failed to ask Rhodopis for information about Egypt and Amasis, but he scrupulously avoided showing the briefest peek at his own designs and mortal failings. It never seemed to matter how cleverly or obliquely she pried. Cambyses was too alert, too much the careful king, even in the sleepy moments after their bed-games had ended. The king's closed nature pained Rhodopis, despite her resolve to remain aloof and unattached.

She turned her troubled frown upon the moon. The month had fled; Khedeb-Netjer-Bona would be expecting a dispatch soon. But thanks to the king's reticence, Rhodopis had nothing to tell. She was almost glad—pleased she had nothing to reveal to the Pharaoh who had shuffled her off into such terrible danger without a second thought. She owed no debt of gratitude or loyalty—not to Amasis or his chief wife. They controlled her only by the threat of danger.

Ah, but what a threat it was! The dark, tangled garden seemed to close around Rhodopis like the thickets of the pine forests in deepest Thrace. Any creature at all might be lurking in the shadows. Lions or leopards, their eyes cold and small, their fangs dripping blood… or men with hard, long knives.

Enough of these dark thoughts, Rhodopis scolded silently. *What good do they do? These musings only make you miserable.*

She turned away from the terrace ledge, ready to return to the lively warmth of the party. But some quick movement on a garden terrace some distance below caught her attention. She remained at her vantage, staring down through the dark. A man was walking through the beds of a lower garden, moving with a deliberate stride even though he carried no light. Rhodopis' stomach churned with fear. Was this her killer, coming so soon to put an end to everything? A moment later, that particular fear passed, replaced by another—quieter and more insidious. It was Phanes who walked through garden—she knew his way of moving by now, his confidence, his Egyptian dignity. Rhodopis watched as he bent over a bed of herbs, plucked a few stems from a plant, and slipped what he'd gathered into a basket. Was the physician gathering herbs for his cures? Or was it a poison he intended to brew? If the latter, Rhodopis had no illusions about who its recipient would be.

She may rightly fear the Pharaoh's assassins, but Phanes posed the most pressing threat to Rhodopis' position and security —maybe even to her life. Unless she could find some way to ingratiate herself with Cambyses—to truly make him trust her, to believe that she was ready to count herself Haxamani first and Egyptian second—Phanes would continue to darken Rhodopis' every thought and haunt her very dreams. How much longer would the loyal physician allow her to dally with the king before he exposed her as an impostor?

I must find some way to beat Phanes to the thrust—strike before he can.

But how? It seemed an impossible task, to place herself—a newcomer to the palace—so highly in Cambyses' confidence that not even the word of his most trusted advisor would turn the king's heart. Her position was utterly futile; despair surged in her chest, choking off her breath for one terrible moment.

Impulsively, Rhodopis knelt in the flower bed. It was damp from winter dew; her knees sank into wet soil, and a chill crept beneath her shawl. The last withered flowers of the season nodded tiredly around her shoulders. She raised her hands to the sky and prayed—first to her familiar Greek gods, to Strymon and Aphrodite, to Dionysus and Apollo and even distant, mocking Zeus. Then she prayed to the gods of Egypt, merciful Hathor and Mother Isis, wise Toth and raging Sekhmet—and to Horus, the war-falcon who had sent her to Babylon on his cryptic mission.

When her list of gods ran short, Rhodopis lowered her hands, trembling and breathless. She had beseeched every deity she could name, and yet she felt instinctively that it was not enough, that somehow she had erred. One desperate sob wrenched itself from her throat before she could calm herself and quiet her thoughts. *Think, damn you—think!*

At that moment, the peace of certainty swept over her, soothing away her fears. Of course, Rhodopis thought with an inward *laugh. You are in Babylon, not Egypt. It's Ishtar you must appease.* The matron goddess of Babylon would surely hear her plea, if no other god would be bothered.

Rhodopis tipped her face up to the crescent moon. "Please, Mighty Ishtar, Leader of Hosts, Lady of Victory, Torch of Heaven and Earth—give me a chance to prove my loyalty to the king. Only one chance; that's all I need. I'll take it, if you provide it. This I swear to you, Lady."

Later that night, long after the new baby's feast had ended and the women had found their beds, Rhodopis remained awake beside her window. She had sat still and silent for hours, gazing out at the stars in the mud-black sky. On the table before her lay a scrap of papyrus—the message intended for Amasis, written in Amtes' careful hand. When the sun rose, the message to Egypt would be carried out of the palace by Amtes, then sent via pigeon to the oasis of Tadmor. From Tadmor, another bird would fly to Memphis with the tiny scroll tied to its foot. The note read simply, "As yet, I have no useful information to report." But although the message contained nothing of value for Amasis or his chief wife, still it was a symbol of Rhodopis' continued coop-eration with Egypt. She couldn't allow Amtes to send it—not yet.

First, she must wait for Ishtar's reply.

෧

Two DAYS HAD PASSED before Rhodopis received her answer from the goddess.

She stood with the other women below the sun-shades in the courtyard, cheering on the king as he drilled with some of his men. The mood was festive and light, as it ever was when Cambyses practiced with his weapons. Rhodopis did her best to ignore Phanes, who stood aloof among the men on the other side of the courtyard. She sipped iced melon juice—she was still astounded at the miracle of ice in the desert, for even in the winter the days were far too warm to countenance it—and nibbled on sweet cakes, and laughed with the harem women as the men grunted and whirled and sweated in the sun, swinging their swords at one another with boyish enthusiasm. A shared contentment flowed around the courtyard in a happy current. All was well, everything in its ordered place—all was maat, as an Egyptian would have said. Despite the sense of shared happiness, Rhodopis could not rid herself of the tension of waiting.

She concentrated determinedly on the king and his military drills. Cambyses believed in keeping fit, both physically and mentally—honed for battle, even if it was unlikely that he would ever personally take to the field again. But, as he had told Rhodopis one night when she lay in his arms, pleasantly tired by their lovemaking, he didn't believe in asking his soldiers to do anything he was unable or unwilling to do. And so, the king drilled as often as duty permitted, parrying and thrusting in the glaring sun, swinging his blunted practice-sword against one opponent or half a dozen at once. He always fought as if his life depended on it, as if the heat and urgency of battles long past returned to him in a surging blood-rush. Now and then, Cambyses used a live sword, and practiced defense with this bronze-studded shield. Those days sent a lump of fear into Rhodopis' throat, for sometimes Cambyses would lift his shield a heartbeat too late, and the tip of a sword would graze his arm or slice a piece from his thigh. The cuts were never severe—the men he fought did not dare attack their king in deadly earnest—but the sight of blood chilled and sickened her.

Today, Rhodopis was grateful that the swords were blunted. Strung up as she was by lingering fear—by the weight of that small scrap of papyrus in her chamber, still unsent—she did not think she could tolerate a single drop of blood falling to the courtyard's stones. It would have set her to screaming like a mad woman, all her terrors boiling over at once. She sipped her melon juice steadily, and watched the men parry and spin. She joined in now and then as the women cheered, and once she laughed, when Cambyses knocked the blade from one of his cursing opponents' hands and sent it skittering across the practice yard. But the pleasant, orderly sense of maat that hung like a gentle haze around the other women never truly touched Rhodopis.

Cambyses' opponent chased after his lost sword, retrieved it, and came swinging at the king with a roar. Cambyses side-stepped him easily, and the women broke into laughter again.

But their merriment cut off abruptly when the guards at the portico, standing watch over Cambyses' practice, leaped

suddenly into action. They drew real blades; the sun glinted off
the well-honed bronze with a fiery flash. For a moment,
Rhodopis thought they intended to attack the king, taking advantage of his moment of vulnerability, armed as he was with an
edgeless practice-sword. The cup fell from her hand, shattering
on the stones, but Rhodopis hardly noticed. She could think of
no reason why Cambyses' men should hate him—but she was
not the only woman who feared for the king's life. Several of his
concubines screamed; someone began to pray loudly, shrieking
out a panicked invocation to Ishtar, begging the goddess to
defend the king. Another woman clutched Rhodopis' arm in
desperate dread, but she did not look around to see who it was.
Her attention was fixed on the Cambyses, and on guards beneath
the bull-crowned pillars.

The guards surged back under the portico—away from the
king. They were not attacking Cambyses after all; they had
turned on someone hidden in the shadows, some threat unde-
tected till now. "Be calm," Rhodopis called to the other women,
"The king is safe!" But the women did not seem to hear her. Their
shouts went on, as did the loud prayer to Ishtar.

A moment later, two of Cambyses' guards dragged the man
out into the light of the sun... and Rhodopis' momentary relief
withered again into cold fear.

The man was Egyptian. There was no mistaking him—the
shaven face, the bare chest covered with the most rudimentary of
shawls, the white kilt hanging to his knees. He jerked against the
guards' restraints, baring his teeth at them, cursing in anger.

Cambyses raised his hand in wordless command. The guards
released the Egyptian. The man straightened his clothing with an
air of grievously injured dignity.

"Ambassador Turo," Cambyses said. A bright streak of amusement colored his voice. "What brings you here, to interrupt my
practice?"

"Apparently I *must* interrupt your practice, if I hope to gain any sort of audience with you. It seems I must be handled like a rabid dog by your guards, as well. You have refused to see me at any audience. This morning—and the day before, and for three days before that—all my requests to speak with you have been most egregiously ignored. *My king.*" Turo spoke the Haxamani tongue well, but he added the title belatedly, with a distasteful twist of his mouth.

Cambyses grinned broadly. "I am a busy man, Ambassador."

Turo eyed the blunt sword in Cambyses' hand, the sweat running down his chest. "I can see as much for myself. But if I must speak to you here, among these scrapping men, and with all your women looking on... then so be it."

"My women always look on," Cambyses said coolly. "One never knows when a woman's sharp eye, or her particular sort of wisdom, might prove valuable."

A murmur of appreciation moved among the assembled women, now that they had regained their composure. Rhodopis held very still, heart pounding. Her blood ran cold as the ice spilled at her feet.

"What is it you want, Ambassador? Be quick; I've many things to see to."

"My Pharaoh has sent me to insist that you withdraw your troops from Edom."

Rhodopis' mind worked furiously. Edom lay between Egypt and the southern edge of Cambyses' empire. It was the last frontier, the final boundary he would break before he invaded Egypt —if he invaded Egypt. The loss of Edom as a stronghold must be one of Amasis' greatest fears.

Cambyses chuckled. "Edom is a contested territory; you know that. So does your Pharaoh. He has no rightful claim on that place."

"Neither do you, my king. And as Haxamanishiya and Egypt are at peace, surely you have no need to maintain troops in the region. Withdraw them, and the Pharaoh will forgive your insult."

"Oh?" Cambyses lifted his blunt blade; he inspected its length casually, tested its weight in his hand. "*Are* these two kingdoms at peace, Turo? Are they truly?"

"You know we are at peace. Egypt and Persia have sealed their alliance with marriages: your two daughters in exchange for the Pharaoh's."

Rhodopis risked a glance across the courtyard. Phanes locked eyes with her, catching her like a fowl in a hunter's snare—the guilty flush of her cheeks, her timid posture. Rhodopis flinched.

Cambyses lifted a hand, summoning more of the guards who lingered in the shadows of the portico. "Come, men—see Ambassador Turo back to his quarters. We will speak of this matter more in the audience hall tomorrow."

"The audience hall?" Turo cried. "Do you take me for a fool? You'll put me off again, as you have for days running! Egypt will not be denied, King Cambyses. We have tolerated insults from your nation for many years, but no longer! If you do not heed my request, and do what is necessary and right—if you do not maintain a true and faithful alliance with the Pharaoh—then Amasis will send your two daughters back to your household in shame, and I will take Amasis' daughter Nitetis back with me to Memphis. The Pharaoh has authorized me to do it."

Cambyses halted his guards as easily as he'd summoned them. The king went very still. He stared at the ambassador, astounded by the threat, silent and tense in his fury. Cambyses opened his mouth, no doubt to pronounce some terrible judgment on the ambassador—perhaps even to declare outright war on Egypt. Rhodopis stepped forward quickly, before the king could speak. As she moved, breaking away from the other women, a quiet certainty filled her. This was the chance Ishtar had provided—this was the goddess's answer to a desperate but heartfelt prayer. Rhodopis must take the chance, must act decisively now. Ishtar had provided a way forward—a path to victory, for She was the Lady of Victory.

Rhodopis went where the goddess led her. She walked calmly across the courtyard to stand before the ambassador—and the startled king. When she spoke, she did so almost without thought, allowing the inspiration of the moment to carry her, praying feebly in the farthest corner of her mind that Ishtar would be merciful, and protect her.

"I am Nitetis, the daughter of Pharaoh Amasis," Rhodopis said loudly, so every man and woman in courtyard and corridor would hear. "And I will not return to Egypt. I am Haxamani now; this is my home, and this is my husband, the king you insult with your shouts and your vile threats. My father Amasis is a weak, ineffectual king. I do not belong to Egypt, nor Egypt to me. I renounce Egypt, for Haxamanishiya is stronger and better. The glory of Ishtar and Babylon will prevail." She added lightly, "You may tell the Pharaoh I said this; it is all one to me what *he* thinks."

With that, Rhodopis turned her back pointedly on the Egyptian ambassador.

Silence hung thick over the courtyard. Rhodopis stared past the women and their sunshades, refusing to look at their faces— for she was certain she would break into hysterical, panicked laughter if she caught a single friendly gaze. She trembled, and her heart thundered so loudly in her ears she thought it would deafen her for good. Then the tension broke; Cambyses' roaring laugh of approval rose up above the sudden exclamations from the women and the king's guards. But all Rhodopis cared for was Cambyses' joyous laughter.

"This is my true wife," the king said. "You heard her words, Turo. Take her message back to Amasis, if you dare, and let the Pharaoh make of it whatever he will."

Rhodopis, her back still turned to the Egyptian, stood straight and proud in the Babylonian sun. Her trembling ceased. Once word reached Amasis and Khedeb-Netjer-Bona, they would curse her name. Perhaps they would truly send the assassin Rhodopis had so feared. But Ishtar filled her with peace; she knew she had acted well, knew she had pleased the goddess.

Better still, Rhodopis knew she had won. Cambyses would trust her now—how could he not, after such a display of loyalty? She had built her own fortress against any accusation Phanes might think to make. For as long as she remained alive—as long as she could avoid an Egyptian killer—Babylon could be her home indeed. The gods in all their strange, unfathomable mystery had brought her here, at last, to a place where she could be welcome and free. Here she was determined to remain.

PHANES' LAMP

CAMBYSES DISMISSED HIS CADRE FROM THE COURTYARD AS SOON AS Turo was led away, grumbling. "I'm off to my chambers," the king said, "to make ready for my supper." But it was far too early in the afternoon for such preparations. Rhodopis wondered whether his confrontation with the Egyptian ambassador had left Cambyses more shaken than he dared to let on. Or perhaps, she mused as she hurried back to her own quarters in the women's palace, he had business at that great, dark writing table, the indoor battlefield that dominated his royal apartment. Was Amasis soon to receive an answer to Turo's threats? Of a certainty, Cambyses' reaction would not include a withdrawal of his forces from Edom.

It doesn't matter anymore, she told herself. *Not to me.* Her heart had grown wings; it fitted gaily inside her chest. In one stroke, Rhodopis had severed her ties to Egypt, secured her place in Babylon, and put Phanes safely out of her path. She could breathe now—she could sleep easily, laugh honestly with the women of the harem. Karânî had called Rhodopis "sister." Perhaps she could finally come to think of herself as part of the king's family. What a deliciously satisfying prospect it was, to find before her a life of freedom and ease, a rich contentment at the end of her long and very strange journey.

But as she walked, Rhodopis noticed the wide-eyed appreciation, the half-amused awe with which every man and woman regarded her. She could tell by the way they leaned toward her that they longed to speak to her. But even if all they sought to offer were words of congratulation or sympathetic encouragement, Rhodopis realized with a sudden chill that she wanted none of it. A singularly bleak thought had risen, dominating her consciousness, and she knew she would not rest easily after all—not until she could decide with a level head whether this new fear could be safely dismissed, or whether it was indeed worthy of haunting her dreams. Word was already spreading like a brushfire around the palace. Far-flung guards and stewards, maids and servants who had been nowhere near the courtyard seemed to know already that the new Egyptian bride had snubbed the ambassador from her own country, repudiating her father before Cambyses and his entire court. If the take had passed from mouth to ear so quickly, how long would it take for news to reach Amasis and Khedeb-Netjer-Bona? Perhaps it would fly even faster than Turo's report. Rhodopis could not rid herself of the sickening fear that somehow the Pharaoh and the chief wife knew already, though of course, that was impossible.

The Pharaoh was bound to find out sooner or later, she thought. *It can't be avoided; you knew that when you stepped forward and spoke. What is it you fear?*

A chilling image answered: a man cloaked in blackness, slinking through the bed-chamber. A knife in his hand, fearfully sharp and wickedly cold, the blade hungering for Rhodopis' blood...

She shuddered, almost breaking into a run as she crossed the garden terrace. *There's no reason to fear. You are exactly where the gods intended you to be—far from Egypt, far from Psamtik, removed even from the Pharaoh's wrath. Surely there's nothing Amasis can do to you now. Cambyses will protect you. You are his loyal wife.*

Tears filled her eyes; she wiped the useless things away. She couldn't ease her fears so simply, it seemed. *If only I could truly believe I am safe,* she thought morosely. *If only I could be sure, for more than a fleeting moment. Then I might have some hope of sleeping through the night.*

A new, fragile hope sprang up in her heart. The goddess Ishtar would defend Rhodopis... wouldn't she. Hadn't Rhodopis been as good as her word? She had seized the opportunity the goddess had presented, ingratiating herself in Cambyses' esteem so completely that no one could doubt her loyalty to the king, to Babylon itself.

But when had gods dealt fairly with men... or women? And who was Rhodopis to Ishtar? A stranger, a bit of foreign refuse blown to Babylon on a stray wind. She was no one—no one at all.

Rhodopis shut herself inside her apartment and threw herself face-down across the bed.

"Mistress, are you well?" Amtes said.

"Yes," Rhodopis muttered into one of her cushions. "Only a headache from the heat."

"Shall I send for iced juice? Or milk?"

"No, no," Rhodopis said weakly. "I need only rest, Amtes. I will sleep a while, and then I'll feel better."

"If you're certain you need nothing... I was going to bathe in the outdoor pool. This is the time of day when some of the servant women use the pool, and I thought I might try it. But if you aren't well—"

Rhodopis looked up at her handmaid with what she hoped was a convincing smile. "Go on; enjoy yourself. I will be well. My headache will clear soon; it's not severe." *And truly, no Egyptian assassin is likely to descend on me in the next hour.*

Amtes frowned skeptically. "I'll bring you food first. Then I'll go."

"I don't want any food, dear one. I couldn't eat a bite."

"You should try, at least. You look pale—a bit wilty."

"Bring me wine, then. It may help the pain in my temples."

"It may make the pain worse," Amtes said sensibly.

"I'll take that chance." *I seem to enjoy taking chances of late.*

When Amtes had departed, Rhodopis rolled onto her back with a disconsolate sigh. She lay staring up at the lime-white ceiling, blinking back tears, trying to order her thoughts. She had been so happy only minutes before, so joyfully assured that her oppression was at its end. Why this dragging weight of fear? Was it a sign? Perhaps her work was not yet finished—perhaps her journey had not reached its end, after all. *Seems as if it'll never stop,* she thought, fighting the storm of sobs that was building in her throat. *Soon as I think I'm safe, and can finally be happy, the gods drag me off to some new, terrible fate.* Would they never cease to play with her?

Surely the gods owed Rhodopis some respite from the endless danger, the harrowing intrigues. Hadn't she been obedient to both gods and men, from her first days in Egypt? When had she ever failed any master, whether mortal or divine? Surely justice was the least reward she could expect.

Surely the gods must protect me—Ishtar, or any other. Surely Cambyses must defend me, too.

Then why this strange, diffuse fear that still haunted her, clinging like a spider's web to her every thought and decision?

Amtes returned from the kitchen with a platter of food. She laid it on the table near Rhodopis' couch. "Roasted pumpkin and preserved figs," she said, brisk and business-like. "Under this clay dome, you'll find a fowl crusted with honey and nuts, and roasted on a spit. Don't ask me what sort of bird it is; it's small, but it looks plump enough. I stole it from the fire before Faidyme could take it."

Rhodopis groaned. "That's entirely too much food, Amtes."

"Eat as much as you can, all the same. I won't have you withering up and perishing on my watch."

"Very well, if it will make you happy. Did you bring any wine?"

Amtes moved her shawl aside, exposing a leather skin slung by its strap over one shoulder. It looked heavy and full.

Rhodopis sat up eagerly. "Wine first. Then I'll eat."

"It would be wiser to get food in your belly before the wine. You don't want it going to your head just now, do you?"

"I promise I'll eat, Mother," Rhodopis said. "Now go and enjoy your bath. The harem ladies will take over the pool again soon; you'll miss your chance."

With one last hesitant look at her mistress, Amtes slipped away. Rhodopis took a long swallow of the wine, and then another. It was sharp and tangy—strong, too, filling her stomach with a pleasant warmth that spread along her veins. A semblance of calm returned to her fevered mind. Rhodopis drank again, slowing her thoughts as she rolled the flavorful wine in her mouth. She swallowed it down only after a long, savory interval. As the warmth inside he redoubled, she thought darkly of the gods—of Ishtar, the Lady of Victory, the stranger-goddess who had answered her prayer when no other god would. *Yet I know nothing about Ishtar. I cannot trust her—can I?—any more than I could trust that ambassador or a stranger in a market square.*

A rap on her door pulled Rhodopis abruptly from the bleak reverie. She tensed. Who could it be? Certainly, Amtes would never have knocked. If it were one of the harem women, come to crow with approval over Rhodopis' display of loyalty in the courtyard, then she would be shouting already through the door, laughing and cheering. She would not remain silent; her unseen presence would not fill Rhodopis with the dread of a creature hunted.

Anger at the intrusion, and at the gods' unwelcome manipulations, surged up inside her. Rhodopis rose from her bed and

crossed the room, never pausing to ask who was seeking admit-
tance. She felt reckless and defiant, and piqued by the wine. If
somehow Amasis had already sent an assassin—and if the
assassin had won his way past Cambyses' guards—then let him
do his task. Rhodopis was in the gods' hands, it seemed, subject
to their strange whims, whether it pleased her or not. She could
do nothing to direct her fate, nothing to forestall her doom.

It occurred to her as she laid her hand upon the bronze latch
that an assassin would never have knocked, either.

When she wrenched the door open, Rhodopis was not
surprised to find Phanes standing on the other side. He said nothing, only gazed at her with silent expectation. As before, he held
his lamp on its slender iron stick, but the flame was not yet lit, for
sunset was still an hour away. Rhodopis glanced down at the
lamp, swinging gently on its three fine chains, then back to the
physician's hard eyes. Evidently, Phanes expected to remain with
Rhodopis until after dark. She stood in obstinate silence, determined to force Phanes to speak first.

"We must talk," Phanes said quietly. "This cannot go on." His
manner was not accusatory, not challenging. In fact, there was
something almost pleading in his voice.

"I will listen, if you wish." Rhodopis stepped back, allowing
him inside her chamber. "But I can't promise I'll say anything in
return."

He ducked his head, an unironic acknowledgment of her
cooperation. "Thank you. Is your handmaid in?"

"She has gone to the bathing pool."

Phanes nodded. He set his lamp on the table, just as he had
done the last time he'd appeared in her chamber. He turned to
face Rhodopis with arms tightly folded beneath his gold-fringed
shawl. "You showed great loyalty to the king," he said, "even in
the face of serious risk to your own person. Word will reach
Amasis—you must know that, surely. You will never be allowed
to return to Egypt."

Rhodopis shrugged. "I have just been thinking the same."

Phanes smiled, a sly, approving expression. "I knew you were hiding a secret, Lady Nitetis, but I did not think you were a party to the cause."

Something prickled inside Rhodopis, running its sudden fire up her spine--mingled fear and sudden, intense interest. "Party to the cause? What cause? I don't know what you're getting at."

"I mean to say... you are no longer loyal to Amasis. You made that much clear."

"I never was loyal to Amasis. Not truly."

Phanes lifted his brows, slowly, coolly. "Not loyal to your own father? That is strange, for a King's Daughter of Egypt."

Rhodopis drifted to her silk-covered couch and sat with a careless air. She spooned up a preserved fig and chewed it slowly, watching Phanes in stubborn silence... waiting.

"You are too shrewd to speak further, I see," the physician said. "That is wise. Wisdom is a rare trait in a person so young."

Still, Rhodopis waited. Let Phanes flatter all he pleased; she would not be moved.

His shoulders drooped a little; he nodded again, pensively, as if settling some internal argument that had raged within for a long time. Phanes sighed, and looked at Rhodopis with a mood of surrender. "My lady, I will make one final offering of peace and trust between us. Will you allow me to sit?"

"Certainly," Rhodopis said.

Phanes sank into a chair opposite her table. Rhodopis pushed the platter toward him, but he raised a hand, refusing the food.

"What I tell you now," he said quietly, "I say at great risk to my own life and safety. I have no reason to trust you, Nitetis—indeed, I do *not* fully trust you, for I can tell you are not what you seem to be... what you *try* to seem. But you risked yourself today, to stand in loyalty with Haxamanishiya and Cambyses. I can at least attempt to act as bravely as you have done. Perhaps if I risk myself yet again—further than I already have—it will be enough to win your trust. And your cooperation."

Phanes paused. He stared down at the floor for a long moment, but his eyes seemed to see through everything—carpet and stone, place and time, as he searched memory and knowledge for the right words to move Rhodopis, to goad her toward his mysterious purpose. After a long silence, he looked up again and spoke.

"Ever since Amasis expelled me from Egypt, and separated me from my wife and sons, I have felt a deep, terrible longing to bring his kingdom down... to destroy the Egypt that exists now, and restore my homeland to its former glory. To bring back Kmet, righteous and true—the Kmet my parents loved, and their parents before them. This is what I have worked for, silently and in the shadows, since I first came here to Babylon and entered Cambyses' service."

Rhodopis sat up straight, leaning to the edge of her couch. That strange, fiery flush had returned, filling her with a shivering energy, half curiosity, half fear. Phanes' words carried such force and directness, Rhodopis felt instinctively that they were true. "Why tell me this?" She felt like a skittish horse, ready to leap up and bolt at the next breath of danger.

"Today you turned your back on Egypt—quite literally. I saw you do it. That makes us allies, Nitetis, whether you realize it or not. We are fighting on the same side."

She clenched her teeth for a moment, but forced herself to speak. "That's where you're mistaken, Good Man. I am on my own side. I care for myself, and I fight no one—long as I can manage to stay out of a fight, at least." She fell silent, swallowing down her anxiety and the loss of control that had come with it— the country speech that threatened to come bursting forth, and her youthful need for protection, deliverance from danger. She was on her own, and no mistaking it. She added grimly, "I've learned better than to trust anyone who claims to be my friend."

Phanes leaned back in the chair, a simple acceptance of her position and clarity. Despite that acceptance, he pressed on. "The world is poised just now in a delicate balance. I'm sure you are aware—clever girl that you are—that only three great powers remain: Egypt, Greece, and Persia. Egypt is weakened, ready to topple—that will come as no surprise to you—and Cambyses is prepared to sweep in, to salvage what remains of its former glory, and use Egypt to further his own ambitions."

Rhodopis tossed her head; the dyed-black braid of her hair slid from her shoulder. "What do I care? Cambyses is not a bad man. In fact, he's a good deal better than some men I've met. He'll rule just as well as any king, I reckon, and better than most."

Phanes blinked in surprise at the slip of her tongue; Rhodopis blushed. Her uncultured ways were emerging too fast for her to conceal them; the excitement and uncertainty of the moment were getting the better of her. *You must slow down,* she told herself. *Think more carefully before you speak.*

"Indeed, he will rule well," Phanes said, pretending he hadn't noticed the momentary disintegration of her nobility. "I have great respect for Cambyses. My loyalty to him is real, but even so, I have no wish to see Egypt become Persia. When Amasis falls— as he surely must, sooner or later—"

"Then his son will be Pharaoh," Rhodopis said. She dragged those words out reluctantly, and they were bitter in her mouth. She barely hid an involuntary shudder. "His son—Psamtik."

"I have a suspicion that the son may be just as dangerous for Egypt as his father has proven to be—though perhaps the dangers Psamtik poses are of a different nature."

She couldn't hide her reaction this time. Rhodopis pulled her shawl tightly around her shoulders, a weak attempt to disguise her uneasiness. "You don't know how right you are."

"Regardless," Phanes said, "when any Pharaoh falls, whether Amasis or his son, I intend to be at Cambyses' side. My great work is laid clear before me, ordained by the gods: by working with Cambyses, the fated conqueror, I will restore the Egypt that once was. I will make Kmet whole again."

Rhodopis sipped from the wine skin, more to calm her cold fear of Psamtik than to soothe a dry throat. But the tartness of the wine perked her up; her curiosity bubbled to the surface. "What do you mean—Egypt as it was? When?"

"Why, before Amasis took the throne, of course." Phanes smiled. "Before his infatuation with Greece began. Shall I tell you what Egypt once was, Lady Nitetis? You are so young; it's reasonable enough that you wouldn't know the story, especially if you've been raised on a country estate by a Greek nursemaid." Phanes' wry tone said he had long since ceased to believe that tale, if he ever had.

She ignored his pointed words, nodding for him to speak. Phanes offered a seated bow of thanks.

"Kmet has a long history," the physician said. "As far back as memory goes, it was a place of equality and freedom. Every man and woman had more than they have at present, even the common people—more work, more wealth, more happiness. To be sure, the noble families and great houses have always existed, but in the times before Amasis reigned, the greater part of their influence was confined to courts and temples. In the cities, in the countryside—wherever ordinary people lived—all people stood equal, and all had plenty."

"*All* equal?" Rhodopis' smile was rather acrid. "You mean all *men* stood equal."

"No, Nitetis... no. Though you may not believe me now, I swear I speak the truth: in those times, women were equal to men in all things—rights, possessions, freedom. This separation of the sexes, this habit of hiding women away, this relegation of women to separate rooms, separate lives... it is a Greek custom. These things are foreign to Kmet, and yet the separation and degradation of women—and many other Greek customs—are spreading like an illness through the Two Lands. Outsized Greek influence is changing what it means to be Egyptian, taking it all away, piece by piece. Is it any wonder that every street in Egypt boils with unrest? Oh, yes, we have heard all about the riots, even here in Babylon. Amasis has indulged his admiration for Greece at the cost of Kmetu identity. Imagine everything the Kmetu have lost, for the sake of the Pharaoh's idle interests... especially the women of Kmet."

Rhodopis nodded. Now it was her turn to stare into the distance, remembering, sorting through the misty visions of memory and experience. It was true that noble Egyptian women always sat with their men at the Pharaoh's feasts; there was no gynaeceum where they dined apart. Hadn't she seen it a dozen times from the dais beside Amasis' throne, where she had perched on display with the other women of his household? That dining together, the mingling of male and female, was a remnant of the old tradition. Why had she never questioned the practice before? The significance had never struck her before—the knowledge that Egyptians, when alone with their own people, behaved so differently from the Greeks?

She nodded for Phanes to continue, but she listened more thoughtfully to his words.

"Terrible poverty afflicts so many people now. Of course, there was always poverty before—it seems to be the way the gods have ordered the world. But only in years when the river's floods failed have the Kmetu known such extremes of hardship. In the days before Amasis, before the tide of Greeks came rushing in, any child born to the poorest farmer could hope to achieve a better life through hard work and clever exploitation of opportunity. But now, a chasm separates the elite and the poor. How can anyone hope to cross such a divide? Amasis' fondness for Greeks —and the manipulations of greedy merchants—has torn Egypt apart. The desires of the few—their hunger for riches, their grasping for power—has thrust far more people into poverty than ever before suffered under that lash."

"Yet Egypt is still one of the three great powers," Rhodopis said. "The nation holds together, despite the changes you say have come. Are those changes truly such a disaster, then?"

"Egypt holds together," Phanes agreed, "but for how much longer? How many more years can this sad state endure? The nation is like a brewer's pot, too tightly sealed. The pressure from that simmering brew builds day by day. What will happen if no one ever breaches the lid of that brew-pot, my lady, and relieves the pressure? Have you ever seen the ruination in a brewer's shop when some careless apprentice seals the pots too tightly?"

"No."

"It's not a sight one forgets soon. The pot breaks—but explosively, like a great knotted piece of wood splitting suddenly in a fire. Shards of pottery fly everywhere, strewn across the room, out into the street—and beer drips and runs down every surface."

Rhodopis smiled tentatively at the image.

"Now imagine," Phanes said grimly, "that it's not beer dripping from every surface. Imagine it is blood. The present state of affairs is a monstrous danger for everyone in Egypt: men and women, little children—nobles and slaves, the Pharaoh and the simplest farmer toiling in the fields. All are in danger—and any of them, or all of them, stand to lose their lives."

Chilled by Phanes' description, Rhodopis said rather coldly, "Then why doesn't Cambyses make his move? Why doesn't he conquer Egypt, if it is ripe for the plucking, and stop the pot from bursting?"

"You don't sound the least bit worried by that possibility—that Egypt could be conquered."

"Should I be so concerned? You heard my words today: I am Haxamani now. I know your wife and sons still live on in Egypt—or so I pray. But Egypt holds nothing for me." *Nothing except Aesop. Does he see this danger, too? Can he leave before it's too late?*

Phanes seemed to accept her excuse without qualms. "Cambyses cannot simply pluck Egypt like a pomegranate from a bush.

It's a vast nation, with many people in it—many soldiers. Even with Amasis lazing on his throne, worshiping his Greek friends and their Greek gods, it would be too dangerous a maneuver for Cambyses. Egypt is broken now into factions, but they would unite at once to stand against an outside threat. Before Cambyses can succeed, something must change within Egypt. Events must fall into place, just so, if our king is to expect a victory—and even then, war is always an uncertain venture. Haxamanishiya did not become a great empire through the reckless actions of hasty or foolish kings. Cambyses learned from his father—his forefathers, too. He is patient, but also watchful. He will act when he sees his best chance, and not a moment before."

"What is his best chance?" Rhodopis asked slowly. "What must change before Cambyses can reach for Egypt?"

The idea of a true and traditional Kmet—an Egypt where women stood equal to men once more—shone before her mind with fierce radiance. If what Phanes said was true, perhaps the old Egypt could live again. With Egypt restored to its former ways, thriving under a more sensible king, the nation's influence might spread beyond its borders. Perhaps even Greece could be altered by a restoration of Egypt. Why not, if Egypt had been altered by Greece? Why should the weight not swing in the other direction?

Rhodopis shut her eyes for a moment, overcome by the intensity of her imagination. She saw before her mind's eye a Greece as liberated as the Egypt of past generations. Women owning property, never fearing destitution if their husbands or fathers died. Women free to dine with men, to talk with them about the world's affairs, whether they were hetaerae or no. She saw women walking about the streets of a shining city, unaccompanied by anyone but their sisters and friends—and girls seated in rows with scribes' tablets on their laps, learning to read and write alongside boys. Women leaving the husbands who beat them. Women who might find justice from sensible king if they were

cheated, wronged... raped. The thought—the mere possibility—
stole her breath away. Could it truly be possible? She had gone
into slavery to save the lives of her siblings—the twin boys, and
little Aella. What more could she do for Aella, and for countless
girls like her?

"Amasis has ingratiated himself with so many powerful
Greeks," Phanes said. Rhodopis opened her eyes, looked at him
again. The passionate intensity had returned to the physician's
his face. His calm yet eager voice wrapped around her mind,
drawing her to him, compelling. "If Cambyses were to attack now,
the Pharaoh would simply turn to Greece for aid. Greece and
Egypt together would be powerful enough to crush Haxamanishiya. But if Greek powers pay little heed to Egypt or Amasis,
they are no threat to Cambyses. The moment our king attacks
Egypt in earnest—"

"Greece will come down around Cambyses' ears,"
Rhodopis said.

Phanes leaned from the edge of his chair. "Precisely. So, then
—when Cambyses sees his chance, his attack must be swift and
sure, all but guaranteed to succeed, before any Greek ally has the
chance to retaliate. The stage must be properly set, you see.
Everything must be aligned, just so. And Amasis must not be able
to alert his Greek friends too soon."

Memories of Thrace—and of her family—flooded into
Rhodopis' heart with a painful rush. Was it simply all this talk of
Greece that had done it, she wondered—or recalling her little
sister? Aella would be ten years old now, or near enough.
Rhodopis remembered dry, sunny days below the pines, when
she and Aella had run up the slope, racing to see who could
reach the patch of wild berries fastest. She had always let her
sister win, holding back, watching golden-haired Aella pull away
from her, flying free as a soft little sparrow in the sun. *What I
wouldn't give up, to go back to Thrace—to those early times, those
simple times. And what I wouldn't give to see my family again.*

Rhodopis' melancholy must have shown on her face. Phanes maintained his silence. When Rhodopis focused on the physician again, his mouth was unmoving, tightly pressed. His eyes were deep with sympathy.

After a moment, Phanes said, "I don't know who you truly are, my lady, or what your real story may be. Perhaps you will never tell me. But I know you are not Egyptian. I can only guess how you came to be in the Pharaoh's harem, a place usually reserved for noble Egyptian ladies or ambassador-brides, like Shamiram and Ninsina. But it is clear to me that you are neither a noble-woman nor a Kmetu. Therefore, I can only speculate." He drew a deep breath, as if reluctant to expose her history without her permission. Yet he persisted, and his words stung Rhodopis relentlessly. "Your family traveled from Greece to Egypt, looking for work, but found none. They perished there, starving in the streets, and to save yourself—"

"They didn't starve," Rhodopis said abruptly. Her voice was edged with fire, the heat of fierce pride and an even stronger pain.

Phanes paused. His sympathetic silence invited her to say more.

"I didn't let them starve." All her pretense at refinement fell away; she surrendered to her true nature, grateful to set down the burden of her disguise. "I'm proud of that, and reckon I've got good cause to be proud." As the unmistakable Thracian twang emerged in her voice, Phanes' eyes widened. He leaned toward her again, eager for more of the tale.

"We came from Thrace when I was only ten years old. My father was a laborer—but he wanted his own farm back in Thrace. There was no silver to buy the land, though, and nothing to trade for it. One day, he heard from a few sailors that there was always work down in Egypt, building for the Pharaoh, and they took all comers who were reasonably young and sound. So off we went to seek our family's fortune.

"My father was not a foolish man, nor was he impulsive. I

believe if we'd come to Egypt a year or two sooner, we would have found all the silver we needed in short order and gone home rich —as rich as Thracian farmers ever can be. But by the time we arrived, there was little work to be found. So many people had come to Egypt, you see, looking for employment, and then there were all the Kmetu who wanted work just as badly. We were hard pressed to make our way, let alone to earn the fare to get back to Thrace again.

"Somehow we managed to keep our spirits up, even though times got worse and worse. My parents always told themselves--use, too--that it was only a matter of months before we had all we needed. Weeks, maybe. Then we'd see Thrace again. We lived two years that way, scrimping and scraping just to stay fed. Then things went from bad to worse. My father was killed by thieves— though even a blind man could see he had nothing worth stealing. But that's the way it is in Egypt, isn't it? Men lashing out at men for no reason at all—'There's a knife in my hand and anger in my heart, so you've got to die.' Simple as that."

"Yes," Phanes said quietly. "It seems all of Egypt had gone that way. I am sorry to hear of your father's death."

Silently, Rhodopis collecting her thoughts. She recalled her father, how full of hope he'd been when they had arrived on Tanis—and her mother, pretty despite her age and the effects of her difficult life. She hoped her mother had found her way back to Thrace, hoped the two thousand hedj of Rhodopis' sale—of Doricha's sale—had been enough to keep her family in comfort. If the gods had any shred of mercy left, Mother had made her way home with Aella and the boys, each child whole and healthy and saved.

"Somehow," Rhodopis resumed, "we managed to get by for another year without Father. I'll never know how we did it, though. My poor mother... She was at her wits' end. When she was as desperate as ever a mother can be, she thought to sell me to a man who trades in flesh—only she couldn't go through with it after all. She brought him to our house—what passed for a house, the dirty little flea-infested hut where we lived. But she tried to turn him away at the last minute, all crying and broken as she was; Mother said she couldn't sell me after all, and the trader must go away without me because she'd changed her mind.

"But I wasn't about to stay, and see my sister and my two little brothers starve—yes, I've two brothers, twins like your sons."

Phanes smiled sadly.

"I told the trader I would sell myself to him, long as he promised to give my family a good price. And he did; he was good as his word. He always was that good, long as he stayed away from the wine. Iadmon was the trader's name. I went away with him—to Memphis—and never saw my family again. I'm sure the gods never mean me to see them, either. I can only pray my mother got Iadmon's money, and made it safely home to Thrace.

"Iadmon told me I wasn't to be a common whore. He had bigger plans for me: I was to become a hetaera, and make a fortune for him, and for myself. Soon as I learned just what a hetaera was, I was ready to learn, and do my best. Not for the money's sake—though a hetaera can buy her way free, you know. I wanted to be a hetaera for the *freedom*, for the way I could move about at will, as other women can't do. With that goal before me, I found the strength to press on. I did my best to forget about my family; I threw myself into my lessons. I was determined to become the best hetaera in all of Egypt. I had nothing else to live for, you see—nothing to hope for, except my goal."

"How old were you?" Phanes said.

"Twelve years, going on thirteen."

Phanes breathed a soft, rather pained sigh. "So young, for such difficult work."

Rhodopis' spirits rose. "But it wasn't hard work—not while I was in Iadmon's house. He was a good, kind master, and he saw to it that I learned—oh, *everything* there was to learn. I liked that part... the learning. And the dancing... I liked that, too. After a year, I'd settled right in, and happy as a slave can ever be.

"But Iadmon, my master... he had his own share of troubles. What man doesn't, I suppose?"

Phanes made a gesture of mute agreement, a sympathetically helpless toss of his hands.

"Iadmon had a rival, you see—Xanthes. I could tell Xanthes wanted nothing more than to bring Iadmon low, to see him humiliated and scorned. He set his sights on me, for he saw that I was Iadmon's treasure, the hope for his future riches. One night at a party, Xanthes got Iadmon so drunk, all his common sense fled. He tricked my master into gambling me away, as if I was nothing more than a fine necklace or a race-horse. I traded hands in the blink of an eye... and that's when my life became truly difficult.

"Xanthes' household was nothing like Iadmon's had been. The other hetaerae were vicious creatures—though I suppose it's none of their faults. We were each trying to survive, weren't we? And each of us set up to be rival to the others, all of us competing for the same rich men, the same money, the same narrow route to freedom.

"I started working in earnest while Xanthes owned me. But I had my share of admirers, and soon enough I was setting by a good, tidy treasure, so I didn't mind the hardships so much. I felt sure I would be free of Xanthes and his vicious girls any day now —another year at most, before I could buy my freedom. But I... I was cheated by a friend. Or someone I'd thought was a friend. She stole all my worldly goods, except the shoes on my feet— beautiful rose-gold slippers, a gift from my patron. She left me with nothing; I was forced to start all over again.

"I was so angry that I threw one of those useless slippers into the river, and would have thrown the other, too, but a falcon flew down and caught up the one I'd tossed away. I learned later that night that the bird was one of Amasis' own, and it had flown back to the palace with my slipper in its claws, and dropped the slipper in the Pharaoh's lap. He took it for an omen, of course, and decided the god Horus had sent him a personal sign. Amasis went out searching for the other slipper—and the woman who owned it. I proved it was mine, for I had retained enough sense to keep the other slipper instead of flinging it into the river. Amasis claimed me for his harem, right there on the spot. I think he was all the more pleased because I'm Greek, but I can tell you, nobody else was glad to see a Greek hetaera in the Pharaoh's household. The harem wasn't an easy place for me to live. I was almost relieved to go, when Amasis sent me away in place of his daughter."

Rhodopis fell silent. She took another draft of wine, long and deep. Her throat had gone quite dry.

"A harrowing story," Phanes said. "You have seen so much, for a woman so young. And you say you were a hetaera; not *any* woman may attain a position so high. That is to say—" he shifted uncomfortably. "A hetaera stands very high for a Greek woman."

"But not for an Egyptian." She raised one brow, unsure herself whether she gently mocked Phanes—or whether she was perfectly in earnest. "Do you fancy yourself better than me, because you're Egyptian—because your people treat their women better than mine do?"

"No," Phanes said at once. "Please don't be offended, and don't misunderstand. I want to know more about hetaerae, you see. They were only beginning to emerge in Egypt by the time I was exiled. What is a hetaera's life like? I know almost nothing about them."

Rhodopis shrugged. It was the life the gods had given her; she knew no other, and she hadn't the least idea how to explain the world of the hetaerae to a man of Phanes' sort. "It was... a life of hard work and danger. I did get to know ever so many rich and powerful men... well, Greek men. The Egyptians didn't often go in for hetaerae."

"No, I suppose they wouldn't. It's a foreign concept to Kmet, but after a time, I suppose it would have caught on among Kmetu men."

"If they were wealthy enough," Rhodopis agreed. "That was the main thing: only the best and highest Greek men could afford the companionship of a hetaera. I do admit, there was something gratifying in the work—something nice and comforting, knowing such powerful men fancied you, and were willing to spend so much money just for the privilege of talking to you."

"Talking?" Phanes smiled wryly.

"You may laugh, but it's true. Any hetaera worth the least speck of silver had to be good at conversation. We weren't simple pornae, up against the wall in some stinking back alley. We were refined, you see—worthy. We had to be. No other Greek women are permitted to eat alongside men, hear their talk of great, worldly affairs, and take part in the talking themselves. We had to know as much as we could learn about the world, and the trades of the men we served, and kings and powers... all the things, anything wealthy, powerful men might discuss together."

"And you said it was dangerous work."

"Yes, but the danger came from the other girls—competition —not from the men. The men were more apt to fall in love with us." She laughed, thinking of the mooning Charaxus. "Though, I suppose that was a special threat all its own. The rest of the work —the dancing and the feasts and lying with men—it wasn't much of a patch by comparison to keeping the other girls from beating you, or cutting you up, or stealing your goods. I look back on those days now, and all I seem to recall is the struggle to survive, to come out on top among Xanthes' hetaerae."

"But if not for Amasis," Phanes said rather slyly, "your life would never have been thus: filled with loss and pain, and you, such a bright young woman, made to serve men in the basest of ways. The Pharaoh and his disastrous policies... the Pharaoh, changing the best of Egypt to suit his taste for Greek culture!"

She shrugged again, outwardly flippant, but a curious tightness was settling in her chest, squeezing her heart tighter moment by moment. Over the course of their conversation, Rhodopis had begun to suspect that her life would have been very different indeed if she had never met Xanthes or Iadmon. And why would either man have made Egypt his home, if Amasis had not welcomed them?

Nothing to be done about it now. My life is what the gods have made it. Where's the sense in dwelling on what might have been?

"I've seen you work your charms on Cambyses," Phanes said. "You are far more intelligent than anyone suspects. Aren't you?"

"Reckon so," Rhodopis said, lifting her chin defiantly. If the gods had made her *this*—a hetaera, a whore—then they had also made her sharp-witted and strong. Strong enough to survive this long as the Pharaoh's spy in Babylon, and sharp enough to turn a fleeting opportunity to her advantage. Hadn't she cause to be proud?

"I need intelligent people like you working with me, hand in hand."

"Doing what sort of work?" Rhodopis asked cautiously.

"The most important work. You can help me, Lady Nitetis. You can restore Egypt to what it once was. You can throw off the Greek shroud once and for all, and bring Kmet back to life... so that no other girl need ever face such a fate."

Rhodopis sat in quiet contemplation. Phanes had placed a good deal of trust in her—indeed, he had placed his life in her hands, by revealing who he truly was and how he had come to Cambyses' service. If such information spread, it would certainly mean death for the physician. Even Cambyses—who may be a respectable man, but was first and foremost a king—would not hesitate to take off Phanes' head for the simple crime of meddling in the king's affairs.

Egypt, the way it used to be, sounds much better than Egypt as it is now. A spark of excitement flared in her breast, despite the obvious danger. But she was less thrilled by the opportunity Phanes laid out before her—the chance to restore Egypt, to return all its women to their rightful place—than by a private ambition of her own. Psamtik. Cambyses would make short work of that monster. And wouldn't Rhodopis savor the chance to lay waste to Psamtik's plans, to destroy his dark schemes for the throne! If Phanes was right, if his plan was a sound one, then Rhodopis could destroy Psamtik utterly, strip him of everything he desired, everything he held dear. She could leave him with nothing—*nothing*. Just the thought of the King's Son made Rhodopis tremble, but this time it was not fear that quivered along her veins. It was a desire hotter and more insistent than any she had known before: a hunger for vengeance against the demon who had raped her. No hunger that had ever plagued her compared to this sudden, predatory longing.

Is this what you mean for me, gods? Lady Ishtar, is this the victory you've planned?

Rhodopis could sense no answer to her fleeting prayer. But buoyed by the shelter of Babylon, the favor of the king and the cooperation of the goddess, Rhodopis embraced her desire for revenge. Oh, yes—she *would* destroy the whole of Egypt, if it could be done at al. She would take it all away from Psamtik, that soulless beast who was so sure of his place in the world, so confident in his power, that he would defile and torture a defenseless young woman with impunity, in his father's own house. Could she really do it—take it all away from him, leave him stripped of everything he valued? Would the gods truly permit it?

With a lurch of power so strong it made her queasy, Rhodopis realized she didn't care whether the gods would permit it. *I'll leave Psamtik with worse than nothing, before I'm through.*

"How?" she finally said. "How can it be done? It's a tall order, to bring down an empire. Especially one as old and large as Egypt."

"Before we had this talk," Phanes said, "I admit I hadn't any clear idea of how to go about it. But now I think I understand how it can be done. It will require us both to work together. And it will require a good deal of bravery. Are you strong enough to face what will come?"

"It will take trust between us, too, I suppose."

"It will, indeed. I've already made up my mind to trust you. Have I made the right choice, Nitetis?"

She looked at Phanes levelly. "My name isn't Nitetis. In Egypt, I was called Rhodopis. And in Thrace, I was Doricha."

He nodded, understanding the confidence she had placed in him, the commitment she had made. "Thank you," he said simply.

"As for being brave and strong—" Rhodopis lifted her chin— "I'm stronger than you think. I've faced more than you'd ever believe, and lived to tell the story. I'll do it, Phanes. I'll help you, if the gods are willing." *And I'll crush Psamtik under my heel, even if the gods aren't willing.*

"Good," he said. His brief grin of triumph slid into another of his sober, thoughtful expressions. He turned a rather grim look on Rhodopis. "I'm afraid you will need plenty of strength for what you must do next. May all the gods grant it."

✺ 13 ✺

THE POINT OF THE SWORD

AMTES HAD RETURNED TO THE CHAMBER IMMEDIATELY AFTER Rhodopis committed herself to Phanes' cause. Freshly bathed, dark hair dripping over her shoulders, the handmaid had stood in silence, watching Phanes with a perfectly unreadable expression. At that moment, it occurred to Rhodopis that no matter how much kindness Amtes had shown over the course of their journey, she did not know her handmaid well enough to anticipate show she would react to the plan. Would Amtes gleefully participate in the destruction of Amasis, and the royal family's legacy? Perhaps. But then, it seemed just as likely to Rhodopis that Amtes be horrified by the notion. Was she the sort of Kmetu who longed to see the Greek plague routed from Egypt at any cost? Or was she the sort who would uphold the Pharaoh no matter what ills be brought upon the Two Lands? Amtes may very well believe that Amasis had been chosen by the gods to enact all their inscrutable purposes. Amasis had paid Amtes well for her services... but did she feel any real loyalty toward the Pharaoh?

Rhodopis could not be certain Amtes would maintain the secret—not until they'd discussed the matter in depth. There was no time now to suss out the watchful handmaid. Rhodopis saw at once that she must protect the plot from Amtes until she could be sure where the woman's loyalties lay. One careless word, and a pigeon might go winging off toward Tadmor, and Memphis beyond, carrying word of Rhodopis' treachery and spoiling everything before she and Phanes had found their chance to act.

Rhodopis had smiled up at Amtes, giving no sign of her inner turmoil. "The physician came around to the women's quarters on some other errand, and I thought I would ask him about my headache."

Amtes tilted her head a fraction, so subtle an expression of doubt that only Rhodopis could have seen it, familiar as she was with her handmaid. *I thought you hated and feared Phanes,* Amtes' dark eyes said. *Yet now I find you alone with him.*

Phanes rose from his chair. "If you like, Lady Nitetis, I can show you which herbs to use yourself. They grow here in the women's garden. Then you need not call on me the next time you have this type of pain—though of course, I am always glad to serve, if you prefer."

"That would be well," Rhodopis said. "If I know which herbs to take, then I needn't trouble you."

Amtes pushed her wet hair off her shoulder. "I'll come with you, Mistress."

Rhodopis forestalled her with a raised hand. "There is no need. Master Phanes and I have had certain... disagreements... in the past, but I believe we see eye to eye now."

Phanes bowed his head in acknowledgment. "Every man and woman in the palace respects you for your commitment to the king, my lady. After today, with Ambassador Turo, there is no one left who doubts you—least of all myself."

"You see?" Rhodopis said to Amtes. "There's no cause for alarm. Come out your hair, and then you can eat this roasted fowl yourself. I had some of the figs, but I'm afraid my appetite hasn't fully recovered." She led Phanes toward her chamber door, chat-

ting light-heartedly. "But perhaps once I try these herbs, I'll feel
right as the summer sun again."

"Indeed," Phanes said, following. "Your appetite will return as
soon as the pain is gone. Two hours, three at most."

Rhodopis had closed the door, leaving Amtes alone in the
apartment.

She and Phanes had indeed walked in the garden, first by the
light of the setting sun, then by the amber glow of his swinging
lamp. They had remained together even as the night's chill came
on, bundled tightly in their shawls, working their way along
every path, climbing from one terrace to the next. When they'd
grown weary, they sat together on a vine-shrouded parapet,
looking out over Babylon glittering in the darkness below. And
through those hours, they had talked and planned, raised every
question and turned over every possible solution, approaching
their plot from every angle either one could conceive. At last,
when the garden was soaked in dew, and the eastern horizon
warmed subtly with the coming dawn, Phanes blew out his
lamp's flame.

"You should sleep," he'd said. "In just a few hours, we must go
and speak to the king."

"I don't think I can sleep. I don't feel tired. I feel..."

"Frightened?"

Rhodopis had considered the word for a long time before
answering. "No. No, I don't think it's fear, exactly. This whole plan
is dangerous—of course it is. The king will be angry; there's no
one to say what he might do. And you... I've no real reason to
trust you, have I?"

"But you do trust me."

She had nodded, thoughtfully. "Yes. Only everything you've
said tonight—it could get you killed, too. But you've trusted me
with all of it. I suppose that's reason enough to trust a man."

"I am quite determined, my friend—I can call you 'friend,' I
hope?—to bring Amasis down. It's a gamble, trusting this plan to

one as young and inexperienced as you. But I have waited a long time for the gods to provide a way. I have remained vigilant; I never gave up hope. I believe I would be a fool not to have faith in the gods, and act on the chance they've supplied. But I will not make you do it, Rhodopis. If at any time you wish to back down, I will honor your decision. You may stop this plan yourself, right up until you stand before the king."

Rhodopis had flushed with the force of her feeling. She thought of Psamtik, forcing her, leaving her no choice. Wasn't that the way of men? So many of them had owned her, used her... stripped all choice away. *Now I have power... or I could have it, if I'm courageous enough to take it.* All she need do was face Cambyses. And believe in Phanes, this strange, passionate man whom she had known for only a few weeks. *Gods, but it's hard to see what's best done.*

She and Phanes had parted with the sunrise, and Rhodopis had promised to sleep—but sleep would not come. Instead, she had sat before her mirror, hopelessly alert and far too anxious, staring at her reflection as morning light flooded the room.

Rhodopis searched her features for traces of the girl she had once been. Where was Doricha, the Thracian child? Where was Doricha the dancer, and Rhodopis the hetaera, tumbling into the beds of one man after another? Where was Rhodopis, the favorite of the Pharaoh? And where was Rhodopis, abused and frightened in the garden grove with the point of Psamtik's knife pressed to her throat? She ran her hand over the smooth skin of her neck. The marks of his knife had vanished from her flesh. They had healed without any outward scar, yet she knew he had left a scar on her spirit. Perhaps that wound would never heal. But looking at herself—to see her own face, eyes red from lack of sleep (but not from frightened tears)— Rhodopis could find nothing of Psamtik's influence. That heartened her. She could not see Lady Nitetis, either, who had lolled so often in Cambyses' arms and heard his words of praise and endearment. Nitetis was gone. After today, she would never live again.

I am none of those past people, Rhodopis realized. A thrill warmed her stomach, growing hotter by the moment. *I am only me, as I am here today, and whatever future the gods may grant me— whether it's death at Cambyses' hands or a long life and old age—it will be my future, my life, because I reached out and took it. Because no man made me do it—not even Phanes. Mine, because I chose it.*

By the pale, soft light of morning, Rhodopis painted her face with delicate colors, soft and fresh, blooming and new. She scented her skin with rose oil, the scent Cambyses loved the best on her skin. She dressed in a robe of petal-pink, sweet and pretty, youthfully innocent. When Amtes rose from her bed and found Rhodopis standing before her mirror, her dyed-black hair falling down her back, her face painted as if for court, the handmaid checked and stared.

"Find that beaded hair band for me," Rhodopis said to Amtes. "I don't know where I left it."

"My lady?"

"The king will be practicing with his sword today in the court-yard. I will go and watch."

"Yes, of course," Amtes said. "You always do. But dressed like this? As if he'll be hearing audiences in the throne room?"

"Cambyses will hear one audience today," Rhodopis said calmly. "A very important one. Come, now—the band is all I need, and then you must go and fetch Phanes. Tell him I say: I am ready."

As ready as ever I can be.

❧

By the time Phanes returned to Rhodopis' quarters, the other women had already departed from the harem to watch the king at his exercises. A curious sensation had long since settled in

Rhodopis' stomach—a queasy buzzing, as of hornets below the ground, but that constant, grating murmur was not fear. It was a strange, grateful anticipation. Ever since speaking with Phanes the night before, she wanted to get this business over and done with as soon as she could—let the gods rain down whatever punishment or reward they would. Now that she had decided to act of her own free will, to take her fate in her hands, she was eager to begin, whatever the consequences may be.

When Phanes knocked, Rhodopis turned to Amtes. She embraced her handmaid impulsively, which Amtes accepted with a startled expression. She patted Rhodopis rather awkwardly on the back.

"Whatever happens today," Rhodopis said, "don't go with anyone who may come for you. If I do not return for you myself, then Phanes will, and he'll see you safely away. Trust no one but him."

"My lady!" Amtes pulled back from the embrace. "What in Hathor's name is happening? You were so strange last night, and this morning—"

"I can't explain, Amtes—not now, though I hope I can explain it to you later. And I hope... I hope you'll be glad, and not curse me."

"Curse you? You're speaking nonsense! What herbs did that physician give you? Has he addled you somehow?"

"There's no more time." Rhodopis squeezed Amtes' hand. "You've been good to me. Whatever happens, I won't forget that."

Amtes tried to follow Rhodopis through the door and out into the corridor, but Rhodopis stayed her with a gentle touch. "Please —you must stay here. I want you kept safe."

Her mouth hanging open in helpless wonder, Amtes shook her head. "I'll wait here until you return, then, if that's what you want. But you *will* return."

Rhodopis smiled at her handmaid and turned away.

She walked with Phanes from the women's quarters, across

the very garden terraces they had wandered throughout the previous night. They made their way together to the dusty, hot flatness of the king's practice yard. Both were tense, both silent; they had spoken every sensible and reasonable word the night before, had carefully rehearsed the parts each must play. It was time now to act—to take the chance the gods had provided, and pray that mercy would be their reward.

When they reached the courtyard, bright with morning sun, Cambyses had already begun his drilling. The women were gathered beneath their sun shades, laughing and murmuring together. Rhodopis felt the first lurch of regret, looking upon the king's women. She had almost become a sister to them. She had almost managed to fit, neat as a weaver's weft, into their glad and easy lives. What would they think of her now? Rhodopis had no way to predict Cambyses' reaction, but she was coldly certain that the women she had come to like so well would despise her. The inescapable fact of it soured her stomach.

Cambyses was fiercely engaged with one of his best soldiers, turning and dodging in the glare of the sun. He brought up one arm even as the other made a rapid slash with his sword; the clang of metal on metal made Rhodopis jump. Then her heart sank. Cambyses was working with his shield today. That meant he was training with live swords.

Rhodopis and Phanes hung back, hidden in the shadow of the portico—just as they had been on her arrival in Babylon. How far in the past that day seemed now! How her life had changed in that handful of weeks... and now it would change again, irrevocably. Neither Rhodopis nor Phanes spoke. She could feel the physician's tension, the faint vibration of his body as the flood of fear-energy swept him. It washed through Rhodopis, too, until every muscle and vein within her screamed at her to run, to flee the palace, to sprint across the desert until at last she found some refuge of safety.

No, she told herself firmly. Her trembling ceased. *I am*

committed now. And Phanes is committed, too. He will not sell me out; he will stand by me. She believed it, and it was some small comfort. She and the Egyptian exile had cast their lots together. There was no going backward now, but at least they would go forward hand in hand.

"Are you ready?" Phanes asked as the king and his soldier whirled past them, their sharp blades flashing in the sun.

"No," Rhodopis said. "But that doesn't mean the time isn't right. We must do it now, mustn't we? I feel waiting any longer would be agony."

"Very well, then. I'll be right behind you."

Rhodopis nodded, swallowed hard... and stepped out into the yard. Time seemed to slow around her as she moved directly toward Cambyses; the sound of his drilling was drowned beneath a fearful, continuous rushing in her ears, like a storm at its wildest pitch, or a mountain river in flood. Vaguely, she was aware of the distress of the women—their shouts and frantic gestures, their pale faces and outstretched hands as she stepped directly into the path of the king and his man—into the path of their flying blades. Rhodopis did not respond to the women, did not even glance in their direction. She sent up a silent plea for their forgiveness and pressed on.

The women's shouts did serve to alert Cambyses, however. He glanced over the shoulder of his guard, caught sight of Rhodopis coming toward him, grim-faced and small. His eyes widened with surprise, even as he raised his shield to deflect his opponent's blow. It fell with a metallic clash that seemed to reverberate inside Rhodopis' head. The next moment, Cambyses backed away, shouting, "Down! Blade down!" The guard stumbled to a halt, lowering his sword. Then he sank obediently to one knee before Cambyses, awaiting the king's next command.

Cambyses brushed past the man. Chest heaving, sweat already beading on his skin, the king smiled in a rather confused manner as Rhodopis stopped, staring up into his face. She had ascended high in the king's favor, she knew. Her display of loyalty, here in this very courtyard, was vibrantly fresh in Cambyses' memory. That was why she must act now—Phanes had been insistent on that point, and very persuasive. She must strike immediately, must make Cambyses see sense in the plan while his feelings for Rhodopis were still as warm as a new bridegroom's.

Rhodopis knew the time was now, yet she could not speak. She clutched her hands with a terrible, tight grip; she trembled as she looked up at Cambyses. Every pleasant night she had spent in his bed flashed through her mind at once, every hour they'd spent in laughter or simple conversation, every wave of pleasure he had made to ripple through her body. Immediately in the wake of that poignant vision, a wrench of regret ripped at her heart. Rhodopis had grown to... well, not to love Cambyses, exactly. But she liked and respected him. She had enjoyed lying with him, talking with him, as she had never enjoyed any other man. She would lose everything now, cast it all away—that glad sense of belonging, her status as a king's wife, even the tentative, fragile roots she had just begun to put down in Babylon.

"Nitetis," Cambyses said, bewildered. "What is it, my rose? You look so pale. Has something gone wrong?"

Rhodopis fell to her knees before the king, lifting her clenched hands in a gesture of hopeless pleading. But she did not lift her face; she could no longer bear to look at him. "My king— my husband! I cannot live with the guilt any longer. I have come to make a confession."

"A confession?" Cambyses spoke quietly, his voice was edged by a sudden frost.

"Yes," she said. "I must confess to you who, and what, I really am—here before everyone, for you have always conducted the business of your kingdom before the eyes of your women. They, too, must know the truth."

With her head bowed low, all Rhodopis could see was the

point of Cambyses' sword as it lowered slowly toward the ground. It came to rest in the dust.

"Speak," he said shortly.

Rhodopis swallowed the great, painful lump in her throat. She would have preferred to make her confession in the privacy of the king's chamber, but Phanes had insisted: the scene must play out before the eyes of as many witnesses as possible. Cambyses was sometimes rash and short-tempered, the physician had explained—but he never lost his composure where his women or his subjects could see. It was a point of pride with him, to think carefully and clearly whenever anyone was near enough witness to his affairs. Cambyses had always pronounced sound, thoughtful judgment when he was observed by his subjects.

Bolstered by that knowledge, Rhodopis pressed on. "My king and husband, I am not what I seem to be." She spoke as loudly as she could, letting every person hear the tale. The women had fallen silent. Even the murmur of the city far below seemed to dim and recede, as if all of Babylon strained to listen. "I am not the daughter of Pharaoh Amasis. I am only a woman from his harem, and a woman of low standing, at that. When you demanded a daughter in marriage, the Pharaoh thought it a grievous insult, for Egypt has never given a daughter to any foreign king, in all the nation's long history. But Amasis also knew that the might of Haxamanishiya grows every day; he could not deny you. He sent me to you, instead of a true daughter. I am the Pharaoh's ruse. And..." She had to breathe deeply before she could force the final confession from her throat. "And I came to Babylon as the Pharaoh's spy."

The women burst out with a startled shout, a wordless exclamation that came at once from more than a dozen throats. A few yelled insults and curses; someone cried, "Strike off the head of that traitorous bitch!"

But Cambyses said nothing. The point of his sword shivered in the dust, a testament to his rage-tightened grip on its hilt.

Rhodopis' face burned with shame. Tears blurred her vision, then dropped into the dust. Through all the preparations she had made with Phanes—rehearsing the words, refining their plan—she had never expected to feel genuine remorse for what she had done to Cambyses.

"How dare you deceive me," Cambyses said, so softly Rhodopis almost couldn't hear him over the sound of the women's protests. "You and Amasis." He spat on the ground, very near where Rhodopis knelt.

Then, with one swift flash, his sword raised. Rhodopis tensed, but her heart stilled, and the peace of certainty came over her. The tears cleared from her eyes. It was over; she had reached the end, the ultimate confluence of fate and strife. She would feel the bite of Cambyses' blade, its cold caress on the back of her neck, and then... nothing.

"Please, my king!" Phanes threw himself down in the dust beside Rhodopis, kneeling in exactly the place where Cambyses had spat. "I beg of you: hear what this woman has to say. I only just learned her story, myself. She came to me in confession, you see, for her guilt weighs too heavily on her heart; she cannot bear it any longer. I told her she must speak to you herself, and confess the truth, for her loyalty to Haxamanishiya is real—as is her devotion to you. My king, you saw her yesterday, repudiating Egypt before the eyes of your court. She has risked the displeasure of the Pharaoh—indeed, she has risked her life and safety—and dedicated herself to you. I beg of you, my king: hear her."

"Speak, woman," Cambyses barked. "And Phanes, hold your tongue. My patience is very thin."

"Pharaoh Amasis is your enemy, my king, but I am not." Rhodopis' throat was quite dry; her words quavered as they came, for Cambyses' sword was still raised. He had not made up his mind to spare her life—not yet. "I am not Egyptian, but Greek—and for years, I lived in bondage in the city of Memphis."

There was a pause. Silence had returned to the courtyard. Cambyses said, "You are a slave?"

"Yes, my king—once. But after I was a slave, I was a hetaera."

Again, that tense, tormenting silence. "Go on," Cambyses said flatly.

"When I was a hetaera, my king, I had access to the most powerful men in all of Egypt. I heard their thoughts, their plans... I could influence them to take up the causes I favored, for all men are susceptible to such manipulations when they lie with a woman."

"I dare say that's true," Cambyses growled. The disgust was plain to read in his voice, and Rhodopis could infer his thoughts: *What weaknesses have I betrayed to this spy while she lay in my arms? Has she sent word already to Egypt?*

Rhodopis continued quickly, before Cambyses could act on his anger. "In truth, my king, it is those men who run the country —the merchants and nobles—not the Pharaoh. He is only the body that warms the throne, but he is too weak and malleable to rule. The Greek merchants know how to use him; they play him like the strings of a harp."

"What is your point?" Cambyses said. "Come to it quickly; the chatter of an enemy offends my ears."

"Yes, my king. My point—my proposition—is this: many of my former patrons are traders with crucial influence in Greece. You know, my king, that Greece is the only ally to which Amasis can turn, if he feels trapped or threatened. Greece is his only friend now, for he has made enemies everywhere else—even in his own court. Throughout Egypt, men murmur against him; they pray for his downfall. I know which men to influence, which to compel. I know how to drive a secret wedge between Amasis and Greece. I can cut the Pharaoh off from his only hope for salvation."

Cambyses said nothing for a long, shuddering moment. Then he said shortly, "Phanes."

"I have listened carefully to this woman's plan, my king," Phanes said. "I believe it is sound—as sound a plan as we may hope or pray to find. Amasis may have sent this woman to you to with the intent to deceive, but the gods themselves brought her to Babylon to serve *you*. We all witnessed how she treated the Egyptian ambassador; we know where her heart lies. What cause did she have to repudiate Amasis? What could have motivated her, except true loyalty to Haxamanishiya? We have waited patiently for the right moment to strike at the Pharaoh. I believe that moment has finally arrived. This woman is better kept alive, my king, and employed in your cause."

Cambyses did not move, did not relax. Rhodopis clenched her teeth, waiting, convinced that any moment she would hear the whistle of the king's sword as it cleaved the air—as his killing blow fell toward her small, defenseless body.

But the point of his sword lowered again, coming to rest in the dust before Rhodopis' face.

"Bring the girl and meet me in my chamber, Phanes," Cambyses said. "We have much to discuss."

II

WATCHER

❧ 14 ❧

EULALIA IN MEMPHIS

THE LITTER SANK TO GROUND IN THE DUSKY COURTYARD. RHODOPIS peeked cautiously through the gap in the thick curtains, taking in the first sight of her new home. The house was small, yet finely built, its two stories and rooftop terrace standing demurely behind a high wall covered in a tapestry of vines. Beyond the garden, thick with many years of growth, the Nile flowed smooth and purple in the twilight.

She sank back for a moment against the cushions, letting the curtains swing shut again. She had kept them firmly drawn, sheltering herself from view, from the moment she had boarded the litter back at the public quay, where her boat had landed earlier that same evening. She breathed deeply, tasting the humid Egyptian night. It was rich with familiar smells of wet vegetation and the spice of winter-blooming flowers. Rhodopis savored her final moments of absolute privacy behind the veil of her curtains. Now that she was back in Memphis, the disguise she had adopted wouldn't last long. Sooner or later, she would be obliged to venture out into Memphian society, and once she did, it was only a matter of time before her face or her voice was recognized. She had a mind to delay that moment for as long as she could.

"Close the gate," she called to the litter-bearers.

"At once, Mistress."

Servants and slaves had called 'Mistress' in Babylon, but the title landed strangely in her ear here in Memphis. She half expected the bearers to chuckle over the improbability— Rhodopis, a 'Mistress!' But those men, like all the rest who would make up her household staff, seemed entirely earnest. *Calm yourself*, Rhodopis thought. *There is no reason for them to doubt you, nor reason for them to suspect who you truly are.*

The entire staff had furnished and vetted by Phanes, on behalf of King Cambyses. Indeed, Phanes had been the architect of Rhodopis' disguise; while she had traveled back across the tedious desert and down the coast toward Egypt, Phanes had worked diligently with ink and scroll, pigeon and rumor, constructing through fiction and innuendo a full-fleshed history —even an established reputation—which Rhodopis now donned like some robe of dazzling glory. She was Rhodopis no longer— nor was she Doricha, nor Lady Nitetis. She was Eulalia: sophisticated, eminent, the high-class hetaera come from her native land of Lesvos to increase an already considerable fortune among the grand old glories of Memphis. Daughter of an elite family, Eulalia hoped to brush elbows with the finest and most powerful men in the world—and thus increase not only her personal wealth, but that of her noble line, too. Such was the story, the shield behind which Rhodopis would crouch, praying it concealed her well enough that she could complete her true task in Memphis and abscond back to Babylon in one piece.

Rhodopis, the simple, fresh hetaera and newcomer to the Pharaoh's harem, may have been unused to such lofty titles as 'Mistress.' But Eulalia would accept such niceties as no more than her natural due. She rose gracefully from the litter, nodding coolly to the guards, and stood for a moment in the courtyard. All its dark plantings were flush with the bloom of the wet season. Rhodopis resisted the urge to pull her short linen cape more tightly around her shoulders. After little more than a month in Babylon, dry and hot as the inside of a mudbrick oven (by day, at least), the chilly damp of the Nile Valley was startling. Moisture hung so thickly in the air, it seemed to Rhodopis that she ought to be able to *see* it. It weighed down her cape and her linen dress, clinging to her skin with an oppressive weight. The sooner she was inside her new house, shut away from the eyes of Memphis, the better.

She nodded toward Amtes, still in the litter. Amtes uncoiled herself from the cushions with a stretch and a sigh. As she stood, the pale glow of twilight fell upon her face, picking out the lines and dots of Amtes' own disguise—black ink, carefully applied each morning to her cheeks, forehead, and chin, an imitation of the strange tattoos worn by the women who had grown up far to the south, beyond the Nile's white-water cataracts. The false tattoos were Amtes' best hope for anonymity—for she, too, risked being recognized by the Pharaoh or his people.

Phanes had approved of Amtes' continued service, though he had spent two days interrogating her, carefully prying and rooting through her every word and gesture until he felt certain she was true Kmetu—committed to the Two Lands entirely, but with no particular attachment to Pharaoh Amasis or his family. Rhodopis had been so relieved to keep Amtes close that she had wept for joy when Phanes brought the news. Amtes woman was fearless, staid—a pillar of calmness and strength, even in the midst of a mad and dangerous world. Once Phanes had given his blessing, Amtes had proven herself remarkably enthusiastic about the restoration of a true, traditional Kmet. She had vowed to resume her work as messenger—this time, dispatching messages to Babylon instead of Egypt. "It is all one to me, which way the pigeons fly," Amtes had said when she'd returned to Rhodopis' chamber after the lengthy interrogation. "So long as I do the will of Kmet's true gods."

Rhodopis took Amtes' arm. They walked toward the little

house, Rhodopis moving with a languid sway, doing her best to minimize her unseemly eagerness to scamper inside and heave a sigh of relief behind a private and firmly closed door. Memphis seemed to intrude all around her. Its noises and smells crowded over the garden wall, surrounded her like the ranks of an army. The calls of merchants, striving to sell the last of their wares before all light vanished from the sky, played thinly against a burst of raucous laughter from a nearby wine-house. Fowls squawked in a neighboring garden, arguing over their roost, and a child shouted at the birds in coarse Egyptian. Mud from the river warred with the odors of goat dung and charred bread, lamp oil and a stray drift of myrrh from some inner-city shrine. How strange it was to be back. Rhodopis had never expected to see Memphis again; to return after a few short turns of the moon seemed all but impossible. Yet here she was, strolling through the Egyptian twilight as if no fears nipped at her heels, as if everything was maat as the moon and stars.

The city's familiarity did nothing to quell the sickness in her stomach. The return trip from Babylon had been far more difficult than her first excursion. Rhodopis had been obliged to travel in considerably less comfort. She was a wealthy hetaera now, not a King's Daughter. Her new identity afforded some luxuries—but not nearly as many as a princess of Egypt could expect. Rhodopis' camel train had been far rougher, less comfortable; she had been forced to ride in the saddle, with her skirts split and bunched up around her thighs, instead of lying in a shaded, cushioned litter. The ships that had carried her down the sea coast and up the long, silver flatness of the Nile had been considerably less impressive than Amasis' boats. Despite the discomfort and hardship, Rhodopis had arrived in Memphis faster than she had expected. She did not know yet whether she must count that speed a blessing or a curse. Certainly, she did not feel adequately prepared to be in Memphis again.

A small staff of servants appeared under the portico as

Rhodopis and Amtes approached. They bowed in welcome, but Amtes sent them off at once. "Our mistress is hungry and very tired from the journey. Lesvos is a long way off, you know. Bring a good meal to her sleeping chamber. Is there a bath built into the floor? Yes? Excellent. I'll have it filled with hot water, and bring the best oil in the house. I will bathe Mistress Eulalia myself, and then we'll take to our beds, and we're not to be disturbed until three hours after sunrise. Mistress needs her rest, after so many trying days."

The staff leaped to obey Amtes' commands. Rhodopis stifled a giggle. "You ought to be the mistress, not I. You were born to command."

"Perhaps I ought to take real tattoos, if they make me seem so imposing."

"You'd have been a great hand at running a stable full of hetaerae."

"Perhaps I'll take up the business once our work here is settled. There's a fortune to be made in that kind of work, so I hear."

"There is, but if we succeed, you'll have to go to one of the Greek kingdoms to run a stable. If Phanes has his way, the Greeks won't hang about Egypt much longer."

Cheerful lamplight filled the sitting room of Rhodopis' small but elegant home. The single, sleek couch, wrapped in blue silk, was finely made, with angular keys of ivory set into the wood at its lower edge. Two ebony chairs stood nearby, waiting for the guests Eulalia might entertain in her home. A spacious table large enough for three to dine dominated the room below a woven wall hanging, which depicted a sea dotted with green islands—a scene from Lesvos, Rhodopis assumed. The scents of rose and myrrh lingered in the air, spiced by a faint breath of cinnamon. It was tasteful and refined, rich without being ostentatious—exactly the sort of home a hetaera would purchase when she was ready to strike out on her own. Phanes had done his work well. Of course, the estate—along with a new wardrobe of clothing, the home's staff, and the litter that had carried Rhodopis from the quay—had been purchased with Cambyses' silver. But every detail of Rhodopis' new life in Memphis had been overseen and orchestrated by the clever physician. Phanes had assured Rhodopis that he would filter all the money through a warren of merchants. His network sprawled across Egypt and Greece; it would take the most inquisitive man months to untangle the threads of her assets and trace Lady Eulalia's wealth back to Cambyses and Babylon. And if the gods were good, Rhodopis would conclude her business long before then.

"It will be at least half an hour before they have food or a bath ready," Amtes said. "Shall we go out into the garden?"

Now that she had huddled in her welcome shelter, Rhodopis was not eager to venture beyond the privacy of the house. But, she told herself sensibly, nothing would come of cowering. Her mission in Egypt was sure to be fraught with danger; she could not live in fear of what may be lurking in her own garden. "Yes, all right. Let's watch the first stars come out." She followed Amtes to the house's rear portico.

The garden, too, was small, but every bit as graceful and pleasant as the rest of the estate. Rhodopis eyed the smooth expanse of river. She wished her garden wall did not extend to the waterside—anyone with ill intent might sneak along the bank and hide in the dense, dark hedges—but she supposed Phanes could not work every conceivable miracle from distant Babylon. A great white spray of stars arced above the Nile. She tipped her head back to take in the whole of the night sky.

"Do you know," Rhodopis said, "the night I left Egypt, I thought I would never see these same stars again. I think I believed the stars would look very different in Persia."

She fell silent, troubled by the pang in her heart. The stars had struck Rhodopis to sentimental foolishness that night. If not for her senseless fretting about the night-time sky, she never would have gone alone into the garden. Psamtik would never have found her. Rhodopis was no fool now. The thought of Psamtik sharpened that wistful stab to a sudden, vengeful hunger. All at once she was ready to begin her work, eager to author his destruction.

"When will you begin entertaining men?" Amtes asked. "You must start soon, my lady. If you don't, no one will believe you're a foreign hetaera, come to make your fortune. At least, they won't believe it for long."

"I know. I suppose it can't be put off—nor do I want to delay. But oh, the thought of it has weighed on me, all along our journey. I'm dreadfully afraid I'll be recognized. And what shall I do if I am?"

"Were you so well-known among rich Greek men, before the Pharaoh took you for his harem?"

She shook her head. "Not especially, though I was on the verge of gaining a sort of fame. There was a disastrous auction at some old fool's garden party. I had an admirer—Charaxus. He bid up my price far too high; that alone nearly made my reputation for me. Talk flew around the city; I almost became a celebrity, just by standing on a garden wall and letting men place their bids. But luck favored me—Amasis scooped me up and hid me away in his harem before my reputation could be made."

Amtes laughed. "What a strange world you hetaerae live in!"

"There may still be men in the city who remember me. Charaxus certainly will, if he hasn't left Memphis... or gotten himself killed. I'm afraid he had more enemies than friends." A sudden recollection of Archidike's face reared up in Rhodopis' memory, cruelly vivid. She shivered, then added quietly, "There are certain others who would recognize me, too, even with my hair dyed black."

And whatever will I do when Archidike sees me? Rhodopis had no answer to that disturbing question. It was all but certain that she would be recognized, soon or late. The game mustn't be up when she was spotted. She must have a ready plan—prepare a smooth, plausible response to the confrontation she knew was coming, and rehearse it well, so no one could catch her unaware.

"This is a lovely garden," Amtes said, bending to inhale the fragrance of a rose. "And the house is a good one. Rich enough to convince anyone, but not too showy. Anything finer might arouse suspicion."

"I only wish I could enjoy this lovely little estate more. I feel all tied up in knots with worry."

"You must trust Phanes... and the king."

And you. Rhodopis turned away from her handmaid, gazing out across the dark river. Moment by moment, the flowers and trimmed hedges emerged from the twilight gloom as the light of the stars increased. Amtes had never given Rhodopis any reason to doubt her. But Rhodopis still felt the sting of betrayal, the pain of a shattered friendship. Despite her reluctance, she must find the will to trust again. She had come back to Memphis a pawn in a dangerous game. If she hoped to survive, she would have to rely on the people who claimed to be her allies. Rhodopis could only pray that the gods would not play her false again.

"I do trust Phanes," Rhodopis said. "He told me his story— how he came to be in Babylon. It was a harrowing tale. I could have exposed him to Amasis through one of your letters, and that would have been the end of him."

"But you didn't."

"Of course not. You know by now, I've got no love for Amasis... or his family." Rhodopis glanced at her handmaid uncomfortably. She said casually, "Have you?"

Amtes snorted. "Phanes worked me over thoroughly, and you know it. It's Kmet I love, not our present Pharaoh."

"I've no cause to doubt you. I suppose... it's difficult for me to put my faith in anyone. You mustn't mind me if I'm wary some-times. I don't mean any offense." She considered Amtes for a moment. "Why did you do it, then? Why go to Babylon, to serve the Pharaoh's ends, if you don't love him?"

Amtes answered without hesitation. "The same reason you went: I had no choice. What is any woman to do, when a powerful man tells her she must go here or there, must do this or that?"

They both lapsed into silence. Out on the river, a night fisherman sang. The tiny boat was too far away for Rhodopis to make out the words, but she could hear the man's voice rise and fall in a comfortable rhythm. He sang as if no one in the world had any cause to worry.

Rhodopis said, "Phanes told me it hasn't always been this way in Egypt. He said that once, many years ago, women stood as high as men in all things."

"That is so. It was before my time, of course, so I don't remember it, but my mother and grandmother often spoke of the way things were before the Greeks came. I would like to see Kmet restored. Maybe the gods will curse me for interfering with the Pharaoh—after all, one must believe the gods put Amasis on the Horus Throne for reasons of their own. But there's no way for me to know how the gods will react until I'm dead and walking through the Duat. I suppose it makes as much sense to do what my heart tells me, as to assume I know what the gods prefer."

"And your heart tells you to do... all that we plan to do? Even to the Pharaoh?"

Amtes smiled coolly. "My heart tells me Kmet must live again. I admit, my lady: you and I do seem unlikely allies in that work— a Greek and a Kmetu."

Rhodopis laughed shakily. "That we do."

Amtes seemed to sense her growing discomfort; she changed the subject, tossing her hair over her shoulder as if they discussed nothing more consequential than the price of figs in the market square. "Did Phanes and the king roast you with questions as thoroughly as they did me? I thought they'd never stop asking me this and that. They pried out every imaginable detail of my life."

"Indeed, they did! After I had confessed myself to the king, he took me back to his chambers, and there he and Phanes spoke to me for hours. The king was ever so angry, and it's no wonder to me. But he kept his temper well. He questioned me on everything —everything he could think to ask. I told him what my position was in Amasis' court and harem, and which other women lived there, and how well I knew the king and the chief wife. And... the king's heir, Psamtik. Then he set in on Memphis, and my time as a hetaera. He wanted to know every moment of every encounter I'd ever had with a man. If I hadn't known *why* he wanted to hear those tales, I would have assumed he found them motivating."

Amtes laughed loudly. "Motivating?"

"You know what I mean."

"Did you tell him everything?"

"Of course," Rhodopis said. "I held nothing back. I had this terrible, prickly sense that if I left out the smallest detail, he would know—and he was already furious enough with me. If I'd made him any angrier, he likely would have killed me on the spot. But I didn't mind telling him. I had already decided the night before, while you were off bathing, that I would commit myself to the cause. I've reasons of my own to wish for the restoration of Kmet." *Or, failing that, at least the destruction of Amasis' power, and any hope that creature Psamtik might have of ruling in his father's place.*

Amtes yawned, stretching her arms above her head in a comfortable way. "I'm glad the king decided to trust Phanes' plan."

"So am I. When the king finally agreed to try it, I broke down and wept with relief. Only I wasn't sure until then, you see, that I wasn't to be killed after all." Now, though, the fate of Egypt hung from Rhodopis' shoulders. It was a great, heavy expectation, and despite her eagerness to cast Psamtik into the Underworld, she felt entirely too small and fail to bear the burden. She had been certain Cambyses shared her suspicion—certain he thought Rhodopis far too young and weak to carry out the work. Phanes, though, had seemed entirely confident in Rhodopis' potential.

Or perhaps, she thought wryly, *Phanes is willing to sacrifice me on the chance his wild scheme will work. After all, he's not risking his own skin.*

"It's good to be back in Egypt again," Amtes said.

Rhodopis murmured a noncommittal response. For her part, she would have preferred to be anywhere else—the tossing sea and blistering desert included. Yet that vicious hunger, the drive to bring Psamtik down, still gnawed at her. The sharp teeth of rage sank into her spirit, making her keen for action even as her heart pounded with fear. Her goal was plain—to drive a wedge between Greece and Egypt—but the way she must go about her work was anything but clear. Somehow, she must endeavor to turn men's hearts and minds in secret, picking apart their alliances with Egypt, uniting them to Persia, so that when Cambyses' blow came and Amasis turned to Greece for aid, the Pharaoh would be left stranded, without a friend in the world.

Simple as that, she thought bitterly. *Easy as blink.* How in the name of Ishtar was Rhodopis to meet enough many Greek men and influence so very many minds? Even if she seduced a different man every night for the next year, her efforts might not be enough to deter an alliance with Greece.

But I can't give up, nor despair. I won't let Psamtik have his throne easy as that.

"Look," Amtes said, breaking into Rhodopis' thoughts. "They've lit the lamp in your room. Your bath must be ready."

"Good. Gods know I need it."

They started toward Eulalia's estate. Rhodopis felt a thrum in her stomach, the first rising rush of confidence, like a flock of birds taking to the dawn sky. "Tomorrow morning we'll begin," she said to Amtes. "You must go to the nearest marketplace and start making friends."

"What sort of friends?"

"Other handmaids, of course—women who work for hetaerae. You'll find them around the peddlers' stalls, buying up cosmetics and perfumes and fine silks. Get to know them. Learn whatever you can from them. But most of all, you must spread the word that a new hetaera has come to Memphis, and that she is ready to make new acquaintances among the better sort of Greeks."

❧ 15 ☙

AN UNEXPECTED APPEARANCE

AMTES WAS AS SKILLED A HANDMAID TO THE HETAERA EULALIA AS she had been to Lady Nitetis, King's Daughter of Egypt. Only a few days after returning to Memphis, Rhodopis had her first request from an admirer—an invitation for Lady Eulalia to attend a very select dinner party on the north side of the city. There she would serve as exclusive companion to a certain young merchant called Drakon. His was a name Rhodopis recalled from parties of the past, though she was all but certain she had never entertained him personally before. Drakon was rising quickly through the opulent strata of Memphian Greeks, it seemed. She hoped his focus was more on his business and his future than on his past. The risk that he might recognize her was not insignificant.

Rhodopis prepared for the party with cool resolve. Amtes draped her body in fine, pale-green silk, blousing out its soft folds here, tying more tightly there with fine wool sashes and belts of thin, soft leather. The effect exaggerated the meager curves of Rhodopis' body, aging her by at least two years. Phanes and Cambyses had certainly provided Rhodopis with plenty of excellent clothes. Her chests and cedar wardrobes seemed full enough

to burst, packed with every garment and guise a high-class, well
established hetaera could hope for. Silks dyed in the most fash-
ionable shades, embroidered at neck and hem; wool so light and
fine it was as soft as the petal of a rose. And linens, of course, for
this was Egypt, after all—linens sheer or solid, pleated or plain,
all made after the most current Memphian style.

"You look brilliant," Amtes said, stepping back to admire her
own handiwork. She turned Rhodopis about by the shoulders, so
the latter might appreciate her reflection in the mirror.

"It *is* positively frightening, how much older I seem."
Rhodopis felt pleasantly surprised.

"I'm not half done yet. Sit down; I can add two more years
with your face paints. Yesterday at the marketplace, I found a
new, darker shade for your cheeks. It will damp down some of
your girlish glow."

"Not too much, I hope. My clients won't like to find a venerable grandmother lying on their couch."

Amtes laughed. "Place a more trust in me than *that*, if you
please."

"Before you paint my face, we had best decide on a hair style."
Rhodopis sighed. "How I wish I could leave it be! I got used to
letting it hang free back in..." She paused, glancing toward her
chamber door. There was always the possibility of a hard-
working servant scrubbing the walls or sweeping the floors, and
although the estate's staff had been carefully chosen by Phanes,
still Rhodopis felt that no amount of caution would prove exces-
sive. "Back in Lesvos," she finished.

"Of course. But loose hair is not the fashion here. Everyone
will think you too strange, maybe even mad, if you don't put it up.
I believe even the men would think something was amiss, and
you know they never notice the details of a woman's appearance."

Rhodopis sighed again, deeper this time. "That's true enough.
Why must we go to all the bother, then?"

"That's an easy question to answer." Amtes worked a bone

comb through Rhodopis' long, black hair. "You do it so you may intimidate all the other women."

"Like a dog pissing on a garden wall," Rhodopis said with a wry smile.

"Exactly. But this new perfume oil smells much better than dog piss. I found it at the market, too. It's made from irises, marjoram, and cumin spice. Put it on while I fix your hair up, like a proper lady of Memphis."

When Amtes had finished her work, Rhodopis chose a necklace from her jewelry cask and held it up to her throat, considering the effect of translucent, milky-pink chalcedony against her soft-green dress and pale skin. She nodded and handed the chain to Amtes. The handmaid fastened the clasp, then brushed her hands together with an air of satisfaction.

Rhodopis smiled at her reflection. Between the artful dressing and deft, subtle touches with the paints, Amtes had managed to make Rhodopis look twenty years old, at least. "I hardly recognize myself. Well done, Amtes. I will have no trouble concentrating on my work, since I won't need to worry that someone might remember me from my early days in the city."

"I'm glad you're pleased," Amtes said. She glanced out the window, noting the low slant of evening sun. "But now you had better go. Your litter should be ready and waiting in the courtyard. It won't do for Lady Eulalia to arrive *too* late for her first appointment."

❧

RHODOPIS FELT secure enough in her disguise that she kept the curtains of her litter tied back, the better to take in Memphis as she progressed along its bustling streets. An alley's mouth, a market with its painted carts and stalls, a particular arrangement of flat, yellow-gold rooftops standing against the sunset sky— each scene was familiar, as ordinary and expected as if she had never left the city. But even with that routine comfort, how strange it felt to return to the north end of Memphis! There all this curious mess had begun nearly four years ago; there, the tangle of Rhodopis' life had tied itself in the first of many knots. A wide lane marked by two pylons, each shrouded in white-flowering vines, caught her attention as she passed. She stared at it for a moment, then, as the lane fell away behind her, she pushed the curtain back farther to look more hungrily. It was the entrance to Iadmon's estate. *Wonder what he's doing now*, Rhodopis thought. *And I wonder if Aesop is still with him.*

As the litter sailed on, Rhodopis turned her back on Iadmon's estate. She would have had to turn upon her cushions and crane her neck if she wanted to see it now. She would not put on such a display of curiosity or longing; Rhodopis had no interested in looking backward. Whatever fate had in store lay ahead—but she could not help wondering how Aesop fared. With a pang of sympathy for her previous self, Rhodopis recalled her own terrible heartbreak when she'd failed to send Aesop word of her departure from Memphis. Did she dare to write him now? Surely it was too risky. A letter might be intercepted, and then everyone would know Rhodopis had returned, and that the hetaera from Lesvos was nothing but an elaborate fraud. The lady Eulalia could not risk breaking that delicate, crucial mask.

Rhodopis could hear the dinner party well before she arrived at the host's estate. Music and laughter reached drifted on the still evening air, raising an unexpected storm of nostalgia in her breast. Her heart seemed to expand, pressing hard against her ribs; she was filled with a sudden, eager confidence. Rhodopis had not expected to miss anything about a hetaera's life. But now she discovered that there was a certain comfort in venturing back into a world she already knew. A well-trod path always seemed safer and friendlier than a trek through unexplored wilderness. Since entering the Pharaoh's harem, Rhodopis' life had degenerated into one unpleasant surprise after another, a seemingly endless sojourn through unknown and unknowable realms. But a Memphian party, attended by wealthy, influential men—ah, that was firm ground, where she might expect to stand at ease, without the least fear of falling.

When the litter landed in the host's courtyard, a gray-haired steward with a ready bow and a soft voice offered his hand, helping her rise. "Lady Eulalia," he said, "I am Solon, steward to Good Man Praxiteles, who owns this estate."

Rhodopis stood and bowed her neck in graceful acknowledgment.

"I am most honored to make your acquaintance," Solon said. "All Memphis hums with talk of you; we are delighted that a hetaera of your standing has come to grace our city."

"You are too kind," Rhodopis said, shepherding her tongue with care. Now more than ever, she must not lapse into her country habits; such an unfortunate mistake would give her away at once. She must maintain the perfect guise of an elite Greek woman. "The honor is all mine; the fame of Memphis and its great men extends to every corner of the world."

"Please, my lady, join Praxiteles and his guests inside. They have already served the wine and fruits. Shall I send for a cup?"

"That would be well," Rhodopis said. She walked with Solon through the halls of the estate, moving ever closer to the music and laughter, the party beckoning and calling. "And would you be so kind as to point out Good Man Drakon? I have not had the pleasure of meeting him yet, but I am here at his special request."

"Of course." Solon ushered her into Praxiteles' andron, an exceptionally large and fine room, spacious and welcoming, hung with dozens of lamps. Praxiteles had clearly built his estate with grand parties in mind. He seemed a popular host, too—at least thirty men lounged on couches or gathered near the garden door, while more than a dozen hetaerae were already engaged in their night's work. "Drakon is there," Solon said, "on the red-covered couch, just to the right of the garden door. Directly across from where we stand—do you see him? The young man with the auburn hair."

There was Drakon indeed, looking exactly as Rhodopis recalled, with his reddish hair falling in an unruly wave over a freckled forehead. She felt a shiver of fear, and gave in to the briefest moment of panic. Was she so recognizable, too? Then she quelled her anxiety with determined effort. She must trust in Amtes' work, and in the mercy of the gods. No one would know her. She would fool them all.

"Thank you, good man," she said to the steward. "I will join Drakon now. Please send my wine over when the pourers arrive."

Rhodopis set off across the andron, moving straight through its heart, head up and dignified as if she had nothing to fear in all the world. Below the gentle refrain of harp and flute, she could hear murmurs rippling, following in her wake. It seemed Solon's greeting in the courtyard had been more than polite flattery: the newcomer from Lesvos truly was an item of interest. Eulalia had only just arrived at her first engagement, but already she trailed mystery wherever she walked. Rhodopis must take care to use that fortuitous renown to her advantage.

But whatever will I do if Drakon knows me at first sight? No—I can't afford to fret now. She set her jaw, rehearsing the deflections and excuses she had planned for just such an occasion. She would not be caught off guard by anyone who recognized her... or anyone who *thought* they did. This evening would work to her advantage; she was fiercely determined that it would. Two servants chanced to carry a great silver platter past Rhodopis as they wove through the andron toward the kitchen. The platter was empty, unused and clean; the servants tilted it to maneuver between two groups of couches, and Rhodopis caught a glimpse of her reflection in its well-polished surface. What she saw there inspired a smile of relief. Her dark hair and brows were entirely unlike the pale, honey-red coloring that had marked out Doricha, the little white lotus of Iadmon's house, or Rhodopis, the blushing country girl from Xanthes' Stable. She looked so unlike herself that had she not been prepared for the sight of her own reflection, she might have started with surprise to find a very different woman looking back at her from the silvery surface.

She reached the red-covered couch and Drakon, who lay easily across it. He was in the act of recounting a humorous story to his companions—it involved an ass in a market square, and a very fat man with a short tunic—but he broke off abruptly as Rhodopis approached. She smiled at him in an artfully constrained way; Drakon blinked up at her for a moment, awe and pride evident in his expression—but no recognition, thank the gods.

Drakon sprang to his feet. He lifted Rhodopis' hand, placed a delicate kiss on the backs of her fingers. "My friends," he said to the other men, "I have the great honor to present Eulalia of Lesvos. You have no doubt heard of her by now. My lady, these are Zosimos and Nikias, my friends and associates."

"How glad I am to meet you all," Rhodopis said. "And to make your acquaintance, Good Man Drakon." She gave her companion a brief yet suggestive look, a coy bat of her kohl-darkened lashes that, to her surprise, set him to blushing. *Red hair like my own,* she thought rather mischievously. *Means he's likely to go just as red in the face at the drop of a hairpin. What fun I can have tonight, toying and jesting with him.*

"Please, join me," Drakon said, gesturing to his couch.

Rhodopis obliged, stretching comfortably along the couch, fitting her body against Drakon's. Surreptitiously, she pressed her backside against his groin, which made the poor fellow choke and splutter as he tried to resume the humorous tale of the fat man in the marketplace. *Strange, how quickly it's all coming back,* Rhodopis mused as the men laughed at Drakon's story. *Almost as if I'd been born for this sort of work.*

She wondered—had the gods indeed made her for this very work? Not a hetaera's tasks—those were easy enough for any woman to master, if she chose. No, perhaps it was her secret work she'd been fitted for: infiltrating Egypt's inner workings, colluding with the might of a foreign empire to bring it all tumbling down, to set to rights what Amasis, in his hubris and carelessness, had overturned. The next moment she cast the absurd idea away with a little laugh—which fortunately coincided with one of Nikias' jests. Surely Rhodopis was not *that* important.

"Tell me," Rhodopis said when she found a natural lull in the conversation, "what is your line of work, Drakon? No doubt all the other women in the city already know, but as I am new here..."

"Our boy Drakon inherited a dye business from his father," Nikias said.

"And expanded it, much farther than Dear Old Abba ever dreamed," Zosimos added.

"He's too refined and humble to brag, so we'll do it for him," said Nikias. "Drakon is now the top dye merchant from here to the Delta. We're all in the same guild, you see, and Drakon has put us all to shame. In another year or two, he'll be the headman of our guild, and will push us all about like the pinched old bastard the gods always meant him to become."

"That's why we're here, flattering him and praising him now, so we'll be in his good graces when he comes to rule us all."

The two men raised their cups, laughing good-naturedly.

"I've done well enough for myself," said Drakon modestly. "I won't deny that."

Rhodopis turned to smile at him over her shoulder, a suggestive and alluring grin. "Fortune has been kind to me; I've found a companion with a reputation to match my own."

"Tell us about Lesvos," Drakon suggested. "How go affairs in the islands?"

"Ah." Rhodopis managed to keep her voice smooth and calm, despite the sudden, panicked leap of her heart. "Have you good men gone often to Lesvos? I know the dye trade is quite popular there."

"Often," Zosimos agreed. "If old Amasis hadn't given Greek merchants such favorable terms here in Memphis, I'd have set up in Lesvos years ago. You can't beat it for beauty."

"Clearly," Nikias said, raising his cup in salute to Rhodopis.

"You are too kind." She lowered her lashes demurely, stalling for time. She had never been to Lesvos in all her life—and had had no need to maintain her knowledge of world events, first sequestered in Amasis' harem and then carted off to Babylon. She must find some way to answer the question without saying anything of real substance—anything that might give her ruse away.

"Of course, Lesvos is beautiful as always," she said. "I am quite homesick for it, to tell you the truth, though Memphis is a very nice city."

"Where does your family live?"

"By the sea," Rhodopis said quickly. She had no idea whether the island of Lesvos had mountains or lakes, plains or forests. But seashores, any island certainly had in abundance. "On the eastern side of the island."

"Near Mytilene?" Drakon asked.

"Not too terribly near," she said evasively, and sipped from her wine cup to hide her sudden anxiety. "My father is a merchant, too—in spices. He has caravans that go from Phocaea to Palmyra every year, and his cassia and cinnamon were the best in the whole region." Those details, at least, she recalled from her childhood lessons with Aesop. She held her breath, praying the men found the story plausible, until they nodded, accepting her at her word.

"If it's not too forward to ask," said Drakon, "how did you come to be a hetaera? A woman such as you, from a well-to-do family..."

"It has been our family tradition for some time," she said.

"Two of my aunts were hetaerae, in their younger days. They went to Phocaea and Pyrassos to make their way—for you know, even in a place as grand as Lesvos, there are only so many men to go around. Islands, you know.... But before they left for their new homes, I admired how lovely and independent my aunts were. I aspired to be just like them, from quite a young age. My father and mother were pleased with my choice; they gave me the best schooling a girl could have. Why, I remember—"

A commotion at the andron's entrance spared Rhodopis from the agony of inventing likely memories of a childhood in Lesvos. Glad for the distraction, she turned with the rest of the men to see what had caused the sudden stir of shouts and uncomfortable laughter—and in an instant, her gladness turned to cold horror. A cat-like shadow had slunk into the room, already jostling and disrupting the natural flow of conversation, the pleasantries of a well-ordered event. Her deep-brown skin was oiled, glittering with golden mica dust; long black hair fell in unbound waves over tense shoulders. And from across the andron, those piercing, hard blue eyes seemed to stab deep into Rhodopis' very spirit. There was no mistaking Archidike—and no way to avoid her.

Rhodopis swallowed hard. She reached for the practiced litany of excuses and deflections, trying to call back every word she had rehearsed over the past several days in the privacy and comfort of her chamber. But nothing came. Like a flock of pigeons loosed from a cote, all her preparations fled from her mind, clattering and chaotic. She could do nothing but turn away from Archidike—casually, without drawing any suspicion by an abrupt or graceless movement. She hoped wildly that Archidike would find some distraction, some prey to toy with elsewhere in the andron—that those all-seeing, fierce blue eyes would not pick Rhodopis out of the crowd.

"By the gods," Rhodopis said casually, "who is that woman?"

"Archidike," Drakon said. He loaded that name with meaning,

though Rhodopis could not quite decide whether she heard scorn or admiration in his voice.

"She has made a stir just by walking in. Shouldn't all women be so lucky?"

"That's Archidike for you," said Nikias. "The gods never made a wilder woman. No one can predict what she'll do from one moment to the next."

"That's the allure of her, I suppose," Drakon said. "I went with her a time or two, when she worked for old Xanthes, but she fairly scared me off. Adventure and surprise are all right in their proper places. A man doesn't those things in his bed."

"Maybe *you* don't," Nikias said, laughing.

Rhodopis risked another quick glance over her shoulder. Archidike was making her rounds of the andron, pausing now and then to sling a back-handed compliment or a flirtatious challenge at the men she passed. And she was edging ever closer to the garden door—where Rhodopis lay with Drakon.

"Every good hetaera must have her style," Rhodopis said. "I take it 'surprise' is what this specimen has adopted for her own."

"I don't think she puts it on as any sort of affectation," Drakon said rather darkly. "That's why she has so many admirers—like Nikias here."

"Oh? Is she quite popular?" Rhodopis was appalled at the flush of envy that coursed through her. *The gods know damnably well, Archidike would still be toiling away for Xanthes if she hadn't stolen my fortune. And if Amasis had never taken me, I'd still be toiling away for Xanthes, too, trying to earn it all back while* she *traipses around the city, pleased as a cock with ten extra tail feathers.*

"I should say so," Drakon said. "Archidike is a rising star in the Memphis sky, though the gods may damn me if I can explain it."

Nikias flexed his fingers into an imitation of a lioness's claws. He raked the air savagely. "That's why!"

"Here she comes," Drakon said.

"Nikias! Hard to believe Praxiteles let a sod like you come to his grand party." Archidike's voice rang like a temple cymbal in Rhodopis' ears. It had been almost two years since she'd heard the woman who had once been her friend; the sound sent a shiver of mingled recognition and revulsion up Rhodopis' spine. She sipped from her wine cup and did not look at the newcomer, praying fervently that Archidike would wander through the garden door and leave her in peace. But just as Nikias was framing a sarcastic reply, Archidike blurted, "What are *you* doing here?"

In that moment, Rhodopis knew she had been recognized. *Curse my luck*, she thought bitterly. *I had hoped I might get by for a few parties at least before I had to dole out any excuses.*

She raised her face languidly to Archidike, but she did not allow her eyes to focus. She couldn't bear to really *see* the other woman's face. "I beg your pardon?"

"Did the Pharaoh let you out of your golden cage?" Archidike said. Then she laughed cruelly. "Or did he throw you out?"

The men looked at one another—and at Rhodopis—with uneasy, puzzled expressions. Rhodopis sat up on the couch; Drakon followed, and made as if to stand. Rhodopis knew he intended to usher Archidike away on her behalf. For a moment, she was tempted to let her companion handle the nuisance of Archidike on his own. But she stayed Drakon with a hand on his thigh. If she, Rhodopis, did not put Archidike in her place now— and do it of her own accord—she would certainly lose the war of rumors and gossip that would follow. She must act decisively, and make Archidike look the fool before word of their confrontation could leave the andron.

In her most cultured speech, Rhodopis said, "I am very sorry; you must have mistaken me for another woman."

Archidike snorted. "I have not, and you know it."

"Archidike," Drakon said coolly, "you *have* made a mistake. This is Eulalia, newly arrived from Lesvos."

"If *she's* Eulalia—" Archidike pointed, one sharp, lacquered nail almost scratching Rhodopis' face— "then I'm an untouched virgin. Even a blind man could see that this is Rhodopis. You all remember—Rhodopis of the rose-gold slippers, whisked away to the Pharaoh's court. What are you playing at?"

Rhodopis laughed lightly. "Now I'm certain you do have me confused with another woman. Or you're jesting with these good men, and with poor me. I've never been to the Pharaoh's palace in my life, let alone his court. I should be so lucky!"

"I'm not joking." Archidike's voice sank to a low, threatening growl. "Nor am I confused. You're either lying, or you've gone mad, and truly believe your own tale."

Rhodopis brushed fluttering fingers against her chest, giving a good show of offense. "I certainly have no reason to lie. Such a thing would soil my reputation, and my family's. Perhaps you have heard of my family; my father is a well-known spice merchant from Lesvos, by the name of—"

"Your family is poor, and from Thrace. And your father is dead."

Rhodopis laughed. "Do I sound like a Thracian? Gods forbid!" The men joined her, though their laughter had taken on a distinctly uncertain note. She turned to Drakon. "Are all the hetaerae in Memphis as coarse as this one—and as credulous? This poor creature is convinced I'm someone else. The dear thing must have an addled mind. I have heard such things can happen."

"What do you mean?" Drakon said.

"Well..." Rhodopis lowered her lashes. "Perhaps it's unkind to speak of it in front of this dear girl, her situation being what it is. But I've heard that if a woman isn't careful who she takes into her bed—if she's not clean, you see—she makes herself susceptible to illnesses. Sooner or later, such afflictions have a devastating effect on the mind. It's tragic, really, for how can it be avoided? One never knows which women are clean or unclean."

Archidike lurched toward Rhodopis; Nikias and Zosimos both reached out at once to restrain her. "You bitch," Archidike spat. "You lying, vile, contemptible bitch!"

Drakon leaped to his feet. "Here, now!" But before he could move toward Archidike, she jerked herself free from the men's hands, whirled, and stormed through the open door into the twilight garden.

"I must apologize," Drakon said to Rhodopis. He was trembling faintly as he resumed his place beside her. "Archidike... no one can predict her, as Nikias said."

Rhodopis waved a hand, brushing away her companion's concern. But inside, she was thrumming with pleasure, relishing the feeling of having sunk a few well-deserved barbs into Archidike's back. "Think nothing of it, my friend. The dear thing will cool her temper, and gods willing, she'll be granted the help she needs. Let's not allow her outburst to ruin our good time."

She reclined on the couch once more, with Drakon's arm around her. But all the night through, as she laughed and jested with her client and his friends, Rhodopis kept one eye on the garden door, poised for the possibility that Archidike might return... and bring the whole construction of Rhodopis' disguise crashing down around her ears.

ANOTHER STARTLING REUNION

THE GODS AND ARCHIDIKE WERE MERCIFUL. THE MERCURIAL hetaera never emerged from the garden—at least, not that Rhodopis saw—being, perhaps, too humiliated by Rhodopis' attack to feel comfortable in the andron for the remainder of the night. Now and then, as Rhodopis conversed with Drakon and his friends, she felt the odd, stray twinge of guilt. It had been very harsh, to suggest something as ruinous as an illness plagued Archidike. But every time that pang of regret stirred in Rhodopis' heart, she smothered the spark of remorse before it could kindle itself to a flame. Archidike deserved what she had received. She had played Rhodopis false, and would have destroyed her career, if the falcon and the Pharaoh had never intervened. Amtes would declare the whole business maat: Rhodopis had restored the balance of her own small, private cosmos by putting Archidike firmly in her place.

Rhodopis had been grimly relieved when Drakon whispered a suggestion that they might leave the party and retire to his own grounds. She wouldn't have stayed to face Archidike's growing wrath for all the gold in Babylon. Alone with Drakon in his beautiful, elegant home, Rhodopis found that all the tricks of her former trade returned with natural ease. She earned not only her payment—the first money she had ever received that was hers alone, with no part owed to any master or keeper of the Stable—but ample and generous compliments from her client.

"I can see why your reputation preceded you," Drakon had said as he walked her through the starlight to her waiting litter. "I understand why all of Memphis resounds with your name. You are the most delightful companion I have ever passed the time with, Lady Eulalia."

Drakon's generosity extended beyond the edge of his bed. He was effulgent with his praise, spreading word among his well-placed friends that the new hetaera from Lesvos was every bit as desirable as rumor made her out to be. Six weeks after her first engagement with Drakon, she had made several new friends among the Greek elite and had worked hard to make each as happy as she'd made Drakon. Better still, she had seen nothing of Archidike since Praxiteles' party. Freedom from that threat, coupled with her success as a hetaera, left a pleasant glow hanging about Rhodopis each night as she climbed, exhausted but satisfied, into her own silken bed.

"But I've no doubt Archidike is still roaming the streets of Memphis," Rhodopis said one morning to Amtes, "busily spreading the word that I am back, and pretending to be someone I am not."

They sat together in the garden, where they could speak without fear of being overheard. A pile of tablets and scrolls was heaped on the table between them—requests for Eulalia's company, sent by some of the finest men in the city. Amtes gave a disparaging grunt as she pored over the contents of the letters.

Rhodopis stirred her breakfast of figs in rose water. "I don't suppose her rumors matter much now, though. Very few hetaerae took any notice of me before; neither did many men. No one else is likely to recognize me. My disguise didn't hold up to Archidike, but Drakon gave no sign of knowing me."

"I hope you're right," Amtes said.

"I suppose I did the right thing at that first party, turning the tide on Archidike. She came out looking like a perfect fool—"

"While the reputation of the great Eulalia of Lesvos grows by the day." Amtes dropped the last scroll on the stack of requests with a pleased air. "I can't keep up with all these letters. It's as if you've worked a spell on the men of this city. All of them insist: they *must* have your company!"

"It's only because I'm still so new." A wash of glumness darkened Rhodopis' mood. "There truly is nothing special about my performances in bed—I know it's true. And I'm good-looking enough, but I'm hardly any great beauty. Once the shimmer of novelty has dulled away, or when a more exotic and fascinating hetaera comes along, I'll lose all my advantage. It worries me terribly, Amtes."

"Why should it worry you?"

Rhodopis sighed. She dropped her spoon into the bowl of figs with a graceless clatter. "Six weeks, and I still haven't found the right allies—the right connections to crumple Amasis' ties with the Greeks. You've been sending your notes to Phanes regularly, I know, but not a single word we've sent has been encouraging."

Rhodopis had tried to soften the blow of her bad news by promising Phanes and the king that she was still working diligently toward their secret end—and that she felt sure of a breakthrough soon. But the truth was, she felt no such certainty. The same fear that had haunted her in Babylon had begun to gnaw at her in Memphis. How long could she fail at her task before the king she served grew anxious, and put her out of the way? Rhodopis had no illusions that Cambyses felt any special attachment to her, no matter how much he had enjoyed her in his bed. Her confession of betrayal had unpicked every last stitch of that goodwill. She must deliver a powerful Greek ally to Cambyses— soon—or she couldn't hope to remain alive much longer.

Oh, why did I ever agree to this? I should have sent Phanes pack-

ing. I could be enjoying a quiet, peaceful life in Babylon right now. I could still be a wife of the king!

"There is nothing for it but to keep trying," Amtes said sensibly.

"You're right. I know you're right." Rhodopis picked up her spoon again and ate steadily, determined to face whatever lay ahead with dignity and grace.

"Well, Mistress," Amtes said, turning back to her stack of letters with business-like efficiency, "you must decide which of these men you will see tonight."

"Whichever is the best connected," Rhodopis said at once.

"They are all well connected. This is Memphis, after all."

"I've attended ever so many grand parties with crowds of guests," Rhodopis mused. "And I've got nothing to show for it. Perhaps this time I ought to take a different path. A small, intimate affair, I think, with a handful of distinguished guests. Or even something entirely private, if we have such a request. Perhaps a different setting—a different mood—will give me the chance I need to bring a man over to the cause."

"Leave it to me," Amtes said. "I'll find just the right client for you. Meanwhile, you must go and bathe, and call one of your servants in; I'm going to send her off to fetch a physician who's skilled with massage. Look at yourself—your shoulders look stiff as stone. You must relax if you're to make it through the next few weeks with your wits intact."

"Just as you say," Rhodopis agreed. She rose and went inside her house to prepare for the evening ahead. She felt resolute as a soldier marching off to war.

۶

THAT NIGHT, Amtes sent Rhodopis off to a small but elegant affair, a gathering of a dozen men of the glass merchants' guild. They were all older fellows, most of them gray-haired with lines around their eyes. As such, they were not given to wild times; Rhodopis felt sure that whatever else the gods may have in store for her tonight, she was unlikely to encounter Archidike at such a dull and dignified party.

The host, Chares, was a pleasant, grandfatherly man with rather stooped shoulders and an endearing creak in his voice. Nevertheless, despite his age, he welcomed Rhodopis with a warmth and charm that made her feel pleasantly secure. As he led her toward the andron, he slipped a small purse, heavy with silver, into her hand.

"I am still somewhat new to Memphis," she said, surprised. "Is it the custom here to pay a hetaera before she entertains?"

"No, Lady Eulalia, it is not. But if you should choose not to slip off with any of my guests," Chares said with a quick wink, "I still want you to be well compensated. I have asked you here for your company, first and foremost... and for your beauty, of course, which so enhances my humble home. You have no obligation to do anything else, unless you fancy it. But I won't see you go without pay, whatever may come."

"I thank you," Rhodopis said graciously. "It is a most kind and thoughtful gesture."

She was, as Chares had said, a general ornament of his party —one of only four hetaerae present. As she was not assigned to entertain any particular man, Rhodopis enjoyed considerable freedom to move about Chares' small but pleasant andron and his larger, more opulent garden. Amtes had chosen well: at such an event, Rhodopis would find ample opportunity to make new acquaintances. Surely one among them would lead to a useful connection between Egypt and Greece.

Chares' guests were as pleasant as their host. They strewed Rhodopis' path with flattery; they took great pains to offer her sweets and savories, fine wine and enjoyable conversation. After a time, someone called, "Let's have one of these beautiful women dance, shall we?" and Rhodopis' heart constricted with painful longing. How she would have loved to dance for an audience again—especially one so refined. But she and Amtes had already agreed that dancing would be too great a risk. Black hair and the very finest clothes might fool Memphis, but a reckless display of a truly unique feature would undo everything in the blink of an eye.

"Do you dance, Eulalia?" one of the guests asked.

She lowered her eyes. "I am afraid not, Good Man. The gods did not bless me with grace—nor with a sense of rhythm." She turned to another of the hetaerae, tall and buxom with nut-brown hair. "But I have heard that Aspasia here dances beautifully."

Aspasia, too, attempted to demur. "I'm no sort of dancer at all. Perhaps one of the other hetaerae—"

"Come, now," Chares said. "I've seen you dance a dozen times, Aspasia. No one can compare!"

"Yes," said one of the other men. "I watched Aspasia dance at Iason's party two weeks ago. I'm sure we would all enjoy a repeat performance."

Cajoled, Aspasia took up a pose in the center of the andron and waited for the music to start. The moment the harp chords swelled, a curious sensation thundered through Rhodopis' body, envy and appreciation twined in a single, white-hot bolt. A flavor both bitter and sweet rose in her throat. She seized a fresh cup of wine from a passing servant's tray and drank deeply, trying to wash the cloying taste from her tongue.

Aspasia's dance was good, and her enjoyment of both music and movement seemed honest enough. But Rhodopis identified a thousand things she would do differently—better—if only she were dancing instead. As the music swelled to its climax and Aspasia spun gracefully back to her starting position, Rhodopis was obliged to press the heel of one foot hard against the toes of the other, forcing herself to remain still. What a torment it was, to sit idly watching, pretending she was enjoying the entertainment without betraying the least flush of envy.

When Aspasia posed to accept her praises, Rhodopis excused herself from Chares' couch and paced restlessly across the andron. She lingered at the garden door, sipping slowly from her cup, hoping her body would soon forget that terrible, compelling itch, the long-suppressed desire to commit every movement and emotion to music. She watched the bats flit over Chares' garden, swift and darting, dipping down through the deep-blue shadows of the night on a sudden spread of angular wings. Her mind wandered through a mist of hopelessly mingled thoughts, shapeless things she could not sort, while the music from Aspasia's dance repeated relentlessly inside her head. With a sudden surge of desperation, Rhodopis recalled how she had danced alone in the desert—on nights very much like this one, violet and blue—with only Amtes' bone flute and the groans of the camels for accompaniment.

A slow, stirring awareness breached her reverie, pulling her back from the edge of darkness. A name... someone had called a name out in greeting, and she knew it well. Rhodopis tensed. She did not turn around, but every sense strained to its natural limit, waiting for someone to speak that name again. A sudden fear chilled and soured her.

It's not him. I didn't hear his name. It can't be him; the gods wouldn't be so cruel.

But when, Rhodopis wondered bitterly, had the gods ever been good to her?

Someone shouted out that name once more, and there was no mistaking it now. "Charaxus! How good to see you, my young friend."

Sickness swelled in Rhodopis' belly. She breathed deeply, trying to calm her frantic thoughts. Her hand tightened on the wine cup, and it shook until a few drops spilled over the rim, trickling down her knuckles. *Think, damn you. Think! Aesop didn't train you to go to pieces at the slightest little fright. And you've faced worse than this, besides.*

So Charaxus was here. Very well; she could not avoided him. Rhodopis understood at once that there would be no point in denying her true identity to him, as she had done with Archidike. Charaxus had been madly in love with her—perhaps he still was. He would certainly recognize her, and no denial would put him off. She could not evade him. She must take this wild horse firmly in hand straight away, and tame it before it could gallop beyond her reach.

While Chares' guests were still greeting Charaxus, Rhodopis set off around the perimeter of the andron, drifting gracefully from one patch of shadow to the next. Two of Chares' friends pulled her into one of their half-drunken jests; she laughed happily at the old fellows' game, then moved on as quickly as she could. She tossed a winsome smile over her shoulder as if she hadn't a care in the world —and all the while her heart rang loudly in her ears. She was terribly, unshakably aware of Charaxus—his familiar form looming in the periphery of her vision, the tenor note of his voice cutting across the murmur and music of the party with invasive force. Finally, Rhodopis slipped behind a large pillar. There, trembling, she waited until Charaxus disentangled himself from his friends, accepted a cup of wine from the pourer, and began to wander through the andron.

She listened to his voice as he made his greetings and his excuses, drawing ever nearer to Rhodopis' hiding place. She swallowed hard, firming up her spine. Then, when he was close enough to her hiding place, she hissed softly.

Charaxus looked around, startled, but he saw nothing. Rhodopis edged out from behind the pillar, letting the light of the nearest lamp fall warmly on her face for the briefest moment. Just as she slipped behind the pillar again, Rhodopis caught the flash of recognition as it lit Charaxus' eyes—a sudden flowering of disbelief, mingled with surging hope and joy.

Quickly, before he could utter any foolish declarations of love, Rhodopis held a finger to her lips. She nodded toward the garden door, then turned at once and left the andron, praying to all the gods that he would keep his mouth shut and follow her. It seemed the shock of seeing her again had rendered Charaxus silent with awe. He slipped out into the evening air behind her, quickly but quietly.

"Thank the gods we can be alone here," Rhodopis said breathlessly before Charaxus could speak. She threw herself into his arms, nearly knocking the cup of wine from his hand. He embraced her tightly, uttering a low, wordless moan of adoration. Rhodopis felt him bend toward her, trying to kiss her; she pushed away from his chest before his lips could find her own. "You can't know how badly I've wanted to speak to you, to send you a message—oh, anything, Rax!"

"Rhodopis, my love—my life! Whatever happened to you? That woman who runs Xanthes' operation—"

"Vélona."

"Yes, that's the one. She is so unpleasant, I must say. After she stopped answering my letters, I went to Xanthes' estate many times and asked to see you, but all that woman would tell me was that you'd gone off to the Pharaoh's harem. She wouldn't utter another word on the subject. It was terribly rude treatment, after I'd been so generous as your patron."

"It's true," Rhodopis said. "The Pharaoh took a fancy to me and swept me off into the harem, but I didn't care for him at all. How could the Pharaoh's household interest me? Oh, Rax!—all the riches in the world can't compare with your love. I've missed you so. I was hoping I would find you, praying I would, once I got out. The Pharaoh let me go, you see, but only if I promised to leave Memphis forever and never come back. He swore his heart would break if he knew I was here, within reach but never to be his."

"I can understand him," Charaxus said huskily. "You're a treasure no man would want to give up."

"But I couldn't leave Memphis—not until I found you again. So you see, I must hide in plain sight. That's why I look so strange, with my hair dyed and all—and it's why I must use a different name now. No one must know it's me, Rax. Amasis will never let me go a second time. If he knows I defied his orders and stayed here to find you, why... I fear very much that he would separate us... forever. You do take my meaning, don't you, darling?"

Charaxus nodded slowly. "It seems the sort of thing a jealous king would do."

"But we're together again now. That's all that matters! And so long as no one ever learns it's truly me, we need not fear Amasis."

Charaxus drew a short, sharp breath, as if his heart pained him. "It truly is you. I'd almost given up hope. I'd thought I would never see you again, and I must let the beautiful dream of our happiness die." His voice quivered with barely restrained emotion. "But we really will be together, after all. You are in my arms..." He embraced her again; she pressed her cheek against his shoulder. "This is no dream. It's real, isn't it, my treasure? We are united once more. The gods have blessed us with their mercy."

"Praise the gods!" Rhodopis said, hoping the break in her voice sounded more like passion than the laughter she felt welling in her chest.

"You will come to me now, won't you? Now that you're free of the Pharaoh and that coarse lout Xanthes."

"Of course I will, darling! Nothing can keep me away. As long as you swear to keep my secret, that is. I could never live with myself if Amasis found out, and... and *punished* you. Oh, Rax! No one must ever know!"

"No, my love... no one shall learn it from me. But Memphis is a danger to us both now. You must come away with me, Rho—"

he caught himself abruptly. "—My love. Leave Memphis with me... not as a hetaera, but as my bride."

"Oh!" Rhodopis said. Her face heated. She should have counted on this, should have seen it coming. If only she'd had more time to think, to plan...! Stalling for time, her mind working frantically, she said, "But where would we go?"

"Why, to Lesvos, of course—to my family's estates. We will be safe there. Amasis cannot touch us. No one—nothing can touch our love!"

The improbability of it! Again, the threat of laughter stirred within her. Eulalia was supposed to be from Lesvos, and here was Charaxus, proposing to carry her off to that very island! *If he has his way, reckon I'll find out whether Lesvos has mountains or not. But I mustn't let him think there's any possibility. It's too absurd to imagine.*

"I can't leave Memphis... not just yet. I've debts to Xanthes that I must pay off. Amasis was going to pay them, naturally, but he won't do it now that I've left."

"I'll pay the debts for you," Charaxus said at once. "You'll want for nothing as my wife. I'll care for you so tenderly, so devotedly. Oh, do let me make you happy, my jewel! It's all I've ever wanted."

Damn him!

She thought quickly. "But I am working to get some of my friends out of Xanthes' Stable, too. I can't leave Memphis until I've helped them set up on the outside, as free hetaerae. I owe them a debt of another kind—a debt of gratitude and honor." There was certainly no one in the Stable to whom Rhodopis owed any such thing, but the emphasis on honor was something the high-minded Charaxus seemed to accept, albeit reluctantly.

"I suppose," he said slowly, "it will have to do, if I cannot convince you to come away with me now. But how long will it take? How much longer must we wait to be married? My heart will burst with the strain of it!"

"Not long, I hope." Rhodopis gazed up at him with wide eyes, smiling her sweetest, most beguiling smile. She could see in the helpless shake of his head, the melting look in his eyes, that her display of innocence and devotion had every desired effect. "Oh, Rax, I'm so happy to have found you! How the gods have blessed us. I don't know how I lived without you, these two long years."

And how in the names of all the cruel, capricious gods will I keep you at arm's length long enough to see my mission through?

17

THE PIRATE OF SAMOS

CHARAXUS ROLLED FROM HIS BED. HE LEFT THE TUNIC HE'D removed lying on the floor where he'd dropped it, and pulled a fresh, clean one from a cedar chest. It hung loosely on his body. Rhodopis watched rather listlessly as he opened the shutters of his bed-chamber window. A river breeze entered, carrying the crisp scent of the Nile. The air held a certain familiar spice, too—the promise of warm weather to come, and all too soon after that, the thick, pounding heat of summer.

Rhodopis did not rise from the bed. She sprawled on her back, sniffing the air despondently, feeling the inevitable advance of the seasons. She had been in Memphis for two months now; winter had all but passed. She had dispatched eight notes to Cambyses and Phanes, but none had contained the message she knew the king expected. This week, Cambyses finally answered. The king's reply was terse: *Deliver a useful connection, if you expect me to find any use for you. Do not delay any longer.* It hadn't taken much insight to read the threat in Cambyses' message. Time was running short. Her body seemed to know it as well as her mind; there was never a moment now when her heart did not race. A constant lump had taken up residence inside her throat;

Rhodopis often imagined it was the tip of Cambyses' sword, pressing, waiting.

"When we reach Lesvos, you'll marvel at the views." Charaxus lounged against the window sill, watching the river flow steadily by. "The Nile is pretty enough, I suppose. It is the greatest river in the world, of course, but even the grandest river is nothing, compared to the sea. The sea around Lesvos is blue as sapphires, dotted with lovely dark islands. It's a sight worth looking at, I tell you."

Rhodopis sighed. She stared up at the frieze carved into the ceiling—storks wading among tall reeds—and allowed Charaxus' happy chatter to recede from her consciousness. His joy at having her back was unfettered. Rhodopis found his attentions more stifling than ever before. Charaxus had thrown a most unwelcome complication into her maneuvers, and the gods knew her work had already been difficult enough to manage. Now she had to spend every third or fourth night in Charaxus' bed, playing at lovers to keep him happy and complacent. One fit of anger or jealousy and Charaxus might very well spill her secret, unmasking the enigmatic Eulalia for all of Memphis to see. Every night she lay in his arms was a waste of precious time—a chance squandered to find and deliver the connection Cambyses expected.

Charaxus nattered on, glad as a hoopoe in a berry patch. "We'll go sailing as often as you like, my love. There are many tiny islands worth exploring—quite private, too, so we can have them all to ourselves, little kingdoms for us to rule. And I know you'll adore my family, when you finally meet them. My mother is the very best woman, kind and gentle, and my sister Sappho—"

If only I had a boat now, Rhodopis thought darkly. *I'd sail away to some tiny island off Lesvos and live in a hut made of sticks and mud, and count myself lucky, so long as neither Amasis nor Cambyses could ever find me. Nor Charaxus, either.*

The thought sent a new tingle up Rhodopis' spine. Ah—a

boat! That was exactly the sort of resource Cambyses' hoped-for man must hold. A fast boat, capable of sailing quickly from Memphis to any Grecian port. And the man who sailed it ought to be well acquainted with Greeks of real power, the sort of contacts who held kings and princes in the palms of their hands. She had met plenty of merchants, and all of them sailed to every port, north and south, that they could reach from the Memphian shore. But they were all so entrenched in their trades that they were content to stay put for most of the year, lounging about the city while hired men did most of the *real* work of a trader.

"Why, that old Samian pirate sailed better than any man I've ever met," Charaxus was saying. "Sappho and I went out on his fastest ship for a lark once, but we damn near lost our lives, or so it seemed to me. I've never seen anything go so fast on the water as that ship of his. I was terrified—I'm not afraid to admit it—but Sappho just laughed into the wind, as if it were no more unusual than riding a horse."

A bitter, ironic smile tugged at her mouth. *A Samian boat, was it?* She couldn't help but remember Iadmon's ship, the *Samian Wind*—the one that had carried her here from Tanis. She turned her mind dully toward those thoughts, reliving her days on the deck of the *Samian Wind*, more as a welcome distraction from her fears than because the memory was particularly sweet. Newly separated from her family—from the only life she had known— her poor, tender, childish heart had attached itself to Aesop's kindness. Oh, she had not loved Aesop, of course. Young as she was, love had never crossed her mind. But he had been good to her. She still thought of him as the only real friend she'd ever had. Rhodopis wondered whether Aesop was safe now, whether he was happy. And she wondered whether she could ever expect to feel safe or happy again.

Charaxus talked on, unaware that Rhodopis' mind had wandered far away. "—But that pirate knew more than I'd given him credit for. I dare say he still does. He had quite the reputation for knowing things no other man ought to know. It was his connections with the rulers he worked for, I believe. He would do a job of work for one, and accomplish what no one else could— his ships were so very fast, he could go where no one else dared, and in half the time it would take anyone else, too—and once he'd earned the gratitude for this king or that, he would use that gratitude for leverage, and extract all sorts of rare things from their treasuries. Clever." Charaxus laughed heartily. "Ah, me. What fun Sappho and I had with him, even if I was sure I'd fall overboard and drown. He's in Memphis now, or so I hear. I ought to find him and see if he still remembers me, though I confess, I'm half afraid he would put me on his boat again, and furl out those great, red sails, and set the thing flying so fast that the wind strips the flesh right off my bones. I'm not as young as I was! I can no longer withstand the rigors of a pirate's life."

Rhodopis sat up slowly. The linen sheets fell away from her naked body; the air was not as cool as it should have been. The summer would be here soon. Time passed all too quickly.

"What did you say his name was, Rax? That Samian pirate of yours?"

Charaxus turned from the window. He smiled rather possessively at her nudity. "Polycrates. Yes, I heard just yesterday that he was here, though no one could say why. Come to do the bidding of one of his friends, I suppose, whatever that secret task may be."

Charaxus left off all thought of Polycrates of Samos; he came back to the bed, stripping off the blue tunic as he went. He dropped it on the floor, atop the other he'd shed earlier that day. Then he slid beneath the sheet and began planting a trail of kisses up Rhodopis' arm. His lips traveled to her shoulder, then to the soft curve of her throat.

Rhodopis pulled back from, shrugging off his attempts to nuzzle closer. "Tell me more about that pirate," she said lightly. "He sounds amusing."

"I'll amuse you far more," Charaxus promised.

"No, *really*, Rax. I can't go again today; you've worn me clean out. A girl needs a rest now and then, you know."

Still, Charaxus persisted. His fingers moved busily under the sheet, teasing Rhodopis' thighs, circling her navel. She gritted her teeth to stop herself from shrieking at him to leave off, to keep his hands to his damnable self.

"I'm curious," she said, affecting a casual yawn. "I've never met a pirate before. What could bring him to Egypt, I wonder? It's a terrible, long way from Samos."

"Oh, Polycrates goes all over the world—wherever he's sent. He'll do for money what a thousand other men will not. That's the way with pirates. They're daring—" Charaxus kissed her neck, "—and adventuresome—" his mouth moved to her cheek, leaving an unpleasantly wet mark "—and so fearless they're *dangerous*." He nipped her earlobe, causing Rhodopis to start, uttering a little gasp of surprise. "But most of all, they're greedy. Enough silver can buy a pirate's hand—and his ship—for any task you can imagine."

Charaxus pushed her gently back onto the mattress. She rolled at once, dodging his hands, leaving him to groan with frustration as he cast his eyes up toward the carved ceiling, begging the gods for patience.

"He must be working for someone here in Egypt, then," Rhodopis said. "Do you think the Pharaoh has hired him?"

"He may be working for anyone in all the world," Charaxus said, rather shortly. "And as for who the Pharaoh has or has not hired, I'm sure you know more than I. You spent so long in the Pharaoh's company, after all."

There was no mistaking the note of bitterness in his words. That was no surprise; Charaxus resented Amasis for having taken his lover away, and although they never spoke of it, Rhodopis could tell the fact that she had lain with the king of Egypt gnawed at his thoughts unceasingly. Rhodopis supposed it was a tall order, for any man to follow one of the wealthiest kings in the world, and expect to impress a woman more. *If he knew how many times I lay with Cambyses—and how Cambyses pleased me—poor Rax would fall dead of envy right here and now.*

"But in truth," Charaxus added, "Polycrates isn't terribly likely to work for the Pharaoh, even if he is a pirate. At least, old Amasis would have to offer him a truly staggering sum to arouse his interest in the first place."

"What do you mean? You said pirates would do anything for pay. What does it matter so much, who hands over the silver?"

"It has been a long time since I've seen Polycrates—much may have changed—but I recall him as an inveterate hater of Egypt, and of all things Egyptian."

Rhodopis prayed the thrill of hope in her breast did not translate to a visible flush of her tender complexion. "Oh?" she said casually.

Charaxus laughed. "Once—some time before that wild sailing trip Sappho and I took with him—Polycrates told me he hoped Egypt would fall in upon itself. It's too old and dusty, he said, like some dark tomb, and tombs never hold anything that isn't dead. Words to that effect; I don't remember exactly what he said, for it was years in the past."

"Surely Egypt isn't as bad as that."

"No, but the Pharaohs have always been hard on pirates up in the Delta—it's an Egyptian tradition—and no doubt Polycrates has been forced to pay heavy tolls to access the Nile and ply his trade. I'm only assuming the reason. All I know is, Polycrates held a distinctively negative opinion of Egypt, the last time we had occasion to talk."

"I don't suppose he is working for Amasis, then."

"Certainly not. If Amasis needed that sort of work done, I am sure he could find more affordable—and more affable—men."

Rhodopis' stomach fluttered. Was this, at last, the chance she needed? Had the gods pierced her dark despair, provided a tiny crack through which some hope gleamed? That glint of possibility was silver-bright, yet slim and fleeting. In Babylon, she had seized a narrow opportunity when Ishtar had presented it. She must do the same now, and trust that the gods would once again uphold her. But even as her heart raced with newfound hope, Rhodopis counseled herself sternly. You can't let expectation run wild. Over the past two months, she had met more men than she could count, hoping each new acquaintance would lead to a breakthrough. And countless times, those fragile hopes were dashed. This Samian pirate might very well prove to be another fruitless branch.

But if I don't try—if I don't meet him myself and find out—the gods might never give me another chance.

Rhodopis rolled back toward Charaxus. She kissed him lightly on the lips. "This pirate friend of yours sounds amusing. I want to meet him myself."

Charaxus cringed, an expression of pure chagrin. "It has been several years since I saw him last. He may not remember me at all, let alone count me a friend. And... he is a terribly coarse fellow, Rhodopis. That is usual among men of his sort, yet still, I hesitate to expose a woman to such a... personality."

Rhodopis laughed; there was nothing feigned in her amusement. "You hesitate to expose me? Me, a hetaera? Any person might say a hetaera is ten times coarser than the very worst pirate on his most offensive day."

"You won't be a hetaera forever," Charaxus said quietly. "You'll be my wife soon, a true lady of Lesvos."

I'll be dead soon, bobbing face-down along the Nile, unless I bring someone useful over to Cambyses' side. "Well," she said with forced cheer, "I'm neither a wife nor a lady of Lesvos yet. If I'm ever to meet a real Samian pirate, I had better do it now, while I'm still a hetaera. Oh, won't you, Rax? Life has been too dull lately. This winter is hanging on relentlessly. I need something to look forward to, or I'll go mad. Let's have a little fun, can't we?" She kissed him again. This time, her kiss was slow and lingering.

"Come, darling. No pirate can hurt me while you're here to protect me. Won't you say yes?"

"Well..." Charaxus hesitated again. Rhodopis beat her lashes, feeding him her most charming and seductive smile. "Well, all right," he finally agreed. "I'll make some inquiries. If he has the time... and if he still remembers me... I'll see what can be done. Anything to keep you happy, my love."

ࢥ

RHODOPIS HAD WARNED herself for days not to become overly excited about the prospect of Polycrates. But despite her sensible admonitions, she couldn't quell the fluttering sensation in her stomach as Charaxus' guests began to arrive at his small, elegant home. She had dressed in her most beautiful gown, a smooth, shimmering silk of carnelian red. She waited just inside Charaxus' portico in a pool of golden lamplight, greeting each guest with dignity and quiet grace as he arrived. It was a task reserved for the mistress of the house in Lesvos, Charaxus had told her. She was acting in the place of a wife, taking on a role she neither wanted nor was suited for—all to please Charaxus. Rhodopis felt as if she were being tried out, like the singers and players who audition before masters of performing troops. Yet that was silly, she thought glumly as she watched another litter arrive in the courtyard. Charaxus had already set his heart and mind on marrying Rhodopis. This was no trial of her capacity or fitness for a wife's work. No doubt, Charaxus intended the role as a sort of gift—a privilege, a treat he assumed Rhodopis would savor.

Rhodopis wouldn't have minded the task if she'd had any real intention of marrying Charaxus. Indeed, she might have been flattered. But as it was, acting the good little wife only made her feel all the more used and confined. She was resolved to play the role perfectly, though. Wasn't she a hetaera? Hadn't she been trained for a hetaera's life, fitted for the position by the best two men in the business—Iadmon and Aesop? And what was a hetaera's life, if not one feigned role after another? She set her mind to play this part without complaint, with all the poise and aplomb of a well-polished hetaera. Tonight would go well; it *must*. She would make it so by main force, if necessary. Nothing— not even Charaxus' sentimental fantasies about a happy life in Lesvos—would ruin the evening.

As they stepped from the litter, Rhodopis greeted the next two guests, gentlemen older than Charaxus by some ten or fifteen years.

"You must be Good Men Dareios and Eusebius," she said. She lifted the vase of rose water that waited beside the nearest pillar. "Please, freshen your hands. I've a towel here for you."

When the guests had dipped their fingers in the water and patted their hands dry, Rhodopis gestured to the servant who lurked nearby, waiting for her summons. "Wine?" Rhodopis said, offering each man a small cup.

"By Zeus," said Eusebius, "it is a delightful surprise to find traditional female hospitality so far from home."

"One never expects such inviting domesticity in Egypt," Dareios agreed.

Rhodopis beamed at them with a gentle, wifely smile. "I will see to it that you enjoy the evening, Good Men. Nothing could make me happier. Please, do go in. The master of the house waits in the andron."

More guests arrived—a fifth, a sixth, a ninth and a tenth. Rhodopis treated every man with the same charm and kindness, but her hopes wilted with each successive arrival. Inside the house, Charaxus had already cued the musicians; a traditional Samian folk song came forlornly out into the courtyard, the sound pooling rather weakly between the garden walls. The kitchen-maid would be making her rounds now, filling each man's cup of wine. The dinner party had begun, but Polycrates of Samos had not arrived.

Rhodopis knew she must return to the andron. Charaxus would be waiting for her. But she couldn't make herself abandon her hope. She lingered by the portico, waiting for the pirate, even as the night grew colder and the moon crept higher in the sky. A half hour passed while she watched the entry gate, praying for the gods to send their mercy. But the courtyard remained empty, and inside, the musicians played on.

A gentle hand touched her shoulder; Rhodopis started.

"Come inside, my love," Charaxus said. "My guests want to see you, and bask in your radiant light."

Reluctantly, Rhodopis followed him inside. She lay beside him on his eating couch, simpering at his guests.

"This is Eulalia," Charaxus said proudly, "the celebrated hetaera from my homeland."

The men murmured their approval. "We thought you had gone and found yourself a wife," one of them said.

Charaxus smiled and squeezed Rhodopis' shoulder. "Perhaps someday soon."

How can any of these fools think me an admirable Greek wife? Rhodopis thought, queasy with irritation. *A proper Greek woman wouldn't linger in the andron. I wonder why Charaxus hasn't sent me off to that dull little gynaeceum he keeps for his female servants. It's where a proper Greek woman would eat her supper, rather than lying about like a whore on a man's couch.*

But of course, Rhodopis could not afford to let her disappointment to show. Charaxus' happiness was of paramount importance—as was his complacency. If he wished to display her like a common porna, even as he played this tedious game of husband-and-wife, then so be it. Rhodopis emanated a glow she did not feel, responding to the men's compliments with as much grace and proper feminine humility as she could conjure up. When they made their jests, she laughed musically and even offered a few of her own, carefully measured to please the palates of these refined and dignified men.

Charaxus seemed to grow more satisfied by the hour as he watched Rhodopis play the hostess in his home. His beaming smile set her secret fury boiling. The gods knew, if she were ever to become his wife, Rhodopis would take no role such as this in Charaxus' home. She would be sequestered away behind thick curtains and stone walls, hidden from the eyes of male visitors, not holding forth in the andron, coaxing laughter from the men as she filled their cups with wine. Did Charaxus want a wife or a hetaera? He could not have both. Such a woman would never be accepted, in either Lesvos or Greek-controlled Memphis.

An hour dragged by, as did the first courses of the meal. The food was delicious and well prepared, but Rhodopis found she could eat very little. Disappointment and anxiety sat like twin stones in her gut, heavy and dry. The servants entered, bearing a palate-cleanser on their trays: bright green cucumbers stuffed with pungent goat cheese. The cheese looked entirely too thick and rich for Rhodopis to handle now. Her stomach lurched at the mere thought. She must find some gracious way to leave the party early. She had played the perfect wife for as long as she could stand; now she wanted only to hide away in Charaxus' bedchamber, where she could give vent to her stormy emotions and weep without restraint over how cruel fate had thwarted every last one of her desperate plans. But just as she was gathering her skirt to stand, a booming laugh rang from the edge of the andron. Rhodopis sat up sharply, staring.

A great, dark-haired man with a curly beard was striding purposefully into the room. Charaxus' steward scurried along behind him, protesting feebly, trying to convince the newcomer to slow down, to give his name, to observe the established protocols of a high-class supper party. For one terrible moment, Rhodopis thought Cambyses had come to Egypt himself, for the express purpose of striking off her head. The newcomer looked so much like the Persian king, tall and broad and bearded.

"I am sorry, Master," the steward said to Charaxus. "I tried to get this man to wait, but he—"

"It's all right, Epaphras," Charaxus said to his servant. "He is here at my invitation, and he has always enjoyed making an entrance." Charaxus rose from his couch and said heartily, "Polycrates! My old friend; you've come after all. It has been too long since I last saw you."

Rhodopis shuddered with relief. She rose, too, forcing herself to do so with grace, fighting the urge to skip across the andron singing. The gods had relented after all!

"I am so pleased to make your acquaintance, Good Man Polycrates," Rhodopis said. She offered a hand. "My name is Eulalia."

Polycrates took his time in kissing the backs of her fingers, staring the whole while into Rhodopis' eyes. "What a toothsome little thing you've got here, Charaxus. A hetaera, eh? Perhaps I'll take her to my bed tonight!" He roared with laughter.

Charaxus shifted on his feet, flushing; the other guests covered their mouths to hide a collective amusement that was perhaps a bit too keen and eager for propriety. *Ah*, Rhodopis thought. *This Polycrates fellow hasn't been in Memphis long, but it seems he already knows it's considered great sport around here to bait Charaxus, the tiresome dandy of Lesvos.* She liked Polycrates straight away.

Recovering himself, Charaxus indicated the empty couch that waited for Polycrates. He called for wine.

"Plenty of it," Polycrates added to the pourer as the young man came forward with his pitcher.

"I haven't seen you for a good many years," Eusebius said to Polycrates as the latter settled on his couch. "I recall we had an unfortunate encounter some time ago, in the Delta."

"We did," Polycrates said. "This was ten years back, at least. Old Eusebius and I had both just moored our ships outside Tanis, at one of the toll stations. He had his crew dressed right smart, all in matching tunics with his colors on display, like some fucking king's flag in the middle of a battle." Polycrates wheezed with laughter. "Eusebius went ashore for some reason or other—to enjoy taking a shit without hanging his arse over the rail of a ship, I suppose—and while he was gone, I coaxed a few of his crew over to my boat. I had good beer and some nice honey wine, and a few pretty girls traveling with me. Eusebius's men came over for conversation, to wait while the inspectors made their rounds. Well, I waved the inspectors over to my ship first. They took stock of my goods—the goods they could see, at least; I've got more than a few hidden compartments on my boats—and they saw Eusebius' men there, painted up in those unmistakable colors like a lot of two-for-a-hedj pornae! 'Right, then,' the inspectors said to me, 'we'll add this lot of cargo to the totals on Eusebius' other ship.' I said, 'Excellent. My master Eusebius has told me to be off as soon as I've passed inspection, for this cargo has to arrive at its destination tomorrow, and we can't spare another hour.' The fools waved me along. I sent all of Eusebius' men back to the shore and sailed away... and Eusebius was kind enough to pay the toll for me!"

Polycrates bellowed with glee again. The other men cast worried glances at Eusebius, but the old fellow was laughing, too. Evidently, time had taken the sting out of the pirate's trick.

Rhodopis observed Polycrates carefully as the next course was brought around. She found she had enough appetite to eat heartily, now; the soup of onions and radishes was delicious. The Samian pirate launched a barrage of jokes and outrageous tales across the andron, proving himself every bit as coarse and shocking as Charaxus had warned he would be. Rhodopis found Polycrates rather amusing. She would have liked to lie on his couch instead of Rax's, if only to goad Polycrates into ever more entertaining comments, and test how deep the well of his shocking stories ran. But of course, she was more interested in the pirate's fleet—and his connections within Greece—than his fascinating array of curses and scandalous tales.

When they'd finished their onion soup, the guests stood, stretching, and allowed the servants to clear away the dishes. The party wandered out into the garden, leaving Charaxus' people to freshen the small andron. There they would while away the time until they were called back for the sweet course. Rhodopis slipped away from Charaxus as the little crowd spilled out from beneath the portico, into the crisp night air. Now was the moment she had been waiting for these days past—these days that had felt like years. Now, at last, she could speak to the pirate alone. If the gods were good, she would work the charms of a hetaera upon him, and Polycrates would be hers.

Rhodopis found Polycrates among the flowers—an improbable setting for the hulking man. He was bent low over a pot of jasmine, sniffing lustily at its sweet, early buds. It was so strange to see a man of his stature worshiping those white blooms like a blushing maiden that Rhodopis giggled as she approached.

Polycrates looked up, grinning rather sheepishly. "You've caught me; I do have a weakness for sweet and pretty things."

"Do you?" She swayed closer. "What other sweet, pretty things do you enjoy?"

"I can tell you one thing—" Polycrates gestured toward the silk sash snugged around her waist. No—he was indicating a place somewhat lower than that. "*There's* a flower I'd much rather smell."

Rhodopis' mouth fell open in feigned shock at his comment. "My good man! That is an outrageous thing to say to a woman of my sort."

"A woman of your sort? You've heard worse, I dare say."

She smiled enigmatically. "Perhaps I have. Shall we walk? There aren't many paths through Charaxus' little garden, but we can at least be off by ourselves."

"D'you fancy being off alone with a man of my sort?"

"Perhaps I do."

Polycrates offered his arm with as much dignity as any of Charaxus' better guests might have done. Rhodopis slid her hand to the warm crook of his elbow. His muscles were firm beneath his rough skin. Polycrates led toward the rear of the garden until they were as far from Charaxus as they could get.

"You haven't been in Memphis long," Rhodopis said.

"No, Lady Eulalia. I try to avoid Egypt as much as my work permits. The tolls and taxes are burdensome, and Eusebius is not always conveniently to hand."

She laughed lightly. "I sometimes find Egypt rather tiresome, myself."

"I must say," Polycrates said, "I find Old Egypt more palatable since it became Southern Greece. I don't miss much about Egypt as it was before."

"Before?"

"In my younger days."

"Ah," she said, plucking a winter flower, smelling it casually, "I thought you had meant before Amasis came to the throne."

"I suppose I do mean exactly that. But some of Egypt's old shortcomings have been covered up nicely by Greek importations. Hetaerae have improved the place immeasurably, for example... and you are among the prettiest I've ever seen."

She tucked her flower into his beard. "Surely you've seen prettier hetaerae than I."

"I have."

Rhodopis gasped with pretended ire. "You aren't supposed to say such things, Polycrates, even if they are true. You ought to insist I'm the most beautiful woman the gods ever made."

He laughed. "That's how the game is played, isn't it? Gods, but I'm glad to be in the company of a hetaera again. I've been on the sea for too long, and then on the river. And though I will admit the ordinary women here in Memphis are well enough, in their way, there's no woman who can compare to a real Greek hetaera —not if you're after a good time."

"Surely some of those ordinary women know how to have a good time."

"The Greeks might. The Egyptians don't," he said shortly.

"You don't seem to have a very high opinion of Egypt."

"Should I? It's a dusty old place, stodgy and all too traditional. The world moves on—the world improves—but Egypt remains, unchanging, like honey in a sealed jar. It's unnatural."

"I understand it has changed rather a lot, under Amasis."

"That it has," Polycrates said. There was something glum in his words. "But the people aren't best pleased. If they had their way, Amasis would have been a king like all the hundreds who came before him. I have no special love for Amasis, but at least he has given Egypt a bit of a stir."

"Shaken it up, you mean."

"Yes, exactly. Now--whether anything new and original grows up out of the dust he's agitated remains to be seen. I don't have much hope; once Amasis is gone, that dust will settle back into its old patterns. All will be as it was before... and before... and long before that."

"I admit that I do find Egypt rather tedious," Rhodopis said. "I miss Lesvos. But I'm here to make my fortune, and there's more silver to be had in Memphis just now than anywhere else."

"I'm here to make my fortune, too. Nothing else could have drawn me back to this dry old dusty place. Well... almost nothing else. Memphis is bleeding silver just now, and that's good for both of us. He may have stirred up the dead old dust of Egypt, but Pharaoh Amasis is not the wisest man who has ever sat upon a throne. His policies have stabbed a hole in Egypt's side, and wealth spills out like blood. The hole will heal itself eventually— that's the way of nations—but in the meantime, I shall stand beneath that gush with the biggest basin I can carry, and catch every drop."

"I have heard some men wonder how much longer Amasis can hold the throne," Rhodopis said casually. "Many of the fellows I go with say this Pharaoh won't last much longer."

"Nor will he. It's a wonder he's held the country together this long, but it's only a matter of time now before the whole damn thing gives way, and one enterprising Greek king or another takes over. Egypt has been dying for generations. You're wise to make your fortune now, while you still can, and then get out before it all tumbles down."

"Which Greek king do you think is most likely to come in and clean up once Egypt falls?" she asked playfully.

Polycrates grunted. "The city-state of Cyrene is still young enough to be hungry. I could see Cyrenian forces mustering a larger army from among the allies, and descending on Egypt... perhaps. And Macedon is at least confident enough to try it, though I can't say whether King Aeropus truly has the interest. The Chrysaorians could make a move toward Egypt, I suppose, though they have always been more interested in defense and trade than empire-building."

"Persia might move toward Egypt," Rhodopis said. "I've heard from many men that their king, Cambyses, is eager to expand his empire."

"Ah, that he is."

"Have you ever been to Persia?"

"I have visited parts of the empire, but I've never been so far as the king's seat in Babylon. Hard to sail a ship across the desert, you know."

"I would love to see it," Rhodopis said. "There's no adventure like traveling, and seeing new lands."

"You like adventure?" Polycrates scratched his thick beard, looking down at Rhodopis with an air of consideration—and definite interest.

She grinned wickedly up at him. "More than you know. But until I can get to the Persian Empire and behold it myself, I'll have to content myself with adventures closer to home. Tell me what Persia is like."

Polycrates recounted a few brief tales from the Persian-controlled cities he had visited. He did appear to have more enthusiasm for those far-off ports. As he spoke, Rhodopis found none of the contempt he had shown for Egypt, and she took it for a good sign. Polycrates might be amenable to her plan. *If I can only find a likely way to broach the subject.*

She returned her attention to Polycrates' stories. "...And two days after leaving Halicarnassus," he was saying, "I made it to Sidon. Now, there is a fascinating city, if ever the gods made one."

Rhodopis blinked in surprise. "Halicarnassus to Sidon in just two days?" She had seen plenty of maps; if what he said was true, the pirate had sailed the route with astonishing speed.

"I've the fastest ships in the world," he said frankly. "*Ships*— not just one. I have acquired an entire fleet of my own in recent years. It's gratifying, to own the sea."

Rhodopis laughed. "You own the sea?"

"I might as well. With a fast ship, a man can go anywhere—do anything, before anyone else knows about it."

"But you can't go to Babylon," she teased. "Across all that desert."

"I don't need to go to Babylon. I'm sure Cambyses' great city is a sight to behold, but I've got good friends in many other places, with palaces that surely rival his."

Rhodopis, of course, had seen Cambyses' palace—had lived inside it, walked among his magnificent gardens, watched the sun set over Babylon below. No other palace could compare; she was utterly convinced of that. But she made a show of being thoroughly impressed. "Do you, really? Tell me who else you know."

"I have done enough work for the kings of Cyrene and your own Lesvos to consider them both good friends... though I doubt they would be pleased to hear me say it. Pirates do not have the best of reputations, my lady. And there are others." He ticked them off on his fingers, casually. "Quite a few well-placed men in Athens; Aeropus of Macedon; and important fellows in Corinth, Megara, and Sparta owe me dearly, as well. I have a few friends, scattered here and there.

"You're playing," she said reproachfully. "You don't know all those great men."

"I do." Polycrates said it so simply, with no hint of his previous puffed-up bluster, that Rhodopis believed he was truthful. The secret spark of hope she had nurtured so carefully flared like a sunrise.

The steward's thin voice called out from the direction of the portico.

"Sweet course is ready," Polycrates said. He offered his arm again. "Though I wonder that Charaxus thinks he can offer anything sweeter than you."

"You must tell me all about these kings you claim know," Rhodopis said warmly. "If I believe you're in earnest, perhaps you and I will go on an adventure together." *I'll be ready to leave sooner than you think.*

18

THE OLD NAME

RHODOPIS ACCEPTED A CUP OF DARK SPICED WINE FROM A SERVING woman as she stepped into Heliodoros' andron. The sharp bite of garlic, warmed by rosemary and tangy marjoram, drifted from the kitchen. She paused, drawing a deep breath, savoring the scent. The odors made her heart leap with unexpected recognition and a curious throb of nostalgic longing. Where had she smelled such cooking before? Ah, yes—in Iadmon's household. *It makes perfect sense*, she thought, *for Heliodoros' cooks to use the same spices Iadmon favored. Both men are both from Samos.*

And tonight's feast would feature the best Samian food, wine, and entertainment that Memphis could offer. Heliodoros had sent word around the city that he intended to host a true Samian feast, with every homeland delicacy his cooks could re-create. Rhodopis had caught wind of Heliodoros' plans via one of Charaxus' guests; the next morning, as soon as the sun rose, she had sent Amtes out to seek an invitation for the Lady Eulalia. Polycrates was likely to make an appearance at any Samian celebration. After getting to know the pirate at Charaxus' select dinner party, Rhodopis felt sure that within his thick, undeniably coarse shell there beat a rather sentimental heart. Polycrates, so far from home, was unlikely to miss the opportunity to bask in the comforts of Samos.

"Eulalia!" someone shouted from among the men's eating-couches. Another fellow called, "Welcome, lady!" She answered with a rather distracted wave, scanning the room for a glimpse of Polycrates' black beard and bullish shoulders. There was no danger of Charaxus appearing at tonight's party—Heliodoros had insisted that only Samian men attend. He would have limited the entertainment, too, but Samian hetaerae were in short supply; he'd had no choice but to broaden his selection of female guests, or risk leaving the men wanting for company. The knowledge that she could go about her business freed from Charaxus' jealousies filled Rhodopis with a delightful sense of fortune. Success was all but guaranteed tonight—indeed, she felt a tickle of joy moving delicately around the edges of her ever-present anxiety. It seemed tonight the gods were on her side. She was determined to win Polycrates' trust and confidence, but she would gladly settle for a mere hour in his bed—anything that would move her closer to securing his ships for Cambyses.

It took only a few moments for Rhodopis to see that Polycrates had not yet arrived. If he had, the andron would be shaking right off its pillars from the drum-like boom of his laughter. *No matter*, she told herself. *He arrived late to Charaxus' party, too.* He would appear sooner or later, and when he did, Rhodopis would be quick with her charms.

She made her way across the andron, undaunted, savoring the rich, spicy wine. The usual ripple of intrigued murmurs followed her—Lady Eulalia inspired interest wherever she went —but Rhodopis could not help but notice that the comments lacked some of the enthusiasm she had generated earlier in the season. Eulalia's novelty was wearing off. Soon she would become a fixture of Memphian life, no longer the exotic newcomer... common as dust in the alleys. It was well she had found Polycrates while her star still shone in the Memphian sky. Once she'd secured the pirate to her cause, Rhodopis could leave Memphis and never look back.

She glided past the small circle of couches were Iadmon lay, talking easily to his companions. Rhodopis did not peek from the corner of her eye at her former master, though the temptation was almost irresistible. She was not surprised to find him here— he was Samian, of course, and it seemed every Samian worth knowing had gathered at Heliodoros' party. The risk that Iadmon would recognize her was slight, yet still, Rhodopis preferred caution. Tonight she would avoid making friends with any man in Iadmon's circle—at close quarters, Iadmon very well might see past the dyed hair and fine cosmetics, and remember the red-haired girl who had once brightened his household with the magic of her dance. This was a large party; Heliodoros' house was a grand one. Providing Rhodopis could maintain a healthy distance between herself and Iadmon, she felt safe enough in his presence. As she passed him by, she could not help but note that he was dressed in the same yellow silk he'd worn the first time she had seen him, as a starving child in Tanis. She brushed one hand down the length of her hip, luxuriating in the water-smooth texture of her own silk, dyed a vibrant red, far finer and costlier than Iadmon's garment. *Iadmon did believe I would rise to great heights. But sure as the sun and stars, he never pictured me climbing this high.*

Rhodopis found a circle of men near the back of the andron. She did not know any of them by name, though one or two had vaguely familiar faces. No doubt she had seen them at parties in the past but had spent no significant time with any of these men, as far as she could recall. There was only one other hetaera among them—a woman nearing her thirties, with rich brown hair and a deeply sun-bronzed complexion. Rhodopis did not recognize her.

"May I join you, good men?" she asked, speaking with the melodious, cultured tones for which Eulalia was known.

"Of course!" One of the men rose eagerly, extending his hand. She allowed him to take her own and kiss it. He was young and attractive, with a bold nose, dark hair, and strong arms. "I am Kleon of Samos," he said. He added with a rueful laugh, "Though, who here is not from Samos?"

"I am not," Rhodopis said, lowering herself gracefully to his couch. "I come from Lesvos."

Kleon's eating-couch was perfectly positioned: she could watch the entrance to the andron as avidly as a hungry hawk, without any show of doing so. When Polycrates arrived, she would make some excuse to her Kleon and his friends, and go to the pirate before any other woman could assert herself. *Though I dare say, no other woman is apt to want Polycrates,* Rhodopis mused. *His beard is like a lion's mane, and his manners are even wilder than that.* He was unlikely to attract the interest of the refined hetaerae at tonight's banquet.

"You are Eulalia—am I correct?" said Kleon. "There has been plenty of talk about the dark-haired hetaera from the islands. I see that rumors of your beauty fell far short of the truth."

She smiled at him gratefully. A servant arrived with a fresh pitcher of wine; Rhodopis took the pitcher and filled Kleon's cup herself. "I am far from home," she said, "but I find Memphis most agreeable. I thought to remain here for a year or two, and then return to Lesvos—or perhaps take up elsewhere in Greece. But Memphis is rather pleasant. Perhaps I will stay after all."

"We would be glad for you to stay on," said her companion. His friends were quick to agree.

You say that now, Rhodopis thought, *but I see how the wind blows. Another month or two, and Lady Eulalia will find herself rather short on invitations to parties.*

"Do you know Lysandra?" Kleon asked, gesturing with his wine cup toward the other hetaera.

Rhodopis' ears twitched. She knew the name, if she had not recognized the woman. Lysandra had a reputation as one of the best hetaerae in Memphis; Rhodopis had often heard the girls at the Stable speak of her in hushed, admiring tones. Lysandra's singing voice was said to be the best the city had ever seen, and she was an admired wit, too. She had bought her freedom after only nine months of service; the woman was a legend among her kind. *It's a wonder I never saw her before*, Rhodopis thought. She tasted her wine, stalling as a chilling thought reared like a cobra in her head. *I must have been at parties with her before... back when Memphis knew me as Rhodopis. It's simply impossible that we never crossed paths.*

Kleon and his friends watched Rhodopis expectantly. She swallowed her mouthful of wine. "I have not yet had the pleasure of meeting Lysandra." She smiled at the woman; what else could she do? "I am certain we'll become good friends."

"Do you know," Lysandra said, "you seem somehow familiar to me, even though you have only recently come from Lesvos."

"I've heard as much from others since arriving in Memphis." Inwardly, Rhodopis cursed. So she had entertained with Lysandra before. Fighting down a flush, she realized Lysandra had almost certainly been at Iason's mask-party, with that thrice-cursed disaster of an auction. All the best hetaerae had attended; with Lysandra disguised, as everyone was, Rhodopis would never have known her. She could only pray that her goose costume had shielded her from Lysandra's eye. "It's strange, isn't it? You know, I have heard tales of people meeting their doubles in darkened alleys, or at night-time crossroads. Bad luck always follows. Let us hope I never meet this uncanny double of mine!" She laughed gaily to ward off a wave of dread.

"I've heard much the same," Kleon said. He grinned mischievously. "Have you ladies heard the story of the cattle drover at the crossroads? It's a real, old-fashioned Samian tale— perfect for a party like this one."

"I never have," Lysandra said.

"But it is rather chilling. Should I tell it, or will it frighten you too much?"

"Do!" Rhodopis said at once. *Gods, please—anything to distract Lysandra from her memories of me.* "I like to be frightened. It's good fun."

Kleon began the tale, but Rhodopis turned her attention at once to the andron's entrance. Her previous sense of happy confidence was melting away, faster than ice in the desert. *Polycrates had better appear soon,* she thought. *I can't just hop up and run away; it'll seem too queer. I'd be remarked on, and thought suspicious—and then Lysandra will set to thinking about me, and she'll realize where she saw me last, and who I am. I must wait here patiently until he arrives. But gods, I feel I'm half in a snare already!*

As Kleon's story went on, Rhodopis could feel, now and then, Lysandra's searching gaze, as if the hetaera could not shake off the certainty that she had seen Rhodopis before. Sweat dampened the red gown beneath Rhodopis' armpits. Was Lysandra wondering, even now, whether there was truth to Archidike's rumors, after all? Surely a hetaera as well-connected as Lysandra had heard Archidike's tale a dozen times already. Was she even now thinking: *Why has Rhodopis returned to Memphis with her hair dyed black, in some feeble attempt at a disguise?*

Rhodopis tipped back her cup, draining it in one long draft; her eyes locked on the entrance of the andron, wide with desperation. In the next moment, she spluttered, almost choking on the wine. A man had entered—one she recognized instantly. But it was not Polycrates—no, not at all. This man was smaller in stature, with dark-brown skin and curly black hair. But he bore himself with as much pride and confidence as Polycrates ever showed... despite the noticeable tilt to his shoulders, caused by the twist in his spine.

Aesop's sudden re-appearance in Rhodopis' life was such an astonishment—and such a relief—that for one dreadful moment she lost all control of her emotions. A sudden, painful lump rose in her throat. Tears burned her eyes; she barely blinked them away before they spilled down her cheeks, ruining her kohl. Kleon reached the end of his story just then; Rhodopis, clutched her necklace as if it were a talisman against evil and batted her lashes. The frightening tale provided a convenient excuse for tears.

"I've upset you!" Kleon exclaimed.

"Dear gods, but it was such a chilling story!" Rhodopis said. She blinked the tears away and smiled. "Do you suppose it's true?" *I wouldn't know; I didn't hear a word of it.*

"Who can say?" one of Kleon's friends answered. "Strange things happen at crossroads in the dark."

"Don't tease the poor dear," Lysandra said. "She's quite over-whelmed!"

Rhodopis watched Aesop make his way into the andron, carrying a scroll in one hand. He handed the scroll to Iadmon on his couch, exchanged a few words with him, then proceeded across the andron alone—coming directly toward Rhodopis, and the corridor's mouth behind her.

Rhodopis smiled at her companions as their chatter went on, but as Aesop drew nearer she stared at him intently, willing him to look at her, pleading with the gods to work their powers in her favor, and *make* him look at her, make him *see* her. Aesop's gaze passed over Rhodopis, neutral, politely blank as if she were just another woman in the crowd. Rhodopis' breath caught in her throat. But in the next heartbeat, his attention snapped back to face. His eyes widened subtly. Ever careful, ever deliberate, Aesop gave no other outward sign of having seen her. His pace did not falter; his expression remained perfectly mute. But his eyes never left her own as he made for the corridor. Rhodopis understood that Aesop was waiting, in his turn, for her to give some sign of having recognized him.

She glanced toward a nearby garden door, then back to Aesop. He diverted at once, turning before he reached Kleon's couch, strolling out into the night. The nearness of her friend—her only friend!—sent a thrill of wild gladness through Rhodopis' body. She waited a few minutes longer, laughing along with Kleon's friends, stroking her companion's shoulder—though every moment was an agony of delay. Then, when a lull came in the men's conversation, she turned to Kleon with an apologetic smile.

"I hope you will forgive me. I feel the need for some fresh air—that story, you know. I'll step outside and put my wits back together, but I will be back, if you'll be glad to have me."

"Of course," Kleon said. "Are you well? Do you need anything? I can send for—"

"No, no." Rhodopis patted his smooth cheek. "Please, don't trouble yourself. I need only a walk in the garden. The turn of the seasons always takes me this way; I fear it makes me susceptible to any powerful mood." She held his gaze for a moment, allowing the suggestion to thrill him. Then she rose gracefully. "It was such a delight to meet all of you. Lysandra—" Rhodopis bowed her head to the woman, then departed for the garden.

The night surrounded Rhodopis with its welcome darkness, its quiet seclusion. Insects, waking as the oncoming summer warmed the earth, chorused in the grasses. Rhodopis made herself walk calmly through Heliodoros' garden, though every impulse in her body screamed at her to run, to find Aesop and throw herself into his arms—and to weep with the joy of reunion. She circled the entire garden and crossed through its whispering heart before she found him. Aesop waited on a stone bench in a small, circular court, half-hidden by an overhanging arbor of vines. She grinned and laughed; a dizzy, frantic happiness surged inside her. Aesop rose to greet her, stretching out his arms; they took one other by the shoulders, both shaking their heads in disbelief, each staring at the other in silent contentment.

"Well!" Aesop said at last. "I thought I recognized that beautiful young hetaera, but I couldn't be sure."

Rhodopis laughed shakily. "It's a wonder you knew me at all, with my hair the way it is." She noticed for the first time that his blue sash was gone. He was dressed like any other Greek man—like any *free* man. "You're no longer...?"

Aesop shook his head. "I freed myself. I am now a man of some small but distinctive influence, I am pleased to say, though I still work most often with Iadmon. He asked me to attend this party tonight, to help him negotiate a new deal with another trader who is here. It was a job of work, I hear—getting Heliodoros to admit me. I am most definitely not Samian."

"Free! I'm so glad for you, Aesop."

"And I for you." Aesop released his hold on her shoulders. Reluctantly, Rhodopis did the same. "Iadmon was inconsolable for a long time after he lost you. He really did think highly of you —not only for the fortune he'd hoped to make, but for your own sake. Your sweetness was missed around the old estate—your bright, charming ways. With you gone, we all felt as if a lamp had gone out in Iadmon's house, and no one could get it lit again. But I think your loss was a call the master needed to hear. He has been perfectly behaved since then. He never over-indulges in wine anymore, no matter who tempts him."

"I'm glad to hear that, too." Rhodopis sat on the stone bench, silent for a moment as a flood of memories scoured her.

Aesop joined her. "You disappeared for quite some time. I tried to find word of you, but news was scarce—and what little word I could find seemed too strange to be believed. Tell me what has happened since we last saw one another."

Rhodopis breathed deeply, filling her lungs with the sweet with the perfumes of the garden. The fresh air seemed to crowd out all the doubt and fears inside her. She released her breath with a long, satisfied sigh. Then she spoke. "I went to live with Xanthes, as you know. I was a part of his Stable and worked for him for a year. Oh, Aesop, so many terrible things happened while I was there." She told him of her friendship with Archidike, of Charaxus and the rose-gold slippers. She told him of the auction—how it had led to Archidike's betrayal, and the hopeless aftermath. "I was so torn up over Archidike, I made as if to throw both of my slippers in the Nile. But the strangest thing happened, Aesop. A falcon scooped one up and flew away with it. I'd never seen such a thing in my life—the sight of that bird, flapping away with my slipper in its talons, was unbelievable enough. But what happened after was more unbelievable still. That night, the girls of the Stable told me how a falcon had appeared at the Pharaoh's feast, and dropped a rose-gold shoe in his lap. Well, I'm sure you heard what happened next. Amasis took it for an omen, and went out into the city, determined to find the woman who owned that slipper. Archidike tried to best me again—I'll never forget her standing before the king, claiming to be the owner of my shoe—but I'd been clever enough to bring the other with me. That proved my identity right enough. Amasis claimed me then and there, and put me in his harem."

"I'd heard the tale of the falcon and the slipper, of course," Aesop said, "but I never imagined it could be true. Even if I had believed it, I couldn't have dreamed that you were the woman Amasis found."

"I can scarce believe it myself," she said, grinning. "And yet I've lived it—all of it. This has truly been my life, though it feels like something from a nursery tale."

Rhodopis' smile dimmed a little.

"There's more to your story," Aesop said softly.

"Yes. And I know I can trust you—*you*, of all people! But oh, Aesop, I'm afraid. And I'm fearful if you know the whole story, you'll think me a liability, and you'll wish never to see me again. So maybe it's better after all if I say nothing."

Aesop took her hand. "Perhaps I can help you, if you do tell me. You need help, don't you?"

"I do," Rhodopis burst out, "ever so much! I've tried to be as clever and clear-headed as you taught me, but... but..."

"You're sixteen years old, my friend. Whatever is weighing on you, it's a difficult burden for a young person to bear."

The starlit blooms of the garden blurred into great, soft balls of glowing light as tears filled her eyes. Rhodopis couldn't stop herself from weeping; the relief of sympathy, of being understood, was far too great.

Aesop patted her back. "You can trust me, Doricha. I will never hurt you, and I'll help you if I can. I swear it by all the gods."

The sound of her old name filled Rhodopis with a surge of emotions, so powerful and sudden she couldn't sort them out. They all wound together, binding in a hard knot somewhere below her heart. She shook her head, surrendering to the relief of a friendly hand and a sympathetic ear. And then, with another deep and ragged breath, she told Aesop everything.

"Once I was in his harem, Amasis got it in his head to send me off to Persia, disguised as the Pharaoh's daughter."

Aesop went very still, waiting for her to say more.

"If he'd only wanted me to go and marry the Persian king, that would have been well enough. What woman wouldn't like to be wife to a king? But he sent me to Persia with a secret task. Amasis is terribly frightened that Cambyses will bring down his armies from the north, and no one will be able to stop him. I was... I was meant to be Amasis' eyes and ears in Babylon. Get to know Cambyses, and then tell all his secrets to Amasis, so he could find some way to stop the Persians from invading."

Aesop's eyes widened, and his lips pressed into a thin line. But he regarded Rhodopis quietly, a calm acceptance of her terrible predicament, and waited patiently for her to say more.

"But once I was in Babylon," she said, "I met a man named Phanes. He's the king's most trusted advisor, and he saw through my disguise straight away. Aesop, there was nothing I could do to deter him—nothing! He was far too intelligent and persistent. But after he told me his great work—the goal he's dedicated his life to

—I found... I found that I wanted to help him after all. And I would have done it, I think, even if Phanes *hadn't* had the power to expose me to Cambyses."

"What do you mean?" Aesop said slowly, cautiously. "What is Phanes 'great work?'"

Rhodopis' voice dropped even lower, a whisper so faint she could scarcely hear her own words. "He intends to overthrow Amasis, and place Cambyses on the Horus Throne."

A tense silence. Finally, Aesop said, "I see. I suppose it's no great surprise, that the king of Persia would seek to conquer Egypt. The way the winds are blowing, Egypt can't continue to stand on its own—not for much longer. But I had assumed it would be some Greek king who claimed the Two Lands, when the time was right, and Amasis was ripe for the harvest. The Pharaoh has made a tidy path for the Greeks, after all. But why do you care for his plan, Doricha? What is this affair to you?"

"It's because of Psamtik that I care." Her voice was level, calm... hard with determination.

"The Pharaoh's son?"

"Yes. He... he hurt me, Aesop, when I was in the Pharaoh's harem. He—"

"All right," Aesop said, squeezing her cold fingers. "I understand. You needn't say any more. Poor thing."

"I'll do anything to stop Psamtik from taking power... from ever holding the least shred power over another person. I never want to see that hideous beast on a king's throne, with a king's crown upon his head. He isn't worthy of such an honor. And I will stop him from taking the throne, Aesop, no matter what I must do. Even if I lose my life in the attempt. Even if I must bring Egypt down with Psamtik."

"Wouldn't it be easier to simply kill Psamtik? If you want to prevent him from taking the throne, I mean."

Rhodopis huffed a near-silent laugh. "How am I to get back into the Pharaoh's palace? And what weapon should I use, that the king's guards can't take from me? No—strange as it seems, it would be easier to topple Egypt entirely than to find my way back into the palace, a free woman, and do away with Psamtik." She paused; the insects sang on. "As I told you, I can scarcely believe this is my life and not some fantastical story."

"How are you to do it? This Phanes man—what has he planned?"

Rhodopis hesitated.

"You can trust me, Doricha. What loyalty have I to the Pharaoh—or to Egypt itself? We who have lived as slaves have no nation, no affiliation, save to one another. I feel much more loyalty to you—a friend—than to any king or country."

"I do trust you," she said. "Maybe it's foolish, for my life seems all danger and fear, and if I have learned anything since leaving Thrace, I have learned that I should put my faith in no one. But I trust you, Aesop. How can I not?" She clasped her hands together, squeezing so tightly that her nails bit into the backs of her hands. "I'm back in Memphis to secure allies for Cambyses. He needs someone capable of driving a great, strong wedge between Egypt and Greece. But I must find that ally soon. My time is running out. If I don't provide Cambyses what he needs, I know I'll wake one of these nights to find a man with a knife standing over my bed. Cambyses is growing impatient."

"Have you thought of anyone yet? Identified any man who might suit your purpose?"

"Polycrates of Samos seems likely," she said. "He has the fastest ships, and his love for silver is far greater than his love for Egypt. But I can't attract his attention—he's so coarse and uncaring. Nothing I try seems to interest him. I attempted to catch his eye at a party a few nights ago, and he seemed amused by me--but no more than he would have been by any pretty woman. He wasn't particularly drawn—not enough that I could hope to influence him. I had thought he would be here tonight. He is Samian, after all. But he hasn't turned up, and now I'm starting to despair."

"I have encountered Polycrates a few times," Aesop said wryly. "He is coarse, as you say, but despite his loud ways, the man has exceptionally refined tastes."

"Has he?" She smiled tentatively. The thought of Polycrates harboring an appreciation for the finer things in life was simply too incongruous.

"Most men of his type do have fine tastes—mercenaries, I mean. Pirates. What else would drive them to seek out ever more fortune? In that way, Polycrates is no different from the merchants and guildsmen, and the sons of rich families who haunt these night-time parties. They all love rare, exquisite things; they all seek wealth so they can buy more silks, bigger houses, more fine wine and beautiful women—all the earmarks of class and status."

"But I've already disguised myself as the finest, most sought-after hetaera in Memphis. Even that hasn't been enough to win more than a kiss on the hand from Polycrates."

Aesop stroked his chin, thinking. "Beautiful women can be had anywhere. A man like Polycrates is lured by rarity. You should dance for him, Doricha. Your dancing sets you apart from other women. It will drive Polycrates mad with desire; no one in Memphis dances half so well as you."

"That's the trouble, isn't it?" Her hopes sagged again. "If I dance, anyone who sees me will know who I truly am. My disguise will be ruined. Archidike already suspects me; I've held her off with slander, but that shield can't hold forever. And Charaxus knows who I am, of course—there was no avoiding him. If anyone else finds out... *when* they find out... rumor will travel back to the Pharaoh's palace. Amasis and his chief wife will kill me if they know I'm back in Memphis, for it can only mean I've changed sides and gone over to Cambyses." She choked back a sob. "I face death no matter what, Aesop! What shall I do?"

"It's true," he said calmly, "the risk is great. Is it worth revealing your identity, to secure Polycrates and his ships? For you are correct: there will be no maintaining your present disguise once you dance."

"If I can convince Polycrates to side with Cambyses quickly, then I can be on my way back to Babylon before anyone in Memphis can catch me. But I can't be sure of him—oh, if only I could be sure! Aesop, what if I dance, but Polycrates won't pledge his ships?"

"That is a decision only you can make—a risk only you can run. I wish I could offer more encouragement than that, Doricha. But I can promise this: I will support you and help you, no matter what you choose."

"Help me?" She swallowed her tears. "You mean in the work —Phanes' plan. I can't ask you to risk yourself, too. The gods put me in this predicament for reasons I can't understand, but you're free of it, Aesop. You should stay well clear."

His voice dropped lower. "I have no great love for Egypt as it exists now. Remember, Doricha: the same system, the same culture enslaved us both—took us from our families, changed both our lives forever. I would rejoice to see Amasis fall. Perhaps Egypt will fare better under Cambyses than it has fared under its present Pharaoh. One thing is certain: Egypt can hardly do worse."

Rhodopis had no strength to resist him anymore. Overwhelmed by the relief of friendship, she threw her arms around his neck, weeping on his shoulder, heedless of the eye-paint she left on his chlamys and his skin.

"We will bring Polycrates to your side," Aesop whispered, patting her back with his warm, gentle hand. "Trust me. We'll find a way."

19

NOW

RHODOPIS CLENCHED HER HANDS BEHIND HER BACK, WHERE NONE one could see. Sharp nails dug into her palms; the bite of pain stilled her as another wave of shivers threatened to wrack her body. That was how she had passed the early evening—holding herself apart from the party's many guests, fighting back shudders of dread as one stark fear after another tumbled endlessly through her mind. The music was her saving grace. She lingered the musicians, allowing the complex interplay of harp, flute, and drum to comfort and calm her. Rhodopis had lived through enough dire circumstances to drop any woman dead from fright, but only once before had she felt so insecure, so certain a brutal end was at hand. That had been the moment she'd knelt before Cambyses, watching the tip of his sword scrape the dusty paving stones of his courtyard. Now she groveled before neither man nor king—she stood poised, outwardly cool, aloof as a star in the sky. But nevertheless, Rhodopis knew she was about to place her life in the hands of another, as she had done that day with Cambyses.

How strange it felt, how disorienting, to stand once more in the andron of her first master. Her head was light, her spirit drifting as if she moved continually in and out of the dream realm. Somehow, Rhodopis felt that Iadmon's andron—indeed, his entire estate—ought to have looked quite different. The place was so eerily unchanged that she half expected to find a blue sash tied around her waist, with a simple white tunic in place of the fine hetaera's gown. After everything Rhodopis had been through, all the varied identities she had worn—the different lives she had lived—how could Iadmon and his home have escaped the touch of time? She blinked uneasily at the room—the same warm light she recalled from earlier days, flickering in the same lamps. The finely made furniture of ebony and inlaid cedar, each piece standing precisely where she remembered it. Even the upstanding guests were the same—familiar faces she could name by instinct, bodies she knew well lounging on the couches. The pale pillars of the andron were a temple dedicated to stasis. Beyond the pillars, the same old gods waited, unmoved, in their rows of little niches.

Three years gone, and nothing here has changed. Nothing, except me. Now Rhodopis was a free woman, not a slave-girl—or at least, she wore the guise of freedom. She would never be truly free, so long as she remained caught between Amasis and Cambyses, between Archidike and Charaxus with their threats of exposure. Superstitious dread milled in her heart. If Iadmon's home was so completely unchanged, then perhaps she was, too. Perhaps she had not hidden as well as she'd thought. Had Amasis known for weeks that she had forsaken Egypt, and had opened her eyes and ears for Persia? The Pharaoh might be biding his time, waiting for a convenient moment to arrest her.

No, she told herself firmly, fighting back another shiver. *You must trust in Amtes' skills. Your disguise is a good one.*

Amtes had done her work especially well this evening. The good handmaid had dyed Rhodopis' hair again that morning, smothering the red-gold that tried to peek through the fading color. Now Rhodopis' intricate braid was darker than a stork's wingtip. Her kohl and eye-paints were perhaps a touch too extravagant tonight, too gaudy for current fashion. But it was critical that Rhodopis evade Iadmon's notice or that of his friends... at least until recognition became inevitable. Between black hair, bright paints, and the richest gown Rhodopis had found among those purchased by Phanes—a flowing silk of a blue so deep it was almost purple—she bore little resemblance to Doricha the slave girl. Yet still, fear persisted.

Why shouldn't I be afraid? Only a half-wit could believe that all is well. If the night went as Rhodopis hoped—as she and Aesop had planned—then the mask called Eulalia would shatter for good. Tonight, Rhodopis would run the first trembling strides in a race against time and rumor. She was not at all certain she was strong enough to win.

This party—this night—had been Aesop's idea. He was a free man now, no longer a part of Iadmon's household in any legal or official sense. Yet Aesop still enjoyed significant influence over the trader's life and business. He had convinced Iadmon to host a Samian party of his own... and this time, Aesop had seen to it himself that Polycrates would attend.

Rhodopis had received word early that morning that Polycrates would dine with Iadmon. She had sat for a long time at her garden window, trying in vain to gather her thoughts. Her feelings had been scattered like seeds before a storm wind—of little substance, whipped this way and that, impossible to catch and hold. Rhodopis had found but one firm thought to which she could cling: *Tonight, I'll run the ultimate risk—my last gamble in Memphis.* If the plan succeeded, she might hope to live. If it failed, all hope would assuredly die.

With that certainty fixed in her mind, sunk deep and cold in the marrow of her bones, she had risen from her fruitless thoughts and turned to Amtes. "I was supposed to go to Charaxus tonight. You must send him word that I can't see him."

"What shall I tell him?" Amtes had said.

"Tell him I'm ill. Tell him *anything*. Tell I hate him, if you like, that I think he's a meddling fool—it hardly matters now, if he knows the truth."

The music bent and slowed. It took on a melancholy air. Rhodopis accepted a cup of wine from a passing servant, more for the distraction than to quench any thirst. She sipped it slowly, never even tasting the vintage, and watched as Iadmon's final guests arrived. Hetaerae moved through the andron, graceful and lithe as herons in river reeds. Now and then, a woman stooped to whisper in a friend's ear, or dropped an enticing kiss on a man's cheek. Servants bore the first course into the andron, carried on great trays of polished wood. But Rhodopis shook her head when the staff approached. Her stomach was far too ill with worry to eat tonight.

A young man crossed the andron, his gaze fixed on Rhodopis. She shifted uncomfortably as he drew near, but she made herself smile at him.

He bowed a polite greeting "Beautiful Eulalia, won't you please join me for supper? I would be most honored to share my couch with you."

"You are very kind," Rhodopis said, "but I cannot."

He chuckled. "I see. Waiting for someone in particular?"

She laughed lightly, looking away, giving what she hoped was a passable imitation of shyness. Let the man think whatever he would. It mattered little, now.

"Lucky man," he said. "If you change your mind—or if he proves disappointing—feel free to find me. I won't change my mind, I promise you."

He left her, and Rhodopis breathed a sigh of relief. Not only was she entirely too anxious to entertain anyone tonight, but accepting company was no part of the evening's carefully laid plans. Tonight she must hold herself apart from all other hetaerae—from all the guests. Tonight she must be the exquisite, unattainable, the rare creature Polycrates craved, the coveted object that would drive him to distraction. If the gods were merciful, it would work as Aesop had promised. She saw her conspirator moving purposefully across the andron, toward Iadmon on his couch. Aesop caught her eye. He gave her a fleeting but encouraging smile.

He seems entirely sure it will all go off without any trouble. Wish I could feel half so confident.

Aesop bent over Iadmon's couch, murmured something in his hear. The master of the household raised himself on one elbow and looked around the andron with a rather suspicious air. Rhodopis' heart sped with a nauseating lurch. She wondered what news Aesop had delivered, what could have put Iadmon in a state of sudden discomfiture. But then a tall, broad, dark-bearded figure strode between the entry pillars of the andron, and Rhodopis understood.

Polycrates had come prepared for Iadmon's party, she noted with dismay. Rather than taking his pick of the women whom Iadmon had invited, the pirate had procured two hetaerae of his own. The women clung to his arms, one on each side. Both were beautiful and delicate; their feminine shapes only seemed to underscore the large size and imposing presence of their Samian companion. And both women were exceptionally beautiful. Their features were well-made, perfectly carved as if by a craftsman of unsurpassed skill. When it came to grace and enticing curves, there was nothing to choose between them. Rhodopis' heart sank lower still as she evaluated Polycrates' two hetaerae. How could she hope to compete? She would never stand apart, when set against such loveliness, such feminine perfection. There was something earthy, something overtly sexual about both women, evident even in the way they stood beside their companion, casually taking in Iadmon's party. An appealing, raw sexuality seemed to rise from their bodies, compelling as the scent of a lotus flower. *How can I expect Poly-crates to want me, when he's already set his appetite for those two playthings?*

Iadmon stood, somewhat stiffly and reluctantly, and went to greet Polycrates.

"Iadmon!" the pirate roared. "You old sack of balls, you. How is business?"

They clasped hands, Iadmon looking rather pale and uncer-tain as he murmured a more genteel response to Polycrates' ebul-lient greeting. Aesop stepped close to his former master, smiling as he spoke to both men, his air bracing and encouraging. Rhodopis wished she were close enough to hear what her friend had said.

Polycrates took his place on the last empty couch; a servant hurried to him, bearing the first-course dish. The two hetaerae who had accompanied Polycrates were obliged to stand, since there was little room for either to lie beside their friend. Poly-crates' booming laughter filled the andron as he greeted the men positioned nearby and offered up his unrefined jests. As he talked, his hand roamed freely over the body of one of his women, fondling her backside in a cursory, almost distracted manner.

With the final guest was present at last; the supper began in earnest. As trays of rich food circulated the andron and conversa-tion rose, Rhodopis shrank back into the shadows between pillars. She did not want the serving staff to approach her again; the mere smell of roasted beef and onions, normally so delicious, was enough to make her gag tonight. She remained cloaked in comforting shadows, shivering, squeezing her eyes shut. The noise of the feast—and of Polycrates' laughter—seemed to roar amid the pillars of the andron.

"Doricha." Aesop's whisper was barely audible, but it was enough to startle Rhodopis. She jumped, pressing a hand to her heart, and turned. Aesop was there in the shadows beside her; he laid a comforting hand on her back. "Are you ready? It's almost time."

She nearly choked on her words. "No, I'm not! I've never been so unready before. Oh, Aesop, how can I do it? Everyone will know me—word will get back to the Pharaoh. How, how can I go through with it?"

He patted her back gently. "Trust in your ability. And trust in the music, too. Let it carry you on, let it guide you—you know how. They'll all think you're wonderful. And you will be wonderful, in truth."

"It doesn't matter what they think. It only matters what... he thinks." She couldn't make herself speak Polycrates' name.

"You will enchant him, too—him, most of all. He'll be yours after tonight. His ships are as good as yours already."

"You don't know that." She croaked with despair. "You can't know it."

"But I know you. I know the magic of your dance. And I know the strength of your spirit, my friend."

"My spirit's weak. Weak, Aesop! I'm all shivery inside; I don't think I can take a single step, let alone dance! I was a fool to think this would work!"

"You are no fool," Aesop said drily. "Your cleverness and careful thought have already carried you through far worse dangers."

"There is no danger worse than this."

"And yet," he said, "there is no way out of this danger, either. No way out, except to face what you fear the most. You must give Cambyses what he needs if you're ever to be free."

She swallowed hard. "What if Polycrates doesn't like me after all? I'll be exposed; everyone will know it's me, that I've been lying all this time, hiding my identity... What then? Amasis will find out, and—"

"At least," Aesop said, taking her hand, "you won't be alone. Whatever happens to you, I will take on the same fate."

She was horrified by the thought of Aesop dying because of her own foolhardy actions. She rounded on him with a frantic, desperate energy. "I can't let you do that—I *can't*!"

"Then you must trust in our plan. It will go well; I know it. You must believe you can make Polycrates want you. Believing is the first step along that path."

The servants cleared out of the andron; Iadmon's guests tucked into their beef and onions. The host's voice rose above the murmur of the feast—and Rhodopis twitched at the sound of her old master's command. "Let us have some entertainment while we eat."

"Get ready," Aesop said.

"No," Rhodopis panted. "I can't do it!"

Iadmon called, "I have brought a dancer for you all to enjoy while we eat. My musicians may begin when ready."

Rhodopis clenched her fists and her aching jaw, shaking her head in mute horror.

Aesop leaned closer. "Now," he whispered in her ear.

On the instant, Rhodopis stilled. That simple word, that friendly order, full of confidence that the girl Doricha could succeed, if she only deigned to try... She felt again the hot sun in Iadmon's garden, the lazy river breeze stirring the fringe of her dancing-belt against her thighs. The memory of a shivering beam of wood came back with such vivid force that Rhodopis threw her arms out to either side, as if to balance herself against a fall. But she wasn't going to fall, of course. Aesop was there beside her, urging her to try, seeing the fullness of her hidden, untapped potential. Fear faded—not completely, but enough that Rhodopis could make herself stand eye to eye with fate. She stepped out from behind the pillar and walked steadily to the center of the andron.

Rhodopis took up the dancer's pose. Murmurs of conversation died back; the room filled with the glad tension of expectation. She could feel it tingling up her spine. Rhodopis was dimly aware that Iadmon had gone very still. His face was turned toward her; there was an amusing strain of disbelief in his posture. But Rhodopis did not look directly at her former master. She gazed beyond Iadmon, beyond the straight white pillars, out into the hall of the gods. She had time for one fleeting prayer before the music began.

Here you have brought me, Rhodopis said silently. *Strymon, Aphrodite, Zeus... Iset and Hathor, Horus the Falcon. Here you have brought me, Lady of Victory, Ishtar of the Blue Gate. I stand at the crossroads of fate. Do with me now whatever you will. I am ready... I am ready.*

The music rushed up to meet her, catching Rhodopis by her raised arms, pulling her up and up into the soaring ecstasy of dance. Aesop had found the very best musicians to carry her through this most crucial hour; the harps and horns sang together in a superb chorus of emotion. She had intended to perform her own, rather seductive variation on a Samian folk dance, rustic and rousing—one she had been certain Polycrates would recognize. But as harmony and counter-melody wrapped around her, surged through her, bore her on a current of feeling, Rhodopis abandoned that carefully laid plan. Rapt and glowing, she heeded the call of Terpsichore, Muse of dance—and chose instead to invent every step and sway, every subtle, precise movement of hand and foot as inspiration directed.

She began by circling the room, just as she had done so long ago, when she had first danced before Iadmon's guests, a nervous and half-trained slave. Now, as then, she paused briefly at every man's couch, forging a connection with gesture and touch—a brief locking of eyes, a slow and suggestive smile. How easily she slipped into the role, that beloved part she hadn't played for nearly two years. Gods, but it felt good to dance before an audience again. Every man and woman present was graced by her flitting nearness, a there-and-gone warmth like fitful rays after a long, arduous winter. Charm and innocence were still evident in her every movement and expression. They were hers by nature, unquelled by the hardships of life, still shining in her eyes like a temple fire despite the long, dark night of her dangerous journey. Rhodopis found her audience eager and keen, once she had led them all into the shimmering new world she made with deft feet and descriptive hands. She even came near Iadmon, bending to reach for him with a brief show of regret. She looked him fearlessly in the eye, and saw the shock of recognition that lit his face, sun breaking through a dense veil of clouds. But before Iadmon could do more than stare, she whirled away, spinning off toward the next man.

Once Rhodopis felt that settling of satisfaction, the calm glow that told her she had woven them all into her spell, she transitioned to the earnest, candid core of her dance. The Muse spoke, and Rhodopis responded, telling the story of her young life through movement and music, rhythm and pulse. She danced the joy of her early life in Thrace, poor but unfettered among the hills and pines. Great, long, reaching strides carried her, as if on a Thracian storm-wind; her outstretched arms were like wings of a gull, flying high and free. With bent back and drooping head, she told of hunger and strife in Egypt. She danced the sorrow of her father's death, the weight of woe that dragged at her, the fear and pain that buckled her. The Muse led her close to Iadmon's couch again, and there she expressed the delicate unfolding of tender new hope. Like a seed sprouting from dreary mud, she grew and stretched and thrived. She reached toward the rising sun, the beautiful prospect it promised—a bright glory of opportunity and prestige. But then—ah!—a great loss, the rending of her hopes. Xanthes. Rhodopis' harsh, jerking movements and the reluctance grimace she wore stood at odds to the fine, flowing music. But she could feel her audience respond to the change, leaning in, ever more engrossed by the turning of her fate.

Archidike was next. Rising to her toes, tottering this way and that as if she sought to flee from a reality too terrible to be borne, Rhodopis danced the pain and incredulity of a friend's betrayal. And then, falling to the floor, clutching her body as if she could wring the sorrow from her agonized spirit, she told of the plunge into stark despair, when her freedom, which had been so close she could all but taste it, was torn away again.

With hands spread like a falcon's wings, Rhodopis painted an image of the still, indifferent river. One by one, she cast her dreams and expectations into the water—and Iadmon's guests followed the arc of their flight, staring, moving their heads as if they could see the dancer's hopes drifting away on a tragic current. And then—the rapid dive of the great, gray bird, the strange intervention of the gods—and Rhodopis, scooped up like her slipper, carried off to the Pharaoh's palace in the unbreakable grip of the falcon's feet.

She moved as if in a dull, stifling dream—trapped in the gilded cage of the harem. She danced her longing for true freedom, for love. She danced her anger at Psamtik, the pain and humiliation of his assault—and her fanged, ravenous hunger for revenge. In the next moment, she broke free, bursting out of the Pharaoh's palace on a wave of hazard and dread... and no small amount of excitement. She danced unfettered below the desert moon, and the land around her—invisible, yet somehow seen by her audience with a magical clarity—turned purple in the peace of solitude and twilight.

When the time came to tell of the passion and pleasure she had found in Cambyses' bed, Rhodopis moved ever closer to Polycrates. Before his avid eyes, she exposed the softness and heat of her flesh—bare inner arm, strong pale thigh—bending and panting, shameless in the heat of her desire. She was absorbed in her own story, giddily freed by its telling—and wild with the triumph of her power. But she did not fail to note the interest in Polycrates' dark eyes, heating from a spark to a flame.

Nor did she miss the way he twitched suddenly, loosing his hold on the two beautiful hetaerae as he leaned toward Rhodopis, his mouth agape with awe. She spun out of Polycrates' reach before he could attempt to touch her.

The brilliant musicians seemed to sense that the dancer's story had reached its end—and Rhodopis wondered faintly, even as she whirled into her final pose, whether this was, in fact, the end—whether now the gods were finished with her, and the knife in the darkness would come. The music ceased. Rhodopis held her pose. As she panted for her breath, her gaze swept the andron. Men and hetaerae alike were clambering to their feet, rushing to acclaim the dark-haired dancer. Shouts of praise crashed like ocean waves against the shore. She saw Iadmon's pale-faced disbelief, the stunned stillness of his body. Rhodopis ignored them all—shocked Iadmon, cheering women, men with their fists raised in excitement. She even ignored Aesop's triumphant grin. Rhodopis saw no one in the room, acknowledged no one, save for the Samian pirate. She offered Polycrates a slow, inviting smile.

He rose from his couch slowly, as if in a dream. The two hetaerae clutched at him, but he shook off their hands. He came to Rhodopis through the cheering crowd, as if some unseen muse guided him, too.

Rhodopis' heart sang with victory. She took Polycrates by the arm.

❧

THEY LEFT the andron together while the room still rang with praises. Neither Rhodopis nor Polycrates spoke, yet she was keenly aware of the urgency burning inside him as they hurried along Iadmon's corridor. Polycrates tried one door after another, and finally found a guest chamber. The servants had prepared it well: a single lamp burned on a table beside a pitcher of wine and two cups. In one corner, raised on a thin iron tripod, a diminutive brazier sent up a pale ribbon of incense smoke.

Polycrates pulled Rhodopis inside. He slammed the door.

"Did you like my dance?" she teased.

His growl of desire was like the purr of some great, lazy lion. "Do you know you're the most exquisite dancer I've ever seen?"

"Surely not. You've been everywhere in the world… everywhere fast ships can go. You said as much at Charaxus' party."

Polycrates moving toward her, one slow step, then another. All this haste was gone now. He had her, like a bird in a snare, and now he seemed to savor the delay of his gratification.

"You are," Polycrates insisted. "The most beautiful, most exceptional dancer in Egypt or in Greece."

"You've been outside Egypt and Greece," she said, pouting mischievously. "What about the Persian Empire? Am I the most beautiful, most exceptional dancer in Persia, too?"

"I'm quite serious. I've never seen any woman move the way you do."

Rhodopis shook her head. The flirtatious pout fell away in a self-deprecating laugh. "That can't be true, Polycrates." It truly couldn't—in Egypt alone, there were hundreds of women better trained than Rhodopis, with years' more experience—but she was glad Aesop had been right about Polycrates' tastes. He had been right that Polycrates would go mad for her, too. *Good old Aesop, clever as always. I should never have doubted him.*

"I must have you," Polycrates said hoarsely. He took another slow step toward her.

Rhodopis bent her neck shyly, demurely. "I am yours for the taking."

Polycrates moved with sudden force, sweeping Rhodopis into his arms. His kiss was rough, insistent—as were his hands, which seemed to be everywhere at once, squeezing, clawing, crushing her against his chest. For one moment, Psamtik intruded in her thoughts, and she tensed—but the next moment he was gone again. Rhodopis found that she liked the ungentle way Polycrates handled her; his force and haste felt like manifestations of her own power, a reflection of her strength and will, long nurtured in secret, fruiting on the vine. His touch was a foreshadowing, too: a glimpse of the wrath to come, the vengeance Rhodopis would bring down upon the heir to the Horus Throne.

Polycrates untied one of the knots at her shoulder. The blue gown slid, exposing her breast almost to the nipple.

"I appreciate women like no other man does," he said.

"Oh, do you?" She shrugged her bare shoulder

"I've sampled far and wide, and you are among the finest."

"Everywhere a ship can sail," she said teasingly.

"I've enjoyed a great many women, Eulalia." He untied her sash next. The gown loosened around her waist, and the incense-smoked air cooled the sweat of her dance. "A great many."

"Do you think to impress me with such a boast?"

"I mean only to say—" Polycrates untied the other knot at her shoulder. The gown gave way entirely, falling to the floor. Rhodopis stood in nothing but her sandals, naked and pale before him. "—that I make it a point to take a woman to my bed as often as I can. But I never truly enjoy it, unless I know I've found the best."

"The best? What sort of woman is the best? Do you mean the most beautiful?"

Polycrates stepped back, the better to look at Rhodopis, taking in the entirety of her body by the soft glow of the oil lamp. His gaze was both appraising and hungry, appreciative and impatient.

After a moment, Polycrates said, "The best woman is not necessarily the most beautiful—though of course, beauty is fine in its own right. But the world is full of beautiful women; mere beauty can't satisfy me. The best woman is an intriguing one—a rare one. I like unusual women."

"Tell me about the unusual ones," Rhodopis said. She turned

slowly, stepping over the fallen gown, moving closer to the lamp so he could see her, every inch of her bareness, as he recited the names of all the women who had pleased him best.

"There was Berenike, who could bend her body into positions you can't begin to imagine. And Euanthe, who could fight any man with a sword or a spear. And Meritamun—yes, and Egyptian —whose skin was whiter than yours, and her hair was the color of dried flax. She couldn't go out by day, for the sun would burn her and blind her; she had eyes of a peculiar color, a haunting, pale red. Melisse could sing sweeter than any bird. Myrrine had a third nipple."

Rhodopis laughed. "You truly do appreciate rarity."

Polycrates nodded, staring at her breasts.

"But I am rarest of them all," she said. It was not a question. "No one in the world dances like me."

"No one," he said hoarsely.

"Do you think I'll delight you just as much as they did, all those unusual women, once you have me under that sheet?" She stepped out of her sandals with quick grace.

"I'm certain you will," Polycrates whispered. "I expect I'll enjoy *you* most of all."

He seized her; the breath left Rhodopis' lungs in a sudden, startled rush as he pulled her against his chest again. She twisted her fingers in his hair and kissed him, blood roaring with triumph.

◈

DEEP IN THE NIGHT, long after moonset, Rhodopis returned to her home in the litter Aesop had prepared. He had sent a contingent of guards, too, to protect Rhodopis on along the route through the North End, for Memphis still boiled with dissatisfaction. Aesop would have been loath to risk her safety at any time, but she was especially valuable now, with Polycrates in her hands.

I dare say there's more reason for the guards, Rhodopis thought. Eulalia was gone forever now, and no mistaking it. Word must already circulate through the city: Eulalia of Lesvos danced every bit as well as little red-haired Rhodopis, the rustic beauty of Xanthes' Stable. In a handful of hours—days at most— Memphian society would connect the story of Eulalia's spectacular dance to Archidike's tale that Rhodopis had returned, and was operating under a false name. *I have perhaps two days at most before Amasis sends his soldiers out to find me.* When the Pharaoh's men came for her, all the guards in Iadmon's household wouldn't be protection enough.

Real as that threat was, it occupied a small, insignificant place in Rhodopis' heart. She still ached and throbbed with the feel of Polycrates' rough, passionate attentions. His panting praises still whispered in her ear. He had called her the best, sworn she was the most wonderful, the most thrilling woman he had ever held. The Samian was hers now. She needed one more night to be sure of him, to enchant him so thoroughly that he couldn't deny any request. Then she would be ready to present him to Cambyses, neat as an offering of figs in a basket.

I'll be gone with Polycrates before sunset tomorrow. Let Amasis do his worst; I don't fear him any longer.

When she reached her courtyard, Rhodopis hurried inside, dismissed the guards, and stumbled through the darkness without bothering to light a lamp. She groped her way to Amtes' bed and shook her awake.

Amtes sat up at once, wide-eyed and alert. The maid's small window admitted just enough starlight for Rhodopis to read her expression—half expectant, half fearful.

"What is it, Mistress? Has something happened?"

"Something has happened, sure as the sun and the moon. But don't look so worried, Amtes. I've got a message for you; you must send it off to Cambyses tonight."

Amtes scrambled out of her bed. She struck a spark to her

lamp; the small room filled with cheerful light. Amtes slid a box from beneath her table, flipped up its lid, and found a scrap of papyrus and a small writing brush. She spread the scrap on her table and looked up at Rhodopis, ready for the message.

"Tell Cambyses," Rhodopis said, "'I have found your man.'"

20

POWER IN HER HAND

RHODOPIS KNEW SHE WAS NOT CLEAR OF HER TROUBLES—NOT YET. But Polycrates' enthusiasm was such a comfort and relief that she slept better than she had in months. Her dreams were sweet and hopeful, suffused with gentle music and the soft, warm smell of honey. She woke late in the morning and lay comfortably abed, contented and quiet, watching the mellow light move by increments across her room. A breeze drifted in from the garden, fresh and invigorating. Winter's chill was almost gone now. It had given way to a rich, spicy warmth that enhanced her easy sense of satisfaction and achievement.

She reflected on the previous night with a quiet inner glow. Polycrates had been hers entirely. The praise he had showered upon her felt more like worship, better suited to a goddess in her temple than a mere hetaera. Rhodopis had no doubt that her roguish pirate would be glad to spend this evening in her company. She would make her offer tonight—promise Polycrates all the silver in Cambyses' treasury if he only pledged his ships to the cause. She could keep fate at bay for a few more hours until she had given Polycrates another taste of her charms.

Rhodopis stretched her arms overhead, yawning, reveling in

the warm flush of success. *Too late now for any knife-wielding killer to sneak into my chamber. Before the end of the week, I'll be sailing north with Polycrates, faster than the Pharaoh's ships can go!*

The chamber door did open at that moment, but it was only Amtes. The handmaid hustled inside and shut the door firmly behind her, pale-faced and scowling. "I'm glad to find you awake, Mistress, though it would be better if you were already up and dressed. What do you think? Charaxus is here."

"Oh..." Rhodopis pressed her palms against her eyes until spots of light bloomed behind her eyelids. "Of course. Of course, the gods would send him to spoil my mood now, just when everything has gone so well for me. What does that tiresome lout want?"

"He wants to speak with you," Amtes said. "And he is none too pleased."

Rhodopis sat up quickly. "Blast him! Can't he leave well enough alone?"

"Evidently he cannot. It was all I could do to convince him to remain in the sitting room like a decent man, and not barge his way in here to confront you directly. Quickly, now; put yourself together. The sooner you handle Charaxus, the sooner he'll leave."

Groaning, Rhodopis dragged herself out of her bed and pulled on a robe. It was not her finest garment, but after all, she had told Charaxus she'd been ill. A simple, serviceable robe would do nicely; no woman wore her best to her sickbed. Amtes combed out her mistress's hair but left it hanging free, spilling own Rhodopis' back in dark, shining waves. There was no sense in putting it up—a woman recovering from a minor illness wouldn't bother, but more to the point, Rhodopis felt no inclination to make herself beautiful for Charaxus. One day more, and she would never see him again. All his silly affection—and his oppressive dreams of taking Rhodopis for a wife—would be left in the dusty tombs of memory.

As soon as she was presentable, Rhodopis stomped through the small estate's hallways and into the sitting room. Amtes was right: the sooner she dealt with her caller, the sooner he would leave her be. Then she could return her focus to the pleasures of the night ahead: Polycrates and his ships, the revelation of Cambyses' plan. She found Charaxus pacing from the portico to the garden window and back again, his hands clasped behind his back, his eyes distant in a face darkened by anger.

"Good morning," Rhodopis said neutrally.

Charaxus stopped abruptly, but he turned to look at her with a deliberate slowness that made Rhodopis feel distinctly uneasy. There was a peevish light in his eye. "Are you feeling well today?"

"Oh, yes. Quite well, thank you. A day's rest was just what I needed."

"I'm glad you've recovered from your illness. Recovered enough to dance at Iadmon's party last night!" He threw those last words at her like a soldier's spear.

Rhodopis felt the color drain from her face; her arms prickled with goose flesh. She had known rumor would move quickly through Memphis, but she had never imagined that word of her exploits would reach Charaxus overnight. *Does Amasis know already, too?*

"What are you talking about?" she said levelly.

Charaxus rushed at her suddenly, white with a desperate pallor. Rhodopis staggered back, appalled by his strange urgency. "I heard the news this morning," he said. "My servants were discussing it. An incredible dance, they said—one of the best anyone has ever seen."

"It was never me! I was here, sick in bed."

He laughed bitterly, spraying a drop of spittle from his lip.

"Really, Rax. There are dozens of good dancers in Memphis. How silly, for you to assume that I—"

"A black-haired woman," Charaxus said, "of your build and approximate age—young, at any rate—who could dance like

Terpsichore herself. With skin as light as alabaster. You can't fool me, Rho—"

She lurched toward him and clapped her hand over his mouth. "Watch yourself," she hissed. "You know the danger I'm in... the danger we're *both* in. *No one* must hear that name—not even my servants."

Charaxus knocked her hand away. "You lied to me. You said you were home with an illness, but you *lied*. I wonder, what else have you been hiding?"

"Why should I hide anything from you?"

A nasty laugh forced its way out between clenched teeth. "That's what I'd like to know. Haven't I been good to you? Haven't I given you everything a woman could ask for? I've even promised to make you my wife—and after you've spent so long as a hetaera, bouncing from one man's bed to the next."

"Indeed; how generous," Rhodopis said drily.

His eyes widened. A dizzying new revelation seemed to dawn on him. "All those reasons you gave for delaying our marriage, for staying here in Memphis... for continuing to work as a hetaera, a *glorified whore*... Those were all lies, too, I expect."

Rhodopis tossed her head defiantly. She had been lying, of course—about everything. But she was not likely to admit it now. "How dare you, Rax! You hurt me so. What else could I be, for the sake of our love, but honest and true? And yet you fling insults at me! It's not my fault I am what I am. The gods have made my fate, as they've made every person's fate, even yours. And you fell in love with me, the hetaera, the glorified porna. I haven't changed one bit, yet suddenly I'm not good enough as I am? Now I'm broken and unclean?"

In the blink of an eye, the anger fled from Charaxus. An expression of great agony came over him; he clutched Rhodopis' hands impulsively, squeezing so hard that the bones of her fingers ground painfully together. She resisted the urge to jerk her hands away. "Whether you were telling the truth or not, I... I can't abide this anymore. I can't stand to know that you visit other men... *entertain* them. You must go away with me to Lesvos. I can have a ship ready to sail tonight. Come away with me, and be a proper woman, a proper wife."

For one brief, wild moment, Rhodopis considered his offer. Charaxus was a fool, and a thorn in her sandal—but Lesvos was a long way off. Suppose Phanes' plan fell apart? Suppose Polycrates would not give Rhodopis his ships after all. She might find safety in Lesvos. She might take another name, shed her history, and disappear quietly into Charaxus' household. She might become a proper, subservient, altogether invisible Greek wife.

But in the next heartbeat, Rhodopis cast the thought aside. If she agreed to marry Charaxus, she would sacrifice forever the freedoms a hetaera enjoyed. Well did she remember Phanes' story of Egypt--the way it had been in days gone by, before Greece had encroached with its confining, oppressive influence. Many dangers still lay ahead; she might yet find that knife in the darkness, another blade pressed to her throat as Psamtik's once had been. But if she died carrying out her task, at least she would die a free woman, acting by her own will, making her own choices. No. The last thing Rhodopis wanted was to become a good Greek wife. *Reckon I'd rather become food for the vultures.*

She pulled her hands free of his grip. "I won't do it. I told you my reasons; I'll stay here until I've fulfilled all my obligations."

"Blast your obligations!" Charaxus clenched a fist; for a moment, Rhodopis thought he might strike her. But then he bit down on his knuckle as if struggling to contain his emotions—or trying desperately sort through the few options that remained.

After a moment, Charaxus seemed to calm himself. He walked slowly to the garden window; Rhodopis relaxed a little. *The storm has passed. He understands me now. He'll go away in a moment—apologize and leave, and in another day or two, I'll leave as well. This mess with Charaxus will be over and done with. He'll forget me, find another woman to be his wife.*

Charaxus did not turn away from the window. He stared stiffly out into the garden and said coldly, "If you do not prove your love for me by leaving tonight and marrying me, then I will have no choice but to tell the whole city that Archidike's rumors are true."

Rhodopis sucked in a silent breath. So Charaxus had heard Archidike's tales. And who else? Did all of Memphis know? Then, in a flash, a gouting flume of anger replaced her icy fear. How dare this vain, mooning lout threaten her! She, who had been an Ornament of the Harem—she, who had been wife to Cambyses, Lord of Haxamanishiya! She would have blessed every god above the earth and below it, if one of them had only risen in that moment to strike Charaxus down. That fawning, spineless creature! Why couldn't the gods simply vanish Charaxus from her presence? Now, in the very next heartbeat!

"You never would!" Rhodopis said, breathless with rage.

Charaxus turned to stare at her. His smile was slow, mocking. "Do you honestly think I won't?"

She spun on her heel, headed back toward her chamber, but Charaxus crossed the room before Rhodopis was even aware that he'd left the window. He seized her painfully by the arm. The horrid, blood-red memory of Psamtik's attack flashed back into her mind; before she could stop herself, Rhodopis whirled and lashed out with all her force. She struck Charaxus hard across his face.

He stumbled back, holding his cheek. Rhodopis gasped at her own audacity. Her hand tingled, imbued with a thrill of power.

"A proper wife would never do such a thing," Charaxus said, low and cold.

"I am not your wife," Rhodopis growled. "I'm a hetaera. And so long as I am still a hetaera, you cannot touch me without my leave. If you had any respect or love for me, you would understand what you're asking me to give up, and all for the *honor* of becoming your wife."

He lowered his hand. His cheek was red, marked by her fury. All his coldness melted away in the face of his sorrow. "Doesn't our love mean anything to you? Anything at all?"

Rhodopis glared at her former lover, every bit as cold as he had been, moments before. "Go; spread your rumor, if it will make you happy. Have me killed by Amasis, if it pleases you. But so long as I am still a hetaera, and still living free, I will not be ordered about by any man."

Anger and despair warred on Charaxus' face, the dark cloud of each emotion eclipsing the other by turns until only an indecipherable darkness remained. Then he turned briskly and left her home.

When he had gone, Rhodopis stood alone in the sitting room. Her breath came in short, sharp gasps; shock at what she had done stabbed through her, followed a strange, fatalistic awe at the terrible events she had set in motion. She had no way of knowing whether Charaxus would make good on his threat. Perhaps by sunset, the streets of Memphis would overflow with a story that corroborated Archidike's unlikely tale. It was possible that his pride was so wounded that he would leave off and hold his tongue, knowing everything between them was finished now. Was he the vengeful sort? Would he prefer to see Rhodopis brought low—even killed—rather than slink away quietly to lick his wounds? She had no idea what she ought to expect from Charaxus—and she was dreadfully afraid to find out.

There was no time to waste. She must secure the Samian fleet now, this very day, or the knife in the dark would surely come.

"Amtes!" Rhodopis shouted, hurrying back toward her bed chamber. She loosened the tie of her robe as she went; by the time she shoved her chamber door open, it trailed out behind her nakedness, half-shed already.

Amtes had been perched on a stool beside the garden window, stitching the seam in a torn tunic. She looked up in alarm, then leaped to her feet when she saw the wide-eyed fear on Rhodopis' face. "What has happened, Mistress?"

Rhodopis tossed the robe across her bed. "Make me beautiful —now. I must go to Polycrates immediately."

"But he hasn't sent for you."

"I don't care; I'm going to him all the same. Be quick! As soon as I've gone, you must send a note to Aesop. Tell him he must prepare to leave Memphis before sunset. My hair, Amtes—help me put it up! Oh, I have to see Polycrates; he must give me his ships today, or everything is lost!"

21

A DISTASTEFUL ERRAND

At Iadmon's party, after his lust had waned and they had fallen into conversation, Polycrates had mentioned that whenever he was in Memphis, he made use of a certain riverside house that belonged to an old friend of his, a wine merchant by the name of Kyrillos. Rhodopis did not know where Kyrillos' waterfront estate was; for all she could tell, it might lie far to the north or south, well beyond the city limits, among the farms and vineyards that fringed the outer edges of Memphis. Wherever the wine-seller's house was, she knew she must find it—and pray that Polycrates was there.

Amtes had called up the litter-bearers while Rhodopis had been busy with her jewelry casks, finding the right adornments to make herself look, once again, like the exquisite rarity Polycrates longed for. When enough jewels winked at her throat and wrists, she hurried back through her little house and out into the court-yard, where the litter stood waiting.

"Remember," she said to Amtes, "you must send that message to Aesop straight away."

"I will, Mistress."

She turned to the chief bearer. "Do you know where to find

the house of a wine merchant called Kyrillos? It's a waterside home, I understand."

"Yes, my lady, I know the place. But it will take at least half an hour to get there... maybe more."

Rhodopis gritted her teeth. Another damned delay. While she crept uselessly through the streets of Memphis, the twin rumors spawned by Archidike and Charaxus ran through the city, multiplying like rats everywhere they went. "Very well," she said, willing herself to remain calm. "Take me to the wine merchant's home, quick as you can."

It took nearly a full hour for the litter to reach Kyrillos' estate. All the while, Rhodopis kept an uneasy eye on the sun. It tracked to its apex, lightening the mid-day sky to pale blue; the sun was declining and the sky darkening subtly toward afternoon before Kyrillos' estate came into view. Although the curtains of the litter shielded her face from the eyes of Memphis, still Rhodopis felt as if everyone she passed was staring—and worse, whispering the very rumors she hoped to outpace, passing the fateful story from mouth to ear.

The litter finally turned into the gate of a riverside estate on the southern edge of the city; the bearers lowered the conveyance with groans of relief, for the journey had been an exceptionally long one. It was all Rhodopis could do to rise from the cushions with dignity and grace, rather than tearing the curtains apart and clawing her way up from the litter in a blind panic. The house was small, though it did boast two stories. It reminded her uncomfortably of Charaxus' estate. A guard stood beside the portico, nearly as brawny as Polycrates himself. The man toyed idly with the hilt of a long knife that stuck up from his leather belt.

Rhodopis approached the guard with a warm, innocent smile. "Hello, good man. I am here to see Polycrates. He is in, I assume?"

The guard chuckled, sounding rather surprised. "Did Polycrates send for you, then?"

"He did," she said. "He was most insistent that I should come this afternoon."

The guard braced his fists on his belt and laughed in full. She blinked in confusion, and for a moment she thought he had seen through her lie and would send her away. But the guard did not seem to disbelieve Rhodopis. He only seemed... amused. He stood aside, ushering her through the portico with a smirk.

The house was empty, though it was very fine and airy, with a comfortably lived-in atmosphere. She passed a small andron, then a reading room with shelves full of scrolls and tablets. Somehow Rhodopis doubted Polycrates found much use for his friend's reading room; he didn't seem like the sort of man who enjoyed the contemplation of philosophy or poetry. Beyond the reading room, she found a short hall and made her way down it. A large door confronted her, painted with fruits and all variety of birds. There was something too lush and showy about the fruits—unabashedly vivid, juicy and ripe. *This is the sort of room Polycrates would choose for his bedchamber, and no mistake.* She pushed the door open.

"It's about time," a woman said from inside the chamber.

Rhodopis froze on the threshold. She knew that voice. Rough, almost growling, but with a sweetness that was at curious odds with its coarser tones.

There, sprawled across the chamber's huge, ebony-legged bed, lay Archidike. A corner of the sheet only partially covered her nakedness; One breast was exposed to view, as was her side, her hip, the firmly muscled leg, flung out casually across the mattress. She rolled over in an unhurried way and looked up at the door—and stopped when she saw Rhodopis. Her face grew harder by the moment.

"Where is Polycrates?" Rhodopis said.

The surprise fled from Archidike's face. A cat-like grin of satisfaction replaced it. "Well. Rhodopis of Thrace. Not many people believed me at first, when I told them you'd come back.

They were all more eager to swallow *your* nasty little story, that I'm unclean. But they're starting to believe now, after that show you put on for Iadmon. Oh, yes. You danced with all your might and mien, didn't you? Rhodopis is certainly back in Memphis *these* days. Or will you still attempt to deny it?"

"I won't deny it," she answered quietly. There was nothing for it now but to own up to the truth. Archidike had caught her out. "But you should know why I had to hide," Rhodopis added. Quickly, she recounted the same tale she'd told Charaxus—that she couldn't bring herself to love the Pharaoh, and so he had released her from the harem on strict orders to leave Memphis, lest he be compelled to take her back again, and never set her free.

Archidike rolled her eyes. Clearly, she found the story less than convincing. "What a fascinating life you lead," she said drily.

"Tell me where I may find Polycrates."

"Craving him, are you?" Archidike stretched, purring deep in her throat. "I don't blame you; he's good. But he sent for me, not you." She paused, blinking up at Rhodopis. "Or did he send for you, after all? He does like two girls at once. More, when he can convince them to play along."

From somewhere outside, on the streets beyond Polycrates' borrowed home, rough shouts rang out, a cacophony of anger and fear. Rhodopis stood like some helpless creature stunned by the blow of a hunter's club—swaying, senseless with the shock, struck cold and useless by a grim certainty that her doom had come. Amasis had tracked her to this estate; his men were circling even now closing in... But in the next moment, she realized the shouts were nothing more than ordinary unrest, the anger that boiled over to run hot and red down every street of Memphis. She shuddered, fighting back the chill in her blood. She was safe this time. But would the next voices she heard be those of Amasis' guards, coming to drag her before the Pharaoh, to face his judgment and execution?

If not Amasis, then Cambyses will do me in. It will take days for Amtes' pigeons to reach Babylon. The only place I'll be safe now is on the deck of Polycrates' ship.

"I'm here on business of my own," Rhodopis said, straightening her spine by main force, staring down at Archidike with eloquent scorn. "I'm not here to entertain Polycrates. And if I were here for that sort of thing, I wouldn't work alongside *you*."

Archidike snorted. "Prudish as always. Gentle little Rhodopis, blushing and cringing away from the men." The hard angles of Archidike's face softened for a moment. She tapped her lower lip thoughtfully. "You should have stuck with me, you know. We could have had the best double act in Memphis, playing off one another that way. You, the delicate flower, innocent and fresh, afraid of being despoiled. And me..." She rolled onto her stomach, kicking her feet lazily in the air above her taut behind. "Ah, *me*."

"It was you who left me." Rhodopis knew she oughtn't to let Archidike needle her, but she couldn't seem to help it. Archidike deserved to hear the truth; she deserved to know what pain her vile acts had caused. "It was you who betrayed me. The worst of it is, you played at being my friend—more than a friend. You're nothing but a sly rat, a filthy beast who creeps about the alleys in the darkness. You think only of bettering yourself—never of anyone else. You don't deserve to be a hetaera. You're nothing more than a common porna at heart."

Archidike sat up. She looked at Rhodopis with such confusion, such frank startlement, that for a moment Rhodopis wondered whether she had remembered their life together in the Stable correctly. "No, Rhodopis—you sabotaged my career for your glory. Cut me out, all to gain a little temporary fame at the auction. And after all that—after you did me such a nasty turn, and dashed my hopes—you still ended up with the wealthiest patron. Then it was off to the Pharaoh's harem, wasn't it!" Her face fell; the glare she leveled at Rhodopis was so dark, so full of naked hate, that a shiver crept along Rhodopis' limbs. "The gods have always hated me," Archidike said. "Well, fuck the gods anyway, and fuck you, too. I'm making my own fortune now—making it my way. You and the gods had both better stay clear of me, if you know what's good for you. I'll walk right over anyone and anything that gets in my way. I've worked too hard, suffered too much, to be denied any longer. I will have what's mine, Rhodopis. I'll have the life I deserve."

Before Rhodopis could frame a reply, she and Archidike both started at the sound of heavy footsteps in the hall. Rhodopis whirled in the doorway, half expecting to see one of the Pharaoh's guards, or perhaps Charaxus, come to finish what he'd started back at her estate. But it was only Polycrates. He was staring down into a pitcher of wine as he walked; he did not see Rhodopis.

"Archidike," he shouted, "I've found your favorite in Kyrillos' cellar—Spartan sweet red. Are you ready for—"

Archidike rolled on the bed, tangling herself in the sheets, purring with low, mocking laughter. Polycrates looked up—and stopped in his tracks at sight of Rhodopis, pale and silent before him. A great, bloody gout of wine sloshed over the rim of the pitcher, splashing on the clean white tiles of the floor.

"Eulalia," Polycrates said. "What a surprise."

"She couldn't stop thinking about you," Archidike said.

Rhodopis gathered her linen cloak tightly around her shoulders. "I'll go. I'll come back later, when you're... not so busy."

"Oh, don't go," Archidike said slyly. "There's no need for it."

Polycrates eyed Rhodopis. Though he stood several paces away, she could all but feel his hands on her, untying the knots of her gown as he'd done at Iadmon's party. The speculative flicker in his eye quickly bloomed to open desire. "No need, surely" he agreed. A grin spread among the thick black curls of his beard. "None whatsoever. Why don't you join us, Eulalia?"

"I really can't," she said quickly. "I must be going. I—"

"Come, now." He moved past her, his shoulder brushing against her own, and set the pitcher of wine on a table. "It's all in fun. And Archidike won't mind, will you?"

"Not in the least," Archidike said, amused.

"Surely you don't—" Rhodopis began.

Polycrates finished the sentence for her. "Want both of you at the same time? Oh, surely I do, my precious delight—my rare treasure. I most certainly do."

Rhodopis hesitated. She swallowed hard, but the lump in her throat remained.

"Never fear," he cajoled. "I'll pay you well for it. I always pay well, don't I, Archidike?"

She thought frantically, *There's no way out.* If she was to have any hope of convincing Polycrates to give her the fleet, she had to keep him happy. And there was no time left to stall. She must take the gamble, or Charaxus—and the Pharaoh—would win.

She stepped into the chamber, loosening her linen gown. It fell to the floor with a whisper. Rhodopis climbed on the bed beside Archidike. She fixed a smile on her face for Polycrates' sake, but she could feel the fire of hatred burning in her own eyes. For a moment, she and Archidike stared at one another, each challenging and furious, each daring the other to back down. Then, with a low, rumbling laugh of anticipation, Polycrates joined them on the bed.

22

CONFESSION

As soon as she could disentangle herself from Polycrates' arms, Rhodopis scrambled from his bed, pulled her gown up, and knotted it hastily over one shoulder. She threw the linen cape around her neck without looking back at Archidike or Polycrates, and hurried from the room. Rhodopis stormed down the hallway, burning with shame, tears blurring her vision. Every moment of that awful encounter replayed itself in her memory, in cruelly vivid detail. Archidike's smug air of victory. The crawling sensation on Rhodopis' skin whenever she had chanced to brush against Archidike. Worst by far was the plain and powerful delight Polycrates took in the other woman. Rhodopis may be the rare, exquisite dancer who had piqued his appetite for the finest, most unusual things... but Archidike was clearly the more desirable plaything, in Polycrates' estimation. He had positively fawned on her, only reaching for Rhodopis now and then, as an afterthought. The whole embarrassing tableau had made her feel like an especially small and wilted radish, served up alongside a roasted goose.

Mortified and afraid, Rhodopis very nearly swept right out of Kyrillos' estate, climbed into her litter, and returned to her home.

But just before she reached the portico, she halted. Charaxus was somewhere out there, prowling about the city, enacting his vengeance even now. If she left without securing Polycrates' ships, everything was finished for good. She had to make one last attempt. Her life—and Aesop's—depended on getting out of Memphis before the Pharaoh heard her name.

Rhodopis turned reluctantly and made her way back through the halls. She found the painted door and stood staring at its bright red fruits for a long moment. She could hear muffled voices inside—Polycrates murmuring in the pleasantly sleepy sensation that always overcame men when their passion was spent, and Archidike, chattering happily, laughing to herself, well pleased with her day's work.

Damn her. Damn them both. How could she get Polycrates alone?

She peered this way and that, searching the hall for a likely hiding place. There was a small closet near the bedchamber, cramped and dark; Rhodopis crept inside. She shut the door carefully and backed up against a row of dusty shelves. Groping slowly, carefully, she found sealed clay jugs beneath her hands—wine, she assumed—and hard, flat wheels of some smooth, waxy substance. They could only be cheeses.

A fine predicament for Lady Eulalia, she thought bitterly. *Cowering in a cheese closet while the Pharaoh hunts for her head.*

Rhodopis pressed herself against the door and listened. The house remained still and silent. She waited for half an hour or more, shifting her weight from one foot to the other, trying to ignore the growing ache in her back. Just as she began to convince herself that it was hopeless after all, that she must return home hope for the best, the hinges of the bedchamber door creaked.

"I'll be back in two days, then," Archidike said.

Polycrates' muffled reply came from somewhere inside the chamber.

"Perhaps we'll have another guest in our fun." Archidike's laugh was thick with cruelty. "Though I doubt we will find another as interesting as... Lady Eulalia."

Footsteps, moving lightly down the hall. Rhodopis waited until she could no longer hear Archidike's retreating steps. Then she counted to fifty and eased herself out of the closet. Just as she emerged, Polycrates appeared, too, whistling happily. He had tied a simple, rumpled white kilt around his waist—the sort Egyptian men wore. It looked perfectly ridiculous on the inveterate Egypt-hater.

Polycrates gave a great start of surprise at the sight of Rhodopis slinking from the wine closet. Then he laughed uproariously. "What, back for more?"

Rhodopis shook her head. "Not for more of... that. Please, Polycrates. I must speak with you. It's why I came today, and it's terribly important."

He paused, considering her earnest face and trembling hands as he scratched his beard. His brows drew together in a peeved frown, and Rhodopis knew he intended to send her on her way. She clutched her hands in a show of pure desperation.

"I'll fall on my knees and beg if that's what you want."

Polycrates sighed. "All right, all right. No need to fall on your knees—you can save that for later. I'll hear what you've come to say, if it's so blasted important. But only over wine and food. I'm famished; the two of you worked me like a horse in the traces. Come along to the andron."

She followed him down the hall. Polycrates sprawled across a couch with a groan of exhaustion; Rhodopis took the couch opposite with considerably more grace. Polycrates called for his servants, and in moments a woman appeared from the kitchen, bowing, resting her hands in the simple sash that marked her as a slave.

"Bring good cheese and the best bread," Polycrates said, "and some of those figs in honey. Is there any more smoked fish?"

"Yes, Master, indeed there is."

"Bring me a great pile of the fish, then." As the kitchen slave turned away, he said to Rhodopis, "Smoked fish is not my favorite, but it's fortifying after any especially taxing exertion."

"Good Man," Rhodopis began, "I wanted to ask you about—"

"Ahh... Archidike," Polycrates sighed. His eyelids slid half-closed, an expression of heavy satiety. "Is she not the most delicious, the most delightful, the most entertaining of women?"

Rhodopis raised her brows and said nothing.

"I had her several times last year when I came through Memphis. After I left, I tried to find another woman who excited me half as much—the gods know, I tried. But I never could. She is like a force of nature. Like a brush fire or a great, raging storm." He sighed again.

"I thought you liked the most exquisite things," Rhodopis said. "I grant you, her blue eyes are interesting against that dark skin, but she can hardly be called exquisite. She's so... coarse."

"I like the most *unusual* things," Polycrates said. "Archidike is certainly unusual. It's not just those blue eyes, though Poseidon knows they are as fascinating and wild as the sea. It's... everything. Every damned and blessed thing about her."

Rhodopis stared at him in frank disbelief. Archidike had always lacked dignity and refinement, ever since her days in the Stable. Some men certainly seemed to enjoy her wild spirit, but few seemed inclined to sing her praises.

"She's like a lioness stalking her prey," Polycrates said appreciatively. "Dangerous."

"Archidike is certainly that," Rhodopis answered drily. Perhaps the gods were amusing themselves by setting up a contest between Charaxus and Archidike. Which tale about Rhodopis would reach the Pharaoh first?

The kitchen slave appeared with a tray of food; she set it on the table between Rhodopis and Polycrates. The pirate tucked into his meal with zest, but Rhodopis could only stare despondently at the food. Time was growing shorter by the moment; the gods laughed in their realm of power, watching the twin snakes of rumor twist ever closer to Amasis—while Rhodopis could do nothing but lie on a pirate's couch, miserably contemplating a wedge of cheese.

"In Miletos, I found a girl called Elpis," Polycrates said, his mouth stuffed with figs and fortifying fish. "I had her for two weeks straight. She had a fearsome streak, just like Archidike—angry and strong, with hard eyes and sharp nails. Ah, very sharp indeed! I thought she would surpass my little Memphian demoness, but when it was time to sail on to the next port, I came very close to forgetting all about Elpis. It was Archidike I thought of instead—hungered for, really. I craved her, with an instinct quite outside the realm of rational thought, even outside of dreams."

Rhodopis made some small, inarticulate noise, trying to hurry Polycrates along the path of reminiscence.

But Polycrates showed no sign of leaving off. He talked on and on, recalling the women who had pleased him best, in ports from Aphaia to Akrotiri, Halicarnassus to Troy. Every woman had been surpassingly beautiful, talented, unique in some distinct and important way. But who among them could compare to Archidike? The wild, the untamable, the unpredictable hetaera with blue fire in her eyes and a mouthful of hateful curses. As Polycrates' lust for Archidike waxed like the full moon, Rhodopis' heart began to beat with unexpected surprise. It seemed Archidike meant more to the Samian than Rhodopis had assumed. She was not just a favorite hetaera. Rhodopis with her dancing, her exquisite rarity, was at best a mere curiosity. It was Archidike who had captured Polycrates' heart. She wondered if Archidike was aware of it yet—or, if she knew, whether she would care.

"There is no one in all the world who can compare to Archidike." Polycrates finished his worship by stabbing a fig with his eating knife. He plucked it from the blade with his teeth and chewed slowly, eyes closed in ecstasy as if the fig held all the sweetness of Archidike's kiss.

"I am surely nothing like her," Rhodopis said. "And you *do* know how to make a woman feel inadequate! Here I am, back for more—and all you can speak of is her?"

"You're not back for more," Polycrates laughed. "You're here to talk to me about this mysterious business of yours, whatever it is that plagues your mind. Talk, then."

Rhodopis saw at once that she could not convince Polycrates to commit his ships in this way—sated as he was, hungering only for the woman he loved. He would laugh her off; he would never believe she could deliver on a promise of Babylonian silver. She would have to lure him back to bed after all. With Archidike gone, she might hope to reignite his passion for the exquisite and the rare. It might be enough to bring him around.

"Maybe I changed my mind," she said lightly. "Maybe I'm back for more, after all."

Polycrates laughed but said nothing.

"When one must share, one never gets quite enough for satisfaction."

He watched her steadily over the table with its half-emptied tray. Rhodopis could all but read his thoughts: *Is she in earnest? Does she truly want me again?*

Rhodopis stood; for the second time that day, she cast off her linen cape. "I am not Archidike," she said slowly, "but surely I have some merits." She untied the dress. It, too, fell once more.

Polycrates came to her with another raucous laugh. He lifted her in his arms and laid her across on his supper couch. Rhodopis scratched his back and shoulders as he positioned himself above her; she bit his arm as hard as she dared, trying to make herself seem as dangerous and unpredictable as Archidike. Anything to bring him to her side, to enmesh him in her charms —anything to get out of Memphis that night.

"You do have merits of your own," Polycrates said, running his hands up her body.

"As do you," she murmured.

"Which of mine do you like best?" He moved her hand to his cock, hard and ready beneath the Egyptian kilt.

Rhodopis squeezed dutifully, but she said, "Your fast ships, of course."

He laughed. "My ships? I don't believe a woman has ever given me that answer before."

"Then that makes me unusual, too."

He shrugged. "I didn't take you for the type of woman who craves the sea. That sort of woman is typically less..." He seemed to be searching for the right word. "Refined."

"But your ships do sound wonderful." She ran her hands up his muscular and rather hairy chest, twined her fingers behind his neck. "I would love to see them. Wouldn't it be a great laugh, to go sailing together?"

"Sailing—where?"

"Anywhere," Rhodopis said at once. "Far beyond Egypt. You said you've never been to Babylon—"

"No ship can make it to Babylon."

"But you could sail to Gebal, and take a caravan across the desert to Babylon. Don't you want to see it? I've heard it's the greatest city in the world—far better and richer than Memphis. You have no great love for Egypt—you told me as much at Charaxus' party, the first night we met. I have no love for this place, either. Let us both go away together. Let us leave Egypt—tonight! I feel so... oh, wild and unpredictable! Come, Polycrates, let's do it before we change our minds."

His hands darted up behind his neck; he seized Rhodopis by the wrists and, quick as a cobra's strike, pinned her arms above her head. The dense, black beard descended upon her mouth. His kiss was forceful, dominating. But his hands pressed harder, fixing her to the couch. When he pulled back from the kiss,

Rhodopis squawked in protest, trying to free herself from his grip.

"So. You want my boats, eh? You're after my ships. That's why you came here today."

"No, I—"

"I am no fool, Eulalia."

"I only want to sail away. An adventure!" She put on a show of pout and tease. "I thought you liked adventurous women."

"No well-bred woman wants to sail off with a pirate like me— not when she's one of the most sought-after hetaerae in Memphis, earning a fortune every night. I doubt even Archidike, wild as she is, would give up so much freedom and wealth to sail from port to port." His scowl deepened. "And you came here today without being called; I never sent for you. You came of your own accord, to try to convince me to spirit you away in one of my ships. Tell me what's truly going on here, Eulalia. Tell me the truth now, or I shall get angry."

Rhodopis bit her lip. A great shudder of surrender passed through her body, wracking her limbs, sending a curious warmth down her spine. What did she have to lose by confessing the truth to Polycrates? Archidike would do her work, if Charaxus hadn't already; the Pharaoh would know all about her return to Memphis by moonrise. Rhodopis' life would be forfeit. She may as well be honest with the man.

She looked up into his dark eyes. "I'm a spy," she said calmly. "I was a hetaera here in Memphis, but Amasis took me into his harem, and then sent me off to Persia to report on Cambyses. Only, once I got to Babylon, I changed allegiance and agreed to work for Cambyses instead."

His shaggy brows raised.

She went on. "I want the Persian king to conquer Egypt, and restore it to the way it was before we Greeks had so much influence. I want Amasis pulled from his throne, and I want his son

Psamtik destroyed." The fire of hate flared in her belly. "I will see Psamtik destroyed, do you hear me?"

The pirate nodded slowly, but still, he said nothing.

"Cambyses is ready to do it," Rhodopis said, "ready to fall on Egypt—but he needs Greek allies. I've been here in Memphis for weeks now, trying desperately to find someone—anyone—who seems likely to make a useful alliance with Persia. Someone who can stop Amasis from getting the help he'll need when Cambyses attacks. I found no such man, though... until I met you. Your fleet, your connections in Greece and Memphis—and you have no loyalty to the Horus Throne. I want you to join forces with Cambyses, and help us conquer Egypt."

Still, Polycrates held his tongue. He continued staring down at her, wide-eyed with some emotion Rhodopis couldn't quite place. It might have been horror. She thought a hungry bolt of greed crossed his expression, too, with a quick, silvery flicker. Then, all at once, he threw back his head and roared with laughter, so loud the andron seemed to shudder. He released her; Rhodopis jerked her hands down to her chest and rubbed her wrists, glaring.

"You hurt me, you brute."

"What a tale!" Polycrates said.

"It's all true—every word." She fought to sit up; Polycrates retreated on the couch, allowing her to scramble upright. "You must believe me."

"I do believe."

"You... you do?"

"It's too absurd a tale to be false!"

Polycrates returned his attention to the figs on his supper tray. He ate one, then another, while Rhodopis sat with her heart thumping, waiting for him to speak. At last, unable to bear the suspense any longer, she said, "Now that you know, what are you going to do?"

Polycrates only chuckled. He stood and stretched with his bare back to Rhodopis. The red tracks of Archidike's claws still showed on his skin. Polycrates lifted his cup of wine, drained it in one long draft. When he lowered the cup, he wore an air of happy buoyancy like some bright-colored robe. "What am I going to do?" he said. "Why, I'm going to overthrow Egypt, of course. What else should a man like me do, when given with such an opportunity?"

Rhodopis did not trust him. She swallowed hard. "You're only teasing me. It's cruel, Polycrates, when my life depends on finding someone to help."

He shook his head. "It's no jest, Eulalia. I'm quite serious. I go wherever the money's best, but the money hasn't been particularly impressive in Egypt for years now. I'm only here now out of necessity—and perhaps, if I'm honest with myself, to enjoy Archidike a few more times before I leave for good. But Amasis is a fool, and Egypt is plagued by this damnable unrest. I expect the pay will be much better under Cambyses than any fares I can hope to earn here in Memphis." He stilled, suddenly thoughtful. "It seems so clear to me now—go to Persia, and sell my ships to their cause. It's a wonder I never thought of it myself, for everybody with the least spark of intelligence can see where Egypt is headed. But the truth is, I would never have thought of it if you hadn't spilled out your confession to me. You funny little hetaera." He laughed again, hearty and amused. "The gods are strange, aren't they?"

A slow, hopeful light crept around the edges of Rhodopis' thoughts, like the morning sun peeking over a misty horizon. She wasn't doomed after all—not yet, not for certain. She scrambled from the couch and snatched up her dress, donning it hastily. "We must sail to Persia as soon as possible. We must leave tonight!"

Polycrates laid a steadying hand on her shoulder. "Why the rush, girl?"

"Cambyses is expecting an ally by now. And he'll be so glad to have you, with all your ships, and all the people you know—here and in Greece. You can influence—"

"You've got some other reason for leaving tonight."

She pressed her lips tightly together. But reluctance and secrecy were only habits by now. She had already told Polycrates the most dangerous and damning tale. What trouble could the rest of the truth make?

"I do have another reason. My name isn't Eulalia—it's Rhodopis. If Amasis learns that I'm back in the city, he'll send his guards after me straight away. There will be no mercy for me, Polycrates—I betrayed the Pharaoh. Charaxus knows who I am, but I angered him this morning, and he went off full of hate, vowing to spread the word that I've returned. And..." She hung her head, unable to look at him while she spoke on. "And Archidike knows, too. Archidike has her own reasons for hating me. She would be very glad to see me hurt, or even killed." She looked up at him again, lurching forward in sudden desperation. "But I would never hurt Archidike, Polycrates—you must believe me! The sourness between us is all due to a misunderstanding. I'll leave her well alone, for your sake, if you'll only help me get away before she can tell the Pharaoh I'm here!"

Polycrates patted her on the shoulder. It felt so strange to receive a comforting gesture from this overbearing man—who had only touched her with the basest lust, until now—that Rhodopis nearly laughed. But there was nothing amusing about her predicament.

"I can't leave tonight," Polycrates said. "Certain arrangements must be made before I can sail. My crew will take at least a day to track down and rally back to the ships; they're scattered all over the wine shops and alleys, sniffing after pornae. There are other details I must see to before I can leave, as well."

Tears stung her eyes. "How long, then?"

"Tomorrow night. I can be ready by then, if I work hard today. You must lie low for one more day. You can do it, can't you?"

"I shall have to," Rhodopis said faintly.

"Good. Meet me at the North End quay tomorrow at moonrise, second to last mooring. My ship is called *Omen*."

"You won't leave me behind?"

He laughed, harsh and loud. "Gods, no. If what you've said is true, I'd best have you beside me. How else can I hope to explain myself to King Cambyses? If I haven't your blessing, he might think me a spy sent by Amasis. Then it would be my head on a spear, instead of yours."

23

AT MOONRISE

THAT NIGHT, COWERING IN HER LITTLE HOUSE, RHODOPIS AND Amtes occupied themselves by packing a large basket apiece for the coming journey. They would be forced to travel light; they could risk no conspicuous parade of goods, streaming out of Eulalia's estate toward the North End quay. Whatever they brought out of Memphis—each necessity for the long journey— must fit within the two large baskets Amtes had procured. The baskets had tightly fitted lids and woven straps for the women's shoulders. Rhodopis would carry one, Amtes the other; whatever they could not hoist onto their backs would be left behind for the servants to claim.

Rhodopis and her handmaid passed a few tense hours by the work, sorting carefully through each possession in the house, weighing its relative benefits and potential uses. In the end, she and Amtes packed a few changes of plain, unadorned clothing, the simplest hygiene goods, and a handful of bracelets and earrings each. None of the jewelry was too grand or rich, for they must be able to trade the pieces with ease in port towns along the way. The bartered ornaments could be used to secure whatever essentials they did not carry out of Memphis. Amtes also packed her writing brush and ink, along with a few scraps of papyrus. She had sent her last pigeon that afternoon, alerting Cambyses that Rhodopis had secured his expected ally, along with a small fleet of fast ships. They both prayed the message would reach Babylon in time.

But it did not take long to prepare for the journey. As night deepened and both women fell idle, Rhodopis carried a bowl of incense out into the garden. She crouched among the flowers, drifting the smoke across her face, praying to Ishtar and a host of other gods for mercy and protection. Now and then, the streets beyond her walls would surge and with angry shouts, and every time she flinched, certain that Polycrates had abandoned her and the Pharaoh had come. Often, she broke into tears, frantic with the strain of waiting. She could do nothing but pray, casting her fears up to the distant white stars.

By the time the incense had crumbled to ashes, Rhodopis was bone-weary with fear. She crept into her bed and slept for a few merciful hours, too exhausted to pray any longer. But morning came relentlessly, and when she rose, Rhodopis was more frightened than ever before. An impossibly long day stretched ahead, bleak and cruel—hours of useless pacing, hours of uncertainty while she waited for moonrise to come. She ate little of the food Amtes brought, and remained beside her window, by turns tearful and emotionless, then somber with acceptance. Polycrates was every bit the pirate, the consummate opportunist. She was painfully aware that he might have found some advantage in selling her out to the Pharaoh, or gratifying his lover Archidike by sealing Rhodopis to her fate. By the time the sun set, she was half mad with tension. She would have welcomed the Pharaoh's guards pounding on her door by that time, merely for an end to the strain.

But at last, the purple shroud of twilight descended over

Memphis. Night's black deepened. The thin, sharp crescent of a white moon edged above the garden wall. When pale starlight limned the first spring blossoms in her garden, Rhodopis breathed deeply. The cool night air filled her, calmed her. For a moment, she half convinced herself it was the first breath she'd ever drawn.

"It's time," Amtes said quietly, coming into the chamber. She had not painted the false tattoos on her face that morning; the disguise was no longer needed. Faint traces of ink remained on her cheeks and brow, eerie, shadowy. Amtes hefted her basket up from the floor, fitted its straps on her strong shoulders.

"What have you told the household staff?" Rhodopis said.

"That you're off to attend a client who prefers late-night engagements. I kept my cape's hood up while I spoke to them, so they didn't see my face and notice my tattoos missing... in case anything goes amiss. If we run into trouble, we must return here to the estate, and take up our old disguises."

"Nothing must go amiss," Rhodopis said hotly.

Amtes tossed a cloak of simple, unbleached linen to Rhodopis. "Put this on."

"And if the servants see me leaving, dressed this way?"

"They'll think it's part of the games you play with tonight's client. In the morning, they will find the letter I've written. It says you've gone back to Lesvos to see your dying father one last time, and you've left all the goods here at the estate to them. That will keep them all well paid through the end of the year. They won't be caught out in any desperation."

Amtes wrapped a long scarf around Rhodopis' head, covering her black-dyed hair. The scarf made a rather skimpy costume, but Rhodopis knew she could shelter better beneath that simple strip of silk far better than she could in the trappings of a hetaera.

Amtes slipped something small and hard into Rhodopis' hand. The latter looked down in surprise. It was a small knife, sheathed in flat, slick leather. Two long, thin braids of dark silk trailed from the sheath.

"In case we are separated," Amtes said. "Tie it around her waist."

Rhodopis did as her handmaid said, then lifted her basket and settled it on her shoulders. She nodded to Amtes. Side by side, they slipped quietly through the darkened house, out beneath the portico, and across Eulalia's small, neat courtyard. When they passed beneath the outer gate, quiet as a pair of shadows, Rhodopis' heart lurched with an uncomfortable sensation of exposure. She pulled the rough cape close around her body, seeking some comfort in its folds, and hurried along the street toward the quay.

Amtes had already scouted the route earlier that day. She led Rhodopis swiftly through the alleys, the empty market squares. Step by hurried step, they pressed on toward the river. They passed through groups of men and women who went about the business of early evening—bearing jugs of water from the river, beating sleeping mats on the street corners, or laughing and jostling as they moved from one beer shop to the next. No one cast an eye in Rhodopis' direction; she moved among the citizens of Memphis, unremarked. Still, although the city appeared to take no notice, Rhodopis couldn't rid herself of a dreadful, sinking certainty she and Amtes were followed. Again and again, she glanced back over her shoulder, scanning the streets for any sign of pursuit. But there was no one—no suspicious shadow darting in her wake, no troop of soldiers closing with their swords upraised.

It's only raw nerves, she told herself firmly as they turned down the final alley. The stars reflected off the river, spread before her now like a great dark swath of polished obsidian. *Only nerves. You're almost there.*

Rhodopis never knew what force compelled her to look back one last time. But when she did, there was no mistaking

Archidike, striding through the alley behind her, uncloaked and exposed, her smile arrogant and mocking.

"Oh, gods," Rhodopis hissed. She took Amtes' hand, pulling her faster toward the river.

"What is it?" Amtes asked stoutly.

"Archidike. She's following us."

Amtes peered back into the alley. Then she set her jaw and picked up her pace. "Keep one hand on your knife," the hand-maid suggested. "That one's dangerous."

They broke out of the alley, onto the broad, flat expanse of the quay. Several boats waited at their moorings; Rhodopis scanned each one as she hurried past, searching for the *Omen*, but she did not see Polycrates' ship. For one panicked moment, she thought the *Omen* was not there. They had come to the wrong quay, or worse, Polycrates had set sail without them. But then she spotted his boat—second to last in its row, as he'd said it would be. The *Omen*'s high, curved prow was reminiscent of the *Samian Wind* that a sob of relief ripped itself from Rhodopis' chest. Polycrates had been good as his word. "There it is," she said, pulling Amtes toward the ship.

Rhodopis heard the rush of Archidike's running feet a heart-beat before the sharp-nailed hand closed on her arm. Rhodopis stifled a scream—of surprise, or anger; she wasn't sure—and whirled to face her attacker. She would have drawn the knife, would have struck at Archidike with all the force of her fury, but Archidike had caught Rhodopis by the right arm, and her right hand was clenched around the hilt. She could never reach Archidike with the blade.

"Don't try to stop me," Rhodopis growled.

Archidike's pale eyes glowed in the starlight, a cold fire. "If you try to leave, I'll go to the Pharaoh. I'll tell Amasis everything."

Amtes lunged at Archidike; the latter turned, and turned again, shoving Rhodopis between herself and the handmaid.

"Haven't you already told half the city?" Rhodopis twisted against Archidike's grip. "Amasis will know soon enough, as it is."

"But he'll know within the hour if you board that boat. He'll send his fleet after you. You'll be killed, Rhodopis—and well do you deserve it."

With a last, frenzied effort, Rhodopis wrenched herself free. Her arm felt bruised, but there was no time to fret. Her fist locked tight on the knife. "I'll be killed either way! You don't know what you're meddling in. This is bigger than you think, Archidike. Leave off; crawl back under your rock and let me go in peace. If you do, I can promise you'll never see me again. I will never interfere with your life or your fortunes. You'll be rid of me forever. Isn't that what you want?"

"Hurry on, Mistress," Amtes said, stepping between Rhodopis and the bristling hetaera. "We've no more time to waste."

Archidike snorted. "Mistress?" To Amtes she said, "Do you know who—and what—your mistress is?"

"Ignore her," Amtes said. She took Rhodopis by the wrist, tried to drag her toward the *Omen*'s ramp. But Archidike laid hold of Rhodopis again.

A man's voice cracked across the quay. "Let go of her!" Rhodopis thought it might be Polycrates. But then recognition flashed along her every nerve, sharp and unwelcome as the pain of a toothache. It was none other than Charaxus; he came pelting down the line of ships toward them.

"Gods give me strength," Rhodopis muttered.

"I knew it!" Charaxus cried, half wounded, half victorious. "I didn't want to believe it, but the evidence was all there before me."

"Evidence? You're talking nonsense, Charaxus." Rhodopis jerked this way and that in Archidike's grip, but the hetaera had locked her talon-like nails into the cloth of Rhodopis' dress. She could not break free.

"All the signs were clear. Yet I didn't want to believe that you could be unfaithful, and seek the love of another man."

Rhodopis kicked out helplessly, trying to shoo Charaxus away. "Get away, you fool!" She was still unwilling to shout, afraid of raising her voice. "I'm a hetaera. You know that; you *know* I go with other men."

"Yes." The word was half a sob. "But I didn't know you would actually *go* with another man. Yet here I find you, trying to board his ship. Trying to *leave*." Charaxus' face twisted in disgust, in harsh disbelief. "And *Polycrates*, of all the foul, rutting beasts in the world!"

Silently, Rhodopis cursed the gods. Then, wrath overwhelming fear, she cursed Charaxus aloud. "You thrice-damned, mindless, shit-pot fool! You followed me here?"

"I saw you leave your house," Charaxus said, speaking quickly. He looked feverish with his awful triumph. "All wrapped up like some lowly maid. I thought you must be sneaking off for a private meeting. But I never thought... *Polycrates!*"

Archidike laughed, but she did not loosen her hold on Rhodopis' dress. "I swear, this is better than honey cakes. I've never seen such a good show, not even in the amphitheaters."

"I won't let you go with him," Charaxus cried. His voice rose to a dog's bay, an inconsolable howl. "I won't let you! You're mine —my love, my only!"

"By Aphrodite's tits, what is going on down there?" At the rough, bullish shout, all of them looked up to the *Omen*'s deck— Amtes, Rhodopis, and her two attackers. There stood Polycrates, the curtain of his cabin swinging shut behind him. In the night's pale gleam, he seemed as broad and stony as a monument. As soon as he recognized Rhodopis under her silk scarf and basket, he leaned over the rail of his ship. "Leave, Charaxus." There was a distinct note of amusement in Polycrates' voice. "This is none of your business now. Believe me; you don't want any part of it."

Charaxus trembled as he answered. "I won't leave her. I love her; she's to be my wife."

"Oh, I am *not!*" Rhodopis thrashed helplessly, side to side. When that got her nowhere, she stamped down hard on Charaxus' foot. He grunted with pain and clenched his teeth, but he did not let go of her wrist.

Polycrates stormed down the *Omen's* ramp. He crossed the quay in half a dozen quick, furious strides then leaned very close to Charaxus' face. "Go. Now," he snarled. "Before I kill you."

Charaxus recoiled briefly; his grip loosened, and Rhodopis pulled free. Polycrates gave Rhodopis a firm shove; she stumbled toward the ramp, slipping quickly into the narrow passage between the *Omen* and its neighboring boat. Archidike, laughing, refused to loosen her hold. Rhodopis dragged her along behind. She could hear Archidike's sandals scuffing against stone as that miserable creature dug in her heels. If only Rhodopis' dress would tear, and set her free!

"Go," Rhodopis said to Amtes, nodding ahead. Obediently, the handmaid strode a few paces ahead. Then, her uncanny composure finally cracking, Amtes bolted alone up the ramp.

Rhodopis strained along the quay, striving toward the ramp, which still wobbled with the speed of Amtes' flight. The next moment, she froze, trembling. There was no mistaking the high, cold hiss that rang out across the quay: the song of a blade sliding from its sheath. She stopped, staring back at the men.

Charaxus had drawn his sword. "Fight me, if you dare," he said rather breathlessly to Polycrates.

Polycrates' hand flew to the hilt of his sword, but he laughed heartily. "Are you so eager to die, little man?"

"Fight me," Charaxus said, quivering, "and whoever is left standing will have Rhodopis forever."

"Now this is a good show." Archidike let go of Rhodopis and backed away, but the hetaera now blocked the only route away from Charaxus. The two men bristled at one another between

Rhodopis and the boat's ramp. Rhodopis could do nothing but cower on the narrow quay, clutching her cloak around her body, waiting for a chance to bolt in one direction or the other.

As Polycrates drew his blade, Amtes dropped her basket on the deck of the ship. She made as if to return to her mistress, but Rhodopis shook her head, silently commanding her to stay where she was. Amtes' face paled, but she remained on board. Amtes clutched anxiously at the rail, leaning over it as Polycrates had one—as if she could will Rhodopis to sprout wings and fly up to the Omen's deck like one of her pigeons.

At least I know Amtes will make it back to Persia alive, Rhodopis thought. All hope for herself had crumbled. *She is known to Phanes; she can explain Polycrates to the king.*

And whether I live or die, Psamtik might yet lose his throne. Remembrance of Psamtik—of the foul creature she had sworn to destroy—flared up, bright and painful, in her mind. She may be a hunted beast, backed into a corner, but she would yet find some way to ensure the King's Son fell from power. She pictured herself dragged before Amasis, harried and abused by his soldiers... but before they ran her through with their bloody swords, might she not find some small chance to sink that tiny belt-blade into Psamtik's throat?

Charaxus chose that unfortunate moment to duck away from Polycrates. He clutched at Rhodopis again. With the memory of Psamtik still hot in her head, she ripped her small blade from its sheath before she could stop to think. She very likely would have killed Charaxus then and there—spilled his blood on the cold stone of the riverbank—if Polycrates hadn't chuckled with pure disdain.

"It will be hard to fight me, man to man," Polycrates said, "with your darling in your arms. Or do you plan to use her as a shield? Release the girl, and I'll oblige you by killing you. That seems to be what you're driving at, after all."

Charaxus shoved Rhodopis behind him. He sprang toward

Polycrates with a hoarse cry of rage. The Samian parried the first thrust of Charaxus' sword, and the next, moving with arrogant ease. But Charaxus' attacks were fierce, unrelenting. He fought with deadly earnest—and why not, Rhodopis thought, dizzy with disbelief. Love itself was at stake.

Polycrates was far larger and certainly more brutal than his opponent, but Charaxus was surprisingly agile. More, fury made him tireless, filling him with an energy and resolve Rhodopis could scarcely credit. He dodged Polycrates' blows like a fly dodges a whisk. Then, as Polycrates lumbered about to face his rapid assault, Charaxus darted in from the side and landed a blow to the pirate's arm. Polycrates grunted with pain and rage.

Gods! Charaxus is a better swordsman than I ever imagined he could be.

He drove Polycrates back, and further backward still, inching the towering, bearded man toward the edge of the quay... and the dark water below.

Charaxus will kill him if I don't do something!

Polycrates could never be talked into giving up the fight, boarding the *Omen*, and sailing away. Rhodopis knew better than to try. His pride was more sensitive than his cock—wasn't that the case with all men? He would see this fight through to the bitter end, even if he died in pointless, wasteful combat. If Rhodopis hoped to get the pirate back on his ship—and to Babylon in one functional piece—she must find some means of forcing him aboard, before Charaxus wounded him so grievously that he could not sail.

The men fought on while Rhodopis wrung her hands, but in the space between two ringing blows of their swords, she heard the low, mocking purl of Archidike's laugh. All at once, Rhodopis knew what she must do. She slipped one hand down to the little knife. Then she stumbled a few steps backward, feigning fear over the men's confrontation, and waited for the right moment to strike. Charaxus forced Polycrates back again, and—yes, now!—

the fight moved past the foot of the *Omen*'s ramp. Rhodopis leaped at Archidike; she pressed the tip of her blade against the hetaera's throat.

Archidike went very still. The laughter died on her lips. She looked at Rhodopis with eerie calm; for a moment they stared at one another, and Rhodopis thought she saw the briefest flash of regret in the eyes of her former friend.

"Come with me," Rhodopis hissed. Now it was her turn to take Archidike by the arm, digging her nails into soft flesh. She shoved Archidike before her, marching her up the boat's ramp while the men went on fighting on the quay below, oblivious to what Rhodopis had just done.

"Take her," Rhodopis said to Amtes.

Amtes obeyed, wrenching Archidike's arm up behind her back. Rhodopis passed the knife to her handmaid. "Keep the blade at her throat. If she tries to break away, kill her."

Archidike laughed, hoarse and dry. "You won't kill me. I know you, Rhodopis. You're far too soft, too tender—the delicate, innocent white lotus."

Rhodopis made no reply; she only stared into Archidike's eyes. She could feel her rage boiling over, all the anger that had long simmered inside her rising to a swift and terrible head. The pain and shame of what Psamtik had done to her—the loneliness, the terrible waiting during her time in the Pharaoh's harem. And Persia—the fear, the awful, snared, trapped-animal feeling that had never left her, never let her rest. She was not Iadmon's precious white lotus any longer. The gods had remade her, fashioned her anew. Archidike saw the truth now; her blue eyes widened with a fearful new understanding. She swallowed hard, her throat moving gingerly against the point of the blade.

"If the gods are merciful," Rhodopis said to Amtes, "I'll be back in a heartbeat. But you must keep Archidike here, no matter what may happen."

Before Amtes could protest, Rhodopis flung her basket off

her shoulders and hurried back down the ramp. She winced and dodged as the men's blades flew, clashing and ringing in the cold moonlight. Charaxus and Polycrates broke apart, only for the most fleeting moment while they steadied themselves for another attack—but Rhodopis did not wait for them to charge in again. She threw herself between the men, arms flung out, face hot with anger in the cool night air. Polycrates was already making his next thrust; his blade whistled past her face, so close she felt the wind of its motion stir the fringe of her head-scarf.

"Blasted crazy slit!" Polycrates cursed. His sword point clattered against quay stone.

"Look!" Rhodopis pointed up at the *Omen*. Polycrates turned —and saw Amtes standing above, Archidike pinioned in her grip. The moon glittered on the blade pressed against the hetaera's throat.

"You bitch," Polycrates snarled at Rhodopis. He hesitated only a moment, bouncing uncertainly on the balls of his feet. He cast a hateful glare at Charaxus, but he slammed his sword back into its sheath, turned without another word, and sprinted up the ramp.

Rhodopis lunged to follow him, but Charaxus seized her at once. She thrashed—and then held perfectly still. A cold, hard bar had pressed across her stomach. Its edge was wickedly sharp, biting through the cloth of her tunic and cape. Charaxus had slung his sword across her body. She turned her head, trying to see his face. But she could only feel his cheek pressed against her own, his hot breath whispering in her ear. "I've gone through too much to lose you again. You will not betray me a second time."

Rhodopis panted with the force of her desperation, but she could not break free of Charaxus. She called up to Polycrates, "Sail! You know what you must do."

Polycrates had freed the hetaera from Amtes' clutches. He wrapped his lover in his arms, then cast a sour look at Rhodopis. But despite his bitterness, Rhodopis could still see the silver flash in the pirate's eyes. He would go to Babylon. Cambyses would pay him well; Polycrates had already made up his mind.

"If you harm a hair on Amtes' head, you'll face the king alone," Rhodopis shouted. "She is your safe passage. She will speak in my place."

"Mistress," Amtes called. The pain in her voice wrenched at Rhodopis.

"You know what you must do." Rhodopis did not know whether she spoke to Polycrates or Amtes, but she was calm now. Charaxus was unlikely to alert the Pharaoh to Rhodopis' double-dealing, as long as she played the part of an obedient wife. Sailing off with Polycrates, at least Archidike could do nothing to harm Rhodopis. The rest of her fate would unspool and weave itself as the gods intended. "Sail on, Polycrates. Amtes knows where to go, and what you must do."

"You're a weak, mewling, blind fucking fool," Polycrates shouted at Charaxus. Charaxus said nothing, but his breath hissed more harshly past Rhodopis' cheek.

Polycrates threw off his lines, and Amtes, her face contorted with what might have been weeping, pulled up the *Omen*'s wooden ramp. The boat glided swiftly from its mooring, out into the wide, flat darkness of the river. The *Omen* would ride the current north, and meet up with Polycrates' other waiting ships, with his crew of rowdy men. If the gods were sensible and merciful—on that count, Rhodopis had no faith—the fleet would arrive in Gebal in two weeks' time. Polycrates of Samos would bow before the king in Babylon before the moon renewed itself again.

And Rhodopis... she would remain in Memphis. Behind Charaxus' firm, hard body (shivering with triumph) she sensed the chaos of the city rising, building, shuddering with the pressure of the people's unrest. Did rumor still stew in that pot of discord? Would it boil over, and send news of Rhodopis to the Horus Throne in a hundred hot runnels of accusation?

As Charaxus hauled her away from the quay, Rhodopis' thoughts were all for Aesop. She must find some way to speak to him. Together, they could formulate a new plan—decide what they must do next. For now, the gods had spoken. Rhodopis would not return to Persia after all.

ABOUT THE AUTHOR

Libbie Hawker writes historical and literary fiction featuring complex characters and rich details of time and place. She lives in the beautiful San Juan Islands with her husband an two naughty cats.

When she's not writing, Libbie can be found road tripping, decorating cookies, and working on her podcast about Jem and the Holograms.

Connect with her below, and don't forget to join Libbie's mailing list (at LibbieHawker.com) to receive updates about new books and get exclusive previews of works in progress.

Follow Libbie on Instagram @libbiehawker or:

www.libbiehawker.com
libbiehawker@gmail.com

Made in the USA
Coppell, TX
16 November 2021